OBSIDIAN KISS

A Sixth Accord Novel

Book One

Lyn Rose

COPYRIGHT

BOOKS BY LYN ROSE

The Honour and Blood Series

The Gate–Honour and Blood, Book One

The Wolf and the Shadow–Honour and Blood, Book Two

The Last Dragon–Honour and Blood, Book Three

The Throne Between Realms–Honour and Blood, Book Four

Standalone Novel

Before the Curse Takes Me

The Sixth Accord Series

Obsidian Kiss Book One

Coming Soon

Venom & Vow Book Two

A Sixth Accord Novel

DEDICATION

For anyone who's ever craved something they couldn't explain.
Take the chance—fate might show you exactly what you were made for.

CONTENT WARNING

This book is intended for adult readers (18+) and contains explicit sex, supernatural violence, strong language, dark themes, and morally questionable behaviour.

If you like it messy, obsessive, and dangerous—welcome.

If not… turn back now.

SUGGESTED LISTENING

Music for the dark, the damned, and the deliciously undone:

This playlist is a pulse beneath the ink —songs that shaped Eden and Nyx, their fire, their bond, their fall.

Scan the Spotify code below to listen.

Open Spotify. Tap the search bar. Click the camera icon. Point it at the code below.

- **"Gods and Monsters" – Lana Del Rey**
- **"Young and Beautiful" – Lana Del Rey**
- **"Beggin For Thread" – Banks**
- **"Control" - Halsey**
- **"Toxic" – 2WEI**
- **"Silhouette"-Aquilo**
- **"Sex and Candy" Alexander Jean**
- **"Crazy in Love (Remix)" – Beyoncé**
- **"Do I wanna know" – Arctic Monkey**
- **"Wicked Game" – Chris Isaak**
- **"Eat your young" - Hozier**
- **"Looking at the Devil" – Seibold**
- **"Monster" – Willyecho**
- **"Feel Like I'm Drowning" – Two Feet**
- **"Dirty Thoughts" – Chloe Adams**
- **"You Put a Spell on Me" – Austin Giorgio**
- **"How Villains Are Made" – Madalen Duke**
- **"Bleed" – Jaklyn Feara**
- **"Obsidian Kiss" – Sunseth**
- **"Seven Nation Army (Melodic Techno)" – Rayyea Noranii**
- **"Get Naughty (Radio Edit)" – Jazzy V**
- **"Shadows Embrace"- Jaklyn Feara**
- **"Ethereal Gaze" – Sunseth**
- **"Fatal Attraction" – Jaklyn Feara**
- **"Chemicals" – Sunseth x After Machines**

- **Vein VIII – Sunseth**
- **Twisted Reflections – Sunseth**
- **Welcome to the Fire – Willyecho**
- **Truth Comes Out – Willyecho**
- **Run – Joji**
- **In the Dark – Reignwolf**
- **"I Was Made For Lovin' You" - from Th..YUNGBLUD**
- **"Close To Me" - Cruelixx**
- **"Quiet" - We Rabbitz**
- **"Dreams" - Alexander Jean**
- **"Mercy on my Grave" - Aventhis**
- **"Welcome to the Dark Side" - Seibold, Neutopia, Leslie Powell**
- **"Scars Don't Speak" - Aventhis**
- **"Power" - Sons of Legion**
- **"Fireborn" - Burn It All - Glum Aleks**
- **"Bound to Roam" – Aven**
- **"Never Enough" - Backroad Raised**

PROLOGUE

Before Edalva had a name, six rulers gathered under a broken moon. Smoke curled through streets still burning from the last war, city bones lit from within, too hot to touch.

No one trusted anyone—not really. They met out of desperation, not hope, drawn together by ruin: wolves tearing through the southern quarter, witches seeding sickness into the water and air, fae turning the river to green glass. Reapers circled the edges, patient as vultures. Vampires fed until restraint snapped, leaving bodies in their wake and fear thick in every street. The humans, slow to act until it was nearly too late, finally felt their world slip out from under them.

Only disaster could make an alliance.

The names meant power, not partnership:

Torran Black—the wolves.

Nyx Ravelle—the vampires.

Lyn Rose

Sevra Wynne—the witches.

Aleria Vale—the fae.

Azariel Klein—from the realm of the dead.

Evelyn Stroud—the lone human at a table set for monsters.

They gathered underground, deep in a flooded terminal where the rails shivered and dripped black water. Every leader brought muscle. Eyes blank. Hands never far from claws, talons, spells.

Above, no one guessed how close the city came to vanishing.

The Accord split Edalva by force—territory edged with curses and old memories. "Break the pact," Azariel's second said, voice echoing off tile and metal, "and the Numina will wake. You do not want their eyes on this world."

No one argued. They all understood exactly what that meant.

When the last signature burned into paper—the deal sealed in ink, blood, and the sting of fear—the city's name settled, heavy and final.

Edalva: a peace built for monsters. It would last. For a while.

Decades later, the first fracture slid in.

A man named Calen walked after midnight, booze hot in his throat, knuckles bruised from the kind of fight you don't talk about. Streetlights fizzed and failed overhead. Sidewalks broken under his feet.

A siren echoed, far off. He kept moving.

The figure came from the opposite direction—just another man under a flickering lamp. Their shoulders clipped as they passed, a casual bump caught on some security feed no one would bother to review. Calen muttered something under his breath, half-turning—then froze.

A sting. Quick. Precise. Like glass slipping into flesh.

His heart clenched hard enough to steal his breath. He gasped once, hand clawing at his chest trying to rip the pain free, but the rhythm was already failing. His knees hit wet concrete.

On camera, it would look like nothing more than a drunk collapsing in the rain.

By the time the stranger vanished, Calen's pulse had stopped.

Elsewhere, the city stiffened.

A wolf found torn by another's teeth.
A Fae heir collapsed, his veins burning with spent magic.
A vampire of old blood drained to nothing by someone who never should have dared.

Impossible murders. The kind that should wake every alarm.

Lyn Rose

But the Council sleeps. Factions pretend peace is holding. No one notices, at first, the tiny wounds hidden on each body—small, precise marks that almost look like nothing.

The injections. The warning. The fuse just lit beneath everything they thought was safe.

CHAPTER ONE

Beneath the Candlelight Veil

Eden

The bass rattled the glass in Eden's hand, every beat a warning. She leaned against the sticky counter, watching the bartender line up shots—five little bullets, silver and mean.

A man pressed in beside her, his breath hot on her ear. His finger traced the bare skin of her arm, slow, possessive, like he owned her already.

"Mmm," he whispered, eyes flickering red beneath the neon haze. "You smell… edible."

Eden's body went rigid. The stink of smoke and sweat smothered the lime and salt in the air. She forced her voice steady. "No thanks. I'm with friends."

Another man slid up on her other side, his grin too wide, teeth too sharp—almost animal.

Lyn Rose

"What about me, pretty thing?" he said, voice low. "Bet you taste even better scared."

The words hit harder than tequila. Something in his gaze wasn't drunk, wasn't human—just hungry.

Her stomach clenched. She dug her nails into her palm, fighting the shake in her hands. The bartender slammed the tray of shots in front of her, a lifeline. Eden grabbed them and fled to her friends.

They didn't notice her laughter was too high, or how her eyes kept darting back to the bar.

The men were still there. Watching. Waiting.

Nyx

The Unity Gala was a lie dressed in silk.

Edalva's elite swept through the ballroom, sharp suits and sculpted gowns on parade, champagne flutes raised, civility stitched tight across their faces. Laughter rippled beneath the chandeliers—bright, brittle. Humans mingled with those they'd flee from if they ever glimpsed beneath the glamour.

Music played, tasteful and low. The lighting was soft, but the danger was absolute. Expensive perfume mingled with nerves and an undercurrent of old blood.

Chandeliers cast fractured light across polished marble—reflections sharp as blades. Every laugh carried the possibility of breaking.

Up on the mezzanine, Nyx Ravelle watched the ballroom with an intensity that charged the air around him. Every detail of his presence was intentional: tuxedo straight, cufflinks glossy black, posture relaxed but never careless. He held a glass of whiskey, untouched long enough to go cool, liking the anchor of it in his hand—a small point of control in a room packed with predators who respected nothing less.

Below, the six factions performed their choreography. Wolves in tailored suits laughed too loudly, their energy barely leashed. One pack leader's eyes flashed yellow for a heartbeat before he mastered himself. Across the floor, Torran Black caught Nyx's gaze, rolled his eyes—a smirk exchanged between old rivals who understood when to play for the crowd.

Witches in sleek dresses and hard smiles discussed biotech and policy with the cold language of surgeons. A Reaper hung at the far wall, quiet as a shadow, enough to hush a circle of overconfident investors. He didn't blink, didn't shift, only waited—as though measuring every vibration for the first sign of weakness.

Nyx tracked it all. The slip of a hand too tight on a glass; the ripple of calculation in Aleria Vale's smile as she dazzled a circle of influencers at the centre of the room, her glamour dialled to a tempest. Every gesture of hers was perfectly rehearsed—a glittering knife in each laugh.

Humans made speeches about harmony, shaking hands with monsters, their smiles strained to the breaking point. Applause rang out, crisp and hollow, skittering off marble like a warning no one wanted to name.

Kain Veyne appeared at Nyx's shoulder, tie loosened, eyes scanning with practiced boredom.
"If I stab myself with this wine flute, will it look like an accident?"
"Only if you do it with grace," Nyx murmured, not looking away from the motion on the dancefloor.
Kain's mouth twitched. "Grace, sure. That's what they'll remember."
"Remind me why we're here?"

Jace Morrow answered from Nyx's other side, voice as dry as the whiskey.
"To maintain the illusion. Let the Sixth Accord believe we play nice. The wolves don't bite, witches don't cast, vampires keep their fangs hidden. Meanwhile—wolf on wolf, a vampire elder drained by kin, a Fae heir burned from the inside out. We dress it up, but the blood is there."
He shook his head. "How are we supposed to keep peace outside these walls when we can't manage it inside?"

Kain shrugged, raised his glass. "Who the fuck knows. Cheers."

Nyx watched a vampire elder lean into air-kiss the mayor's wife, his shadow jagged against marble.
"It's all theatre," Nyx said. "None of them remember what war costs."

"They will," Kain answered, quietly this time, eyes tracking every door. "When it falls apart."

Nyx finally tossed back the whiskey, let the glass clink down on the rail.
"I've stayed long enough."

Kain arched a brow. "If you leave now, fate might throw someone into your bed. You wouldn't be so tense if you just let go once in a while."

"I don't believe in fate." The words sounded emptier than he intended.

Jace straightened, ready. "You want cover?"

Nyx shook his head. "Let them see me leave. Give them something to talk about."

And he turned his back on the glittering room, stepping into the night—unaware that everything was about to crack open.

Eden

The women spilled out of the bar in a knot of laughter, heels clicking, umbrellas forgotten. Rain slicked the street, neon smearing in the puddles.

Her chest tightened when she spotted them—the same two men from the bar. They trailed a few steps behind… then kept going, sauntering up the road until the shadows swallowed them. Relief steadied her breath. Maybe they were gone.

Her friends hugged her tight, one by one. "Congrats again, Eden!"

Engines started. Doors slammed. Before the last car pulled away, a friend leaned out the window. "You sure you're, okay?"

"Yeah, I'm fine. Just waiting for my cab."

"Want to share our ride?"

She shook her head with a smile she didn't feel. "No, it won't be long."

"Congrats again, Eden!" her friend called as the car rolled away.

Nyx

Nyx stepped out into the night just as rain began to fall.

Edalva's skyline cut the clouds to ribbons, each tower and spire a jagged threat. The rain gathered the city's scents— wet pavement, distant smoke, damp electricity. Neon shivered in scattered puddles. Far away, sirens keened through the dark.

A closer sound pulsed just beneath—a heartbeat that didn't fit the rhythm. The pulse hit him like resonance, a note buried in his own chest answering back before he could stop it.

He didn't know her name. Hadn't seen her yet. But he would. That much, something in him already knew.

The weight of the ballroom dropped away. No cameras, no masks—just streetlight and rain, the honest hush of the city at night. He stood beside his car, tracing the roads with his senses, catching the new note of danger in the air.

A voice drifted over, tired and young:
"Yeah, I'm fine. Just waiting for a cab."
"Want to share ours?"
"No, It won't be long."

He glanced over. A group of women said their goodbyes under the awning of a bar, high heels and laughter mingling with the rain. One name lingered in the damp air:
"Congrats, Eden!"

They scattered, leaving her alone beneath the streetlight. She checked her phone. Her face—a flicker of impatience, of stubbornness. Whatever she saw, it made her shove the phone in her pocket with a muttered, "Forget it. I'll walk."

Her footsteps were sharp, definite, steady until she disappeared past the glow. Nyx listened—caught the faint echo, a metronome in the wet silence.

Two men watched her from farther down, melting from shadow to substance. One caught the other's arm, eyes glinting through the gloom.

Eden's pace slowed. Her chest tightened. She recognized them—faces from the bar. They'd been waiting.

Nyx didn't move. He listened. City noise faded into the background, the new focus cutting through everything else. Tension radiated from the men as their laughter dropped in pitch, becoming something private and predatory.

He stepped off the curb. His stride was smooth, unhurried, a shadow following a hunter.

He paralleled Eden on the other side of the street, merging with the dark, keeping watch. Every few steps the pulse returned—hers syncing, then slipping away again—like something testing the edge of a tether he couldn't see.

Their voices carried.

"You made it easy."
"Shoulda taken the cab, sweetheart."

Eden's spine stiffened. She pressed on faster—her heels now staccato, echoing with the start of something like panic. She turned a corner, instinct searching for escape. One streetlight flickered ahead, shadows thickening at the mouth of a side street.

She took it, not yet knowing it was a dead end.

Lyn Rose

Nyx felt the coil inside him tighten. The Accord chained him to law, to patience. Her safety was supposed to be none of his business—not until real violence started. Trouble was the dark thing deep inside him didn't care about treaties. Its hunger flared sharp and sudden, a voice inside: Yours. Now.

Eden's footsteps slowed as the alley closed in. A chain-link fence blocked her way, garbage bins spilling rainwater, rot thickening the air.

The men blocked her exit. One stepped forward, close—too close. He leaned in, breath hot and sour on her skin, and inhaled slowly at her neck.

"Mmm. You smell good," he whispered, voice thick and sleazy. "Where you running off to, pretty one?"

Eden flinched, arm darting into her bag. She fumbled, found the pepper spray, hand shaking but determined.

"Get away from me," she snapped, brandishing the can.

The man rocked back, eyed the spray, then snorted with a crooked grin. "That's cute."

Without warning, she pressed the trigger. The mist caught him straight in the face. He screamed, stumbling away, hands clawing at his burning eyes.

The second moved faster. As she turned, he slammed her against the wall—hard. Brick jarred her skull, rain and blood streaked her vision, senses swimming with pain and shock.

Lyn Rose

His grip was bruising at her waist, fingers fumbling at the band of her jeans, making his intent horribly clear. His breath rasped hot at her ear, sour with cigarettes and stale sweat, his mouth curling into a cruel, hungry smile.

She thrashed—kicked, clawed, tried to scream. Panic sealed her throat, breath breaking in jagged gasps as she bucked against his grasp.

In the darkness, Nyx felt his fangs descend, breath cutting sharp. The rhythm he'd felt on the street now slammed through him, matching her heartbeat exactly—an alien harmony that burned and steadied him in the same breath.

His hands shook, fists clenched so tight his claws nearly pierced skin. The monster inside him howled, rising and wild, vision staining the world blood-red. Protect or consume, it demanded—and for a heartbeat, he nearly let it loose.

The man jerked back suddenly—lifted, slammed into the alley wall with inhuman force. He didn't have time to scream a warning. Bone cracked, a sickening, final sound. The threat vanished as quickly as it appeared.

Eden staggered, unsteady. Her knees went soft, hands shaking so hard she dropped the spray.

The alley was silent but for her gasps and the patter of rain. The bodies—gone. Blood and the faint charge of magic hung in the air.

She stared, breath shallow, searching the shadows, sure someone—something—was still there.

A shape lingered just out of reach, watching: Nyx.

Her scent drew him, fierce and forbidden. It spoke of power, survival, something not-quite-human. A primal hunger coiled inside, closer to breaking loose than he'd let himself admit.

For a moment, he didn't trust himself to move closer. He fought it, jaw clenched, nails digging moon-shaped crescents into his palms.

He could walk away.

But when Eden's legs gave out, he was moving—before the rest of him caught up.

The decision wasn't thought, wasn't mercy—just the same pulse dragging him forward, the unseen chord between them tightening until motion was the only relief.

Eden

The wall hit harder than she expected.

Or maybe it was her head—the shock sharper than memory held.

Everything spun sideways.

Her ears rang; her vision blurred and swam. She blinked once, twice, but the alley spun—a smear of dark shapes and too many shadows. Her fingers scraped brick as she pushed upright, but one knee buckled. She caught herself, heart hammering.

Where—

She spun slowly, hands searching the air.

Nobody. No men. No laughter. No weight on her skin.

The alley was dead silent. Still. But not empty.

The air pressed heavy, thick with something unseen and waiting.

Her heart kicked against her ribs, her scalp slick with cold. When she touched it, fingers came away sticky—dark crimson against the flickering streetlight.

"What the fuck…" she whispered, voice cracking. She didn't recall running, didn't remember being pulled away.

Her pepper spray lay a few feet off. She staggered, snatched it up, backing herself into the wall, lungs burning as breath came fast and shallow.

Thoughts shattered inside her head like broken glass.

I fought. I tried—God, did I black out? Did I hit my head that hard?

She closed her eyes briefly to steady the chaos. The chill pressed in; the silence thickened unnaturally.

A faint sound whispered behind her—soft footsteps slipping through the rain, the faint scrape of a shadow shifting near.

"Who's there?" Eden's voice cracked as she raised her pepper spray defensively, eyes wide and searching the darkness. Silence stretched tight, pressing in like wet velvet.

Her legs quivered, knees folding like a dropped veil.

Before she could fall, strong hands closed around her— steady, firm. His grip at her waist was firm but careful, heat searing through the cold, warmth, his touch rewired the air itself.

For a split second, her heart stuttered—then his chest answered. One rhythm, not two. Her pulse beating where his had been silent for centuries.

"No, don't touch me," she gasped, panic flaring bright in her gaze.

"It's okay," came his low, smooth voice—dark and certain, a quiet promise. "I won't hurt you."

His words rolled over her like thunder beneath velvet, steadying the storm inside her.

She tensed, muscles wound tight, but his hold never faltered or tightened. Slowly, the sharp edges of her fear softened.

Lyn Rose

The unbearable weight pressing on her chest eased just enough for ragged breaths to find their rhythm.

Around them, rain poured in thick silver sheets. The alley's grime blurred like a shadowed canvas beneath a spotlight. His scent cut through the damp—clean linen with something wild and ancient lurking beneath, like the earth exhaling beneath the city's decay.

Eden's eyes traced his face—hair smooth and slicked back, features carved from midnight and stone. His eyes, dark as obsidian, held storms and silence in equal measure. He was a guardian shaped by shadow and quiet strength, impossible to ignore, impossible to fully read.

In that suspended moment between heartbeats, as the city listened and waited, Eden understood—

Nothing else was certain, but here—in his unwavering hold—she was not alone.

She didn't trust him yet—not fully—not after everything— but she felt, just barely, that her fight wasn't over.

He helped her upright without hesitation, one arm firm around her waist, the other steadying her shoulder. She felt small next to him. Smaller than she liked.

"Hospital," she managed.

"I know."

He didn't ask. He simply guided her carefully back up the street to a black car that gleamed like it cost more than her law degree. The door opened like it recognized his hand.

Rain streamed off its surface like quicksilver, streaking down the mirror-shine paint.

The leather seat was warm, carrying the faint, expensive scent of new upholstery—polished hide and clean resin; the kind of smell that whispered money.

She barely registered the ride—just lights blurring past the window and the quiet tension of the man beside her, a man trying not to be noticed but impossible to ignore. When she closed her eyes, she could still smell him—clean, wild, a little dangerous.

Every bump in the road thrummed through her skull, but his presence steadied her more than it frightened her.

The car stopped.

Then she was at the emergency entrance. He helped her out, still silent.

She looked up at him one last time, dizzy but grateful.

"Who are you?" she asked, her words slurring now.

He met her eyes.

Didn't answer.

Lyn Rose

He just stepped back, spoke quietly to the nurse—something about covering the bill—and vanished into the night before Eden could get another word out.

Inside, a nurse clipped sensors to Eden's wrist, watching the monitor flicker. For a heartbeat, two separate pulses synced—steady, identical. Then the second line blinked out. The nurse frowned, tapped the screen, and moved on.

Outside, only the rain remained, striking the pavement where her blood had dripped, thinning it to pale rivulets that slipped into the gutter, the city swallowing the secret whole.

CHAPTER TWO

The Pull Between Strangers

Nyx didn't look back.
Not at the hospital.
Not at the girl.
Not at the blood drying in a jagged, black-red seam along his shirt cuff.

He just walked.

His polished shoes clicked sharply on the rain-slick pavement, catching stray shards of streetlight that fractured the dark like broken crystal. His tuxedo clung damp and heavy—a ghost of the gala he'd left behind.

The antiseptic tang from the ER clung like a second skin, crawling up his throat, mixing with the metallic ghost of her blood. Even the rain—cold, constant—couldn't wash it away. It plastered his hair to his skull, drilled icy needles down his collar, hissed against the asphalt in a voice that wanted him gone, wanted to erase the night itself.

Streetlamps flickered overhead, light bending around him like the city itself sought to render him invisible.

He should have left her.
Should have turned away, as he'd done a thousand times before.

But he hadn't.

Her scent lingered—a blazing brand seared into his senses, sharp and undeniable.

He could taste it like a bitter memory at the back of his throat.

He felt it in the hollow ache between his ribs, imagined her heartbeat beneath his hands, frantic and fragile.

He wondered if she'd felt the same pull—that tight thread of something tangled between strangers

He'd seen beauty before. Hell, he'd broken beauty before, left it in pieces and never once looked back. But she—she was something else. Not just beautiful. Unsettling. Dangerous in a way that went beyond the curve of her lips or the look in her eyes.

It wasn't how she'd stared at him like he was safe. It was the way something inside her had hooked into him—sharp, deep, a thread wound so tight it thrummed in his chest. Like a song he'd forgotten, drawing him closer, daring him to remember. A memory of warmth he'd been denying for years.

A war that twisted with every breath of rain and every whisper of her presence—one part demanding he disappear into the night as he always did; the other urging him to stay and fight for something buried, maybe lost, but stirring like embers beneath the ash.

You're slipping.

The thought cut in, cold and clinical. The kind of truth he couldn't ignore.

He slid into his car, slammed the door, stared out through a windshield smeared with rain. The city outside blurred into a mess of neon and shadow, streetlights bleeding into puddles. He tried to forget her. Tried to forget the way her voice had trembled when she asked his name, like she might believe him if he answered. Tried to forget the way her blood smelled—hot, sweet, laced with something that didn't belong.

The wipers dragged once, smearing water into distorted streaks, like they were trying to wipe Eden from his mind.

Nyx had secrets older than most nations. He'd saved strangers before—wiped his hands clean, vanished into the night. But her? She'd left something behind. Not in the alley.

In him.

He sat there, unmoving, the engine idling, the car thick with the imprint of her—blood, adrenaline, and something softer, a scent that curled under his tongue and refused to let go. He'd trained for centuries to separate hunger from instinct, to walk through a blood bar untempted, to taste and never crave. But her—just that thin streak of blood on the leather seat, the way it soaked into his coat—had him thinking about licking it clean.

Not for thirst.

For something worse. Something deeper. Something old and wrong and impossible to name.

Fuck.

He thumbed open his phone, punched in Kain's number with shaking hands.

"Sir." Kain's voice, clipped and cool, like he hadn't been waiting for the call all night.

"I want the car cleaned. Internally. Tomorrow."

Silence then. "You… spilled something?"

"A human bled on the seat."

"…Was this consensual or should I be prepping a cover story?"

"Just clean it." He dragged a hand down his face, nails scraping flesh. "And find me whatever you can on a woman named Eden."

Kain exhaled, a hiss of static. "Big city, Nyx. You have a surname, age, blood type?"

"I said Eden."

"And I'm saying, how the fuck are we supposed to track a first name? We don't even know how it's spelled—"

"Use our contacts. I don't care if you bribe a hospital registrar or threaten a god. Do it."

Silence.
Then: "On it."

Nyx hung up. Pulled onto the road, tires shrieking over wet concrete, and turned toward the only place that ever felt like silence—Duskwatch.

The mansion loomed from the northern rise, black stone and curved glass rising out of trees and mist. It wasn't visible from the street—nothing about Nyx ever was—but the structure stood three stories tall, brutal and elegant, watching over the city like a predator in the dark. Floodlights shivered across the driveway, catching raindrops like shards of falling glass.

The gates unlocked at his approach, sensors recognizing him instantly. Iron slid back smooth as silk, the kind of technology that whispered wealth and absolute control.

Rain hammered the windows. Inside, it was still. Too still. No lights. He didn't need them.

Nyx moved through the cavernous halls, quick and silent, like if he didn't keep moving, he'd turn around and hunt her. His footsteps echoed on marble, a lonely sound in all that space. In the bathroom, he peeled off his jacket, then his shirt. The fabric stuck to his skin where her blood had dried—small but insistent, a reminder. His fingers slowed at the cuff, not to unfasten it, but to look.

A smear. Barely visible. Most vampires wouldn't have noticed.

But Nyx wasn't most vampires.

He raised the cuff to his nose and inhaled—slow, deep, like he'd been drowning and only her scent could save him. His blood surged instantly—hot, wrong, desperate. His fangs snapped down, sharp enough to split flesh. His jaw locked, every muscle tight, every instinct screaming:

More.

But beneath the hunger, something else coiled—desire, raw and unruly. He let out a low, feral sound, part breath, part growl, and pressed his palm flat against the marble just to keep himself anchored. The cold seeped into his skin, a reminder that he was still in control.

He hadn't reacted like this in centuries. Not to blood.

Not to anyone.

His body throbbed, hard and aching, so deep, her blood alone had marked him. Claimed him.

This isn't normal, he told himself.

But his cock was already straining against his slacks.

And he hadn't even tasted her.

He dropped the shirt into the sink, like it might catch fire in his hands, and refused to look in the mirror. Because if he did, he wasn't sure who—or what—he'd see staring back.

He turned the shower on instead. Heat surged up in a rising cloud, filling the small room with steam as he stepped under it, letting the burn swallow the night clinging to his skin.

The phone buzzed again, this time not Kain but Stroud. He let it ring until the marble echoed with its absence. Reports of a witch dead in her apothecary, veins scorched black. A reaper initiate gone missing from Mortus' edge. Two low-market Fae, traders everyone knew by face, found collapsed in the stalls where glamour usually kept humans blind. The Accord wanted answers.

Nyx didn't pick up. He wasn't ready to hear about other blood when hers was still singing in his veins.

Eden

The fluorescent lights buzzed, relentless and cold. Eden shifted in the hospital bed, wincing as the new stitches tugged at her scalp. Her head swam, heavy and off-kilter, like she was listening to the world through waterlogged ears. Shadows crawled across the ceiling, blurring the sterile white into uneasy grey.

Every blink felt too slow, the world lagging half a second behind her body.

The nurse had said she'd been lucky—blacked out only a few minutes, nothing broken. Lucky. The word tasted sour. Her palms ached, raw from scraping concrete, from pushing away a man who wasn't there anymore. She kept glancing at her hands, half expecting to see evidence of something stranger than blood.

A knock.

Two detectives stepped in—plainclothes, badges glinting, eyes bloodshot and wary. The woman led.

"Miss Marlowe," she asked, voice soft but edged with steel, "We know this isn't ideal timing, but we'd like your statement while everything's fresh."

Lyn Rose

Eden nodded, slow, the movement sending a ripple of pain through her skull. Her tongue felt thick, words stuck behind her teeth.

"Okay. Yeah. Sure."

They pulled up chairs. The man flipped open a battered notebook. "Can you walk us through what happened?"

She told them what she could—the bar, her friends, the decision to walk alone. The alley. "I didn't mean to go that far," she said, voice thin. "I just… I don't know. I was trying to get away."

"And then?"

"There were two men," she whispered. "They followed me. One shoved me. I hit my head." Her hand hovered over the stitches, protective.

The detectives traded a glance. The woman pressed, "And how did you get to the hospital?"

Eden's mind blanked, then flickered—images, sounds, all out of order. A pulse of rain on metal. The scent of expensive cologne. Hands catching her before she hit the ground.

"I don't know exactly. I was losing consciousness. I remember… someone caught me before I fell."

"Someone?"

"A man. In a tux." The words felt ridiculous, but she couldn't unsay them. "He was—tall. Quiet. Terrifying, but not like… a monster. Just—" she paused, searching, "powerful. He smelled like rain and money. He scared the men off. Or—" she shook her head, at a loss, "they were just gone."

The male detective frowned. "Gone?"

"Yeah. One second, they were on me. The next, nothing. Just gone."

"And this man? He brought you here?"

She nodded. "He walked me to a car. Black, expensive. Drove me to emergency. Paid the hospital. Then… disappeared."

"Did he give a name?"

She shook her head. She remembered asking. She remembered the way he looked at her—longer than necessary, like weighing something she'd never understand. Then he left.

The woman closed her notebook. "We'll check the street cams. See if anything comes up."

"Do you think you'll find him?" Eden asked, voice barely above a whisper.

"We'll try," the man said. "But the city's full of men in suits and silent exits."

Lyn Rose

They discharged her just after three a.m., stitches bandaged, paperwork signed in a shaky hand. The headache throbbed behind her eyes, deep and pulsing. Outside, the city was washed in pale light, sharp enough to make her squint. The air smelled different after rain—a little cleaner, but lonelier too.

Mara was waiting at the curb, arms crossed, anxiety rolling off her in waves. "Oh my God, Eden." She rushed over, pulled Eden into a careful hug. "You said concussion. Not 'nearly murdered.'"

Eden managed a tired smile as Mara held her tight. "I'm okay."

"You're not okay. You have stitches in your head."

Eden shrugged, sliding into the passenger seat. "I have painkillers."

They drove in silence. Mara's hands gripped the steering wheel hard enough to leave imprints. The radio played low, some old pop song that didn't match the night at all.

"You're not actually going to work today, are you?"

"I have to." Eden's voice was quiet but steady. "New client. Big case. I already rescheduled once."

Mara shot her a look. "You got assaulted. You can take a day."

"I'll rest after I win," Eden said, a small, stubborn grin tugging at her lips. She tried to focus on the future, on the world of contracts and arguments—anything but alleys and strangers.

Mara groaned. "Fine. But call me if you need anything. Promise."

Eden nodded.

Maybe she meant it.

But as soon as she shut the door behind her and climbed the stairs to her apartment, her thoughts weren't on Mara, or healing, or rest.

They were on the man in the tuxedo—

the one whose name she didn't know,

whose face she saw in flashes,

and the blood she couldn't remember bleeding.

She stood in the quiet of her apartment, hand lingering on the door, listening to the hush settle around her. For a long moment, she just breathed, replaying the alley, the impossible rescue, the certainty that something had changed.

And outside, somewhere in the city, Nyx Ravelle stared into the dark, haunted by the same memory, the same impossible pull—a thread stretched tight between strangers, waiting to snap.

Lyn Rose

Morning cut in—too bright, sunlight slipping through thin curtains that couldn't quite keep the world out. The city's hush sounded wrong, like it had decided nothing bad had ever happened.

Eden woke to her alarm's shriek, heart already racing. Pain flared behind her eyes, antiseptic clung to her skin and hair. She pressed the stitches above her ear and winced. Memory came jagged—men's laughter, wet brick, rain sliding down her jacket, a stranger's hands catching her before she fell. Fear lived under her skin now, restless and sharp.

Her phone buzzed. Unknown number. She forced her hand steady.

"Eden Marlowe."

A voice calm to the point of cold. "Detective Halloran, Edalva Police. You gave a statement about an assault?"

Her pulse kicked. "Yes."

"Need you to come in today—details in the hospital report don't line up. Nothing urgent, but sooner's better."

"What time?"

"Ten-thirty, if you're up for it."

"I'll be there."

Click.

Lyn Rose

Silence pressed close again, the air suddenly heavy. She braced herself on the table, swallowed two painkillers with warm water that tasted like metal.

Then she called work. "Hi, it's Eden Marlowe."

"Eden! Oh my god, are you okay?" Lara's voice burst through the line, too loud, too distant.

"I'm fine." A lie. "Just following up with the police."

"Don't rush back. The Wilkins family will be fine.

 I'll push your meeting."

"Thanks. I'll come in later."

"Promise you'll eat," Lara said, gentler now.

"I'll try."

She hung up and stood. The floor felt cold, her steps echoing like the apartment was listening to the lie in Eden's tone. Early air drifted through the open window—salt, exhaust, the faint sweetness of blooming flowers—but each scent felt warped, sharpened.

She dressed like it might protect her: black stockings with seams, a charcoal pencil skirt, white blouse. Her fingers trembled, so she focused on each button until they behaved. In the mirror, something gold flashed across her pupils— gone before she could be sure. She stared anyway, half expecting a stranger to look back.

Lyn Rose

Keys in hand, she stepped into the hall.

The world outside looked scrubbed and new—shop awnings drying from last night's storm, flower boxes spilling violet petals across the pavement. Yet as she walked, the normal rhythm of morning faltered.

Two men in suits lingered by a café door, conversation dying as she passed. One's eyes caught hers—too bright, wrong for daylight. A woman brushed her arm on the curb and recoiled, hurt, like she'd been burned. Eden muttered an apology, but the woman was already gone, heels clicking too fast.

The air thickened, it was hard to breathe. Maybe trauma, maybe nerves. She told herself she just needed caffeine— something ordinary, something normal.

The café smelled of burnt beans and sugar. She joined the short queue, ordered a flat white, palms flat on the cool marble counter.

"Let me get that for you," a voice said behind her.

She turned. The man stood close—polished shoes, dark suit, eyes the colour of old amber.

"That's kind, but I've got it," she said lightly.

He smiled. "Then maybe let me buy you lunch instead."

"I appreciate it, but no."

"Dinner, then. One drink?" His tone softened, but the air between them sharpened.

"I said no."

He leaned in, close enough that she felt his breath at her throat. His nostrils flared. "You smell…" The rest dissolved into a low growl, deep enough to rattle her bones.

Eden froze. The café noise collapsed around them—no chatter, no music, just that sound crawling under her skin.

The man blinked, straightened, dropped a few coins on the counter, and walked out—too fast, too quiet.

Her coffee arrived with a clatter. She thanked the barista automatically, fingers shaking as she lifted the cup. The taste was ash.

Back outside, sunlight poured hot over her shoulders, but the chill ran deeper. Faces seemed to follow her. Shadows stretched long in her wake.

Eden wrapped her arms around herself and hurried un—certain now that whatever had started in that alley hadn't ended there.

CHAPTER THREE

Beautiful Enough to Own Him

Nyx

Sleep never came easy. Not for Nyx. Not for centuries.

A few hours—restless, thin as tissue—were all he managed, just enough to keep his mind from fracturing, never enough to dull the memory. Her blood on his hands. Her body limp in his arms. The colour of her pain haunted every flicker of his half-dreams.

He gave up before dawn. The city outside wasn't dark or dripping anymore—it was pale gold and sharp, sunlight crawling over the skyline like an apology. He stood at the window, bare-chested, watching morning carve the world clean. It didn't help.

He showered in silence. The scalding water seared his skin, but it couldn't burn away what clung to him. Memory steamed up from his pores, insistent. He dressed with mechanical precision: navy slacks, open collar, sleeves rolled to the elbow. Flesh bared like he wanted to feel something real again. The jacket slipped over his shoulders like armour, but it couldn't muffle the low ache in his chest.

Maybe it was hunger. Maybe that explained the way his mind kept circling her—teeth bared around a memory that wasn't supposed to matter.

Bare feet on marble, he crossed the penthouse to the kitchen. The hidden fridge opened with a coded click. Red light. Glass shelves lined with blood packs. He scanned the labels without interest until he found one marked AB-negative—rare, pure, the kind of vintage that should've satisfied anything.

He poured, watched the light slide through the crimson, almost beautiful. He drank. Smooth. Perfect. Tasteless.

Not what he wanted. Not what haunted him.

The glass hit the sink, the sound too sharp in the quiet. He pressed the garage button in the lift. Today the Jag waited—sleek, black, precise. The engine's low snarl vibrated up through the steering wheel, almost grounding him. Almost.

The drive to Virex was quick. The city glittered under early light—too clean, too loud. The tower rose like a blade, slicing sunlight into mirrored shards. Twenty-five stories of glass and secrets.

He stepped inside. Voices greeted him, but everything sounded too bright, too close.

"Mr. Ravelle—"

He nodded once.

Sera, efficient as always, fell in beside him, heels sparking across marble.

"Morning, sir. Coffee's on its way. You've got three investor briefs, a flagged Biotech contract, and a priority message from the Accord."

Her tone tightened. "Stroud's called twice—sounded… less than patient."

He gave a dry smile. "She's never patient."

Then something hit him—sharp, electric. A sudden *pull* in his chest, like static crawling beneath his ribs. The hallway wavered. The air thinned. For a split second he wasn't in Virex at all—he was somewhere else.

Sunlight. Coffee. Fear. A scent.

Gone as fast as it came.

He stopped walking. Sera turned, confused. "Sir?"

He blinked it away. "Nothing."

But his hand lingered on his sternum trying to steady the aftershock.

He moved to his office, shut the door, and the hum of the building vanished, leaving him with silence and that phantom rhythm still pulsing under his skin. He picked up his coffee, black and scalding, but didn't drink it.

He was still staring out the window—still trying to name that foreign heartbeat—when the phone buzzed.

He didn't check the caller ID. He already knew.

"Stroud," he said.

Her voice came in cold and sharp. "Bodies. Two factions. One Fae collapsed in daylight—no wounds. A wolf found in an alley, throat torn out. Looks like self-defence."

Nyx's jaw worked slow. "You could've led with good morning."

"You could've answered last night."

A silence stretched between them, brittle as glass.

He exhaled. "I was busy."

"Busy working or busy brooding?" she shot back. "Doesn't matter. I need your eyes on this before the wrong people start asking the right questions."

Nyx's jaw worked, slow and tight. "Where?"

"Vestry Market. Logged time, three a.m. Wards are up. Humans are being redirected, but that won't hold. I want your eyes on it before the wrong questions start."

He let the silence stretch, knuckles white on the desk, then: "I'll pull surveillance."

"Good. And Nyx—find me something we can act on. If this spreads, the Accord won't hold."

She hung up.

Vestry Market still smelled of rain and fried oil, banners sagging between stalls that should have been selling dumplings and cheap lanterns. Instead, the whole street was cordoned off, glamour thrumming low and steady, turning human eyes aside with whispers of broken pipes and gas leaks.

Nyx stepped through, his shadow bending the wards to let him pass. Accord enforcers lingered in tight clusters, their expressions rigid, eyes hard. He didn't speak to them. He didn't need to.

The first body was sprawled in the open street. A Fae trader, known to every stallholder. His skin was pale, veins blackened to glass, eyes wide and scorched from within. The faint stench of burned glamour still clung to the stone beneath him, the echo of magic that had turned on its wielder.

Lyn Rose

Nyx crouched, scanning with predator precision. At the hollow of the collarbone—small, clean, almost invisible—was a puncture. Too neat for a fight. Too quiet for a death. He logged it, jaw tightening.

He hovered longer than he should, rain soaking his hair, the city's neon reflected in the slick puddles gathering under the corpse. The Fae's mouth was parted, lips twisted in a silent scream, and for a second Nyx could almost hear it—echoing back through the alleys, a shriek carved into the bones of the city. The stench of spent magic burned his nose, a chemical tang that lingered, oily and wrong, like copper and rot layered together. He forced himself to breathe through it, but each inhale made his stomach clench tighter. Around him, the enforcers kept their distance, faces pale, one of them crossing himself, knuckles white on a charm that would do nothing here.

"Where's the other?"

An enforcer shifted, unease flickering. "Wolf. We moved him off the street. It was… ugly."

Nyx followed the scent before they could gesture. Down a rain-slick alley, near a delivery door, a body slumped against the wall. Broad-shouldered, teeth bared, claws still extended like he'd died mid-lunge. His throat was torn open, the killing blow messy, desperate.

Blood streaked in arcs across the bricks, black in the shadows, glistening red where the light hit. The wolf's eyes were still open, glassy with the last flickers of rage and terror, jaw locked in a snarl so real Nyx could almost see the moment it happened—a friend turning, a heartbeat's warning, then violence so fast it left nothing but ruin. The claws had scored the alley wall, deep scratches etched into the stone, desperate and animal. The wolf's chest rose and fell, but only in Nyx's imagination, because the violence still vibrated in the air. The smell here was thicker, primal— blood, wet fur, panic.

A survivor sat on a crate nearby, jacket ripped, one eye swollen almost shut, claw marks raked deep across his face and arms. The copper tang of blood clung to him, sharp and raw. His voice cracked when he spoke.

"We were just leaving the market. He was fine. Then someone brushed past us and—it was like he wasn't him anymore. He snapped. Rabid. Came at me like I was prey. I tried to talk him down, tried to—" His voice broke, his gaze sliding to the body. "I had to stop him. He left me no choice."

His hands wouldn't stop shaking. Blood oozed from the gouges across his knuckles, fingers twitching remembrance, replaying the fight. His breath hitched, wild and uneven, and he looked everywhere but at Nyx, as though the truth might change if he just refused to meet his eyes. Rain dripped from the end of his nose, mingling with the blood on his shirt. The survivor's pack mark—Greywatch, Nyx noticed, the tattoo still fresh—stood out on his forearm, a streak of black ink blurred by sweat and blood.

Nyx's eyes narrowed. "What pack are you with?"

Lyn Rose

"Greywatch," the man rasped. "Other side of the river." His fists tightened, bloody knuckles shaking. "We'd been friends for years."

Nyx crouched beside the dead wolf, turned the arm with steady hands. At the crook of the elbow—there it was. A needle mark. Small. Precise. Almost invisible. He snapped a photo, jaw clenched.

He stared at the mark, a pinprick lost in a web of veins, but all he could see was intent—a cold, clinical violation. This wasn't random. This was a message. He catalogued the rage in the wolf's body, the violence still etched into the shape of him, and felt an old, familiar chill race down his spine. This was what happened when someone played god with monsters.

"Not an accident," Nyx murmured.

He straightened and pulled out his phone.

The wolf answered groggy, voice rough. "Nyx? It's early— what the fuck. I had way too much to drink—"

"A wolf. Dead. Vestry Market," Nyx cut him off, voice like a blade. "His throat ripped out. I have the survivor. He swears they were friends, heading home. Then someone brushed past them. The wolf snapped—rabid. Attacked his own. The survivor's torn to pieces but alive. He killed him in self-defence. Black… I found a needle mark. Crook of the arm. I think he was injected with something."

He kept his tone flat but inside, adrenaline was surging, every instinct screaming for action, for violence, for answers. The rain hammered the alley, thunder rolling overhead, The city on guard and watching, waiting. The survivor shivered, his face a mask of shock and grief, and Nyx could feel the weight of every eye on him—enforcers, ghosts, the city itself.

Silence. Then the sound of drawers slamming, boots hitting the floor, a woman's voice in the background. *What is it?* Black's reply was low, clipped steel: "Get dressed. I'll be there in twenty." The line went dead.

Nyx didn't stop. He thumbed through to another number.

"Ravelle," Aleria Vale purred, velvet even at dawn. "Why am I lucky enough for an early morning wake-up?"

"Fae. Trader. Vestry Market." Nyx's tone was flat, surgical. "Collapsed in the street. No wounds, no struggle. His own glamour burned him out from the inside. And I found a needle mark at his collarbone."

The silk snapped from her voice. "What the fuck are you saying?"

"Someone's injecting them. It flipped a wolf rabid. Burned a Fae alive. Different outcomes, same cause. This wasn't chance. It was deliberate."

Her breath hissed through the line, sharp as glass. Then, "On my way." She hung up without another word.

Nyx slid the phone back into his pocket, the weight of it heavier than steel. Two bodies on the stones, one survivor scarred for life, and the certainty curling in his gut: someone was moving through Edalva with a syringe, and the Accord wasn't ready for the storm it would bring.

He lingered in the alley, rain soaking him through, eyes fixed on the blood spiralling across the concrete. The city watched—faces in windows, a hundred small judgments folded into the gutters. He wanted to scream, to rip the world apart until he found the hand that had done this. The survivor wouldn't meet his gaze; shoulders hunched, guilt and pain braided through him, braced for another strike. Nyx forced the rage down, tamped it into something cold and precise. There would be time for violence later.

Boots carried him away from the market before the sun was fully risen. By the time he reached the Jag, his jaw was iron, his hands restless against the wheel. He hit Stroud's line.

She answered on the first ring. "Report."

"Wolf injected, put down by his own. Fae burned from the inside out. Both carried needle marks. This isn't faction infighting, Stroud—it's deliberate."

Silence. Then: "Find me proof, Ravelle. Until then, I've got corpses, panic, and no names to hang them on." The line cut.

The Jag snarled through the rain back toward Virex.

He'd barely stepped into his office when Sera appeared in the doorway, tablet in hand. "Sir. Edalva PD on line one. They said it's about surveillance footage. Lorne & Carrick are reviewing it."

Nyx's teeth clicked together. Another fire, another mess. "Patch them through."

"This is Ravelle."

A detective's voice: clipped, efficient. "Detective Renn. We need your expertise on a case. City cam footage—grainy, fogged. The victim's family wants transparency. The files are being reviewed at Lorne & Carrick. We'd prefer you there."

Nyx checked his watch, the second-hand slicing time thin, his senses sharpening, his body wired for the next explosion.

"Hold a moment."

"Sera. Clear my schedule for three hours."

"Yes, Mr. Ravelle."

He returned to the call. "I'll be there in thirty."

Thirty minutes later, he stepped into Lorne & Carrick— modern lines, old money, the air thick with power and the faint scent of polished wood. A receptionist gestured him to the elevators without a glance. A young associate, sharp- suited and forgettable, led him to the boardroom.

Steel, slate, tinted glass—the city's heart disguised as a conference table. The detectives stood as he entered.

"Mr. Ravelle," Renn said, extending a hand. "Thanks for coming."

Nyx shook it, eyes already scanning the room for threats. "You have the footage?"

Then—

The scent hit him like a pulse: warm citrus, soft jasmine, clean skin, and rain. Not blood, but something that made his fangs ache and his thoughts fracture.

Eden.

His fangs lengthened, a pulse of hunger and something darker surging through him. Every nerve ending came alive, skin humming. His cock thickened hard against his zipper in a rush so violent he had to subtly shift in his chair, jaw clenched so tight he thought it might crack. He was painfully, humiliatingly aware of every inch of his body— how close he was to losing it, how easy it would be to let the monster off its leash.

Fuck.

It was her. No doubt. No question. That scent was carved into him now—buried in the deepest part of him, a memory he could taste.

And then—

Lyn Rose

The door opened.

And she walked in.

He didn't blink. Didn't breathe. If his heart still beat, it would've stopped. The world seemed to narrow, the air shimmering, every sound amplified and distant at the same time.

She was a fucking vision.

Black pinstripe skirt, tight and high with a slit that flashed creamy thigh. White blouse tucked in to show every curve. Her breasts moved with each step, restrained but bouncing softly beneath silk. Hair pinned up, a few dark curls loose around her jaw. A bandage on her temple.

And those legs—stockings lined up the back, black pumps clicking like a metronome made to destroy him.

The memory hit like a live wire—her skin against his palms, her legs locked around his waist, heels biting into his shoulders. The taste of her, hot and forbidden, crashed through him.
Heat spiked—sudden, vicious. The images came sharp and unwanted, every nerve begging to break rank, to tear the mask away and make her his.

He hissed low under his breath, the sound nearly lost beneath the hum of the boardroom, but it vibrated through him, dangerous and raw. He adjusted again, pulse hammering, the burn of restraint nearly unbearable. Control slipping, so close to the edge he could feel it in his bones.

She stopped—just a flicker—her eyes locking on him.

Recognition hit her like a flash fire. The alley. The blood. His arms catching her before the world went black.

She stiffened for half a second. Then blinked, tucked it down behind a sharp, professional mask. Her spine straightened. Her face smoothed.

And she smiled. Calm. Courteous.

But it was too late. He'd seen it in her eyes.

She remembered.

Her grip on the document case tightened until her knuckles blanched, the tension echoing the strain in his own body.

Nyx's body reacted before his mind could stop it. Every sense sharpened, every nerve ending flared to pain, his skin prickling, heart pounding in his throat. He tried to look away, failed.

She was the storm that pulled at every instinct he'd spent centuries mastering.

She smiled. Not sweet, not coy—just professional. But it hit him like a punch, the impact radiating through his chest to his gut, to his groin.

If he'd had blood in his cheeks, it would've rushed south. One smile and three centuries of discipline nearly shattered.

The others noticed. He knew they did, even if they pretended not to.

Eden cleared her throat, voice smooth as velvet over steel. "Hi, I'm Eden Marlowe, junior associate at Lorne & Carrick. Thank you for joining us, Mr. Ravelle."

He managed a nod, mouth dry, tongue heavy.

She gestured to the screen. "Our client's son collapsed on his way home. Twenty-three years old. No history, no drugs in his system, no trauma. The coroner listed it as sudden cardiac failure. The footage is the only lead, and the family wants answers."

Her gaze flicked to the detectives, then back to Nyx. "It's nearly useless, but if anyone can clean it up, it's you."

His throat was dry. "Of course," he said, the words scraping out. "Show me."

She turned, bent to plug in the device. The skirt hugged every line of her, the slit parting just enough to reveal a flash of thigh. His vision sharpened, the room blurring at the edges as he zeroed in—senses so overloaded he thought he might break.

A low growl slipped past his teeth before he could leash it, a sound animal and hungry.

Lyn Rose

Everyone turned.

Nyx stood abruptly, fighting the urge to run, jaw tight enough to splinter. "Excuse me. I need a moment."

He didn't wait for permission, just walked out, pulse hammering. The hallway was glass and ice, but it couldn't cool what burned in him, the ache beneath his skin like a fever.

He pressed a hand to the wall, fingers splayed, breath shallow. Hands shaking, he pulled out his phone and called Kain.

"Boss. How's the lawyer party?"

"The name I gave you last night. Results?" His voice was a rasp, barely controlled.

A pause. "Nothing with just Eden. But—"

"Marlowe. Junior associate at Lorne & Carrick." The words came out low, rough, like a threat or a plea.

That landed.

"Yeah. Okay. That narrows it. Give me five."

"Two," Nyx bit out, and hung up, the phone trembling in his grip.

He leaned against the wall, jaw locked so hard it ached, breath coming in shallow bursts. The urge to break something, to tear out of his skin, was almost overwhelming.

This wasn't simple attraction. Wasn't even fascination.

It was pressure, cracking the armour he'd spent centuries forging. No one had rattled his control like this since his blood was new and wild, since even before he'd learned how to be a man, not a monster.

It wasn't claim.

But it was close. Too close.

He shut his eyes, forced three slow breaths, and let the icy air burn through him. When he finally stepped back into the boardroom, he wore his calm like a mask—careful, cold, unbreakable.

Eden was adjusting the display, her fingers quick on the touchscreen. The detectives looked up, but said nothing— professional enough to keep their curiosity leashed.

He sat.

This close, he could smell her again.

Not blood. Not metal. Warm citrus and soft jasmine. Clean soap. Rain. Nothing dangerous. Nothing overt.

But it crawled under his skin all the same, a hunger and a memory, his body remembering before his mind could catch up.

Eden spoke, voice steady. "I've queued the footage. The resolution degrades every ten seconds—we're hoping your team can recover something usable."

Nyx nodded. "Play it." His voice was steady, but every muscle was tight as wire.

The room dimmed. Footage flickered across the screen— black and white, low-res, the usual city grime.

A neighbourhood street. One figure walking home, hood pulled up against the drizzle.

The image stuttered. Grainy. Distorted.

Another shape passed close—too close. A shoulder brushed. Nothing more.

The young man clutched his chest. Staggered.

Then dropped.

No warning. No struggle. No clear cause.

Just a body on wet concrete, twitching once, then still.

The camera blurred, static striping the frame.

Almost nothing to see. Almost nothing to prove.

Lyn Rose

Renn cursed under his breath. The other detective asked Eden to forward the footage to the central archive.

She tapped a command. "Virex will receive a duplicate copy with full metadata."

Nyx didn't move. "I'll start enhancement this afternoon." He was grateful for the distraction—for anything to keep him from looking at her.

The room stayed silent a beat longer than it needed to.

Then Renn nodded to Eden. "We'll leave you to it. If Ravelle needs anything, you'll facilitate?"

She nodded. "Of course."

Nyx stood, already gathering his jacket. But before he could turn, her voice came again—lower, quieter, and with far too much certainty.

"Can I have a word?"

He stopped. Turned.

The door clicked shut.

Eden

Her stitches still throbbed, dull under the fluorescents. Painkillers kept her steady enough to stand, but the boardroom lights felt merciless—too bright, too sharp for a skull that still rang with yesterday's impact.

She turned, locking her gaze on him—and suddenly the room felt smaller. Thicker. Like the walls were closing in.

He stood still. Too still. Like his body was the only thing not betraying the truth underneath.

"It was you," she said.

Not a question. Not a plea.

A truth.

"The alley. The tux. You—" her voice caught, just a breath, "—you caught me."

No flicker of denial. No shift in his expression.

But something passed between them. Sharp. Silent. Hot.

She swallowed. Her mouth was dry, but the rest of her… wasn't. God. No man had ever looked at her like that. Not with violence barely caged beneath restraint. Not with hunger so deep it made her thighs press together without thinking.

Her heart pounded, too hard. She forced her voice calm.

"The cops took my statement last night. I… told them what I remembered. That someone helped me. Someone in a tux." She stepped forward, controlled and deliberate, though her legs didn't feel steady. "If it's alright, I'd like to give them your name. Just so they can take a proper statement. Confirm the sequence. You weren't listed on any records, but someone covered the hospital costs. That was you, wasn't it?"

His silence confirmed everything.

She exhaled once, careful.

"I don't like owing debts I can't repay."

The words were innocent. They didn't sound like what she meant. But the look in her eyes did.

She meant thank you.

She meant why the fuck can't I stop thinking about you.

She meant I want to feel your mouth on my skin.

His eyes hadn't left hers.

She wondered if he could hear the blood in her veins.

Smell the slick heat between her thighs.

Because she felt it—deep, low, coiling heat.

And underneath all of it, that same awful, magnetic pull.

Something wasn't right about him.

And she didn't care.

Eden drew a breath, steadied herself—and stepped closer.

"Please…" Her voice was softer now, real. "Can I take you to dinner? Just a thank you."

His eyes flicked to hers, unreadable.

"I mean it," she went on, pushing past the thrum in her chest. "I don't know what would've happened if you hadn't been there. I keep thinking about it and—"

Her throat tightened. She didn't cry. Not ever. But the words felt thick, like grief brushing against a door it wasn't meant to open.

She looked down, exhaled hard. "Just dinner. That's all."

Then—he moved.

Just one step.

But it brought him too close.

His body didn't brush hers, not even a whisper of contact— but the heat of him hit her like a stormfront.

And when she looked up—

His pupils were blown wide. Jaw locked tight. Like holding himself back took more effort than violence ever had.

Lyn Rose

He inhaled.

A sharp, silent pull.

And something changed.

His eyes darkened.

Like the scent of her had hit him wrong.

Or too right.

Because under the clean notes of her skin and perfume, her body was betraying her. Arousal crept up between her thighs, heat soft and slick, and she knew—knew—that he could smell it.

She took half a step back, breath catching.

But he was already moving.

"I'll contact you," he said, voice hoarse.

Then he turned.

And walked out.

Not slow. Not casual.

Like if he didn't leave right now something inside him would break.

The door slammed behind him.

Lyn Rose

Eden stood still, heart hammering, skin flushed, breath trembling in her lungs.

What the hell was that?

And why did part of her crave to chase after it?

CHAPTER FOUR

She Was Already Under His Skin

Outside, Nyx didn't head for the car. He stood at the edge of the curb, pulse still wrecked, the city roaring around him. He could taste her on the air—citrus and adrenaline, lightning and sin.

He hated that it steadied him.

He hated that it called to him.

Across the street, the tower's mirrored windows caught his reflection: composed, immaculate, lying through its teeth.

He straightened his cuffs, forced a breath, and muttered to no one,

"Pull yourself together."

Then he vanished into the daylight.

Lyn Rose

The city hit him like a slap.

Wet concrete. Hot exhaust. The low, restless thrum of morning traffic echoing through Edalva's inner district. Nyx stepped out of Lorne & Carrick, every muscle wired, a live current running beneath his skin. He felt like he'd just walked off a battlefield, adrenaline still spiking, senses dialled to eleven. She'd smiled. Asked for dinner. Said please. And her scent—gods, that fucking scent—still clung to him like a bruise, sweet and sharp and impossible to shake.

His phone buzzed.

Kain.

"Got it," his second said, voice lazy as ever. "Pulled the file. You were right—she's not just pretty. She's impressive. Sending it to your secure inbox now, but here's the rundown."

Nyx said nothing, just stalked toward the Jag, boots echoing on the sidewalk, trying to outpace the memory of Eden's smile.

"She's twenty-five. Graduated top of her law school cohort. Undergrad with honours—political science and criminal justice. Fast-tracked at Lorne & Carrick. Basically, a prodigy. Five-seven, sixty-one kilos, hair almost black, hazel eyes with gold. O-negative." Kain paused, letting that sink in. "Lives alone in Westmere, second floor. No family. Emergency contact is a college friend—Alana Finn."

Nyx reached the car, metal cool beneath his palm, heartbeat thumping in his throat.

"And boss… there's something weird. She's had four medical incidents since sixteen. All unexplained collapses. No cause, but always off-the-charts adrenaline. You think she's triggering?"

Nyx didn't answer. "Just email me the file."

He slid behind the wheel, hands tight on the leather, and drove. The Jag cut through traffic like a whisper of violence, city blurring past in streaks of light and shadow.

Virex Tower – Private Office, 19th Floor

His office was all hush and shadow, screens the only light. He liked it that way. The city outside burned—grey and gold and hungry for secrets. He ignored it. Sat. Rolled up his sleeves. Opened Kain's file. Forced himself not to rush.

Subject: Eden Marlowe.

He clicked. The dossier spilled out, cool and clinical. But the words ran hot in his blood.

CONFIDENTIAL DOSSIER

SUBJECT: Marlowe, Eden Elise
DOB: 11 September 1999
AGE: 25
HEIGHT: 170 cm (5'7")
WEIGHT: 61 kg (134 lbs)

Lyn Rose

EYE COLOR: Hazel (gold variance)
HAIR COLOR: Dark brown (Level 2 Black Spectrum)
BLOOD TYPE: O-negative
ADDRESS: 22b Lyon Crescent, Westmere
OCCUPATION: Junior Associate, Lorne & Carrick LLP
CURRENT POSITION: Legal rep under Marcus Halden (Partner)

EDUCATION:
• Bachelor of Political Science (High Distinction), Edalva University
• Minor in Criminal Justice
• Juris Doctor (Dean's List), Edalva University—Graduated 2025

MEDICAL HISTORY (FLAGGED):
• 4 incidents: 2016, 2017, 2021, 2024
• Sudden collapse, adrenaline spikes, temporary aphasia
• No neurological findings
• Most recent: laceration, concussion, this year 2025, 24hrs ago

Nyx's jaw ached. O-negative. The rarest—and the most dangerous. His hands curled into fists. This woman, this blood, this pull—he hadn't felt anything like it in a century. Maybe longer. Those flagged incidents, too neat, too strange. Patterns that didn't fit. He didn't trust coincidence. Not anymore.

He shut the file, but the unease didn't leave. Her scent, her voice, her smile. That name—Eden. Not just her blood calling. Something deeper. A chord he didn't want to name. He was in too deep already.

He closed the dossier. Not because he wanted to. Because he had to.

But her face hung in his mind, sharp and bright. Eden Marlowe. Brilliant. Disciplined. Human. And not fucking normal.

He drew in a breath, slow and hard. His body didn't care that she wasn't here—his blood still stirred, teeth itching with memory.

Enough. Focus.

He tapped open the Lorne & Carrick file, the one Eden had queued in the boardroom. Encryption peeled back, legal tags stamped across the metadata. The footage stuttered to life— grainy, blurred, every frame struggling to hold its shape.

His gut went cold. Not an alley cam—this was a neighbourhood street, shaky feed from a corner unit. One victim. Human. Collapsed mid-stride after someone brushed too close.

He'd thought the law firm's request was routine, a human mess he could clean and close. But this wasn't routine. This was the same pattern bleeding into places it should never have reached.

He'd been wrong.

Lyn Rose

He scrubbed through the file again, slower this time. No flash. No weapon. No spell. Just one man walking home down a quiet street, grain crawling over the frame like static snow.

Nyx narrowed his eyes, leaning in. The raw feed was garbage, but garbage could talk if you knew how to listen. He keyed in his personal protocols—grain reduction, light normalization, spectral balance. Code spilled across three monitors, pulling the image apart pixel by pixel until the noise bled thinner.

"Come on," he muttered. His fingers flew. Refraction scan. Frequency isolation. A full-spectrum overlay to catch what the human eyes—and human tech—never could.

The feed stuttered, sharpened, stuttered again. Heat mapping popped red across the man's chest. Wrong variance. Too sudden. Too sharp.

Nyx looped the moment on repeat, every frame slowed to a crawl. He pushed the normalization harder, pulling detail from shadows, bleeding contrast until outlines trembled on the screen.

And then—he saw it.

Not absence. Not failure. A hand. Quick, clinical. The faintest jab at the man's collarbone, so fast the untrained eye would've missed it completely.

The victim clutched his chest, staggered, and went down.

Lyn Rose

Nyx's jaw locked. "Shit."

The victim was human. But the method—the needle, the precision, the aftermath—was the same violation he'd already logged in the wolf and the Fae. Different bodies. Same trigger. It wasn't random—it was deliberate. Whoever was moving through Edalva with a syringe wasn't discriminating.

And Eden was standing right in the middle of it. Handed the mess, told to polish it, made the face of a case that should never have touched her desk. A junior associate thrown into the dark without knowing the dark was real.

Nyx's pulse drummed harder. He knew how this was supposed to work. Supernatural deaths never landed in human firms. The Department flagged them, rerouted them, scrubbed the records, glamoured the witnesses. Mortals weren't meant to see the edges of what lurked in Edalva, let alone carry the files into boardrooms.

But here it was. A human collapse with a supernatural fingerprint, shoved into a mortal firm like it was clean, like it was ordinary.

His hand slid into his jacket, pulling his phone free. One photo glowed on the screen: the wolf in the alley, arm turned, the needle mark at the crook of the elbow. Small. Precise. Cold as intent. He flicked back to the paused frame on his monitor—grain scrubbed, light normalized, the faint silhouette brushing past the human victim before he folded to the pavement. Same brush, same timing.

Lyn Rose

Not coincidence.

Connection.

He leaned closer, freezing the grain-scrubbed frame again. Not a vampire. Not a Court reaper. Not Fae, not witch. Nothing catalogued, nothing known. New. Or old enough to be legend.

Adrenaline hummed through his veins. Something had moved in the open, left its signature, and still almost slipped away. But he'd seen it now. He wasn't letting go.

Nyx sat back in the chair, her scent still clinging to him like smoke. Eden had been given the file. Pulled into this. Not by design. Not by destiny.

Because someone had let a classified case slip through the cracks. And that changed everything.

He opened a secure line. The six-point sigil spun, then locked. Evelyn Stroud answered, her voice cold and clipped.

"Ravelle."

"I was called into Lorne & Carrick this morning," Nyx said. "Human law firm. You know the one."

A pause, then her voice came back, sharper. "Yes. I know it. What the hell were they doing with you?"

"They asked me to de-grain city footage. A human male— collapsed under unusual circumstances. No drugs, no trauma, no history. Just… dropped." His jaw tightened. "I scrubbed the feed. It wasn't cardiac arrest. It was interference. He was injected. Same puncture profile as the wolf and the Fae."

The silence that followed was loaded, dangerous.

"You're telling me we've got wolves, Fae, and now a human—same method?"

"Exactly." He flicked her the files: the still from Vestry, the blurred human frame, the cleaned overlay showing the moment the man clutched his chest. "Same vein mark. Same collapse. It isn't isolated, Stroud. Someone is moving through this city with a syringe, and they don't care what blood it finds."

Her breath hissed across the line. "Shit. That's too much coincidence to ignore."

"Too much to be chance," Nyx said flatly.

"I'll lock the files down," Stroud replied, steel threading her words. "And Ravelle—keep this buried until we've got a name. No panic. Not yet."

The line cut, leaving the weight of her curse hanging heavy in the room.

The call ended. Nyx stared at the dark screen.

He hadn't mentioned Eden. Didn't plan to.

The last place he wanted her was in the middle of this. She should've been far from it—untouched, unknowing. Not standing in boardrooms with corpses in her files and death at her fingertips.

But his mind kept circling her anyway. The way she'd looked at him. The way she'd smiled. And the fact that she'd been holding evidence that should never have reached human hands.

He pushed the thought down and hit Kain's line.

"Start digging," Nyx ordered, voice like iron. "Pull every flagged death in the city from the last six months. Instant collapses, unexplained causes, clean tox screens. Anything that doesn't add up."
"On it," Kain said, already typing. "I'll pull from Accord servers, Virex logs—and even the human systems. The ones Stroud doesn't know exist."

"And cross-check all factions," Nyx added. "Any wolves, Fae, witches turning on each other without cause. Any hint of new drugs or injections on the street. If someone's dosing them, I want the trail."

"Copy that. I'll call when I've got it."

Nyx killed the call, jaw tight.

This wasn't just data anymore.

It was her.

He let the screen fade. Mind racing, pulse pounding. He shouldn't contact her—should stay away, let the thing pass, let her fade. But the footage had touched her. That meant risk. And he couldn't stop thinking about her.

He tapped a message to Kain. "Send her a contact request. Virex signature. Professional channel. Legal representation protocol."

"Eden Marlowe?"

"Yes."

"Message?"

"I'll write it."

He typed, fast and direct, didn't let himself hesitate:

Subject: Surveillance Review – Additional Debriefing
From: Nyx Ravelle
To: Eden Marlowe

Eden,
Further analysis of the footage has revealed anomalies requiring additional context. I'd like to discuss findings and implications in a secure setting. As you were the presenting counsel, your insights are relevant.
Dinner, tonight. 7 p.m.
The address is Vire's—private suite.
I'll send a car.

To be clear: this is not a date.
— N.R.

Send. No second read.

He pinged dispatch: "Pickup – Eden Marlowe. 6:30 sharp. Westmere District. Confirm safe pickup."

Vire's wasn't random. Sleek, invitation-only. Part-owned by Nyx himself—though few knew it—and by Torran Black, the city's Alpha wolf and one of the rare few Nyx considered an equal. Private suite, shielded, no recordings, no scent trails, no intrusions. No interruptions.

Three hours.

Not nearly enough to get her out of his head.

Eden – 5:02 p.m. | Lorne & Carrick

The notification blinked into her inbox like any other. She clicked it, not expecting much—then froze.

From: Nyx Ravelle
Subject: Surveillance Review – Additional Debriefing
Dinner. Vire's. Private suite. Not a date. Professional.

Her heart tripped, missed a beat, then hammered back harder.

"Oh my god," she whispered.

She stood so fast her chair screeched. Walked in a frantic circle. Then did it again.

Was this normal? No. Obviously not. But also—yes? She'd asked him to dinner. He'd just gotten there first.

With a car. And a private suite. At Vire's.

Vire's. The place you couldn't get into unless you were royalty, rich, or cursed. Which, apparently, he was—maybe all three.

She snatched her phone, called Liv.

"Eden?"

"I have two hours. Two hours, and I have no idea what to wear."

"…What?"

"He's picking me up. At six-thirty. Car. Fancy dinner. Not a date but you know it is."

"Back up. Who's he?"

"Nyx Ravelle."

Long silence. Then:

"THE TALL ONE FROM THE OFFICE?"

"Yes."

Lyn Rose

"The one with the hands and the jaw and the voice—"

"YES!"

Liv shrieked. "I'm getting wine. Where are you?"

"Walking out now. I'll be home in ten."

6:03 p.m. | Eden's Apartment

Two wine glasses down. One outfit rejected. Hair up, then down, then half-up. Liv sprawled on the bed, eating crackers, scrolling TikTok.

"He said it's not a date," Eden muttered, staring into the mirror. "But he's picking me up. At seven. To talk about surveillance anomalies. With eye contact."

"Which means it's absolutely a date."

Eden swatted her. "I'm trying not to hyperventilate. Be helpful."

"Wear the dress. The red one."

"It's too much, not professional."

"It's perfect. Sexy but sharp. Like you didn't try, but also like you could destroy a man if you wanted."

Eden glared. "I don't want to destroy him."

"…Liar."

Lyn Rose

She didn't argue. Instead, she pulled on the dress. Tight at the waist, low in the back, classy in front—legs for days, neck bare, sleeves painted on. She added heels. Lip stain. A brush of perfume, light and expensive.

Still felt underdressed.

But also… ready.

Her phone buzzed. A driver texted: Outside. Black car. Take your time.

She stared at herself in the mirror, nerves and curiosity and a little thrill all tangled together.

Whispered, "It's not a date."

And walked out the door.

The city moved on, unaware that its lines had just crossed.

Two predators, same enemy, neither ready to admit it.

Nyx watched daylight fade across the glass, pulse steady but wrong.

Eden stepped into the waiting car, curiosity outweighing sense.

What waited at Vire's wasn't dinner.

It was the start of something that would change the city—

and neither of them could see it yet.

Lyn Rose

CHAPTER FIVE

It's Not A Date

The black car waited at the curb like it had been carved from shadow—sleek, low, windows tinted to obsidian. No logo. No driver visible. The streetlight caught the gloss just right, turning it into a dark mirror reflecting the restless city.

For a second, Eden hesitated, breath catching—not just from the night's chill, but from something deeper, a pulse beneath her skin that whispered of a connection she barely understood. The night carried the ghost of rain—clean asphalt, cool air—but the city itself was dry, glittering.

The car wasn't just waiting. It was watching.

Then the back door opened. Not by hand—automatic. Like the car itself had decided she was ready, like it was part of the plan she didn't fully understand yet.

A driver in a dark suit stood nearby, crisp and anonymous, the kind of man who blended into shadows, but whose presence whispered control. "Miss Marlowe?"

She nodded. "Yes."

He held the door with a subtle but firm gesture. "We'll be arriving at Vire's shortly. Mr. Ravelle is already on-site."

Already there. Of course he was. Always one step ahead.

Eden slid into the backseat, the door closing with a whisper of expensive engineering. The interior was unreal—soft black leather that seemed to swallow her, dim ambient lighting that barely touched the surfaces, and quiet music pulsing through the cabin like a heartbeat she could feel deep beneath her skin.

A bottle of water rested cool in its holder, beside it a bottle of unopened champagne—casual decadence, like they were always prepared to celebrate or seduce.

She chose the wine, poured a glass, and knocked it back in one gulp—numbing the nerves before they could take root.

A digital screen lit up on the partition ahead; it glowed softly, displaying her name and destination like a personal invitation.

It didn't feel like a car. It felt like being handled. Controlled. Protected. And if she was honest—a little bit of that control was electric, thrilling. A strange warmth bloomed low in her chest, confusing and unwanted, something tugged at her from the inside, stirring things she wasn't ready to face.

She tried not to overthink it. Failed spectacularly.

The city slipped by in streaks of light beyond the glass, neon blurring with the wet night. Her fingers twisted in her lap, restless. What was he going to say? What had he really found in that footage? The image of that man crumpling on a quiet neighbourhood street burned the back of her mind. One moment walking home, the next—gone. She didn't know why it unsettled her so much, only that it felt wrong, unnatural. Like something had reached through the world and plucked his life away.

And why did she care more about the way he'd looked at her than the content of any goddamn video? That look—sharp and unfinished—lingered in her chest like a spark she couldn't smother.

Was it real? A connection? Or just her mind reaching for something that was never there?

The ride lasted only ten minutes, but it was enough to make her skin prickle, her pulse race. She touched up her lipstick with shaking hands, smoothed the fabric of her dress like it could armour her, practiced slow breaths that came uneven and quick. When the car finally pulled up to Vire's, the driver stepped out, opening the door once more, the offer reminded her of a gateway to something dangerous and beautiful.

Lyn Rose

She stepped into the cool night air, heart pounding so loud it nearly drowned out the faint pulse of jazz that drifted through the marble-veined walls of the private suite.

The suite overlooked the city's edge—a panorama of glittering lights and distant shadows. All glass, dim lighting, and a faint hum of music that felt like a secret whispered just for them.

Nyx stood by the table, posture calm, drink untouched. His presence was a steady flame in the quiet room—controlled, deliberate—but Eden swore she could feel the storm beneath it. That coiled tension. Like something barely leashed. It mirrored the wild pulse pounding through her own chest.

He didn't pace. Didn't fidget. But every line of his body was keyed to war—coiled, ready, electric.

Then—

Her.

Not a scent. Not a sound.

But something in the air shifted, like a subtle gravitational pull, a sudden tilt in the balance of the room. The invisible thread between them thrummed, a silent song neither fully understood but both felt deep in their bones.

Nyx

The moment she stepped inside, the world seemed to fracture, pulse and wait.

She didn't see him move.

He moved to the tinted glass, eyes tracking her through the reflection—sharp, precise, predator and king. And then he saw it.

The wolf.

Big. Cocky. One of Black's younger enforcers—swagger wrapped in a tailored suit. He worked Vire's security, thought the city was his playground.

He stepped in front of her, voice low, words lost to the tension.

Then—

He leaned in.

Nyx's fangs dropped like blades sliding free in his mouth. His jaw locked hard. His entire body froze in that terrifying way predators do before they strike.

The wolf inhaled her—bold, hungry, like he could claim the scent for himself.

"Mm. Don't you smell good—" The wolf's hand slid to her arm.

Lyn Rose

Red.

That's all Nyx saw.

The rage didn't rise like a wave. It detonated. A shockwave of pure, blistering fury.

Nyx was across the floor before thought could catch him.

He didn't walk—he moved like violence made flesh.

One hand shot out, snapping around the wolf's shoulder, squeezing hard enough to grind cartilage beneath his grip.

The wolf turned, ready to bark back—

Until he saw who held him.

The smirk vanished like smoke.

Nyx's voice cut cold and sharp as ice and iron.

"You touched her."

The wolf swallowed hard, eyes flickering with primal fear. "I didn't know she was—"

Mine.

The word sang through Nyx's blood, echoing in his skull like a death knell. Mine.

But he didn't speak it.

Lyn Rose

Didn't need to.

The boy's eyes widened, the flicker of survival flashing bright.

He dropped into a crouch—not out of respect.

Out of pure, raw terror.

"I'm sorry. I didn't mean—"

"Leave."

One word.

Command.

The wolf scrambled, tripping over his own feet in his rush to vanish into the crowd.

Every gaze in the lounge flicked away at once. No one wanted the vampire's eyes on them.

Nyx didn't watch him go.

He was already looking at her.

Eden stood frozen. Shoulders tight. Breath shallow.

But her scent—gods—her scent rushed into him like wildfire.

Arousal, layered with fear. Sweet. Floral. A hint of sweat.

Real.

It hit him so hard he had to dig his nails into his palm just to stop himself from grabbing her and dragging her upstairs, where no one could see.

She hadn't even said a word.

And still—

He reached for her.

His hand went to the small of her back, steadying, guiding.

Soft skin. Warm. Smooth.

She was warm against his palm, perfect, like she'd always belonged there.

And fuck—the image of the wolf's bloodied face from Vestry flashed unbidden in his mind. Rabid. Injected. Another needle mark in another body. And now this fool, daring to touch what was his. The two threads tangled together in his gut, fury burning hotter with every breath.

His body ignited like lightning crawling beneath his skin.

Muscle, nerve, need.

He felt good just from touching her.

And that only made it worse.

Lyn Rose

Because someone else had.

That wolf had.

That thing had breathed her in and touched her arm, looked at her like prey, like he had any right to sense what belonged to Nyx.

Nyx had never been ruled by his instincts.

But they were snarling now.

Tear his throat out. Mark her. Take her.

Instead, he said, "Come."

Not a request.

And she followed.

Eden

She didn't mean to hesitate. But her legs weren't entirely hers.

The room felt off—like the air was charged, humming, tuned to a frequency no one else could hear. Something had shifted.

Lyn Rose

And that man—the one who'd tried to flirt with her—was now crouched on the floor like he'd seen a ghost. No, not a ghost. A god.

A terrifying, furious god made of shadows and silk.

What the actual fuck just happened?

She hadn't seen Nyx move. One second, she was politely dodging the wolf's terrible pick-up line—the next, there was silence.

Then violence.

Not loud. Not messy. Just… precise. Controlled.

And everyone in the room had felt it.

Especially her.

Her pulse was skittering like a live wire under her skin. Her mouth dry. Her body… hot in places it shouldn't be.

His hand pressed gently against the small of her back. Not rough. Not demanding. Just… there.

Grounding her.

Possessing her.

She should have been angry. Confused. Afraid, even.

But instead—

She followed.

Without thinking. Without resistance.

Like something inside her had already decided:

That man was danger. But also safety.

And somehow, impossibly…

hers.

He didn't let go until they were inside the suite.

And even then, he only released her because if he didn't—

He wouldn't stop at just her back.

Nyx opened the door to the private suite and stepped aside, his hand still lightly resting at her spine.

Not possessive.

Just not ready to let go.

Not yet.

He moved to her chair and pulled it out.

Old manners.

Older instincts.

Eden didn't look at him.

Didn't speak.

Just sat—

Back straight. Shoulders squared.

Like a soldier awaiting trial.

Not defiant.

Not broken.

But somewhere in between.

Her hands smoothed her skirt out of habit, the motion stiff. Robotic.

Like she wasn't sure if she wanted to run—

Or see what would happen if she stayed.

Her scent told him everything her body didn't.

Fear. Arousal. Curiosity. Pride.

And beneath it all… that thread.

Familiar. Deep. Ancient.

Nyx stepped around the table and took the seat opposite her.

Calm on the surface.

But inside, his blood hadn't cooled.

He flicked his fingers once—barely a motion.

A waiter appeared like he'd stepped out of the walls.

"Bring me Black," Nyx said quietly. "And a bottle of wine. Her choice."

The man bowed and vanished.

Nyx let the silence hang.

He didn't speak.

Just watched her.

Watched the way her hands stayed perfectly still in her lap— even as the vein at her throat fluttered like a snare drum.

Watched her eyes avoid his—not out of submission, but strategy.

Pride, he thought.

She wouldn't lower her chin. Not even now.

Good.

Staying strong would keep her alive.

Lyn Rose

Eden looked over the wine list like it meant something.

Her fingers traced the edge of the leather menu, deliberate. Slow.

Buying time.

"I'll have the red," she said at last, lifting her gaze to the server. "The merlot."

Nyx nodded. The man was gone before the last syllable left her lips.

The bottle arrived almost too fast.

Poured in silence.

Her glass—dark ruby, clean-edged, with a floral bouquet.

His—deeper.

Thicker.

Not quite wine.

She noticed. Of course she did.

Her brow furrowed. Then smoothed.

She probably thought it was the light.

It wasn't.

Lyn Rose

He lifted his glass, but didn't drink.

His gaze had already shifted—fixed on the door.

He felt him before he saw him.

Black.

Alpha of the Blackthorne Pack.

One of the only wolves Nyx trusted.

Brutal. Loyal. Feral in the old ways.

The man strode in with a grin already cutting across his face, one hand lifted in greeting—

Then he caught the scent.

Mid-step, Black froze.

Nostrils flared.

Smile gone.

And his eyes locked on her like a bullet fired point-blank.

His pupils dilated.

Breath hitched.

One step forward—then stopped.

Every line in his body coiled tight.

Nyx saw it.

Saw the alpha instinct punch through his friend like a lightning bolt.

Nyx didn't stand.

He just spoke, calm and quiet.

"Eden Marlowe, this is Torran Black. Black, Eden."

Eden blinked, startled but composed. "Nice to meet you."

Black didn't respond.

Just looked back at Nyx, one brow raised—what the fuck?

Nyx stood.

Straightened his cuffs.

"Excuse me a moment," he said to Eden, his voice calm—measured, but impossible to ignore.

He led Black out the side door into the narrow hall between the suites.

The moment the door clicked shut behind them—

"What the fuck is she?" Black hissed, voice low, jaw clenched. "She's not entirely human."

Nyx's teeth bared before he could stop the sound—a low growl rattling in his chest.

"I know."

"You can smell that?" Black barked. "That's not just blood. It's alive, Nyx. Like… pure fucking magic. Like something designed."

"I said. I know."

Black stared at him, eyes wild.

"And you brought her here?"

Nyx stepped in closer, face inches from Black's.

"She's mine," he said coldly. "That's all you need to know."

Black blinked, took a slow step back, hands raised. "Alright. Damn. Didn't know you'd claimed anyone."

Nyx didn't answer.

He hadn't.

Not formally.

Not yet.

But fuck if the thought didn't burn behind his teeth like a brand.

Black's footsteps faded down the hall, but the air between them stayed charged—too thick, too alive.

Nyx closed his eyes for one slow breath, tasting her still on his skin.

If this was the start of a claim, it was already too late to stop it.

CHAPTER SIX

Claimed in Silence

Nyx returned to the table like nothing had happened.

Not flustered.

Not apologetic in the way most men were when they disappeared mid-conversation.

Just calm. Composed. Like a storm that had already passed, leaving a charged silence in its wake.

The restaurant lighting shifted subtly—candles burning lower, shadows gathering around the booth like smoke. Somewhere above, a violin hummed beneath dark jazz, the low thrum of bass pulsing faintly through the floor. The air grew electric, warmth and wine mixing until the night seemed charged with something unspoken.

Nyx moved with precise stillness as he sat, adjusting the cuff of his shirt before lifting his gaze.

"Apologies," he said, voice like velvet stretched over steel. "Business."

Eden nodded slowly. "Sure."

She didn't press. Didn't ask why "business" had looked a lot like tension, like barely restrained violence. Why it had involved the man who'd stared at her like she was something rare—or wrong.

She'd learned not to poke when it came to powerful men and strange silences.

Menus appeared—sleek leather and crisp paper—delivered by two servers who moved with too much grace to be casual staff.

Both smiled.

Both spoke in smooth tones.

But it wasn't the words that made her skin crawl. It was the way they inhaled. Not openly. Not obviously. But with a hunger barely masked, like they were tasting the very air around her.

One passed behind her and slowed—just a fraction. The other handed Nyx a menu, but let his gaze slide to Eden's throat. His nostrils flared. His tongue darted briefly across his bottom lip before he caught himself and stepped away.

Eden stiffened.

Lyn Rose

Nyx's jaw flexed—sharp, deliberate. She glanced at him. He was watching the servers like a general eyeing soldiers who'd crossed an invisible line.

Then his eyes returned to her.

"Eden," he said, the name low, almost gentle. "Tell me about yourself."

She tilted her head, wary. "Like what?"

"Family. Where you're from."

Simple questions. Normal ones. But his tone wasn't casual. And the way he asked—it didn't feel like small talk.

It felt like a test. Like a file being built in real time.

Still, she answered.

"I grew up here. Edalva. My parents died when I was little—car accident. No siblings. I was placed in the system. Bounced a bit, then landed with a good placement for the rest of school. A couple foster siblings, but we're not close." She sipped her wine, not meeting his eyes now. "I don't usually talk about it. Not because I'm sad—just… people get weird."

Nyx didn't interrupt. He took in every word, every pause, every edge she tried to smooth over.

No known bloodline. No anchors. Medical flags. O-negative. Dangerous.

Lyn Rose

He nodded slowly, offering no opinion—just filing it away.

"You're not what I expected," he said.

Eden gave a dry laugh. "No one ever means that in a good way."

Nyx just looked at her—unblinking, unreadable. "I did."

And suddenly, the quiet wasn't so quiet anymore.

She cleared her throat, chasing the ghost of a smile with another sip of wine.

"I never got to thank you," she said softly. "For what you did the other night."

Nyx tilted his head slightly. "You don't need to."

"I do." Her voice steadied. "You didn't just scare them off. You carried me. Drove me to the hospital. Paid for everything. You… saved me."

A server arrived at that moment, quiet as a shadow, and placed down two plates—one seared duck, the other lamb, both finished with dark glaze and delicate edible flowers. Another server refilled her glass without asking. The bottle was older than her entire legal career. The air thickened with the scent of rosemary, smoke, and something richer beneath it all—something like earth and iron.

Nyx didn't speak right away. He adjusted the angle of his knife, then said, "I was leaving the Unity Gala. Saw two men following you. I didn't like the way it looked."

"And you followed them?"

"I did." He sliced into his lamb, calm and methodical. "By the time I reached the alley, they had you cornered. You were bleeding. Dazed. So I acted."

"You didn't call an ambulance."

"No." He took a bite, chewed, swallowed. "The hospital was close. An ambulance would've taken longer. And I could cover your care."

Eden hesitated, then picked up her fork. "Still… thank you."

He inclined his head slightly. "You would've done the same."

She didn't answer. Maybe because she wasn't sure she would've.

Silence stretched—comfortable, then tense. Just the soft clink of cutlery, the rustle of linen. The candle between them burned lower. Her glass was refilled again, the wine sliding red as rubies in the crystal.

"That case I was working on," she said. "The one from the footage you pulled. Did you get a chance to look?"

Nyx's thoughts tightened around the truth.

He'd seen the injection site.

The collapse.

The pattern.

And he knew exactly what it meant.

How much did he tell her without painting a target on her back?

He placed his fork down, methodical and controlled. "Yes. And it was deliberate."

Her breath hitched. "So… he was murdered?"

He nodded, slow. "Looks like it."

Eden stared at him, the world narrowing to the space between them.

Nyx exhaled once, almost soundless. "And there may be others. Same signature. Same method."

Her face paled. "Someone is moving through Edalva injecting people to death?"

"Yes." His voice stayed calm, but the truth underneath it wasn't. "Edalva Police have opened a murder investigation now."

That was it. The line he'd allow her to see.

Eden swallowed hard, the memory of the man collapsing replaying in brutal clarity. The suddenness. The violence hidden in something so small.

Nyx didn't fill the silence. Didn't soften it.

He just watched her, eyes steady, something protective coiled under his stillness.

They finished the meal in a quiet that hummed like static. Eden drained her wine, heat curling low in her stomach, but the knot in her chest didn't ease. The food was perfect, but none of it grounded her.

It was Nyx—dangerous, unreadable Nyx—who held her in place, who kept pulling her deeper even as he tried to shield her from the dark.

Across from her, he sat impossibly composed, now sipping a far darker liquid than wine. She'd stopped wondering what it was.

"So…" she began, swirling what little remained in her glass. "I have to ask."

He looked up, amused.

"What exactly is the infamous Mr. Ravelle known for? Besides… showing up in alleys and saving lives?"

Nyx tipped the edge of his glass toward her. "That depends who you ask."

"Come on." She leaned in. "Give me something. Business? Power? Scandal?"

He finished his drink in a single, smooth pull. Then, at last, he poured himself some of her wine—red catching the candlelight like blood in glass.

"Technology," he said. "Corporate negotiation. Acquisition."

A pause. "And privacy."

Eden arched a brow. "That sounds like the résumé version. Not the tabloid one."

"The tabloid version doesn't matter."

"Because it's false?"

"Because it's noisy."

She hummed, lips curving. "You're very good at saying a lot without saying much."

Before he could answer, a voice broke the rhythm.

"Well, this looks cozy."

Torran Black returned like a storm in slow motion—coat open, tie gone, mischief leaking from every grin-lined edge. The air behind him smelled of night air and expensive whiskey.

He gave Nyx a lazy nod, then turned all his charm toward Eden.

"I owe you an apology," he said, pressing a hand to his chest with theatrical remorse. "For earlier. I was… surprised."

She smiled, the warmth immediate. "That a woman was sitting at the table?"

"With him, yes," he said, flashing a smile in Nyx's direction. "But more specifically—a woman of such beauty… and intrigue."

Then he reached down and took her hand, warm fingers wrapping around hers with theatrical care.

"Allow me to make amends."

Before she could stop him, he lifted it and kissed the back—slow, deliberate, gaze flicking sideways to catch Nyx's reaction.

Eden laughed, low and dangerous. "Careful, Mr. Black. I bite."

"Noted." He winked. "You two should come by the club tonight. First drink's on me. You look like you could use some trouble." He looked at Eden and smirked.

Nyx didn't move, but his eyes sharpened.

Torran gave him one last sideways glance. "Keep an eye on this one, Ravelle," he said, voice velveted with warning. "She might get snatched up."

Then he strolled away—already halfway into the darkened lounge, where candlelight met shadows like old lovers.

Nyx turned back to Eden.

"Would you like to go somewhere else?"

Her answer came with a crooked smile and the last sip of her wine.

"Absolutely."

As they stood to leave, Eden murmured something about needing the restroom. Nyx's eyes didn't leave her as she slipped down the corridor, heels tapping a slow, steady rhythm against the marble.

The second she vanished from sight, Nyx's phone was already in his hand.

"Kain. Jace," he said, voice low and clipped. "Club X. Torran's waiting inside."

No hesitation. No wasted breath. Just orders, cold and precise.

He slipped the phone away the moment Eden reappeared, fingers trailing through her hair like a touch of armour. Her lipstick was freshly reapplied, her eyes gleaming with a mix of curiosity and something sharper—the kind of look that tasted like wine and danger tangled together.

Without a word, Nyx closed the distance, his presence folding around her like a shadow.

She matched his pace as they moved toward the entrance. "Do we need to pay or…?"

He cracked the door open with one hand, the other pressing gently to the small of her back—a silent claim, a quiet promise. "I own part of this place," he said, voice flat. "Torran's the face. I'm the ghost."

Eden let out a low whistle. "No wonder the service feels… different."

Outside, the night had thickened. City lights flickered like distant stars against the sleek black glass of the cars lined up. The air was cool, sharp enough to slice through the lingering warmth of her wine.

The same black car waited, polished and silent. The driver stepped out without a word, opening the door like it was a gateway to another world.

Eden glanced at Nyx once—just once—before sliding inside.

Nyx circled to the passenger side and eased into the seat beside her. The door clicked shut, sealing them in a bubble of quiet.

The city pulsed past, Edalva's skyline glowing gold and indigo through the tinted windows, alive but distant.

She shifted, throwing him a sidelong look, laced with amused suspicion. "So, what's the real deal between you and Torran?"

His mouth barely moved before the car slowed, gliding to a stop at the velvet-roped entrance bathed in neon blue

CHAPTER SEVEN

Desire Wore Her Skin

The car slowed to a stop, its engine humming low like a deep growl.
Outside, Club X pulsed with light—neon bleeding blue across the pavement, shadows and gold laced in smoke. A velvet rope held back a sea of bodies pressed tight against the entrance, all heels and heat and hunger.

The moment Nyx stepped out, the crowd parted.
The bouncer—massive, silent—unhooked the rope without a word and bowed his head.
And then, from either side of the doorway, two men appeared.

Eden straightened.
One moved like smoke: tall, razor-sharp, with eyes that scanned everything and gave away nothing. The other was broader, golden-skinned, and already grinning like they'd just walked into the best kind of trouble.

They flanked Nyx like it was instinct. Like they'd always belonged there.

"Eden," Nyx said, his voice low as the city behind him. "There with me. Kain." He nodded at the grinning one. "And Jace."

Jace gave her a nod—nothing more.
But Kain bumped her shoulder, all charm and sparks. "Nice to meet you. Now let's have some fun, yeah?"

She blinked. Smiled. "I like you already."

The four of them stepped inside—and the world devoured her.

The music hit first.
"Bleed" by Jaklyn Feara pulsed through the air, thick and seductive, the bass slow and heavy enough to crawl under her skin. It wasn't just sound—it was heat. Pressure. A dark velvet rope pulling her deeper with every beat. It filled her chest, echoed in her bones, made her fingertips twitch with the urge to move.

The lighting inside was low and deliberate. Deep purples. Blood reds. White flashes stuttering across the crowd like lightning trapped under crystal. The scent of sweat and perfume curled in the air—sweet, spiced, feral.

The dance floor stretched out like a living thing. A mass of bodies swaying, rolling, grinding. Velvet-lined walls shimmered in the dark, catching pieces of the beat and throwing it back as colour and sound.

Eden faltered for half a second, drawn to it.
The rhythm. The heat. The way the music seemed to pulse through her like a second heartbeat.

Heads turned.
A woman at the bar froze, eyes widening, nostrils flaring. A man leaning against a mirrored pillar tipped forward, eyes fixed on Eden like he'd caught a scent he couldn't shake. More followed. Dozens.

She felt it—like a current shifting toward her, attention drawn in slow, hungry waves.

Nyx felt it too.
His eyes darkened immediately, pupils narrowing to slits as the black overtook their silver. His jaw flexed once—and then he reached for her.

His hand slid into hers, cool and commanding. Possessive.

The heat of his touch knocked something loose inside her.
It wasn't just protection.
It was a warning.

She didn't pull away.

Then: "There you are," came a voice behind them.

Torran Black materialized from the haze, flanked by two women in dresses so tight they looked painted on. His shirt was open at the collar, sleeves rolled to his elbows, hair raked back like he'd already danced, drank, and kissed too many people tonight.

He clapped Nyx on the back. "Thought you might get lost."

Then, to Kain and Jace—quick handshakes, familiarity. And finally, to Eden—another grin. "Welcome to the other side."

He turned on his heel, motioning them to follow. "Booth's waiting."

Black led them through the chaos like it belonged to him. The crowd parted without touching.

The music thickened, darker now—Obsidian Kiss by Sunseth threading through the speakers like desire, soaked in sex and something far more dangerous.

They reached the VIP level, tucked high on a mezzanine overlooking the dance floor. Their booth was a sunken half-circle of black velvet and smoked glass, backlit in flickering indigo. A private bar gleamed behind it—silver-rimmed decanters, crystal tumblers, glass as dark as ink.

Eden sank into the booth beside Nyx, her legs brushing his. The table vibrated softly with bass. Below, the floor moved like water—bodies grinding, arms rising, sweat gleaming under fractured light. She couldn't look away. It was like watching a heartbeat.

The music. The rhythm. The people. They weren't dancing—they were becoming something. One breath. One pulse.

Trays arrived—shot glasses, seven of them, rimmed in silver dust and filled with a warm amber liquid that shimmered faintly under the light.

Without a word, Nyx picked one up and held it out to Eden.

She took it. Their fingers brushed. Electricity.

Around them, the others grabbed theirs.

Black lifted his glass. "To the night," he said, smirking.

Kain added, "And to whatever we forget before morning."

They all knocked them back.

The shot went down warm, burned bright, then bloomed into something sweet, almost floral—like honey soaked in fire and dusk.

Eden's eyes fluttered. "Oh my god," she murmured, leaning closer to Nyx. Her breath ghosted over the curve of his ear. "What was that?"

He froze.
She was too close. Too warm. Too alive.

Her breath on his skin sent a bolt of hunger through him so sharp it bordered on pain. His hand on the table curled into a fist.

As he turned to answer, his mouth brushed the side of her head—his nose trailing down the column of her neck, where her pulse beat like a second heart.

He inhaled.

"Fuck," he whispered, the word low and ragged. "You smell good."

Eden tilted her head, just a little—inviting.

His fangs dropped.

He didn't even feel them at first.

He was seconds from sinking into her, from tasting—

Nyx wrenched back, breath sharp. "It's called a Bloodlight."

He straightened, hands in his lap, shoulders tense. Eyes locked on the opposite wall like it might hold him together.

Jace, silent until now, shifted closer and leaned in, murmuring something only Nyx could hear—measured, grounding.

Across from them, Black raised a brow. He'd seen enough. His grin curved like a blade.

He turned to Eden, voice smooth and laced with heat.

"Another drink, gorgeous?"

She smiled, slow and unbothered by the compliment—it was friendly.

"Yes, please."

The next round of drinks burned sweeter, smoother. Eden was buzzed—floating, glowing, fuck-it-all good. The bass had melted into her bloodstream, the lights strobed like stars just for her, and the velvet booth cradled her like some decadent dream she wasn't ready to wake up from.

She laughed at something Kain said—something reckless, probably. The words didn't matter. All that did was the music: heavy, hypnotic, luring her out of her seat and into the riot of lights and sound, something urgent and wild fluttering in her chest.

"I want to dance," she said, half to herself, half to anyone who might have been listening.

Kain grinned, sharp and easy. "Then let's fucking go, little one." He rose with a flourish, hand out—and Eden took it, letting him guide her away from the table. His grip was steady, warm. Safe, even. But as she moved with him, she couldn't help noticing it didn't make her shiver the way Nyx's touch had earlier, when his fingers had brushed hers, brief and electric. Where Kain's hand steadied her, Nyx's touch had unsettled her, pulling something invisible tight within her, a strange tether strung between them that she felt now, faint but taut, even as she tried to ignore it. Eden shook the sensation off, pushing herself deeper into the noise and light, determined to let the night sweep her away.

She didn't see Nyx tense, didn't catch the razor glint in Black's smile, or the hungry flash in the eyes that followed her into the club's shifting heat.

Kain spun her into the thick of the crowd. Eden let herself move, wild and free, letting the pulse of the music swallow thought. There was a strange weight to the air, a kind of electricity rolling over her skin—a sense that every eye was tracking her, every breath held just a second too long. She passed through bodies, spinning, hips loose, her laughter rising in defiance of the heaviness pressing in from all sides.

It felt like the whole room tilted toward her, the crowd swelling tighter, gravity bending, strangers pressing closer than seemed natural. Someone's hand—bigger, rough— found her waist uninvited, pulling a startled gasp from her lips. It was gone in an instant, Kain shouldering himself in between, steady as stone, his glare enough to send the stranger stumbling off. Eden barely had time to process what had happened before the music swept her up again, spinning her back around, Kain's arm a barrier and shield.

Yet she kept glancing over her shoulder—toward the booth, toward Nyx—half-expecting to find his eyes burning along her skin. There was something about him she couldn't explain, something that had her searching the crowd for a single face, even as she let Kain whirl her through the mass of dancers. The feeling of that invisible tether, pressing her to stay close to Nyx, tugged at her, magnetic like any step away might snap it for good. But she forced herself to let go, to get lost in the rhythm, to laugh until every strange tension faded to a background thrum.

The club's energy only grew stranger, more focused, the press of bodies relentless. If Eden had looked closely, she might have seen the momentary ripple of the crowd parting—shadows bending, heads turning, recognition flaring something—or someone—was making its way through the dark, inevitable as a tide. But Eden kept her eyes shut, pulse fluttering, smile wide, her only intention to dance.

She didn't notice the song shift, the way the music melted into something slower, darker, thick as honey and just as dangerous. She just moved, letting herself surrender to the night—never realizing just how much the night was watching her.

If she had looked up, she might have noticed the world changing. But for now, all she felt was the spell of her own joy, the last spark before everything would finally, inevitably, ignite.

CHAPTER EIGHT

The Taste That Undid Him

Nyx

Nyx tracked Eden the moment she slipped from the shadows in her red dress. He saw her—really saw her—every dangerous inch. For a moment, the world stilled; tension crackled, every sense sharpening to her movement.

Across the table, Kain met Nyx's eyes and smirked, curling Eden in closer. "I've got her, boss," he tossed back, grinning wide, all show and something darker beneath. He swept Eden from the booth and out onto the floor.

Kain spun Eden into the heart of the crowd. Her laughter rang out, wild and free—a spark in the night. She let herself go, light and reckless, letting the music claim her. The bass pounded through her, and with every spin, some strange electricity raced beneath her skin. She chalked it up to good wine and a great song.

She didn't notice how every eye tracked her. The supernatural crowd pressed in, unable to help themselves— voices fading, bodies shifting, drawn to her laughter like moths to a flame. The lights looked sharper, the air thicker, hungry eyes gathering too close. Kain's grip at her waist turned steel, his body moving into a protective orbit, even as the restless energy around them sharpened to a dangerous pitch.

Back at the booth, Black let the shadows settle, his gaze steady on Nyx. He watched the floor, took in the ripple Eden caused, and smirked, low and knowing.

"You better claim that, mate," Black said, casual but with iron in his bones. "It's not just us that can smell her."

Nyx didn't answer. Couldn't. His gaze was locked on Eden, everything else drowned to a low thrum. The flicker of her red dress under the lights was all he could see. Centuries of beauty never moved him like this. This was gravity with a heartbeat. Something primal twisted inside him—hunger, yes, but something darker: possessiveness, protection, a warning pulse that scraped the edge of fear.

He watched the way Kain spun Eden through the crowd, her head thrown back, laughter slicing through the noise. That sound hit Nyx like a blade—equal pain and relief. He wanted her out of there. He wanted her safe, and closer, untouched by anyone but him.

The air in the club shifted—tension mounting like pressure before a storm. He gripped the polished railing, hands cracking wood, pulse hammering against the music. Predator eyes tracked Eden, called by something old and wrong that had nothing to do with scent or sex—just raw, impossible allure. The pull snapped between him and her, straining, alive, and more than it should be.

Then the song changed: "Fatal Attraction" by Jaklyn Ferra. It hit slow and dangerous, pouring danger into every corner.

Nyx snapped. He descended from the booth—he didn't walk, he prowled. The crowd parted, then submitted. Conversation died, fangs retracted, no one daring to stand between him and what was his. Even the DJ missed a beat as he passed.

He caught glimpses of Eden through the bodies—hair wild, mouth open, lost in laughter, oblivious to the chaos she'd spun into the room. The dance floor felt new, molten, as she turned and found him, her eyes looking as though she'd been waiting all along.

He was already there—claiming her waist, pulling her close. Their bodies lined up, her arm falling around his neck, her shiver setting off a detonation in his chest.

The world fell away. He bent and caught her mouth, not gentle but burning. Her surprise melted into hunger, her laugh shattering into a gasp. She pressed into him as the room spun, every thought reduced to heat, want, and the shock of recognition. She tasted like wild summer, like every forbidden thing he'd ever chased and every danger he'd ever needed.

Lyn Rose

The club stilled around them, supernatural's shrinking from the spark that burned on the floor. It wasn't just lust. It was a shift—a raw signal sent through the dark.

And inside Nyx, undeniable and savage, was the truth burning him clean: mine.

He could feel the air thickening as murmurs broke into growls. Two vampires edged forward, eyes gone feral, scenting the heat still on the air.

One moved.

Too fast.

Nyx tore from the kiss, spinning, hand raised. His voice cracked like thunder.

"Back."

The vampire ignored him.

Then everything exploded.

Nyx moved—feral, lightning-fast.

He slammed the man to the floor with a force that cracked the tile beneath them.

The shockwave rolled through the club—bodies recoiling, glasses tumbling, a collective gasp that snapped into screams. The predator's eyes rolled white, veins spider-webbing black across his jaw.

Lyn Rose

Stone shattered. Glass rang. The bassline choked under the roar of violence.

Eden flinched, heart jackhammering. One moment the room had pulsed with music; the next, it was chaos. A man—no, something that looked like a man—convulsed on the floor. People screamed. Others froze, transfixed. The air burned with static and fear.

Kain appeared beside her out of nowhere, sharp and controlled. "Stay behind me."

"What's happening?" she shouted over the noise.

He didn't answer, just shifted his stance, scanning the crowd like he was expecting more. The lights flickered, catching on glass and blood. It didn't look like a bar fight—it looked like a nightmare tearing through silk.

And then Nyx moved again. Or maybe he'd never stopped. She couldn't tell—only that the air bent around him, every eye dragged toward the violence that followed.

Kain chuckled from the edge of the floor, flashing a grin at Eden.

"Now this is a night out."

Jace was already moving. He stepped beside Nyx, sharp and silent, and took Eden's arm with quiet authority.

"We're leaving. Now."

Lyn Rose

He guided them through a side door Eden hadn't noticed before.

The noise fell away behind them like a dream unravelling. Nyx's jaw was still clenched tight, pulse thundering in his ears. He scanned every shadow, every glint of fang, half-expecting another attack. His hands shook, a tremor he could barely hide.
Outside, the cool night air hit them like a balm.
The car waited.
Jace opened the door.
Eden slid inside, pale, eyes wide.
She didn't speak.
Nyx followed, closing the door behind him, the scent and taste of her lingering still on his lips.
She looked at him, breathless.
"What the fuck just happened…?"
She blinked, shook her head, like trying to clear fog from her mind.
Was that real? She thought. Or was it… the drinks? The lights? The music?
Nyx said nothing.
He just watched her.
She didn't speak.
Not at first.
She just stared forward, lips parted slightly, breath shallow and catching, she couldn't pull enough air into her lungs.
Then, soft and distant:
"I… I don't feel well."
Her voice was slurred. Fragile. Like sinking beneath the surface of deep water.
A flush crept up her neck, and for a moment, she looked like

she couldn't breathe.

Not wine.

Nyx knew the signs—too much adrenaline. Overstimulated nervous system. A system on the edge, crashing hard.

He turned sharply toward her, already shifting in his seat—

But it was too late.

She'd tilted her head back, eyes fluttering closed.

He watched her—still, vulnerable, cheeks flushed from the kiss, the chaos, the lingering heat of it all.

Her chest rose and fell in shallow, steady waves.

Then her head lolled gently to the side… and rested against his shoulder.

He froze.

Not because of the touch.

Because of the trust.

She'd fallen asleep against him.

She didn't know what he was.

Didn't know what he could do.

What he wanted to do.

He swallowed, the ache in his throat suddenly unbearable.

He could hear her heartbeat, steady and trusting. That trust was a blade, sharper than any hunger.

He exhaled slowly. Reached up, brushing a loose strand of hair from her face, smoothing it behind her ear.

Without thinking, he lowered his mouth and pressed a kiss to her temple.

Soft.

Reverent.

His.

The car slowed.

The gates to his estate slid open with a quiet hiss, the tall iron doors parting with a sigh of relief.

They pulled into the private garage beneath Duskwatch, where the light was low and golden, cast by recessed panels designed to keep everything discreet.

The driver stepped out and opened Nyx's door without a word.

Nyx shifted carefully, lifting Eden into his arms she felt like she weighed nothing.

Her head lolled against his chest, hair falling like ink across his suit.

She didn't stir.

He carried her across polished obsidian tile toward the waiting elevator.

The doors whispered open.

Inside, glass walls shimmered with shadowed crystal, offering fleeting glimpses of the mansion's steel, stone, and night-touched glass—Duskwatch was designed to keep the world out and hold secrets within.

The elevator rose silently.

It opened directly into Nyx's bedroom.

The space was darkly opulent.

Obsidian floors gleamed beneath black silk sheets.

Mirrors angled to catch slivers of moonlight.

A fire burned low in the hearth, flickering blue-white behind tempered glass.

Nyx laid her down gently, her head resting against the pillow like it belonged there.

She didn't move.

The red dress clung to her skin in a way that tightened his throat.

Slowly, gently, he crouched and reached for her feet.

One heel.

Then the other.

Slipped off with care.

His fingers brushed her ankle a moment too long before he stood.

He reached behind her, finding the zipper at the base of her spine.

He hesitated.

Then pulled.

The dress parted.

He slid it down her body, slow and deliberate, revealing black lace beneath—minimal, elegant, lethal.

She breathed but didn't stir.

Nyx stood frozen, drinking in the sight of her in his bed, in his home.

His shirt was in his hands before he realized.

He pulled it over her head carefully, guiding her arms through the sleeves, like she were porcelain.

The fabric hung off one shoulder, the hem brushing the tops of her thighs.

She looked like she belonged there.

Like she was meant to be there.

His.

The pull was brutal.

He stepped back before instinct betrayed him, teeth aching from restraint.

He could feel his hunger scraping at the inside of his ribs, a beast desperate for release. He forced himself to retreat, to put cold stone and steel between his body and hers.

Down the hall, the kitchen was clinical and cold—matte black counters, stainless steel appliances.

A button, flush with the wall, revealed a hidden room bathed in cold red light.

Shelves lined with blood packs, their labels a catalogue of craving.

Nyx poured himself a crystal tumbler, fingers steady despite the storm raging beneath his skin.

Steam rose from the glass.

He drank.

Heat flooded him.

Not enough.

Never enough.

His phone buzzed.

Jace.

"She's safe," Nyx said quietly.

"I know she will be," Jace replied. "But after you left, the floor didn't settle. A wolf went down hard—full turn, rabid. Black's pack tried to restrain him, but his friend had no choice. Throat torn out before they could pull him clear. Dead before he hit the ground. They found a puncture at the collarbone."

Jace's tone shifted, lower now. "The vampire you put down—he's still alive. Black's men dragged him out and locked him down. Whatever's in him acts like a designer infection—fast, targeted, turns rage up to maximum and severs motor control. We've got him contained, but he's volatile."

"The rest of the crowd scattered. Some still looked half-starved, sniffing the air as they left. Fear's running deep now, Nyx. Every faction felt it tonight."

Nyx's jaw tightened, the glass in his hand creaking.

"Good. Keep the vampire sedated, but don't drain him. I want venous draws every four hours—CBC, tox screen, metabolic panel. Run for all known compounds, then sequence for unknowns." His tone sharpened. "And get me a biopsy from the injection site before tissue degradation sets in. I want to know what's binding to their cells."

He paced once, shadow cutting across the kitchen floor.

"As for the wolf—send the body to Haven's cold storage. Preserve everything. Heart, liver, neural tissue. Full histopathology. If this is a vector, I want the map before anyone else."

A pause. Then, quieter, colder:

"Fresh blood, Jace. No contamination. If this thing spreads, I need to know how it rewrites them."

"No worries, boss," Jace replied. "We've got the wolf on ice already."

Nyx's jaw ticked. "Good. And the vampire—we won't keep him near the Pack. I'll be there tomorrow to review him myself. Then he goes to Virex Med, full containment. Our team will handle the assays."

Lyn Rose

Nyx didn't say anything else.
He hung up.
Then dialled again.
Black answered on the third ring.
"Ravelle. Thought you might call."

"She's with me."

"I know. Nyx…" Black hesitated. Then, quieter: "She's not normal, mate. You know that."

"I know."
"The wolf went rabid. Not one of mine—came in from a pack outside the city. His friend tried to pull him back, but had no choice. Dropped him clean. He's gone."

Black's voice roughened, low and edged with disgust. "The vamp though… fuck, Nyx. He's alive, if you can call it that. Nyx's jaw flexed. "I'll be there tomorrow. He doesn't stay in your Pit. Once I've reviewed him, he moves to Virex Med. Containment, full assays, full control. Until then, keep him alive."

Black grunted. "Aye. But my wolves are twitchy with that thing caged under my roof. He's raving, clawing the walls, chewing his own bloody arm. Nyx. If that's a plague, it's smart and cruel."

I've never seen anything like it."

A pause, heavier now. "And then there's her."

Nyx stilled.
Lyn Rose

"Whatever she is… it's not just blood. It's story. The room changed when she danced. I've seen wars start with less."

Nyx's jaw clenched.
"Send me the bill."

"She's worth more than broken tile and bruised egos."

A sharp slam of the glass echoed in the quiet kitchen.
Nyx exhaled, resigned.
"She's sleeping now."
Black grunted.
"Yeah, well… hope she stays that way. I'll keep the whispers quiet. But you're not the only one who felt it."
The call ended.
He stood in the dark kitchen, blood cooling in his throat, the taste of her still on his mouth.
Nyx leaned against the counter, teeth grinding, fury a storm in his veins. He hadn't wanted Eden near this, not even close. And tonight, she'd been the eye of the fucking hurricane.
He stared into the dark, the memory of her heat pressed against his body, the chaos still reverberating through his bones. The city outside was quiet, but inside him, everything was breaking apart. He closed his eyes, listening to the echo of her heartbeat, promising himself that whatever storm was coming, he'd burn the world before he let her be touched by it again.

CHAPTER NINE

The Taste of Control

Eden woke in the softest bed she'd ever felt.
Sheets smooth as skin. Mattress like a cloud.

Her body sank into it like it had been made just for her. Her limbs felt heavy, loose, boneless in the best way. The air smelled like night and something darker—cedarwood, smoke, and…
Him.

She stretched, fingers brushing the cool silk sheets, savouring the rare feeling of safety.
And then it hit.
Dinner.
The club.
The kiss.
The crowd.
The fight.

People moving like animals. No—worse. Like they didn't obey the same rules of gravity. Or physics. Or control.

The way he had moved.

She sat up too fast. The room spun.
"Easy," came a voice from the shadows. "You're safe. You're at my place."

Her head snapped toward it.

He stepped from a darkened corner of the room, shirt unbuttoned, sleeves pushed up, a crystal glass in one hand filled with something amber and smooth. He crossed to her with that same quiet power, sat on the edge of the bed, and drank the entire glass in a single pull. Like he needed the burn. The distraction.

She watched him—really watched him—and the memory of the club settled heavier on her chest. Her breath caught. The way he'd slammed that man. The growl. The scent. The way everyone backed down.

Not normal.

She flinched—just barely. But he saw it.
Saw the flicker of fear. Of doubt.

His eyes didn't waver.

Eden turned her gaze to the window. The light outside was pale, filtered through deep tint. Maybe midday. Maybe not.

Lyn Rose

She couldn't tell. The place felt like a fortress, shut off from the world, cold and formidable.

Then she looked down.

She was wearing one of his shirts.

Her stomach dipped. Heat curled low in her abdomen.

It smelled like him.

Woodsmoke. Sin. Power.

And then her body betrayed her.

Her core clenched, warmth blooming between her thighs. Her nipples hardened, pushing visibly against the soft cotton fabric.

She gasped—and his nostrils flared.

His gaze dropped. Darkened.

"Sweetheart…" he said, voice dropping a full octave. "When you do that, I barely have enough control to stay away."

Her breath caught. Her face flushed deep crimson as the realisation sank in.

He could smell her.

She went to shift away, hide, something—but he leaned forward and dragged his knuckles gently across the blush rising on her cheek.

"So beautiful," he murmured.

She leaned into his hand before she could stop herself.

His breath caught.

Then slowly, with a careful steadiness, he tilted her chin up until their eyes met.

"Eden," he said, voice low and true. "You're safe with me. But I do need to talk to you."

Her heart thudded.

She could still feel the weight of his hand on her cheek, the way he'd looked at her—like she was something sacred. Or forbidden.

Her mouth opened before she could stop it.

"Did we…?" She swallowed. "We didn't—?"

Nyx blinked.
Then he laughed.

Not cruel. Not mocking. But low, warm, and infuriatingly male.

"Sweetheart," he said, shaking his head, "if we did, it wouldn't be something you forgot."

Heat slammed into her. That voice. That line.

She tried—tried—to scowl. To pretend she didn't want to push him on the bed and climb onto him.

But her lips betrayed her. A twitch. The threat of a smile.

He saw it. Of course he saw it.

She shoved back the covers and sat up straighter.

"I should freshen up."

He tilted his head, amused. "Of course."

She stood slowly, his shirt hanging off her frame, brushing mid-thigh. Her bare legs hit the cool floor, and she didn't dare look at him.

Behind her, she felt him move.

Nyx rose—unhurried, deliberate—and walked past her without a word.

Predator calm.

And as he passed, he deliberately leaned in, inhaling softly. Just enough to make her shiver.

He groaned. Groaned.
Like he was in pain.

Her face lit up like a furnace. She practically power-walked behind him to the bathroom, refusing to look at him.

He stopped in front of a door at the end of the room—barefoot, effortless—and held it open like he owned time.

She stepped past him.

At the last second, she turned.

He was smiling.

Not smug.
Wicked.

The door closed between them.

And she was alone.

Breathless. Burning.

And in so much trouble.

The bathroom was stunning.

Dark stone floors. A glass rain shower. Black marble sinks with matte gold fixtures.

Everything was sleek, shadowed, and utterly masculine. His.

Eden gripped the edge of the vanity and stared into the mirror.

Flushed. Sleep-tousled. Still wearing his shirt.

And her underwear.

God. He'd undressed her.

She dragged a hand through her hair, trying to focus, but her body buzzed like it was still in that club—still feeling his hands on her waist, his mouth on hers.

Nyx Ravelle was a problem. A beautiful, terrifying, intoxicating problem.

Her skin burned.

Without thinking, she stripped and stepped into the shower.

The taps were elegant—chrome and black—and the moment she turned them, a blast of cold water hit her like ice.

She gasped, bracing both hands against the glass as the chill poured over her, trying to cool the wildfire under her skin.

It helped.

A little.

She stepped out, dripping.

Everything in the bathroom still smelled like him—his soap, his cologne, his air.

She opened a drawer and found a black towel. Thick. Soft as sin. She dried off quickly, wrapped herself in it tightly, and gathered her things—her undergarments, his shirt—and opened the door.

She stepped out of the bathroom wrapped in black.

The towel was thick, soft, clinging to her still-damp skin as she crossed the threshold. Her hair dripped in slow trails down her back. She walked carefully, hyper-aware of every inch of herself—and of him.

Nyx stood near the wall, arms at his sides, gaze unreadable.

He didn't speak. Didn't move.

But she felt the heat in the room shift.

He nodded toward the bed.

"There's something for you to wear. In the bag."

That was all he said.

Eden's heart kicked harder as she crossed to the bed, the towel brushing against her thighs. A matte black shopping bag sat neatly on the sheets, like it had been there for hours, waiting.

She pulled it open.

Lyn Rose

Inside: folded black jeans, a soft dark shirt, and—

Her fingers hesitated.

Black lace.

Underwear.

The exact style she'd worn the night before.

Her mouth went dry.

He hadn't asked.

But he'd noticed.

Her whole body went hot again. Not just embarrassed—
aroused. She bit the inside of her cheek, trying to breathe,
trying not to imagine the way his eyes must have lingered.
Noticed the cut. The details.

Behind her, she could feel his silence like a shadow.

She didn't turn around. Couldn't.

She swallowed and tightened her grip on the towel.

"Thanks," she said, quiet, almost too quiet.

She wasn't sure if he heard her.

But she was certain—absolutely certain—that he knew.

Lyn Rose

Nyx

She stepped out of the bathroom like a goddamn fantasy
wrapped in black.

His towel clung to her damp skin, hanging just low enough
to threaten, just high enough to torment. Her bare legs
caught the light. Droplets still traced paths down her thighs.
Her hair was wet—long, dark, curling slightly as it dried.

She didn't look at him.

She didn't have to.

He felt the shift in the room. The heat. The need.

Nyx swallowed hard, his throat suddenly dry.

He kept his hands at his sides, jaw tight.

"There's something for you to wear," he said, gesturing
toward the bed. "In the bag."

That was all he could manage.

She moved across the room, silent. Each step pulling the
towel tighter over her hips. He stared—helpless—at the way
it hugged her, the soft curve of her back, the bare stretch of
thigh that had no business being on display in his bedroom.

She opened the bag.

Paused.

Lyn Rose

He saw the moment she found the lace. The shift in her breath. The flush rising down her neck.

She knew.

She knew he'd noticed what she wore last night.

Her scent hit him a second later—hot, sweet, flaring with fresh arousal.

His fangs ached.

Nyx closed his eyes. Just for a second.

Control.

It was slipping.

And fuck, he wasn't sure how much longer he wanted to keep it.

Nyx's hands curled into fists at his sides.

If he stayed, he was going to touch her.

Not maybe. Not eventually. Absolutely.

And not gently.

"I'll give you some privacy," he said, his voice rougher than he wanted. Controlled, but only just.

He turned before she could answer.

Walked out the door without looking back.

The moment it clicked shut behind him, he dragged in a breath through his nose—and finally, he could breathe.

Her scent wasn't gone. Not completely. It clung to his skin, under his tongue, buried in his memory.

But it wasn't flooding him like it had in the room.

Out here, in the long, darkened hall, he could think again. Could feel the thrum of blood beneath his skin without the edge of snapping.

Just a towel.

That's all she'd been wearing.

And still, she'd nearly unraveled him.

Nyx pressed his palms to the wall and exhaled.

He'd fed. He'd held the line. He hadn't touched her skin. He hadn't bitten her.

But the scent of her arousal was still echoing through his blood like a drug he wasn't allowed to taste.

And it was only a matter of time before he lost the war.

CHAPTER TEN

Every Warning Said Run

The door creaked open just enough for Eden to slip inside, the soft sound swallowed by the stillness of the hallway. Nyx stood with his back to her, the glow from his phone casting sharp shadows across the angular planes of his face. His voice was low, steady, deliberate as he spoke into the receiver. "...clear my schedule."

There was a pause, punctuated only by the faint click of the call ending. He turned slowly, already sensing her presence, his eyes finding hers without a word. Eden offered a tentative smile and glanced down at the clothes she now wore—jeans and a soft black shirt that felt like armour after the night's chaos.

"Thanks," she said quietly, nodding toward the outfit. "For the clothes."

Nyx dipped his chin once in acknowledgment. "Come. You must be hungry."

Lyn Rose

She followed him into the house, stepping into a world that felt both alien and strangely familiar. The space was breathtaking in its precision—clean lines that cut through shadow, surfaces so polished they swallowed light whole, walls of smoked glass and dark stone. It was beautiful, but in a way that felt controlled, like every detail had been calculated and placed with exacting care. There was no mess, no softness—no sign of the warmth that most homes carried. Yet, despite the sterility, Eden didn't feel unwelcome. There was a quiet invitation in the way the space held her, like it was waiting for something to break through the cold.

They reached the kitchen, where Nyx moved with effortless grace behind the counter. His motions were practiced, almost mechanical—chopping onions, slicing peppers, cracking eggs with precision born of repetition.

The sizzle of bacon hit the pan, filling the air with a mouthwatering promise, but Eden barely noticed. She perched on a tall black stool, resting her elbows on the counter, chin cupped in her hand, watching the rhythm of his hands.

Without warning, Nyx was beside her. She blinked up, startled by the sudden closeness.

A smirk tugged at the corner of his mouth. "Where'd you go?"

Eden hesitated, then squared her shoulders, finding some thread of courage. "Listen… Nyx. Thank you. For dinner.

For the club. For everything." Her gaze locked with his. "But I need to go home."

His expression didn't crack, but something shifted beneath the surface—a flicker of confusion, then surprise, and finally a trace of something she couldn't name. Still, he said nothing, so she pressed on.

"Believe me, it's not you. It's just—last night was… weird. And it's not the first time I've had nights like that. Weird seems to follow me."

"I keep trying to piece it together," she said, rubbing her temples. "It's all flashes—glass, shouting, someone's eyes going white. I can't tell what was real and what I imagined. Everything after that… fog."

She let out a soft, tired laugh—more a breath than a sound. "I think I just need to sleep it off. Reset."

Nyx was silent for a beat, then his shoulders relaxed, the tension easing. "Come sit at the table," he said, voice softer now. "I'll answer your questions."

Questions? Eden blinked, surprised. She hadn't asked any— not out loud, anyway. But something in his tone made her pause. Maybe she did have questions. Maybe she just hadn't realized it yet.

She followed him, sliding onto a chair at the sleek table. Nyx placed a golden omelette in front of her with quiet precision—folded perfectly, like a masterpiece from a five-star kitchen. Then, without ceremony, he set another plate for himself.

He poured her a glass of orange juice, the bright liquid a sharp contrast to the muted tones of the room. Only then did he sit, folding his hands, eyes fixed on her.

Eden glanced down at the food. "Okay… you cook?"

"I do a lot of things," he said simply.

She took a tentative bite. The eggs melted on her tongue—rich, creamy, with hints of herbs and a subtle spice she couldn't quite place. She looked up, catching him watching her. Not cold, not intense—just focused.

"I meant what I said," he murmured. "You're safe here."

She nodded, swallowing hard. "I believe you. I just…" She hesitated, then pushed forward. "You saw what happened last night. People were acting like animals. Like they smelled something. And you—"

He didn't interrupt. He just listened.

"You moved like nothing I've ever seen," she continued, voice dropping lower. "And the man you slammed into the ground? He got up like it didn't even faze him."

Nyx's expression didn't shift, but his fingers drummed once against the rim of his glass—controlled, deliberate.

Her words cut deeper than she knew. He pictured the wolf, veins blackened, thrashing until his own packmate tore him down. The vampire chained, gnawing his own arm like something had rewritten his hunger. And now her— remembering the way she'd gone pale, how she'd whispered *I don't feel well* before sleep took her on his shoulder.

Different symptoms, same echo. A pattern forming. A vector. Someone was pulling strings, and she was already caught in them.

"I don't know what I saw," Eden said, voice barely above a whisper. "But it wasn't normal."

A heavy silence settled between them.

Finally, Nyx spoke. "You're not wrong."

Her breath hitched.

"I'm not going to lie to you," he added, "but I'm also not going to explain something you're not ready to hear."

She frowned. "Try me."

He studied her for a long moment, head tilting slightly—not dismissive, but weighing. Then he asked, "Let me ask you something first."

Her breath caught.

"The things you said before. About this not being your first weird night." His voice was steady. "What did you mean?"

Eden's fork hovered midair, forgotten. She hadn't meant to say it aloud. She set it down, exhaling slowly.

"You'll think I'm crazy," she said finally.

Nyx smirked, repeating back her words. "Try me."

She smiled, relenting, her shoulders sagging a little. "It's little things. Things that shouldn't add up—but they do."

Her fingers circled the rim of her glass. "Men always say I smell good. Even when I'm drenched in sweat. I went running once—no perfume, hair tied back, literally panting—and some guy followed me saying he liked the way I smelled. Said it was 'intoxicating.' Like, what the hell? I was a walking puddle."

She shook her head, half-laughing. "It's always like that. Too much attention. Too much… something. Alana—my best friend—used to come on my dates just to keep things normal. Even when we didn't sleep with them, the guys never wanted to leave. She'd walk them out, all smiles, and they'd follow her like she'd hypnotised them."

She grinned, shaking her head again. "And then I'd never hear from them again. They just disappeared." A snort. "Knowing Alana, she probably threatened them."

"Ahhh," Eden said dreamily. "Fun times."

She glanced up, more serious now. "But lately it's worse. Guys don't just flirt—they breathe me in. Like they can't stop. If I say no, they push harder. It's like rejection scrambles their brains; they lose control. I've had to call cabs from bathrooms, bolt out the back of restaurants. I don't know what it is, but it scares me."

Her voice softened. "And it's not just guys. Once, a woman on a train leaned in and told me I 'smelled like power.' Another called it magic. One dude, dead sober, said I 'smelled like a wet dream.'" She scoffed. "I didn't ask."

The humour faded.

"In high school, I passed out in theatre class. Just collapsed. They said my adrenaline was through the roof—but I hadn't moved. No drugs. No condition. The tests came back clean."

She swallowed. "It's happened four times now. Same pattern. Most recently? At work. Mid-meeting. Just dropped."

Nyx didn't speak. But she could feel his stillness. His focus.

"Sometimes I walk into a room and people just… react. They stare. Or go quiet. Or too loud. Like they feel something I don't. I don't know what to make of it."

She shrugged. "I'm just a normal girl trying to survive in a big city."

Eden wiped her fingers on the napkin and shifted back. "Do you mind if I use your restroom?" Her voice was light, trying to push away the heaviness between them.

Nyx rose without hesitation. "Not at all."

As he passed her, his phone buzzed sharply in his pocket. He pulled it free, checking the screen, and something in his posture tightened—still controlled, but taut.

He gestured down the hall. "Second door on the left."

"Thanks," she said, standing.

He answered as she stepped away. "Talk to me," he said, voice low and urgent.

Jace's reply was grim. "Two more deaths. Different districts. Different methods."

Nyx's jaw tightened. "Go on."

"First one's the same—puncture wound at the collarbone. Heart failure in under two minutes. Same chemical trace, same injection signature."

"And the other?"

A pause, then Jace's voice dropped. "No wound. No poison. Nothing physical at all. Accord medics said it looked like… burnout. Body emptied from the inside. No explanation yet."

Nyx's gut turned cold. Two patterns. Two killers. One they could track, one they couldn't. Yet.

"I'll send the location. You need to see it."

"On my way."

When Eden returned, Nyx stood at the table, all business again. The softness from before was gone, replaced by the sharp mask she'd come to recognize.

"I'm sorry," he said, voice clipped but sincere. "I have to go."

She nodded, unfazed. "Seems like you're always getting calls."

His gaze held hers a moment longer than expected, then a rare, quiet smile curved his lips. "Would you have dinner with me again?"

She blinked, surprised. "Tonight?"

"Yes." A pause. "But here."

She glanced around the sleek, obsidian palace. "Umm… sure," she managed.

That smile again. He stepped close, taking her hand without hesitation—a grounding touch that stole her breath.

"Come," he said, guiding her to a mirrored panel she hadn't noticed before.

It shimmered, sliding open to reveal an elevator.

They descended two floors.

When the doors slid open, Eden's breath caught.

Rows upon rows of gleaming black cars filled the space—sleek, dangerous, immaculate.

Her eyes landed on one instantly—the obsidian coupe from that first night, the hospital run, the blur of lights and blood.

Nyx opened the door for her.

She slid inside, fingers grazing the cool leather, the memory of that night stirring anew.

He circled to the driver's seat and slid in beside her.

He turned with that rare grin. "You ready?"

She couldn't help but smile back. "Always."

The engine purred to life.

The garage doors peeled back into the wall, nearly invisible.

The car slid out smooth as ink into the bright light of the day.

As they drove, she glanced back once.

His house rose above the city like a silent sentinel.

Below, Edalva sprawled out, a glittering circuit board of light.

It must be breathtaking at night, she thought, still smiling unknowingly.

She stared out as the skyline receded and the sprawl of the city told a story she hadn't yet finished reading.

His home overlooked it all—like a king on a throne.

Beautiful, distant, and utterly alone.

Her thoughts snagged when he spoke.

"This is my street," she said before she meant to.

Nyx didn't answer.

He drove on—smooth, unhurried—like every mile brought him closer to some unseen purpose.

When he pulled to the curb, her stomach twisted.

He cut the engine.

Then it occurred to her, she had never given him her address. "How did you know where I live?" she asked.

"My driver picked you up last night. Got the address from Lorne & Carrick," he said smoothly.

It made sense.

Still… something about the way he said it left her throat a little dry.

Lyn Rose

Before she could respond, the door hissed shut behind him.

She watched him move—sleek, composed—but as he passed the driver's side, something in him shifted. His head lifted, shoulders squared.

Then, without warning, he opened her door.

"Second floor, right?"

She blinked, nodding slowly.

He didn't hesitate.

His hand, warm and steady, settled on the small of her back, guiding her toward the stairs.

It wasn't possessive.

Not quite.

But it was aware.

Like he listened to every creak and whisper the building made.

She thought he was being a gentleman.

Until they reached her apartment.

The door was ajar.

Her stomach dropped.

Lyn Rose

"Alana?" she called, voice thin. "Is that you?"

No answer.

She reached for the handle—

Nyx was faster.

He pushed her back with one firm arm and stepped inside.

The moment he crossed the threshold, something shifted.

A flicker.

A breath.

Not human.

Before Eden could react, Nyx was across the room, slamming a figure against the wall, one hand wrapped around its throat.

It didn't look human. Not entirely.

Nyx bared his teeth, low and lethal.

"Who the fuck are you?" he growled. "Why are you near what's mine?"

He didn't wait for an answer.

He slammed the intruder face-first into the hallway wall, gripping its throat, already dialling.

Lyn Rose

His voice dropped low, dangerous.

"Stroud. Fae. Unregistered. Male." A pause. "Get Aleria Vale over here now before I rip his fucking throat out."

The words snapped Eden from her daze.

She hovered near the doorway, pulse hammering in her throat as he ended the call and turned to her.

"Police are on the way," he said. "Grab what you need. You're staying with me."

She blinked. "Wait—Nyx, I can call a friend. I'm fine. It's not—"

"You're safer with me." His tone brooked no argument.

His phone buzzed again.

Without looking, he answered.

"Kain, Jace—get to 22b Lyon Crescent. Westmere. Now."

He ended the call and slipped the phone into his pocket, turning back to the intruder still limp against the wall.

The creature made a low noise—neither human nor animal.

Eden tore her gaze away, moving to her room, shaken but not scared.

This wasn't her first break-in.

Lyn Rose

Twice a year, usually.

Nothing stolen.

Just doors left open, lights off that she swore she'd left on.

She'd changed locks, filed reports, moved on.

But this—

This was different.

She packed in silence—laptop, files, a few clothes.

Her hands moved on autopilot, but her mind replayed the scene again and again.

Nyx moving faster than she could follow.

His voice, low and lethal.

That growl.

And the words—

Why are you near what's mine?

A shiver rolled down her spine.

It should have scared her.

Should have made her run.

Lyn Rose

But it didn't.

Instead, it tightened her stomach.

Made her breath catch.

And stirred something deep—dark, unspoken, and terrifying.

She wasn't sure what scared her more.

The break-in.

Or the way she hadn't hated the sound of being claimed.

Lyn Rose

CHAPTER ELEVEN

Nothing Felt Real Anymore

Kain was the first to push through the cracked door, stepping inside like he owned the place. His eyes barely flicked around before they locked onto Eden. A grin spread across his face—easy, familiar, almost reckless.

The air shifted, thickening, the room felt like it was getting smaller like it braced for trouble.

"Well hey there, troublemaker," he said, nudging her shoulder with a smirk. "Whatcha gone and done now?"

Despite the lingering tension in the air, Eden couldn't help but smile back, a bitter twist curling in her chest.

Her pulse fluttered, breath catching like a secret ready to spill.

"Me? Innocent and sweet."

Kain laughed, loud and unapologetic.

But the sound scraped against the tight silence that had settled.

"Yeah, right."

But then Nyx turned.

His presence cut through the room like a sharpened blade.

His gaze sliced through the room icy—cold, sharp, and absolute.

The air seemed to thicken, the laughter died in Kain's throat. His grin vanished in an instant.

The weight of Nyx's stare made the space shrink, like the walls pressed in.

"Noted," he muttered, stepping back like he'd been burned.

Nyx didn't break eye contact. He jerked his head once, the smallest tilt toward the far corner of the room.

Kain caught it immediately, the cocky grin nowhere in sight now.

He followed Nyx a few steps off, their voices low, words swallowed by the hum of police chatter in the hall.

Meanwhile, Jace slid into the gap Nyx had left.

His movements were smooth, calculated—an anchor in the swirling tension.

He stepped toward Eden, his tone even and professional, drawing her attention away.

"Miss Marlowe," Jace said smoothly, scanning the room without seeming to. "Anything missing? Electronics, files, jewellery? Or just disturbed?"

Eden blinked, startled by the sudden precision in his tone.

Her hands trembled slightly, clutching her bag tighter—a shield against the unknown.

"I—I don't think anything's gone. It looks… rifled, though. My desk, some shelves. But nothing obvious."

Jace nodded once, pulling a small notepad from his jacket and jotting down details, the motion calm and practiced.

His pen scratched softly—each note a small tether to reality.

"What about damage? Any signs they were looking for something specific?"

His eyes flicked to hers—steady, grounding—keeping her anchored while the low murmur of Nyx and Kain's private conversation drifted unheard at the other side of the room.

In the corner

"What's up?" Kain asked, voice pitched low.

Nyx's reply was colder, deeper.

"I've got to check the vampire. He's locked at Blackthorn now, but I want him transported out after this—" he gestured at the shattered door, the cops, the chaos "—because there's more going on here than a simple break-in. I need an hour, maybe two. Distract her. Lunch, coffee, I don't care how. Just keep her safe."

Kain's grin twitched back.

There was a flicker of dark amusement, but his eyes held something sharper—respect, maybe fear.

"Now that won't be hard."

Nyx's growl cut him off, a sound that made the walls vibrate.

It was low, primal, a warning carved from years of command.

His voice dropped to that register again, deep and absolute.

"Keep your mind on the job. I want eyes on her every second, Kain. Even if she goes to the fucking toilet. Do you hear me?"

For a heartbeat, Kain looked like he might push back.

But then he exhaled, shoulders bowing slightly in recognition of what Nyx was in this moment—not just a friend, not just Ravelle, but the King of his House, and this was his house now too.

"Of course, boss."

Nyx's gaze slid back to Eden. She was speaking quietly with Jace, unaware of the storm gathering around her. His jaw tightened, the decision locking in.

"I'll figure out what the fuck is going on," he muttered, more to himself than anyone else.

When Nyx returned to them, Jace straightened and looked up from his notes.

"What's the play, boss?"

Nyx's voice was clipped, all business and steel.

"Once the cops clear out, I want this place sealed tight. Surveillance everywhere—windows, doors, roof. Find out who owns this block. Now."

Jace didn't hesitate.

"On it."

Nyx's gaze flicked briefly toward Eden, then back to Jace.

"And I'll be at Virex within a few hours. I need to assess something first."

Eden stood frozen, clutching her laptop bag like an anchor.

It wasn't the break-in that rattled her most.

Not even the intruder Nyx had pinned moments ago like a trophy.

It was this—the way everyone fell silent at his command.

The gravity in his voice.

The way he moved through the apartment like a general surveying a battlefield.

It was… terrifying.

And strangely magnetic.

Her pulse hammered in her ears, breath shallow and quick.

She swallowed hard, fingers tightening around the strap of her bag hoping it could hold her together.

Before she could sort through the swirling thoughts, a sharp knock on the broken door jolted her.

The world shifted again.

Not just cops.

Not uniforms.

Evelyn Stroud.

The Head of the Department.

The woman who appeared on every press conference when the city's blood ran too hot.

Eden had seen her on screens, in hearings, in the glare of live feeds.

But never in person.

Now, here she was. Black coat snapping tight at the waist, heels clicking like a metronome. Her presence sucked the air from the room—sharp, commanding, unyielding.

And right behind her—

No.

It couldn't be.

Aleria Vale.

The actress.

The legend.

A woman whose name was whispered like a secret in high society.

Eden felt her stomach flip sideways, a cold twist of unease settling deep in her gut.

Something was happening.

Something bigger than a break-in.

Lyn Rose

Stroud stepped forward, dismissing Kain and Jace with a single, sharp nod. They melted into the shadows behind her like ghosts.

"Nyx," she said, voice cool and clipped.

He turned, shoulders squared, but didn't answer immediately. Instead, he shifted, stepping half in front of Eden—silent, immovable.

Eden stepped out from behind him, forcing calm into her voice though her throat felt tight.

"Hi. Eden Marlowe. I work for Lorne & Carrick."

Stroud blinked. Just once. Enough to betray surprise.

Then her expression reset into a mask of professionalism as she extended her hand.

"Well, Eden. Seems someone's taken a particular interest in your apartment. No other units touched. No forced entry. No witnesses. Clean."

Eden's brows rose, heart skipping.

"You already know that?"

Stroud's smile was tight, knowing.

"We've talked to the residents. Done a sweep."

"Have you got somewhere to stay?" Her tone shifted, a hint of kindness breaking through the steel.

Before Eden could answer, Nyx's voice cut in—low, firm.

"She's staying with me."

The air shifted.

Stroud's eyes flicked to Nyx—sharp, assessing. A silent conversation passed between them, charged and unreadable.

Eden felt the floor tilt beneath her, the room suddenly smaller and colder.

Then a new presence swept over to them.

"Nyx, darling."

Aleria Vale glided forward like a shadow made graceful, heels silent on the floor. Her beauty was a weapon—sharp enough to cut, mesmerizing enough to wound.

She kissed Nyx on both cheeks, familiar, intimate, like she belonged to his past—or maybe still did.

Eden's stomach clenched, a knot tightening as she swallowed the sudden rush of jealousy and confusion.

Aleria Vale.

More than an actress. A goddess of the city's darkest stage.

And here she was, tracing the edges of Nyx like she held the script to his secrets.

Their voices dropped into a murmur—too low for Eden to catch—but the air between them thickened with something electric and dangerous.

Aleria's fingers brushed Nyx's arm, lingering too long before retreating. She tilted her head, laughing softly—a sound that held promises and warnings.

Nyx gave a rare half-smile in return.

Eden felt like an intruder watching a private scene, uninvited, invisible.

Her breath caught, muscles tightening as a flush of vulnerability crept up her neck.

Aleria turned her head slightly, nostrils flaring—the faintest intake of breath. A flicker of surprise crossed her face, quickly schooled into composure. Then her gaze settled on Eden, sharp and appraising. Not cruel, just measured—it was like assessing a scent she couldn't quite place, weighing its significance in a single glance.

And in that moment, Eden understood.

This wasn't just a break-in.

This was a world.

One she'd stumbled into unarmed.

Lyn Rose

And nothing in it was normal.

She stood a little apart from the others, arms folded, phone clutched in her hand like it could anchor her. The apartment looked like her life—familiar and ransacked. But it wasn't just the shattered lock or overturned bookshelves.

It was the people now standing in it.

Stroud. The Head of the Department. Talking quietly with Nyx like they knew each other well. Like they'd faced situations much worse than a standard break-in.

Aleria Vale, too. Famous, flawless, the kind of woman whose name came with perfume ads and award shows. She'd glided in like she belonged there, kissed Nyx on both cheeks, and leaned in to speak low near his ear.

Eden tried not to stare.

Of course he knows them. He's a CEO. He's got money, power, connections. It makes sense. This isn't weird. This is just… high society weird. Not conspiracy weird.

And yet, something itched under her skin. A feeling she'd had her whole life—the kind that said you're missing something important.

She needed to do one normal thing. Just one.

Eden slipped down the hall toward her bedroom, pulled out her phone, and dialled her best friend.

Lyn Rose

It went to Alana's voicemail.

Figures.

She left a message anyway. "Hey. I'm okay, I just—my place got broken into again. I'm safe, I'm with someone. Not like that. I'll explain later, I promise."

She ended the call and tucked the phone into her bag, exhaling a slow breath. Just a moment. That was all she needed. A breath to steady herself.

Nyx

She was gone.

He turned, expecting to see her where he'd left her—just behind him, near the wall, close enough to watch but not close enough to hear.

But the space was empty.

His pupils contracted, muscles tightening with a tension that clawed at his chest.

His hand twitched at his side, instinct flaring like a warning pulse through his blood.

"Nyx?" Aleria's voice, smooth and precise, brushed against him like a practiced note. But he barely heard her.

Lyn Rose

Where the fuck had she gone?

He inhaled—not with his lungs, but with every fibre of his being—and there she was. Her scent threaded faintly from the hallway. No panic. No fear. Just space. Just… absence.

He didn't like it.

Didn't like the way his chest tightened or the way his jaw clenched as Stroud kept talking beside him.

I turned my back for two minutes.

And she slipped away.

"She's not a prisoner," he muttered to himself, but the words tasted like a lie. Because every bone in his body wanted her where he could see her. Where he could guard her. Where no one else could touch her.

Aleria tilted her head. "She's not normal, Nyx. You're feeling it more than the rest of us, aren't you?"

He didn't answer. Just turned, abruptly, and walked.

Past the officers. Past the broken doorframe. Down the short hall without a word.

A man on a mission.

Eden

She sat on the edge of her bed, phone loose in her hand, trying to remember how to breathe like a normal person.

What the hell had just happened?

Her apartment—broken into.

Her files—rifled through.

Nyx—unrecognizable when he moved, when he growled. When he claimed her.

And now people in suits and silence, who looked at Nyx like an equal. Like he was one of them.

This wasn't just a break-in.

And deep in her gut, Eden knew… this was more, this was about her.

She didn't hear him approach.

Not until the floor creaked.

She looked up sharply—and there he was.

"I just needed a second," she said, voice shaky but trying to steady.

"I didn't mean to—"

"You weren't where I left you." His voice was quiet. Deeper than before. "And I didn't like it."

There was no accusation in his tone. Just raw honesty. And something else, coiled and dangerous, buried beneath the words.

Heat, maybe.

Possession.

She didn't move.

Didn't breathe.

Then Nyx crossed the space and sat beside her—not close enough to crowd her, but close enough to make her heart skip a beat.

He reached for her hand, slow and deliberate.

Turned it gently in his grasp.

And pressed a kiss to her wrist.

Her breath caught.

"Kain and Jace will have everything handled," he murmured, gravel-soft. "Doors replaced. Surveillance up. By the day after tomorrow, no one will get within ten feet of this place without setting off six kinds of hell."

Lyn Rose

His gaze held hers. "But I need to step out, sort a few things. Kain will take you to lunch, keep you safe."

Eden shook her head, quick. "No, Nyx, it's fine. I'll go see a friend. You don't need to babysit me."

His jaw ticked, but instead of arguing, he bent again, brushing his lips across the inside of her wrist—slower this time, deliberate, trying to brand the vow into her skin. She froze, mesmerised.

"If you don't want lunch with Kain," he said quietly, "he'll take you to the Lennar instead."

Her brow furrowed. "The Lennar?"

"Yes, the hotel. I own it. Top floor. Highest security in the city. I'll drive you there myself if you prefer."

"Nyx, that's—" She exhaled. "That's not necessary. You've already done more than enough."

He gave a single nod, not quite smiling. "Then trust me for a little longer. I need to know you're safe."

Before she could press the argument, he leaned in and kissed her. Light, fleeting, just enough to steal her breath. She sighed into it, pulse stuttering.

When he pulled back, his voice dropped lower. "I won't be long."

She nodded, dazed, heart hammering.

Lyn Rose

"Good," he said softly, rising to his feet. "Come. Let's get back to the others."

They stepped back into the ruined living room.

Eden still held his hand.

Nyx didn't seem to notice.

But Aleria did.

Her eyes flicked downward—not judgmental, but aware. And when Eden let go, the ghost of his touch stayed branded against her palm.

The famous woman turned toward her.

Ethereal in a tailored coat of silver-grey and black. Blonde hair like soft liquid gold, caught in an intricate braid, eyes like polished obsidian.

She extended a hand.

"Eden," Aleria said smoothly. "It's lovely to meet you."

Eden reached out automatically, old instincts kicking in— polite, composed, professional.

But the moment their hands met, Aleria inhaled.

Not a loud breath. Not a gasp.

Just a whisper of a scent taken in.

Lyn Rose

Her smile faltered. Only for a second.

Then she turned sharply to Nyx, gaze flicking over him—unreadable.

He met her eyes. Said nothing.

Aleria adjusted herself like she'd been snapped from a trance, and turned back, flawless once more. "Apologies. I'm Aleria Vale."

Eden's mind stuttered. She recognised her when she first walked in but Aleria Vale. The Aleria Vale.

"Nice to meet you," she said automatically, channelling every ounce of courtroom control. "I'm Eden Marlowe."

Aleria's smile warmed. "So I've heard."

There was a beat.

Then Eden said, carefully, "I understand Miss Stroud being here, given the circumstances. But… respectfully, I'm not sure why you're here."

Aleria's lashes lowered, amused. "Curious thing, isn't it? I'm not quite sure either. But when someone like you gets tangled in our world… I like to be informed."

Eden stiffened. "Your world?"

Aleria just smiled.

Nyx's hand found the small of Eden's back again. Subtle. Protective. Claiming.

And Eden felt it—that she was being looked at not like a victim, but a variable.

Something new.

Something dangerous.

Aleria's words lingered in Edens head.

Then: a clipped voice cut in from behind.

"Vale."

It was Stroud.

Sharp-suited and sharper-eyed, Evelyn Stroud crossed the room with a calm that radiated authority. Not the loud kind. The kind that came with knowing every secret in the city— and exactly who to bury if they talked.

She stepped between them, all cool elegance and iron.

"Aleria was asked to attend as a favour to me," Stroud said evenly. "The Department appreciates her discretion in matters of public interest."

Eden blinked. "Public…?"

Stroud turned, her smile polite—but razor-thin.

"What happened here was unfortunate, Miss Marlowe. The investigation is ongoing, but your safety is our priority. You were lucky Mr. Ravelle was nearby."

Aleria gave a feline little smirk but said nothing more.

Stroud continued, smooth and controlled. "As of now, the Department is closing this matter. You've already given your statement. Should anything else arise, I'll be in touch. In the meantime—" she glanced at Nyx "—thank you for stepping in."

Eden tried to speak. To ask more.

But Nyx's hand pressed slightly firmer at her back, a subtle nudge.

And Stroud's eyes made it very clear: this conversation was over.

Nyx's gaze lingered on Eden for a heartbeat longer, jaw flexing, then he gave the barest nod toward Kain.

Kain stepped forward, grin sliding back into place like armour. "Come on, gorgeous," he drawled, offering his arm with theatrical charm. "I'm starving. Let's grab lunch before I waste away."

Eden blinked, startled, but before she could answer Kain had already hooked her gently toward the door. Nyx didn't stop him. Didn't even look her way. He just let her go.

The betrayal stung, small and sharp. She glanced back once, eyes catching Nyx's, searching for something—explanation, reassurance—but found only stone. Like a child being shepherded away from the grown-ups' table, she let herself be steered out, her mind a tangle of What the hell is going on? But she didn't resist. Not yet.

The door shut behind her. Silence pressed in, heavier now that she was gone.

Nyx turned back to the room—Stroud standing like a blade in heels, Aleria lounging with poise that dripped calculation, Jace watchful at his shoulder. The air tasted of iron and dread.

Stroud was the first to break it. "You think this was connected to last night?"

Nyx's tone was ironclad. "It wasn't coincidence. Someone breached Club X—a secured Accord venue—dosed a vampire under my watch, and now Eden's apartment gets hit within hours. Same city, same night. That's not chance."

Jace folded his arms. "And the wolf. Dead before sunrise. Injection mark confirmed. Same compound shows up in the Vestry Market victims too. Three deaths, all unaligned, all traced back to the same molecular tag."

Aleria tilted her head, her smile sharp but thin. "Deliberate, then. Not coincidence. Something's drawing this chaos to her."

Lyn Rose

Nyx's eyes darkened, voice dropping into a growl that vibrated the glass. "And if that's true, then the city isn't on the verge of panic—it's already there. They just don't know it yet."

The words hung, heavy and absolute.

Stroud's jaw tightened. "Then we contain it. Quietly. Before the factions catch wind."

But Nyx's silence said it all—containment was already slipping. The wolf torn apart. The vampire raving in Blackthorne's Pit. The bodies at Vestry Market cooling in Haven's morgue. And Eden… right at the centre, whether she knew it or not.

The dread was a living thing now, thick in the air, and none of them dared name it aloud.

CHAPTER TWELVE

The Pit

The car ate the miles in silence, sunlight flashing over the hood as trees blurred past.

Nyx drove, hands steady on the wheel, jaw tight as stone, every muscle coiled beneath his skin. Jace sat in the passenger seat, his gaze fixated on the blur of forest beyond the glass, eyes reflecting the cold, muted light. Neither spoke. There was no need. The weight in the car was enough—the kind of silence that carried everything words couldn't hold, dense and suffocating.

Gravel crunched under the tires as the Lodge came into view, its timber-and-stone frame rising from the morning mist like a fortress carved out of the mountain—ancient, unyielding, grim. The drive curved wide, flanked by cabins still dark. They had stood dormant for months—silent, untouched—ever since the Pack's women vanished.

Nyx cut the engine before the car had fully stopped. He was already out, boots striking gravel with a hard, purposeful rhythm, coat trailing behind him like a shadow. Jace followed, closing the door with a muted thud that echoed too loudly in the stillness.

The Lodge loomed larger with every step, tension crawling through its beams. Black's enforcers lined the porch and drive—broad-shouldered men, some bare-chested despite the cold, muscles corded like drawn steel; others in rolled-sleeve shirts, every one of them taut and ready. They didn't pace. They stood like fixtures—watching, waiting. Predators holding the line while the rest of the Pack stayed away, their empty cabins a quiet reminder of everything that had been taken.

And though their bodies stayed human, the wolf was in their eyes—a sharp, restless gleam that tracked Nyx with silent warning as he moved toward the door.

Tyren, Black's second, stood like a sentinel at the top of the stairs, arms crossed, posture rigid and solid. His gaze flicked once to Nyx, then to Jace—sharp, assessing. The air between them hummed with unspoken recognition, threaded with history and caution.

Beneath it all, Nyx felt it. Pressing. Wrong. Heavy. Like the Pit itself was exhaling poison through the bones of the Lodge, a sickness feeding on shadows and fear.

And then Black was there.

At the top of the steps, shoulders squared, arms folded, jaw carved from granite. His presence was a low gravitational force that sucked all light and sound toward him. His voice rolled down like a growl dragged over broken glass, rough and dangerous.

"'Bout time. That thing's tearing itself apart. And my Pit with it."

"Come on. I'll show you."

Inside, Black led them through the heart of the Lodge. What waited above was beauty—vaulted timber ceilings, polished stone, firelight catching in glass and brass. A mountain retreat refined and dangerous, the kind of place that made you forget how wild the world outside could be.

But beneath that beauty ran bone.

They passed through a hall lined with carved beams and narrow windows rimmed in frost, then down a stairwell hidden behind an ironwork gate. The air shifted—cooler, heavier, the scent of cedar giving way to damp stone and cold metal. Torchlight burned blue along the walls, flickering like captured lightning.

The further they descended, the more the Lodge changed. The warmth above faded to silence, the kind that had weight. Stone corridors slick with condensation replaced wood. The smell turned metallic—blood, sweat, and something older still, a rot that crawled into the lungs.

The Lodge swallowed them whole.

Wolves moved aside as they passed, their eyes tracking every step, hackles twitching. Even the walls seemed to breathe, the shadows stretching and coiling with each torch flare.

They turned down a narrow passage cut straight into rock and began the final descent. The air thickened, copper-sharp, tasting of iron and confinement. The silence wasn't silence at all—it pulsed with muffled growls, the rattle of chains, the rasp of something alive and furious below.

The Pit wasn't just a cell.

It was a wound carved into the mountain's heart.

The stairwell opened into a cavernous chamber, its walls slick with condensation, light spilling from iron sconces that burned low and cruel. The smell hit first—copper, bile, decay—burning the back of the throat.

And in the centre, chained to the stone floor, was the vampire.

He was ruined flesh wrapped around fury. Every muscle taut to the point of tearing, veins crawling black like poison up his arms, across his throat, into the whites of his eyes. His lips were torn from his own fangs, blood smeared down his chin, slick and warm. The sound he made wasn't speech. It wasn't even animal. It was a screech, high and raw, vibrating in the bones, shaking the very air.

Lyn Rose

The second Nyx stepped into the chamber, the vamp lunged.

Chains screamed, stone cracked, the weight of four enforcers bracing against the anchors just to hold him down.

Black's voice was a low rumble, a growl from the depths.

"He hasn't stopped. Not once. He's been trying to tear his way out since we locked him in."

Nyx's gaze didn't waver. He stepped forward.

The vampire thrashed harder, froth flying from his mouth, eyes rolling white with madness. The enforcers cursed, straining against the pull of chains. One lost his grip, slammed back into the wall. The vamp nearly surged free—

Until Nyx spoke.

"Stop."

The word wasn't loud.

But it carried.

The thrashing stilled.

The scream cut short.

Chains went taut but unmoving, every muscle locked mid-rage.

The enforcers staggered back, staring.

Lyn Rose

Nyx walked closer, voice calm, steady, inexorable.

"Still. Calm."

The vamp's chest heaved, ribs straining against skin stretched thin, but he didn't move. His gaze locked on Nyx—wild and burning, but caged inside invisible walls.

Nyx crouched, slow, deliberate, pulling a sterile kit from his coat. The syringe glinted under the harsh light, cold and clinical.

"I am going to approach you," Nyx said, each word measured and deliberate. "I am going to draw your blood. Do not move."

The vamp shook, a tremor running through his limbs, but the compulsion held.

Nyx stepped close, knee on the stone, sleeve rolled back as he swabbed an arm slick with sweat and blood. He found the vein, slid the needle in—

And the control shattered.

The vampire roared, eyes blazing red, body convulsing with unnatural strength. His head snapped forward, teeth catching Nyx's hand, tearing skin with a savage bite. Blood spilled, hot and immediate, a searing line of pain.

Nyx growled, the sound ancient and dangerous, and backhanded him with enough force to crack stone. The vamp's head snapped sideways, blood spraying the floor.

Lyn Rose

Jace moved, hand to his weapon—

"No." Nyx's voice thundered, steady despite the blood dripping from his hand.

He yanked the plunger, filling the vial with thick, corrupted blood, then reached for the second syringe—longer, darker. He plunged it into the vein and depressed the sedative.

The vamp jerked once, twice.

Then sagged.

Nyx didn't wait.

He pulled a blade from his belt, slicing clean across the injection site, carving a square of flesh and tissue free.

The enforcers recoiled at the precision of it, but Nyx wrapped the sample in sterile gauze, tucking it into a steel case at his side.

He stood, wiping his bloodied hand against his coat, eyes black as pitch.

"Keep him restrained until containment arrives," Nyx said, voice cold as steel.

He was already dialling, stepping toward the stairs.

The line clicked.

"Virex Med. Containment."

Lyn Rose

"Prepare a cell," Nyx ordered. "Immediate transfer. You'll have a live subject in under an hour, sedated but volatile. Venous samples en route, tissue confirmed. Lock him down until I arrive."

He ended the call without waiting for a reply, already climbing back toward the light.

Jace followed in silence.

"We'll have answers before the day's out. Or we'll burn the city to get them."

The Pit's chains rattled once behind him, metal singing like a warning.

And then the Pit fell quiet at last.

Eden

The restaurant was all glass and sunlight, perched high above the harbor like it was designed to show off. Boats carved trails through the glittering water, sails snapping, engines humming, the entire trade route alive with motion. Edalva's veins, she thought, pulsing with money and power just like its streets at night.

Eden sat back in her chair, sunglasses shielding her eyes, the sun warm on her skin. It should have been perfect. It looked perfect. But her mind refused to let her sink into the calm.

Kain was talking—something about a fight he'd nearly gotten into on the way here, delivered with that reckless grin of his. She smiled at the right times, laughed when he nudged her with a joke, let him carry the conversation like she was riding the current instead of swimming against it.

But inside? Inside she was still in her apartment, the door splintered, Nyx's hand on her back, Stroud's cold eyes, Aleria Vale's perfect smile.

She sipped her drink, the citrus sharp on her tongue, and her thoughts ran on repeat.

Nyx. The way the room bent around him. The way he moved like every decision had already been calculated. The way his eyes had burned when she slipped from his sight for two minutes.

The words he'd said. You weren't where I left you. And I didn't like it.

Heat crawled up her throat at the memory. She told herself it was control, protectiveness, his world colliding with hers— but the way he kissed her wrist before leading her back to the others? That hadn't been business. That had been something else. Something dangerous.

Kain reached across the table, flicking her menu down with a playful snap. "You're not even listening, gorgeous."

She forced a smile, shaking her head. "I am. Boats. Fights. Something about you being the hero."

Lyn Rose

"Always," he said, flashing teeth. His tone was light, but his eyes weren't. They flicked past her, scanning the deck, the waitstaff, the movement below. Easy grin, restless hands. Eden realised with a small twist in her stomach—he wasn't just keeping her company. He was working.

And that made it worse.

Because if she was being "watched," it meant there was something to fear.

Her fingers toyed with the edge of her glass. She tried to play it off, to tell herself this was normal—lunch, sunlight, laughing with a man who clearly enjoyed the game of making her smile. But beneath the sunnies her gaze kept darting back to the harbor, to the water, to the glittering surface that looked like freedom but felt like a cage.

Last night at the club—what she'd felt when the room turned. The way eyes locked on her, like she was the only thing alive in the building. And then that vampire… getting up after Nyx smashed him into the floor. His veins blackening, his scream carving through her bones.

Her stomach tightened.

Weird always followed her, but never like this. Never with her life on the line.

Kain leaned back, stretching, sunlight hitting the curve of his jaw. "See, this is better. Food, drinks, no creeps breaking into your place. You look good out here."

Eden smiled faintly, lifting her glass. "It's easier in daylight."

But even as she said it, her thoughts snagged on the truth. The daylight was an illusion. Last night was real. Nyx was real. And whatever world she'd stumbled into—it wasn't letting her go.

She glanced sideways at Kain, who was now charming the waitress with a grin, all swagger and warmth. He looked normal. He acted normal. But she'd seen the way he deferred to Nyx. The way even his jokes cut short when Nyx's gaze sharpened.

They were all playing a game she didn't know the rules to.

Eden tilted her head back, letting the sun burn her face through the sunglasses, pretending for a moment she could soak it all away.

But the truth pressed in any way.

Why me?

Nyx

The car ate up the road, its engine a low growl beneath the weight of silence. Jace rode shotgun, eyes flicking from the map on his phone to the endless sprawl of Edalva's outskirts. Nyx gripped the wheel tighter than he needed to, jaw set, thoughts circling like blades.

Lyn Rose

The city blurred into industrial blocks, warehouses standing like broken teeth against the skyline. Sirens had faded. No press. No Department uniforms. Stroud hadn't wanted noise on this one.

That told Nyx everything.

They turned down a narrow access lane. Sunlight flashed off metal and glass, glinting off the medic vans parked in a crooked line. Accord medics moved carefully, faces grim, gloves slick in the glare. The smell hit first—not just blood. Something hollow, scorched, wrong.

Nyx killed the engine. He stepped out into the stillness, coat trailing, boots crunching gravel. Jace followed, his silence sharpened to a knife-edge.

The body lay crumpled against a loading dock wall, arms splayed, head tilted back eyes distant, staring at a sky that wasn't there.

Nyx slowed. His shadow fell across the corpse.

Not a corpse. A husk.

Skintight over bone, eyes collapsed inward, veins raised like black wires burned through the flesh. Mouth frozen open in a silent scream. Clothes untouched. No wounds. No blood. Nothing left.

It looked less like a death and more like an unravelling.

"Fuck," Jace muttered, breaking the silence at last. "Looks like someone scooped him clean."

Nyx crouched, gloved hands steady as he inspected. He pressed two fingers against the neck. No warmth. No blood pressure. No residue. Nothing.

The void itself stared back at him.

"Not drained," Nyx said low. "If it were a frenzy, there'd be tears, tearing, blood loss. This is… different." His hand hovered just above the chest, he could feel it in the air. "Like the soul was sucked out."

Jace's jaw tightened. "Witch work?"

Nyx shook his head once, sharp. "No burn marks. No tether. No ritual signatures. Whatever did this—it wasn't coven."

Jace exhaled through his teeth, scanning the edges of the dock. "Then who the hell does that leave?"

Nyx stood, the weight of the night pressing on his shoulders. He stared down at the husk, at the slack jaw, the

clawed-in fingers, frozen mid-tremor.

"Something new," he said finally. His voice was calm, but his eyes burned. "And it's hunting."

Nyx straightened, the hard midday light cutting across his face, sharpening every line into something merciless. He pulled his phone from his coat, thumb already moving.

Lyn Rose

Nyx thumbed the call through, eyes on the wet road.

"Kain," he said when the line clicked alive, his tone clipped steel. "I'll be back at Eden's apartment in ten. I'm taking her to Virex with me. Meet us there."

He ended the call before Kain could reply.

The next number rang only once.

"Stroud."

Her voice was cool, precise. "Report."

Nyx's jaw flexed. "The vampire at Virex is contained. Labs are running the samples. The wolf's body is at Haven—same compound signature. But we've got something else. Another killer."

Her tone sharpened. "Different vector?"

"Yes." His voice was flat. "Different. No wound, no toxin, no bleed-out. Accord medics are calling it burnout, but the body's… empty. Like something stripped it clean from the inside."

Silence settled, heavy and exact.

"Confirmed?"

"Confirmed." His knuckles whitened on the wheel. "Two killers. Two methods. Twelve hours apart."

Stroud exhaled through her teeth, measured but hard. "Then we escalate. I'll pull assets—quiet ones. This stays off record."

"Understood." He killed the call without goodbye.

The car cut through Edalva's veins, sunlight flashing off wet asphalt. Beside him, Jace was silent, watchful, already cataloguing logistics in his head.

Nyx didn't look at him. His mind was already at the apartment.

Ten minutes, he thought. Ten minutes, and Eden would be back in his line of sight.

Because whatever had been brewing these last few days— she was standing too close to the fault line.

The coupe rolled to a stop at the curb, engine low and predatory.

Nyx's hands were still clamped white-knuckled on the wheel, but his chest felt like it might cave in from the pressure inside. Too many bodies today, too much blood. And through it all, the single thought tearing him apart— Eden.

He killed the engine, shoved the door open, and stepped out.

And there she was.

Not tucked away, not hidden behind glass or steel, but right there on the pavement. Leaning against Kain's car, head tipped back as the morning sun poured over her. Her hair—black as midnight, long, straight, and impossibly sleek—caught the light like spun obsidian. A laugh slipped free—soft, lyrical, unguarded—and it struck Nyx low, brutal and consuming.

It wasn't a gut punch. It was heat, sharp and unbearable, like her voice had wrapped around his cock and tightened with every note.

Relief slammed through him, savage and consuming, nearly buckling his knees. She was safe. Warm. Breathing. Here.

But with that relief came the hunger. The desperate, maddening need to touch her, pull her in, bury his face in her neck and never let her go. Every inch of him screamed for it.

His jaw locked, teeth grinding, as he forced the mask back into place. King. Predator. Controlled. Not the man about to shatter just from the sight of her smile.

Kain glanced up, grin half-cocked, lazy as sin. "Bout time, boss. Thought you'd left me babysitting all week."

Nyx ignored him. His eyes never left Eden.

And she—she turned at the weight of his stare. Her laughter caught, lips parting, sunlight still woven through her hair. For a heartbeat, the world narrowed to nothing but that look.

The storm in his chest quieted. Just for a moment.

CHAPTER THIRTEEN

The Truth Always Leaves A Mark

Nyx closed the distance between them in three strides, his presence blotting out the city behind him. His gaze locked on Eden, molten-dark, unreadable.

"Ready?" His voice was low, almost intimate, though it carried the weight of command. "We're going to Virex."

For a moment, she only stared—entranced, caught in that undertow she never seemed able to fight. Her throat worked once, and she nodded.

He extended his hand, palm open. Her fingers slid into his without thought, and he pulled her gently but firmly against him before steering her toward the waiting car. Every step was deliberate, claiming, like she already belonged at his side.

Lyn Rose

At the curb, he opened the rear door, guiding her in with a steadying touch. Then he circled the car, nodding once at Jace and Kain before slipping into the driver's seat.

The ride was silent but thrumming with tension.

The car purred to a halt outside a towering structure of dark glass and steel. Virex Industries loomed like a modern fortress—its sharp edges catching the afternoon light. The air still carried a faint metallic tang, the scent of rain rising from sun-warmed concrete.

Eden barely had time to unbuckle before Nyx was already out, the soft thud of his boots striking the wet pavement. He moved with purpose, coat shifting around him as he came around to open her door. She hesitated, afternoon sunlight glancing off the car's surface and the lingering damp in the air, then took his offered hand. His grip was warm and steady—a quiet anchor amid the city's glare.

Without a word, he led her to the entrance. The tall black double doors were slick with rain, reflecting shards of sunlight off their surface. Nyx pulled a small device from his pocket, its metal cool against his fingers. A soft click echoed, reverberating through the hollow silence, and the doors slid open with a mechanical sigh.

Eden blinked against the sudden shift—the sterile scent of polished stone and wealth washing over her. "Seriously?"

Nyx's mouth twitched, the ghost of a smile breaking through the shadow of his jaw. "Welcome to Virex."

Lyn Rose

Inside, silence reigned—a thick, almost tangible quiet that wrapped around them like a shroud. Dimmed lights cast long, angular shadows across marble floors gleaming like frozen glass. The scent of cold stone mingled with the faint hum of the building's pulse, a low vibration beneath the stillness.

He clicked the device again, moving to a sleek wall panel. His fingers, cool and deliberate, danced over the smooth surface, entering a short string of numbers. A soft chirp confirmed the alarms had been disarmed—a quiet exhale in the air.

He led her down a wide hallway lined with darkened glass. The world beyond was veiled, sunlight reduced to a faint, distorted shimmer. For a moment, it felt like the city itself had been shut out—nothing but shadow and silence beyond the walls.

They stepped into a private elevator, doors sealing them in with a whisper. The air inside was cool, mechanical with polished metal. The soft hum beneath their feet matched the quick rhythm of her pulse.

When the doors opened, Eden stepped into a space that mirrored Nyx—sharp lines, polished surfaces, an elegance too precise to be accidental. The obsidian tiles reflected muted light; smoked glass framed the room like a mirage. Matte black accents absorbed sound, swallowing even breath.

He gestured toward a leather couch by the windows. The faint scent of worn leather mingled with his cologne—dark, clean, and quietly disarming.

"Make yourself comfortable," he said. "Can I get you something to drink?"

She shook her head, already pulling out her laptop. The cool metal of its casing grounded her. "I'm okay, thanks."

As Nyx walked away, the atmosphere shifted. The temperature dipped, the air thickening with the low electric hum of the security wing. Server towers lined the walls like silent guardians, their blinking lights pulsing in coded rhythms. The faint scent of machines and electricity sharpened, mingling with the sterile cold.

The main console waited, a dark void until Nyx pressed his palm to the reader. Cool surface. Quiet spark.

A flicker—then the room breathed. Data cascaded in encrypted layers; Virex nodes flared faint blue like distant stars. Most CEOs never touched their own security. Nyx wasn't most CEOs.

He pulled the flagged segment—01:12 A.M., Club X, mezzanine. The worst of the chaos lived off-frame, but the ripple was there: Eden cutting through the crowd, the air around her changing shape. Kain sliding between her and a hungry vampire. The scrape of claws on leather. Nyx descending—predator pressure turning the room taut.

He scrubbed back, paused, zoomed. Frame by frame.

Not just hunger in their eyes. Something nearer to awe.

Like instinct remembered her before reason could.

He killed the audio after the filtered murmurs—*she smells like… that's not human… what is she——*and opened a secure line.

"Containment."

"Sir."

"The vampire from Blackthorne goes to Virex Med. Maximum sedation. Secure cell. ETA?"

"Forty minutes. Blood and tissue in transit—chain logged."

"Prep cold storage for the wolf's organs. Heart, neural, liver. Full histo. I want the vector mapped before anyone else."

"Yes, sir."

He cut the call. The servers hummed.

Two killers. Two methods. Eden at the centre when it began.

He forced that thought down and opened another encrypted channel—this one tied to a morning flag. The feed scrolled cold and clinical:

• Injected case: Blackthorne wolf—sealed in Haven.

• Injected case: vampire—raving in chains, Virex collection inbound.

• Outlier: collapsed downtown—no wound, no poison, no bleed-out. Body looked hollowed from the inside. Medics called it burnout.

Something threaded them; he couldn't see the seam yet.

Beyond the glass wall, the building stilled—everything waiting, except her. Eden Marlowe, curled on the black leather, sunlight edging her hair like fire. Unaware.

He exhaled and pulled her file again—not curiosity, confirmation. Club X footage flared back: Eden in red, laughing; the crowd freezing mid-animal. Wolves stiffen. Fae go statuesque. A vampire's jaw locks as scent hits.

He slowed it.

Not attraction. Biological.

A trigger.

He routed into Virex Med. Blood type: O-negative. Rare, clean—and burning hot in the hormonal read, calling to things better left sleeping.

Cross-refs: adrenal spikes. Pheromonal markers. Unnatural bonding response.

A second window bloomed—old, half-buried archive on the darknet. He keyed the terms with clinical hands and an unsteady pulse:

O-negative.

Uncontrolled scent reaction.

Spontaneous bond initiation.

The system blinked.

Hit.

TheraGen.

Not a faction. A lab.

Shut down nearly a decade ago. IVF-based. Unregulated. Blacklisted across three factions.

Fragments decrypted:

Project Thera — Internal Roster

Most data corrupted or erased.

One line survived.

Subject Ref: E.M.

Reactivity: Untested.

Predicted Outcome: Volatile bond potential.

E.M.

Eden Marlowe.

The server's hum turned to static. He didn't breathe.

This wasn't coincidence.

She wasn't random.

She'd been made for this.

The alert hit—shrill, clean.

INTRUSION DETECTED.

"Shit." He slammed the keys—firewalls up, hard lockdown.
The screen flickered as code curdled and spread like rot.

Someone had buried this for a reason.

And someone knew he'd just unearthed it.

He contained the breach, ripped core data into a secure
offline node, and isolated it from the rest of Virex's system.

The screen dimmed.

Silence.

Only one line remained in quarantine.

Lyn Rose

THERA_GEN_SUBJECT_EM_REDACTED

But something else lingered.

A remnant file, hidden beneath layers, encrypted in metadata.

Just a phrase.

Barely a whisper.

Laç de Sânge.

The words scrolled across the corner before blinking out.

Nyx froze.

Not a name.

Not a warning.

A myth.

One he hadn't heard in years.

Not since old blood houses still whispered secrets.

Not since the Blood Courts silenced anything they couldn't control.

A bond that asked no permission.

Waited for no logic.

Lyn Rose

It just was.

Violent.

Rare.

Absolute.

Born not of love.

But of need.

Survival.

Fate.

Nyx grabbed his comm.

"Jace."

The younger man's voice came instantly.

"Sir?"

"I'm sending you something. A name. Laç de Sânge. Find every trace. Old blood court archives, fringe science, folklore. I don't care how deep it's buried. Dig it up."

A pause.

"Understood."

"And Jace—don't share it. Not with Kain. Not with anyone."

"Copy that."

Nyx hung up.

Cleared logs.

Flushed access tunnels.

Wiped search paths from every node connected to Virex.

Then he sat back.

Cold.

Fingers still wrapped around Eden's name.

She wasn't a spark anymore.

She was the fuse.

He whispered—

"…what the fuck are you, Eden."

He returned to the office like a shadow slipping back into its master.

Silent.

Controlled.

But not calm.

Lyn Rose

Not anymore.

She didn't hear him at first.

Eden was still on the couch, her legs curled beneath her, laptop balanced on one thigh as her fingers moved with absent focus. Her hair fell over one shoulder, catching the light like liquid shadow.

Her pulse—steady.

Her scent—impossible.

He leaned against the doorway, unseen.

Watched her.

Smelled her.

Felt the pull like a cord wrapping tighter around his ribs.

His body reacted before his thoughts did—pupils narrowing, hunger low and deep behind his ribs, the ache to taste, to take to mark. He felt his canines press faintly against his upper lip and exhaled through his nose, trying to suppress the beast pacing beneath his skin.

She shifted slightly, her shoulder tilting—exposing the soft skin of her throat.

Heat surged.

Not bloodlust.

Lyn Rose

Not entirely.

Something older.

Worse.

The need to claim.

To consume.

To keep.

She looked up then, catching him watching her.

And smiled.

Small.

Almost shy.

But real.

The kind of smile that kicked his thoughts sideways and made something primal sink its claws deeper.

A flush bloomed across her cheeks.

Not fear.

Heat.

Recognition.

Lyn Rose

He didn't move.

Didn't speak.

Just watched her watching him—the space between them suddenly thick with something unspoken.

Something inevitable.

Eden.

He stepped into the office without a sound, the door clicking shut behind him.

Eden didn't notice.

Not at first.

She was still on the couch, screen dimmed, her laptop resting quietly on her lap now. Maybe she'd stopped working. Maybe she was just pretending to, needing a moment of stillness in a world unravelling too fast.

He leaned against the desk, watching her in silence.

Her heart—a quiet thrum, steady but unsure. He could hear it as clearly as breath, feel it like heat against his skin. She shifted slightly, sensing the weight of him before she looked up.

Their eyes met.

Lyn Rose

She straightened, uncertain, the question clear on her face.

He didn't speak. Not until he'd forced his instincts back into the cage where they belonged.

"Are you alright to leave?" His voice was low. Unreadable. But steady again.

Eden nodded, rising and slipping her laptop into her bag.

"Of course."

He opened the door, let her pass, and followed.

The city was bathed in deep blue now—Sunday evening settling over Edalva like a slow exhale.

Nyx drove in silence, one hand on the wheel, the other resting near the gearshift. Eden sat beside him, quiet, thoughtful. Neither of them broke the stillness. The hum of the car, the occasional flicker of passing lights, the soft breath she took when they began to climb—all of it felt fragile somehow.

Like any word might shatter it.

They reached Duskwatch just as the stars began to creep out from behind the skyline. The gates opened silently, and he pulled into the private garage with a soft purr of tires on polished stone.

Then he cut the engine and looked over at her.

"Come," he said, his voice gentler this time.

"I'll show you the best place to see the city."

He stepped out and came around to her door, offering his hand without thinking.

She hesitated only a second before slipping hers into his.

Warm.

Small.

Real.

His fingers closed around hers, and something deep in him settled.

He didn't let go.

The lift glided upward with barely a sound.

Fourth floor.

The doors opened to glass and air and light.

Eden gasped.

A full-wall window stretched from floor to ceiling, revealing the heart of Edalva in all its glittering glory—buildings like silver teeth, streets like veins of fire, the horizon soft with the last breath of daylight. The room itself was a luxury dream: an indoor pool cast in black tile, steam rising from a recessed hot tub, lounge chairs and soft lights that glowed like candle flame.

But it was the view that stole her voice.

She stepped forward slowly, until she stood at the edge of the platform, palms brushing the glass.

"It's… unreal."

He watched her from behind.

Watched how her breath caught. How the city shimmered in her eyes.

She didn't know he'd moved closer until she felt him—his presence like gravity pulling just behind her.

She turned to glance back at him—and he was close.

Closer than before.

The space between them barely existed.

Her heart skipped.

He didn't touch her.

But he could have.

He was so close his breath stirred the hair near her temple.

And then he leaned down, just enough that his voice slid along her skin.

"You like the view."

It wasn't a question.

And it wasn't just about the skyline.

Her throat tightened.

"It's… beautiful."

She felt him watching her, felt the shift in the air. The gravity between them tugged tighter.

His hand lifted.

Fingers hovered just above her jaw, like he meant to touch her—but didn't.

She swore the heat from him alone could set her alight.

But then—

He blinked.

A breath.

A curse under his breath she couldn't catch.

And he stepped back.

Lyn Rose

Distance.

Again.

"Let me show you the rest of the floor."

She didn't move.

Didn't breathe.

Just stood there.

Jaw tight.

Skin flushed.

Dying inside.

Because whatever that was?

It wasn't over.

It was just beginning.

CHAPTER FOURTEEN

Lac de Sânge

The elevator chimed softly, and Eden's breath hitched before the doors even opened.
She recognized the hallway instantly.
The polished floors. The obsidian walls. The hush of wealth and secrecy.
His floor.

Her fingers tightened slightly around his as they walked. He didn't say anything. He didn't need to.

When he opened the door, the room welcomed her like a memory—sharp, clear, strange. The bed was made now, the black sheets sleek as glass, the throw folded with surgical precision. It should've felt cold. Distant.
But somehow, it didn't.

The blanket looked softer than mink. The kind of thing you sank into and didn't want to leave.

Nyx moved ahead, crossing to a cupboard on the far left near the ensuite—the same one she'd showered in that morning. Gods was that only today?
It felt like another life.

Eden stood still a moment, her body catching up with her mind. Her heels clicked faintly as she slipped them off. The moment her feet met cool floor, a shiver slid up her spine.

Nyx noticed.
He didn't speak—just opened the cupboard and pulled out something dark and loose. One of his. A sweater, maybe. A cardigan.
He walked over and held it out.

She blinked down at it. "I'm fine. I have my own."

His gaze caught hers—steady, unreadable, but not cold.
"I like you in my clothes."

She stared at him.
No smirk. No edge of flirtation.
Just honesty. Blunt and quiet and devastating.

She pulled the sweater over her head.
Soft. Warm. Too warm.

His scent wrapped around her like a second skin—cedar, cologne, and something darker she didn't have a name for. Heat bloomed low in her belly, spreading like wildfire. Her skin prickled beneath the fabric, an ache that wasn't just warmth but something sharp and hungry. Her pulse thundered in her ears, quick and uneven. It wasn't just desire—it was like her body was waking up from a long sleep, catching fire from the inside out.

And when she looked up…
Nyx was watching her like he might combust.

He moved before she could speak—not fast, but deliberate, his footsteps near silent on the dark marble tiles. He stopped beside her, leaned down, and let his mouth brush the edge of her ear.
"The only thing better than seeing you in my clothes," he murmured, voice a rasp of velvet and hunger, "would be seeing you out of all of them."

Eden's breath caught hard in her throat. Her cheeks flushed so hot it burned. Her whole body ached, like electricity thrumming just beneath her skin. She wanted to reach out, to close the space between them, but part of her trembled with the fierce sharpness of wanting something she couldn't fully grasp.
But she didn't move away.
Didn't blink.
Didn't breathe.

Not when he leaned back just enough to meet her eyes— deep, dark, ravenous. Not when he brushed a single knuckle down the edge of her cheek, dragging heat in his wake.

His lips parted as he inhaled her scent.
And groaned.
Low. Raw. Like it cost him to hold back.

Then his hands were on her waist—strong, insistent—
pulling her to him.

She didn't resist.

She went.

Her breath came shallow, her heart a war drum in her chest.
But her hands moved like they'd always known the way—up
his chest, along the line of his shoulders, fingers sliding into
the dark hair at the base of his neck.

She felt fire crawl beneath her ribs, an ache that wasn't just
want but need—raw, relentless, alive. Every nerve screamed
for more, her pulse a frantic rhythm hammering against his
stillness.

Then—he felt it.

Her heartbeat.

Not through the air, not through her body—through his.

A dull, impossible thud in his chest.

For a split second, it matched hers.

Steady. Strong. Alive.

Nyx froze.

He hadn't felt a heartbeat in centuries. Not his own. Not
anyone's inside him.

Lyn Rose

And yet—there it was, syncing to hers like an echo that shouldn't exist.

The shock burned through his restraint, loosening the careful edges he lived by. His breath dragged rough through his teeth. Something ancient stirred—hunger, yes, but something older, heavier, dangerously close to *wanting*.

He bent his head.

She tilted hers.

And then…
He kissed her.
No hesitation. No apology.
Just fire and hunger and the kind of claiming that rewrote the rules of what she thought a kiss could be. His mouth was warm, demanding, parting hers like a vow. Her knees went weak. Her fingers tightened in his hair.

And everything else—
Vanished.

Eden
The kiss didn't stop.
Couldn't.

Because the second his mouth found hers, she wasn't sure she remembered what air was supposed to taste like without him.

Her body was burning from the inside. It itched and ached in ways that made her dizzy and raw. The heat pooled low and spread, a relentless fire she couldn't cool. She was hungry for him—more than skin deep—an ache that clawed through every nerve ending and tore at her control.

Nyx pressed in, slow but firm, like gravity meant nothing if she wasn't beneath him. His hand slid around her waist, the other already finding her hip. She felt the heat of his palm through the fabric—his sweater—and then he was walking her backward. Each step deliberate. Controlled. Until her back hit the wall with a soft thud and he didn't stop moving.

His kiss deepened. Rougher. Hungrier.
Like he'd finally broken the leash.

Then—
His hands slipped beneath the sweater.
Her breath hitched.
And then lower—beneath the blouse he'd chosen for her that morning, fingers dragging fire up her bare skin. It should've startled her, but all she could do was gasp and arch into the heat of him. His touch was gentle and raw all at once, calloused thumbs brushing the underside of her ribs like she might vanish if he didn't feel her fully.

When his thumbs grazed just under her bra, her knees almost buckled.
"Nyx—" she moaned.

He growled. Actually growled.
And kissed her again like he owned her pulse.

Lyn Rose

Nyx
He wasn't thinking anymore.
Couldn't.

The second she pulled that sweater on—his sweater—he'd
fucking lost it.
The scent of her. The sight of her. The sound of her breath
catching when he touched her.
It short-circuited whatever restraint he had left.

She was in his space. In his clothes. In his arms.
And it wasn't enough.
Would never be enough.

He kissed her hard, hungry, like he could imprint himself
into her mouth. Her lips parted like she was made for him,
and when her back hit the wall, he didn't hesitate.

He needed to feel her.
Not above clothes. Not in polite touches.
Skin.

His hands slid under the sweater—his—then under the
blouse. The fabric bunched easily as his fingers found her
bare waist, then higher. Smooth, warm, alive.

She gasped. Moaned his name.
He loved that sound coming from her lips.
Gods, her skin. Her scent. Her voice. The way she arched
into his hands instead of pulling away.
She wanted this. Wanted him.

Lyn Rose

The connection flared. Deep. Ancient.
Her blood sang to his. Called him closer. Claimed him
without permission.

He bent his head to her neck, breathing her in, brushing lips
against her pulse point.
"Your heart," he whispered raggedly, "it's driving me
fucking insane."

She didn't move. Didn't speak.
Just looked at him with those wide, dazed eyes and offered
herself.

And his control snapped.

One hand fisted in her blouse, the other cradling her neck as
he kissed her again—deeper, rougher, teeth scraping her
lower lip like he wanted to drink her in.
But he didn't take more.
Not yet.

Because as much as he wanted her…
He wanted her willing.

He pulled back—barely.
Both of them breathing like they'd run a mile.
Still touching.
Still burning.

"Say something," he rasped, voice hoarse. "Or I'll tear down
every last wall you've got."

Eden

Her breath was still caught in her throat when he pulled
back.
Chest heaving. Skin flushed. Lips swollen.
She blinked up at him, dazed, drunk on whatever the hell
that had just been.
"Why did you stop?" she whispered.

Nyx's jaw tensed. His fingers still hovered near her waist,
like he hadn't quite convinced himself to let go yet.
His voice was low. Gravel and restraint.
"Because you don't know me yet. And I want you willing."

She didn't hesitate.
"Nyx, I am willing."

That did it.
That nearly undid him.
A muscle jumped in his jaw. His pupils dilated—black
devouring gold.
For a split second, he swayed toward her again, breath hot
against her mouth, and her body lit up like a live wire
waiting to spark.

Nyx

His phone buzzed.

A brutal, shrill cut through the air that barely reached him over the roar in his blood.

He didn't want to move.

Didn't want to stop.

Didn't want to do anything except press her back against that wall and taste the parts of her that had been haunting his every thought since the fucking alley.

But the phone kept buzzing.

With a guttural sound—more animal than man—he pulled back, jaw tight, eyes dark. His hand left her waist reluctantly, the other still braced against the wall beside her head, like if he moved too fast, he'd lose the last shred of control keeping the beast in its cage.

He didn't look at the screen.

Just answered.

"Nyx," he growled.

Jace's voice crackled through the speaker. "Found what you wanted. Laç de Sânge—file's in your secure inbox. And the samples? Not back yet. Lab's running slow."

Nyx's tone dropped, lethal and cold. "Tell them it's top priority."

"Done," Jace said without hesitation.

Lyn Rose

Nyx's throat worked. "Good." He hung up.

Slowly, he looked back at her.

She was flushed. Chest rising and falling in sharp little breaths. Lips kiss-bitten. Hair mussed from his hands.

And gods, gods, she was looking at him like she was still on fire.

Still his.

Still willing.

"Come," he said, extending his hand. "I was making you dinner."

There was something almost cruel in the contrast—his voice rough, his body still screaming to claim, and yet the words so calm.

He saw the flicker in her eyes. Frustration. Hunger. A hundred unspoken questions.

She didn't speak.

Just slid her hand into his again.

He exhaled. Not relief. Not ease.

Just a thin, fragile line of control.

For now.

Eden

He led her by the hand, Like nothing had just happened. He acted like he hadn't just kissed her like he needed it to live. And like his hands hadn't scorched her skin moments ago, tracing lines that still burned beneath her clothes.

And she was still trembling—shaking with a heat that ran deeper than mere desire.

The kitchen was sleek and cold—marble counters, matte black cabinets—but the moment Nyx stepped inside, it shrank, the air thickening, charged and dangerous.

He let go of her hand.
She missed the contact instantly, the loss like a physical ache.

Without a word, he moved to the fridge, pulling out two thick, dark steaks that looked like they belonged in a gallery, not a kitchen. He never asked how she liked them. Seasoned with quiet ease, he set the pan aflame.

The scent hit her—warm butter, sharp rosemary, something smoky and rich that wrapped around her like a promise.

He laid out salad with a careful hand, dressing poured into crystal like a sacred ritual. On the stove, a dark glossy gravy simmered quietly.

"Steak?" Nyx glanced over his shoulder.

Her voice caught, fragile and raw. "Yeah. That's… perfect."

No smile, but a flicker—almost a crack—in the armour at the corner of his mouth.

She moved to the island, leaned on the cold marble, trying to tame the wildfire still raging in her veins.

Nyx worked like he fought—silent, precise, dangerous. Flipping the steak with a sharp flick of his wrist, pouring sauce with reverence, then finally setting down plate, cutlery, and a crystal tumbler filled with something amber and burning.

He slid her plate forward.
"You, okay?" His voice was softer now, but still edged with something unspoken.

Eden looked up, caught in the gravity of his proximity. Too close. His eyes were darker, deeper, shadows pooling beneath them. His jaw was tight—taut with tension.

"I don't know," she admitted, voice low and honest. "You keep kissing me like I'm yours. And then you keep pulling away."

Nyx hesitated, silent for a long moment.
Then, quiet but certain: "Because you are. But not yet."

She swallowed hard, the words hanging between them.
"That's not how this works."

A flicker of heat sparked behind his eyes, dangerous and raw.
"No. It's how I work."

His tone softened, almost tender.
"I want you willing, Eden. Not just aroused. Not just curious. I want you to know what you're giving yourself to. Who you're giving yourself to."

Lyn Rose

Her breath caught. Whispered, "And if I already do?"

His throat moved with a swallow so audible it was a confession. Control wavered, radiating off him like heat off sunbaked concrete.

He leaned in.
His lips brushed her ear, voice a ragged whisper.
"Then I'm fucked."

CHAPTER FIFTEEN

The Truth, He Owed Her

Nyx

He set the plates down with quiet precision: rare steak, salad,
a dark jus still steaming in the bowl between them.
Eden's gaze flicked from the food to him, lips parted like she
wanted to ask something but hadn't found the words.
He didn't give her the chance.
"I'll be right back," he said smoothly, already moving.
"Going to grab a bottle of wine that pairs better."
She nodded, brushing her hair behind her ear, still looking at
him like she was trying to solve a riddle with no pieces.
He left the kitchen and headed straight for the lower floor—
not the wine cellar, not at first.
The blood storage was discreet. Hidden behind a reinforced
panel keyed only to his biometric scan. Inside: his
emergency supply. Black-sealed. Unmarked. Nothing
decorative.
Just survival.
Nyx cracked the top off one of the pouches and drank.

Not slow. Not refined.

Like he'd been starving.

Because in a way, he was.

She was in his space. Wearing his clothes. Still flushed from his kiss. Still tasting like surrender. And every cell in his body was howling.

The blood dulled it. Barely.

He took a second, hand braced on the fridge door. Let the chill bite into his skin.

Then turned, crossed the cellar, and pulled out his phone, unlocking the secure app.

A new encrypted message waited—Jace's reply.

SUBJECT: Re: Laç de Sânge

He opened it.

Laç de Sânge—Blood Tie. Documented three times in vampire history. Bond forms without feeding, mating, or consent. It is instinctive, irreversible, and known to occur only under rare biochemical or magical conditions.

Symptoms:

– Increased aggression toward perceived threats

– Hyper-attunement to subject's presence

– Psychic bleed (early-stage)

– Shared emotional resonance

– Impulse control failure in feeding/mating instincts

All three confirmed cases ended in one of two outcomes:

– Death of one or both parties due to volatility

– Permanent claim, sealed by mutual blood exchange (rumoured to anchor the bond)

Additional theories link Laç de Sânge to selective bloodlines—potentially manipulated through magical or genetic interference. No modern verified reports exist.

• J.

Nyx's grip tightened around the phone. His reflection in the cellar glass looked half-wild, jaw clenched, fangs half-dropped.

He looked back at the wine rack.

Selected a red. A vintage red aged in smoked oak, subtle enough to play nice with seared meat, bold enough to hold his attention.

And walked upstairs knowing what she was. What they were.

He re-entered the kitchen quietly, wine in hand. Eden looked up, brows drawn.

"You were gone a while."

"Everything okay?"

Nyx uncorked the bottle. Poured without blinking.

His hands moved slower than usual. Controlled. Measured.

"Had to search the back racks."

He set her glass down. Their eyes met.

The heat hadn't left the air. It had only thickened.

Outside, the city sprawled beneath them, a constellation of lights twinkling through the floor-to-ceiling windows. The night breathed softly—distant car horns, faint murmurs, and the occasional pulse of neon signs flickering against the dark.

Inside, the room was cool, the faint scent of oak and stone mingling with the weight of what hung between them.

Eden

She took the wine, but didn't sip.

Just watched him.

And when he finally sat across from her, calm like nothing had happened—like he hadn't just dragged her to the edge of something primal and then left her there—she set the glass down.

"Nyx."

His eyes lifted to hers. Still storm-dark. Still unreadable.

"I need to say something," she said. "And I need you to not shut down or vanish behind that perfect CEO mask you wear like armour."

His jaw twitched.

She pressed on. "Whatever's going on between us—it's confusing. And intense. And I'm not saying I don't feel it, because I do. But I'm not going to be toyed with. I'm not some girl you can pull in and then push away like nothing happened."

She drew a breath. "So if you're not interested, say so. If you are… then let's actually figure out what that means. But no more cryptic riddles. No more half-truths. I'm done guessing."

Silence.

Heavy. Absolute.

Then Nyx stood.

Slowly.

His chair scraped gently against the marble.

He moved to the window, wine glass untouched, back to her.

For a second, she thought he might walk away again—disappear into shadows like he had every other time things got close.

Lyn Rose

But then he turned.
And something in his eyes cracked.
"I am interested," he said.
Her heart kicked.
"In fact, interested doesn't fucking cover it."
He took a step forward. Then another.
"In all my—" He cut himself off. "In all the years I've
walked through this world… no one has undone me like
you."
Her breath caught—but he didn't stop.
"I have met kings and murderers. Seen love born and
destroyed. Felt hunger, wrath, devotion, and apathy. And
through it all, nothing—nothing—has touched me like you."
Her fingers tightened around her glass.
"You call to me," he said, voice rougher now, like gravel
under velvet. "You pull at me. Past sense. Past instinct. Past
reason."
Another step.
She couldn't move. Couldn't speak.
"I want to possess you. Own your body. Own your soul."
His voice dropped to a whisper, but it hit harder than a shout.
"I want to devour every breath you make, burn for every
sound that leaves your mouth. I want to carve your name
into my fucking blood."
She couldn't look away.
"But I am terrified that if I touch you again," he said, quieter
now, "I won't be able to stop."
A silence fell. No music. No clock ticking. Just her breath
and his. Tangled.
Eden's voice, when it came, was small. "All the years?"
He met her gaze.

She filed it away.

Later.

She stood, heart racing, breath uneven.

His words still echoed—real, loving, terrifying in their honesty.

I want to possess you. Own your body. Your soul. You call to me… and I don't know how to silence it.

Eden didn't move for a long moment. Just watched him—the man who had just ripped his control wide open for her to see.

Then:

She crossed the space between them. Slow. Certain.

Her voice was quiet when it came.

"Then touch me."

Nyx didn't move. Not at first.

He stared at her like she was the last star in a dying sky. His jaw was tight. Too tight. Every part of him coiled and breaking.

Then he stepped forward—slow, deliberate—and cupped her face in both hands.

"You don't know what you're asking for."

She blinked up at him, breath catching. But she didn't pull away.

"Then tell me."

His hands trembled.

"I was born in 1786."

Her lips parted—confusion flickering, then disbelief. But he didn't let her speak.

"I haven't aged since 1811. I've lived through wars your history books skip over. I've buried empires, lovers, friends. I've walked cities that no longer exist. And for over two hundred years, I've never wanted anything the way I want you."

His voice dropped to a near growl.

"You drive me mad, Eden. Your scent, your voice, your fucking heartbeat. Every instinct I have—the monster in me—wants to mark you, bite you, ruin you."

Her breath was ragged now. Still, she didn't move.

"But I won't take you blind. I won't take you unless you know. Really know."

She shook her head once, dazed. "Know what?"

He leaned down, close enough she could feel the heat rolling off him, smell the blood still lingering in his breath.

"You are not just some woman I want.

You are my Laç de Sânge."

She flinched. "What is that?"

"Blood tie. It's a myth among my kind. A bond so rare most don't believe it exists. It overrides logic. Overpowers control. It's sacred. It's damning."

He stepped back, barely, like it pained him to put even a breath of space between them.

"And you were made to be this."

She froze. "What do you mean, made?"

"Your blood. Your scent. It was engineered, by a company called Biotech, I have a file at Virex for you to read. You're not just my weakness, Eden. You're every predator's."

Then softer—not to scare her, but because the words could shatter:

"And if I touch you now, there's no going back."

Eden didn't move.

Didn't speak.

Just stood there, glass in hand, staring at him like the air had shifted around her.

Nyx saw it all in a flash—the way her spine stiffened, the subtle flare of her nostrils, the flicker of something primal beneath her confusion.

Not fear.

But something like alarm. Like instinct telling her to run, even as something deeper told her to stay.

"Eden." His voice was lower now. Gentler. "I know this sounds… impossible."

She blinked slowly, lips parting just enough to whisper, "Laç de Sânge."

The words felt heavy on her tongue. Foreign. Sacred.

He nodded once.

"It's not a fantasy. It's not a story. It's real. And rare. A bond older than any law—written in blood, forged by something deeper than will."

"I didn't expect it. I didn't ask for it. But the moment I saw you, it began."

Eden shook her head. "You're talking like—like we're fated or something."

Nyx didn't smile. He didn't blink.

"We are."

That landed like thunder between them.

Eden backed a step before she realized she had. "You're saying this isn't just… chemistry?"

"No." His eyes burned into hers.

"This is biology. Instinct. Blood. You unsettle the air around you. Every supernatural you pass feels you. And me—"

His voice roughened, almost a confession.

"I feel you to the marrow. Like something ancient in me woke up and remembered your name."

She gasped, eyes wide. "You're not—" The word caught in her throat. "You can't be."

The taste of it turned to iron on her tongue.

"What are you saying?" Her voice broke. "I didn't ask for any of this."

 "I know," he said quietly. "And that's why I haven't taken it. Haven't touched you beyond what you gave freely.

 I would rather burn than make you feel owned."
Her throat worked. Her chest lifted with a shallow breath.
"Why me?" She repeated.
His answer was steady. Real.
"I don't know. But, I'm sure. I'd bet eternity on it."
Silence stretched.
Her throat worked. Her breath came shallower now, but not from fear. From the weight of what he wasn't saying.
From the shadows still hiding behind his eyes.
"You said this is instinct," she murmured. "That it's real. Old."
Her fingers curled tighter around the wine glass.
"But what are you, Nyx?"
That stopped him cold.
He didn't move. Didn't speak.
So she took a breath, steadied her voice, and asked the real question:
"You're not human, are you?"

Silence pulsed between them.
And then he stepped forward, slow and deliberate—the predator unmasked, but still choosing patience.
"No," he said.
"I'm not."

The words struck like a crack in her bones.

Her knees almost buckled. Her stomach turned. The room suddenly felt too small, the air too thin.

Not human.

A thousand images surged: his strength, his stillness, the heat of his hands, the way the waiter had looked at her like prey.

Eden gripped the table edge.
She wanted to run. To scream. To deny it.
But her voice wouldn't come.

Instead, she stared at him—at the man she'd kissed, the one who had saved her—and everything she'd doubted clicked into place.
The cracks became clarity.

She didn't sit.
Didn't sip her wine.
Just breathed—jagged and raw—and watched him, heart pounding like it was trying to escape her chest.

Lyn Rose

Curiosity.

Want.

Fear.

A pull she didn't understand and a need for truth that wouldn't let her look away.

"You're not human," she said again, voice low. "And you've lived—what, centuries?"

Nyx didn't answer.

He didn't need to.

She took a breath. "You knew Evelyn Stroud. Personally. Aleria Vale kissed your cheek like an equal. You walk through locked doors like they're nothing. You smell things. Sense things. And—"

She faltered.

A beat of silence.

He waited.

Something tugged, unspooled in her mind.

Dinner.

That moment before the waiter arrived. No alcohol yet. Just water. And that dark glass beside his hand—filled with something too thick to be wine. Almost black. "She'd stared too long, blinked, convinced herself it was the shadows.

A trick of the eye."

But it hadn't been.

Her pulse lurched.

He hadn't been drinking wine.

Eden's breath hitched, caught somewhere between disbelief and a surge of something raw and electric that prickled beneath her skin.

Lyn Rose

Her fingers tightened around the wine glass, knuckles whitening as the words washed over her like a rising tide she couldn't hold back.

Two hundred years. A blood bond. A claim made without consent. The weight of it pressed down on her chest, making it hard to draw air deep enough to steady the shaking in her limbs.

Her heart hammered—not just with fear, but with a fierce, aching pull that twisted in her gut. The scent of him, the memory of his touch still burning on her skin, ignited a fire she couldn't control.

Heat pooled low and spread, an ache so sharp it made her shiver despite the warmth of the room.

The room tilted for a moment, the edges blurring as her mind raced to catch up with the impossible. She felt exposed— raw, like a nerve laid bare. His words weren't just words. They were a reckoning.

"I am your Laç de Sânge." The phrase echoed in her mind, heavy and sacred and terrifying.

She swallowed hard, tasting metal on her tongue, her throat dry and tight. The image of the bond—blood and fire, fate and biology—seared itself into her thoughts. She wanted to pull back, to run, but an invisible tether held her rooted, trembling.

The cold glass in her hand felt slippery, distant, like it wasn't hers, like it belonged to someone else.

Her breath came uneven, shallow. Every nerve ending buzzed with a fierce, aching want she didn't understand but couldn't deny.

When Nyx's eyes locked onto hers, dark and fierce, she saw the war waging inside him—the hunger, the fear, the desperate need to protect her even as he burned to claim her. Her chest tightened again, a mix of longing and raw vulnerability. The man standing before her was both, predator and prisoner of something older than time itself. And just like that, the fragile control she thought she had shattered.

"I'm not some girl to be toyed with," she whispered, voice trembling but steady, "but I'm not letting go either."

His confession, his centuries of solitude and restraint, hit her like a thunderclap. Her pulse raced, the heat in her veins rising, her skin prickling with the knowledge that she was caught in something vast and terrifying.

Her body reacted before her mind could catch up—goosebumps rising, breath catching, lips parting slightly with the need to speak and the fear of what might come next.

When she finally asked the question—the one that dared to cut through all the shadows—her voice was low, almost broken.

"What do you drink, Nyx?"

The answer came slow. Final.

"Blood…"

The word hung in the air, thick and dark.

A shiver ran down her spine. Her breath hitched again, this time with a mix of awe and a raw, aching need that left her feeling dizzy and exposed.

Everything she thought she knew about the world—and about herself—fractured and reformed in that moment.

And deep inside, where the bond pulsed unseen, her body whispered its truth:

She didn't want to run.

Lyn Rose

She wanted to stay.
No matter the cost.

CHAPTER SIXTEEN

Craving, Claimed, Changed

"Blood," she whispered again.

The word tasted metallic now. Heavy. Real.

And as it left her lips a second time, her mind shattered open.

It came in flashes. Violent, raw, undeniable.

The alley.

That night.

Two men—laughing, circling—and then gone. No screams. No struggle. Just gone. She'd told herself she was too drunk, a hit to the head, too scared. That she'd imagined the speed, the blur, the way one of them slammed into brick like he'd been thrown by something inhuman.

Nyx had been there.

He'd taken her to the hospital. No ambulance. No explanation. Just him. Watching.

Then the law firm. The conference room. That moment his eyes locked on hers and the air left her lungs like he'd stolen

it. The way her skin prickled before she even saw him.
How he'd looked at her.

The dinner.
That drink.
Not wine. Thicker. Darker. A glass he kept close, never
touched, not in front of her. She'd chalked it up to lighting,
shadow, her imagination.
But it wasn't.

Then Torran Black. How the man had flared—eyes, nostrils,
something other—then turned cold. Sure they were friends,
but he was controlled. Like a wolf rolling onto its back
before a bigger predator.

And the club.
The dance floor.
The way people moved when Nyx stepped near—not with
awe, but fear. Respect. Deference. The way the crowd parted
like the sea, and the air itself changed around him.
Fast. Too fast.

The man at the door who nearly pissed himself when Nyx
growled. The man in her apartment, dangling like a doll
from Nyx's hand, feet off the ground, choking under that
low, guttural snarl—
"Who the fuck are you?"
"Why are you near what's mine?"
Mine.

Image after image after image —
The puzzle she hadn't known she was building finally

snapped into place.
Her knees buckled.
Not fully. Not dramatically. Just a tiny shift—like her bones
couldn't hold the weight of this new truth.
She caught herself against the table, knuckles whitening.

Nyx

"Eden."
His voice was there—low, sharp, immediate.
Then he was there.
One second, she was alone in the echo of her unravelling
thoughts. The next, his hands were on her arms, steadying
her with supernatural speed and frightening care.
"Hey—" His touch was light, grounding. "You're alright."
But she wasn't.
Not really.

And suddenly the heat of him—the scent she'd grown to
recognize even when he wasn't near—was too much. Like
standing too close to a fire that wanted not just to warm, but
consume.
She stepped back.
Small. Quiet. But deliberate.
His hands dropped like she'd burned him.

Something flickered across his face—a crack in the storm.
Not anger. Not confusion.
Hurt.

Real.
Raw.

He masked it in the next breath, eyes shuttering like blackout curtains drawn across a window. But she'd seen it.
And that, somehow, knocked the air harder from her lungs than the truth ever could.

Eden took a breath. Then another. Then finally looked up.
Nyx hadn't moved—still standing where she'd stepped away from him, jaw tight, eyes carefully blank.
But she'd seen it.
That flicker. That ache.

She stepped forward.
"Nyx… I'm sorry," she said, voice gentler now. "Listen, this is a lot. I'm not running. But I've had so much weird in my life that never made sense—until you. And now all of its crashing into place like a puzzle I didn't know I was holding." *This was written in my blood.* That truth coiled through her, sharp and ancient. But the choice? *That was mine.*

His throat worked. "I understand."
"I just… I need some space. Some time."

He nodded once. Clipped. Controlled. "Of course."
"Do you have… a spare room?"

His eyes flicked up to meet hers—sharp, unreadable—and then he turned and gestured silently for her to follow.
She did.

Lyn Rose

The hall outside his bedroom stretched only a few steps before he stopped at the next door. He pressed his palm to a subtle sensor. The door clicked open.
Eden stepped inside—and blinked.

The space was starkly different than the rest of his home. Still dark floors, still obsidian trim. But the bed was framed in pale wood, the fireplace a soft white stone. Plush rugs covered the floor in smoky greys and ivory. Candles—real ones—stood waiting on the mantle, unlit but inviting. The air smelled faintly of cedar and lavender.
Like peace.

She turned, touched by the quiet warmth of it. "It's beautiful."
Nyx didn't reply.
He just stood in the doorway—tense, unreadable again. Something about him looked sharper in this moment. Like the control cost him more now.

"Thank you," she said quietly.
He inclined his head once. And then—
The door closed softly behind him.

Nyx

The moment the guest door shut, Nyx didn't pause.
He walked—deliberate, silent—down the hall and into his office. The door hissed shut behind him. Inside, the room welcomed him with cool glass, low light, and the faint hum

of encrypted systems still running.

He sank into the chair behind his desk. Hands braced against the edges.

He didn't touch the wine. Didn't look at the half-finished code file Jace had sent.

Instead, he stared at the monitor.

And finally opened the secure document.

Jace had sent everything—discreetly, of course. A scan of an old medical journal from an underground archive, watermarked TheraGen Internal Use Only. The section on Laç de Sânge had been flagged, annotated, translated into three languages.

But it wasn't the bond that made his breath still.

It was a reference three paragraphs down.

Subject viability correlates to genetic tampering via Series Thera.

Blood attraction spike: 170–230%. Risk of predator convergence confirmed.

Project termination pending. Survivors flagged for monitoring.

Nyx exhaled slowly. His fangs had dropped without him noticing.

Series Thera.

He whispered it to himself. A name hidden in time.

He scrolled further—redacted blocks, corrupted data, virus signatures Jace had half-contained before sending.

He ran a hand through his hair, jaw flexing.

Whatever Eden was… they'd built her to be irresistible. To him. To anything like him.

And now that he knew?
He couldn't un-know it.

He closed the file. Didn't shut down. Just sat there, jaw clenched, eyes burning through the screen.
Outside, the city glowed like a hearth. Inside, he was all winter.

Eden

The fire in the guest room cracked softly.
Eden lay curled beneath the heavy covers—but warmth didn't reach her.
Not really.
The room was beautiful. Safe.
Calming in every way Nyx wasn't.
And yet she felt like her blood was made of ice water.
Like her veins knew something she didn't.
She pulled the blanket tighter.

He'd said engineered. That she'd been made to be like this.
Like bait.
She hadn't thought about it in the moment—not through the heat of his voice, the ache of his confession. But now, alone in the quiet, it echoed.
"You were made to be this."
Not chosen. Not fated. Made.

Her throat tightened.

The wine sat untouched on the bedside table. Her laptop was shut. Her phone dark.

She lay there in a silk nightgown, firelight flickering across bare legs, heart hammering like it didn't belong to her.

So much weird in her life—people reacting to her without reason. Collapses. Flagged medical files. The way strangers sometimes looked at her like she wasn't real.

She turned on her side, clutching a pillow.

Was she even herself?

The room was too quiet. Her thoughts buzzed like static beneath her skin.

She didn't know who she was anymore. Not really.

Not after everything Nyx had told her. Not after what she'd felt.

But gods—she wasn't afraid of him.

He made her feel… steady. Real.

Even when the ground shook beneath her, his presence wrapped around her like gravity—pulling, constant, impossible to escape.

She'd asked for space.

She still needed it.

Lyn Rose

But the truth she hadn't said out loud?

She didn't want distance from him.

She wanted distance from everything else.

The danger. The blood. The lies.

Because when she looked at him…

She didn't feel like a weapon.

She felt like a woman.

And she wanted.

And still… she hadn't run.

Didn't want to.

Didn't know what that said about her—or about the man on the other side of the wall, who made her feel like she was standing at the edge of the world…

…and if she jumped, he'd catch her.

Or burn trying.

She closed her eyes.
Sleep didn't come.

Lyn Rose

Nyx

The fire hissed softly in the hearth in his room.
He sat low in the armchair near the flames, glass in hand,
shirtless, sweatpants riding low on his hips. The third
whiskey burned slower than the last. He welcomed the sting.
Across the room—the wall.
The one that separated them.
Her room.
He stared at it like he could will it to collapse. To dissolve
into smoke and ash and stop being the goddamn barrier
between him and the only thing his body had ever craved
with such desperation.
Her scent was everywhere.
On his shirt. In the sheets. In his bloodstream.
Laç de Sânge.
It wasn't just a myth anymore.
It had a name. A shape. A history of ruin.
And now it had a face.
Eden.

He drank again.
His phone buzzed on the table.
He didn't look right away. He knew the distraction would do
nothing to quench the fire under his skin. But when it buzzed
a second time, he reached for it.

Black: Checking in. Heard about the break-in. You want my
wolves to run doubles?
Nyx: No. It's handled.

He barely had time to put the glass down before it buzzed again.

Jace: All upgrades to Marlowe's apartment complete. Full sweep done. Cameras, locks, pressure alarms. Remote access routed through your firewall. Also—
Pause.
Found the building owner. Private syndicate. Took five minutes.

Nyx stared at the message, jaw tight.
He typed with one hand.
Nyx: Buy it.
Jace: Already done.

The phone went still.
Nyx exhaled. Not relief. Not victory.
Just the ache of something just out of reach.

He stared at the wall again.
And thought, burn.

Eden

She tried to sleep.
She tried.
But her skin was too tight. Her blood too loud. Every time she blinked, she saw his face. Heard his voice saying You were made to be this.
She finally gave up.

The air in the guest room was too still. Too soft.
She padded out barefoot, wearing only her nightgown—
black, simple—the kind meant to keep cool under pressure.
Shame it did nothing for the heat crawling up her legs.

The kitchen was her aim.
Water. Something. Anything to put out the fire now licking
down her spine.

But she slowed as she passed his room.
The door was open.
Just a little.

And there he was.
Framed by the windows, bathed in the city's dim silver
glow. Shirtless. Muscled. Tension thrumming in every line
of him like a beast barely held in check. His back was to her,
broad and scarred and powerful—and she swore her knees
actually weakened.

Her body betrayed her.
Instantly.
Wet.
Throbbing.
Hot.

He inhaled—sharp. Sudden.
"Fuck."
His voice was gravel, low and wrecked.
"Eden…"
He didn't turn. Just stood there, the muscles in his shoulders
pulling tight.

"You smell fucken divine," he growled. "And if you stand there much longer, I will take you."

Her breath hitched.
She should've run. Should've backed away.
She walked in instead.
And shut the door behind her.

Nyx turned. Slowly.
His chest was a map of war and beauty—lines of old scars across inked muscle. One tattoo stood out: a circle etched over his left pec, knotted like Viking runes and ancient blood rites.

Eden's mouth went dry.
Her voice was barely a whisper.
"What does that mean?" she asked, gaze fixed on the ink.

His eyes—already dark—went pitch-black as he stepped toward her.
"I'll tell you," he said, voice low, "Right after I'm done with you."

Nyx

He handed her the glass.
Not wine this time. Whiskey. Smooth. Dark. Human.
His fingers brushed hers.
And he felt it—the tremble, the spark. The way her pulse jumped at his touch.

Lyn Rose

Still, he didn't move too fast.

He tipped her chin up with two fingers, slow, kind.

"Are you okay?" he asked, voice rougher than he intended.

Concern etched deep across his face, trying to mask the war raging just beneath his skin—the one between protect and possess.

She looked up at him, eyes wide, searching.

And what she found there—beneath the hard eyes and shadows—was care. Real, brutal, terrifying care.

She didn't answer.

Not with words.

She leaned forward, slow. Pressed her cheek against his bare chest.

Skin on skin.

And that was it.

His undoing.

Her warmth sank into him—soft, slow, all-consuming.

His hand flexed at his side, but she didn't pull away.

She just… breathed.

And he shattered.

He set their glasses down blindly, not caring where they landed.

Then his arms were around her.

Pulling her back to him.

Palms roaming.

Down her back. Over her shoulders. Arms. Every inch of soft, heat-wrapped skin he could touch.

And then his hands found the curve of her hips.

The soft round of her ass beneath the nightgown.

His fingers dug in.

He groaned.

The sound was low, guttural—a sound no man should make. No human man, at least.

His whole body vibrated with it—hunger, lust, a need that went deeper than desire.

He held her like a storm barely chained, breath heaving, every muscle tight.

"You have no idea," he growled into her hair, "what you do to me."

Eden

She couldn't think.

Not with his hands on her like that.

Not with his chest under her cheek—warm, solid, real. The steady thud of where his heart should be pounding, echoed through her bones, and for a man who said he didn't age, he felt so alive.

Then he moved.

And she melted.

His hands were everywhere. Worshipping. Claiming. Gentle and rough all at once.

When his palms found her backside, the groan that left him didn't just make her shiver—it broke something open inside her.

She gasped, her body arching into him instinctively, like her blood remembered something her brain hadn't caught up to yet.

He was vibrating. Shaking.

The control he always wore like iron was gone.

She felt his breath at her temple, hot and ragged.

Lyn Rose

"You have no idea what you do to me."
Her lips parted. "Then show me."

Nyx

Nyx didn't need words.
Her presence alone was his undoing.
The second she stepped into his space—nightgown clinging to her curves, pulse wild and scent heady with want—something in him snapped. Not violently. Not suddenly. But like a tether burning away, leaving nothing but need in its place.
He crossed the room in three deliberate strides, each one heavier with want. The whiskey—first his, then hers—was nothing but a delay tactic, a flimsy excuse to keep from touching her. But when her head rested on his chest, everything shifted. That wasn't comfort. That was permission. Glasses hit the table, forgotten. Their eyes met, locked. And in the next breath, he had her in his arms—like he'd been waiting centuries for her to say yes without saying a word.
The black delicate nightgown bunched at her thighs, her bare legs wrapping instinctively around his waist. His hands gripped the curve of her ass, fingers flexing like he needed to memorize the shape of her—of what was his. She moaned, soft and breathless, when his lips crashed into hers.
This wasn't gentle.
It wasn't slow.
It was the kind of kiss meant to ruin—open-mouthed, breath-stealing, possessive. Her hands tangled in his hair, tugging

Lyn Rose

hard, like she wanted to pull him even deeper into her.

He growled against her mouth, moved to her jaw, then lower—his tongue tracing the curve of her neck, the spot just above her pulse.

And fuck, that pulse.

It thundered under his mouth, singing to something ancient in his blood.

His fangs lengthened, scraping against her skin—not piercing, not yet—but close enough to drag a gasp from her lips. She tilted her head for him, breath hitching, body trembling with every inch of surrender.

He groaned—low and feral—and pressed her back against the nearest wall. Her legs tightened around him. He could feel the heat of her through the thin barrier of lace she wore, the way she rocked against him without realizing she was doing it.

Her scent flooded his senses—lust, warmth, hers—and it dragged a sound from his throat he barely recognized. He was losing control. Fraying at every edge.

His claws extended—half instinct, half desperation—and with a sharp rip, he tore her nightgown open down the front. She gasped, the cool air teasing over her now-exposed breasts, her nipples tight peaks against the sudden chill. The ruined silk pooled at their feet, forgotten.

"Fuck," he rasped, voice thick. "You're…"

Words failed him.

She was flushed. Glowing. Breathing like she'd run a marathon. And still—still—she looked at him like he was the only thing she needed.

One hand braced her against the wall. The other dragged up his chest, slow and electric, until her palm pressed to the bare skin over his heart.

His heart wasn't beating—but the growl vibrating through his chest felt like it was.

Her body shifted against his, and the friction sent a jolt down his spine. Her lace was soaked. His cock straining so hard his pants were barely holding him back.

He let his head fall to her shoulder, panting hard, fighting not to sink into her. Not to bite. Not to tear through the thin layers between them and take everything.

"I can smell your want," he whispered, voice wrecked. "I can feel it. And I—gods, Eden—I want to drown in it."

She shivered.

Pressed closer.

And when her lips found his again, wild and hungry and aching—

He stopped thinking entirely.

She was still against the wall, breath heaving, skin flushed, lips swollen from his kiss.

Nyx lifted her like she weighed nothing, her legs still wrapped instinctively around his waist, and carried her to the bed. He laid her down gently, reverently—but his eyes burned with something far from soft.

She lay there, needy and wrecked, her nightgown, torn and discarded, somewhere on the floor. Her thighs glistened, slick with proof of what she wanted. What she needed.

Nyx knelt on the floor beside the bed.

When she looked down at him, eyes glassy with lust, she saw his fangs just peeking beneath his lips.

Her body responded—heat surging, pulse thundering. She was soaked for him.

He leaned in, inhaled deeply, and groaned. "You smell like

fucking heaven."

His mouth pressed a hot kiss to her inner thigh. Then
another. Then his tongue traced a line up where her arousal
had trailed—slow, claiming, obscene.

Eden moaned, hips arching toward his mouth.

He growled low and kissed her again, this time higher. Then
his tongue flicked over her clit—once, then again—and her
moan broke open into something breathless. He sucked
gently, then harder, and licked her like a man starved, tasting
every ounce of her pleasure.

Her hands clutched the sheets, legs trembling, her whole
body unravelling under the weight of his mouth.

Just when she thought she might shatter, he pulled back. She
whimpered, the loss of contact like being torn from the sun.

He replaced his tongue with two fingers, sliding in easily,
finding her soaked and clenching. He pumped slowly at first,
then faster, dragging pleasure from her in broken gasps.

His mouth returned to her thigh, to the spot where her pulse
beat like a war drum under her skin. His tongue lapped at the
promise there. His thumb pressed to her clit, circling in
rhythm with his thrusts, and her body began to tighten again,
desperate for release.

His fangs lengthened.

She didn't see—but she felt it.

The sharp scrape of them against her skin.

She gasped—more shock than pain—and thrust her hips
needing release.

He stayed where he was—lower, at her thigh—and sank his
fangs in just as she shattered around his fingers.

Her scream was guttural. Beautiful. Wrecked.

Her body clenched violently, spasming around his hand as

her orgasm tore through her like a tidal wave. And he drank—deep, slow, reverently—his body trembling from the taste.

Her blood was unlike anything he'd ever known.

Like starlight.

Like honey.

Like a drug that burned clean through his veins.

He groaned into her skin, nearly undone, nearly lost.

When her aftershocks finally began to fade—when her legs trembled but stopped shaking, when her fingers loosened in the sheets—he pulled back with a staggering effort.

He licked the wound closed.

And somehow, gods only knew how, he didn't take more. Didn't sink back in. But...

Nyx did climb her body like a man worshipping a goddess at the altar of his undoing.

She watched him—blood on his lips, fangs still out, eyes black as obsidian. His cock jutted forward, thick and hard, a weapon forged by hunger and fate. He looked down at her and smiled, not soft, but reverent. Possessive. Starved.

And then he entered her.

Eden arched, breath ripping from her lungs as he groaned—a deep, guttural sound torn from his chest. The slick warmth wrapped around him like a vice, soft, wet and perfect.

He moved slowly at first. Controlled. His mouth grazed her skin—her throat, her cheek, her collarbone—and every touch came with a whisper:

"You're mine."

"So perfect."

"You were made for me."

His rhythm deepened. Less measured. More primal.

His hips began to grind, rocking against her overstimulated clit with every thrust. Eden cried out, her hands gripping his shoulders, nails biting skin. Her body opened to him, welcoming every inch, every push, every sound he made. The growling started low in his chest, building with each thrust—his control thinning.

And then, as he bottomed out, balls deep, as her body trembled on the edge of release, his mouth found her throat. His fangs pierced slowly. Deliberately.

She screamed his name.

Nyx roared as he came—hips jerking, cock throbbing, spilling deep inside her as he drank. Her blood hit his tongue like fire and starlight, and it pulled orgasm after orgasm from her body.

She broke apart—again and again and again—screaming, sobbing, shaking.

His name was all she knew.

When he finally stopped drawing from her, when he licked the wound closed with a final groan, he rolled her gently, cradling her against his chest.

Her heartbeat thundered against him. His arms held her tight.

She was breathless. Glowing. Wrecked.

And inside him, something ancient shifted awake again—the thing that had clawed open in that alley and refused to go quiet.

CHAPTER SEVENTEEN

Blood That Binds, Power That Breaks

Eden's head rested on his chest, breath soft and uneven. One hand lay curled against his sternum, her leg draped over his—skin to skin, soft warmth against burning heat. The fire flickered low in the hearth, casting a soft amber glow across their tangled forms.

Nyx lay still beneath her, one arm wrapped around her bare waist, the other drifting slowly—almost absently—down the curve of her spine. Each stroke was gentle, rhythmic. A grounding gesture, though the storm inside him was anything but calm.

"Nyx?" she murmured.

"Mmm." The sound was lazy, sated—bone-deep contentment wrapped in gravel.

"Can you tell me something?"

He opened one eye, the barest sliver. "Now?"

"The Accord," she said quietly. "The factions. Who runs what? I want to understand."

That got his attention.

He shifted, just enough to see her eyes. She wasn't teasing.

"Alright," he said. "Quick and dirty."

"Vampires?"

"We control tech. Property. Old money. Virex is ours. Vires too."

"Wolves?"

"Security, hospitality, nightlife. You've been to their clubs."

"Fae?"

"Beauty, media, fashion. Anything with glamour. They sell the fantasy."

"Witches?"

"Medicine. Biotech. The health sector—both above board and not."

"Reapers?"

"Law. Death rites. Enforcement." He paused. "And secrets."

"And humans?"

His eyes sharpened slightly. "The ones in power know. The rest? Just live in the world we built."

"Then it struck—a ripple sharp as wire, electric and wrong."

He stilled, fingers halting mid-stroke.

The second came harder. Hotter. Like fire blooming in his veins.

Eden shifted, murmuring something soft, unaware. Still floating in the afterglow.

Nyx's jaw clenched.

Her blood—fuck—it was moving through him now. Not just flowing. Moving, like it's alive. Invading.

Her blood wasn't just in him. It was rewriting him.

His pulse thundered. Not from exertion. Not lust. Not hunger.

Power.

Raw, coiled, ancient power surged beneath his skin, streaking through every nerve like lightning searching for ground. His senses didn't just sharpen—they spiked. Sight fractured, too clear. Hearing split into layers. The fire's flicker cast reflections like a thousand razor-thin cuts across glass. Every molecule in the room—every breath of hers—burned into clarity.

His eyes slammed shut. His fangs throbbed, full and aching. His cock twitched, already hardening again—unreasonably fast.

He groaned, low and rough, a sound pulled from somewhere primal.

Eden looked up. "Nyx?"

He couldn't answer.

He pressed the heel of his hand to his forehead, trying to force the surge back down.

But this wasn't just arousal.

It was evolution.

He could feel her blood humming inside him—like a second heartbeat.

It wasn't just addictive.

It was changing him.

His eyes opened, vision glowing with a faint red shimmer. The room blurred at the edges, strange and sharp all at once. When he exhaled, the breath came out in a visible puff—the room hadn't chilled.

Lyn Rose

He had.

His body was overclocking. His metabolism tearing through the shift. This wasn't just heightened instinct—his abilities were unlocking.

And Eden… she was still lying there, bare and beautiful.

So innocent. So unaware.

So breakable.

"Nyx," she said again, quieter this time. "What's wrong?"

He swallowed hard. "Your blood…"

He didn't finish.

Because then it slammed into him.

A crackle under his skin. A flash of fire behind his eyes. Like something ancient waking in his bones.

And then—

It hit.

Nyx bolted upright, the sheet falling away. His bare skin burned. His cock throbbed—not from want, but from something deeper.

Primordial.

Lyn Rose

Her blood had stirred every instinct. Every hunger.

He staggered to his feet, chest heaving, hands flexing uselessly at his sides—and then roared.

It wasn't human. It wasn't vampire.

It was ancient.

His fangs punched down, slicing his lower lip. His eyes flew open—not gold, not black—but something unnatural. Icy. Bloodshot galaxies collapsing inward.

He could smell everything.

The soap clinging to her skin.

The faint iron in the air from the fire grate.

The copper in the nails holding the wall beams behind them.

And he could hear.

Not just Eden.

The city.

Someone laughing three blocks away. A child crying to her mother near Lyon Crescent. A man whispering in a hotel bed halfway across Edalva.

His head jerked toward it. Eyes narrowing.

And then—it happened.

He moved.

Not ran.

Not sped.

Stepped.

From the edge of the bed to the doorway—through space—
with a sharp crack of displaced air.

One moment he stood naked at the bed's foot.

The next, he was at the ensuite door, catching himself
against the marble frame, panting.

That wasn't speed.

That was something else.

Something terrifying.

He gripped the basin, fingers crushing the porcelain.

Behind him, Eden sat up fast, the sheet clutched to her chest,
eyes wide with confusion.

"Nyx?" Her voice wavered. "What's happening?!"

But it wasn't just a voice.

Lyn Rose

It was everywhere.

Not heard.

Felt.

Her words didn't strike his ears—they hit his chest. His head. His bones.

Nyx are you okay?!

He winced, stumbling back into the mirror. The glass cracked. Her voice was inside him.

Inside.

Her blood was still in his body.

And it was changing him.

Then—

Euphoria.

Not bliss. Not relief.

Something purer. Something brighter.

It hit him like an explosion behind his eyes—a surge of sensation that detonated through his spine and rippled through every nerve ending.

Better than any drug.

Lyn Rose

Better than sex.

Better than the most perfect orgasm he'd ever pulled from a willing body.

It was freedom and fire.

Possession and peace.

Nyx staggered, groaning again—this time not from pain or power, but from the sheer rightness of it.

Of her.

Of the blood now fused to his.

He pressed both palms to the sink, panting, body shaking with aftershocks. His reflection in the fractured mirror barely looked human.

And for once… he didn't care.

He felt alive.

More than that—

He felt invincible.

Eden stood in the doorway of the ensuite, barefoot, wearing one of his black shirts—too big on her frame, brushing high on her thighs. Her damp hair clung to her neck. She hadn't meant to find him like this.

But she couldn't ignore the sounds—the roar, the shatter.

The mirror was cracked.

The sink? Splintered where his hands had braced too hard.

And Nyx.

Nyx looked like something risen from ancient myth.

Naked, glowing with a power she didn't understand, eyes wild and fangs still down.

He didn't hear her approach at first. Not with the entire city still whispering in his skull.

But he felt her.

Soft footsteps on stone. The shift in air. The way her scent curled through the room like a balm—or a match dropped into oil.

"Nyx…" she whispered.

He turned his head slightly—slow, controlled. But the crackle of restraint was obvious in every line of his body.

"I'm okay," he rasped. "I think."

She stepped closer, tentative but unafraid. Her eyes flicked over the cracked mirror, then down to the tension in his arms, his chest rising too fast.

"You don't look okay."

He huffed a laugh, but it came out broken. "That obvious?"

Eden hesitated only a second more—then crossed the final step between them. She reached out, one hand pressing lightly to the centre of his back, between his shoulder blades.

His breath hitched.

"Nyx," she said softly, stepping in. "What happened?"

He turned, slow. Controlled only in theory—every muscle in his body coiled, vibrating like a held note.

"I don't know," he said, voice hoarse. "It's your blood. It's... doing something to me."

"And blood doesn't normally have this effect," he cut in, sharper than he meant. "Not even a fraction of this."

His hands flexed uselessly at his sides. Eden's hand was still on his back. Warm. Anchoring.

The euphoria still surged through him, but his head... it was beginning to clear. Just enough for the weight of what had happened to settle. His blood was still thrumming, his senses sharpened to a razor's edge—but beneath it, focus began to bite through the haze.

Nyx turned from the shattered sink and cracked mirror and faced her.

Lyn Rose

"I need to go to Virex," he said, voice low, urgent. "I need Biotech on this. I need answers. I need this processed."

He crossed the hall, keyed open a secure drawer, and pulled out a sterile blood kit.

One quick draw. Centuries of practice. Dark blood filled the vial, steady and slow.

He grabbed his phone, thumb already moving. "Jace. My blood. Uploading now. Full spectrum panel—priority."

"Got it," came the reply. "Running it through Virex systems. You'll have results when you get here."

Nyx sealed the vial and slid it into the cooler unit near the door—already moving, already three steps ahead.

Then he dialled again. "Kain."

"Boss," came the quick answer.

"Get Sevra Wynne from Biotech. I want her at Virex. Thirty minutes."

A pause. Then: "Now?"

"Yes, now," Nyx snapped.

Kain hung up without another word.

Eden was still standing near the ensuite—his shirt loose on her frame, worry clouding her features.

He crossed to her, his tone gentler now. Urgent, but not unkind. "Come on, baby. Get dressed. We need to go."

She nodded, silent, already moving toward the closet. No questions yet. Just that look in her eyes—concern, confusion, and something deeper.

Minutes later, they stepped into the lift together. The doors closed with a soft thunk, and the descent to the garage began.

The drive was quiet.

Too quiet.

The kind of silence that wasn't peaceful—but heavy. Coiled. Like the city had stopped and was waiting.

She blinked down at their joined hands.

Then looked at him.

He glanced her way, and smiled—that soft, rare smile that felt like a secret only she got to see.

"It's okay, baby," he said gently. "I'm sorry I scared you."

His thumb brushed over her knuckles, slow and reassuring.

"We'll get to the bottom of this. I promise."

Then he lifted her hand to his lips and kissed it—not rushed. Not out of habit.

Lyn Rose

Deliberate.

Reverent.

Her chest squeezed, emotion tightening her throat.

But behind the warmth… behind the gentleness in his voice…

She could feel it—a flicker of unease that didn't match his smile. Like a shadow beneath sunlight.

It wasn't just instinct. It was him.

She could feel his anxiety like it was her own—taut, coiled, waiting.

And somehow, Eden knew.

This wasn't over.

There was more to come.

The drive ended in silence—not the comfortable kind. The kind that buzzed under the skin. That warned of things not yet said.

Virex towered above them, dark glass and steel lit with a faint, ominous glow. Eden swallowed. She wasn't sure if it was nerves or something older stirring in her chest.

Nyx pulled into the underground bay. Kain and Jace were already waiting.

Lyn Rose

As the engine cut, Kain moved toward the passenger side, reaching to open Eden's door.

A sound split the air—low, deep, and unmistakably feral.

Kain froze.

Nyx's growl echoed off the concrete walls, dark as thunder. His door slammed, and he was around the car in one step, a blur stepping between Eden and anyone else.

Kain lifted both hands, backing off instantly. "Alright, alright. Just trying to help—"

Nyx didn't reply. He didn't need to. His hand found Eden's, threading his fingers through hers like a brand. She could feel it—not just the strength, but the need. The claim.

He unlocked the private access with a biometric scan and shouldered the door open.

"Stay close," he said, not looking back.

She did.

Not because she was afraid.

Because some part of her knew—if anyone touched her now, Nyx wouldn't just snap.

He'd burn the fucking world down.

The lift opened onto the top floor with a soft chime. Sleek, silent, and cold—like everything inside Virex. Nyx didn't speak as they crossed the wide corridor. His grip on Eden's hand didn't loosen. Not once.

He led her into his private office—not the boardroom—and let the door shut behind them.

"Stay here," he said, voice low. "You're safe in this room."

She nodded, watching him move with surgical purpose. He stepped to the secure terminal, entered two different passwords, and activated the internal print server. The lights from the screen bathed his face in eerie blue as he pulled up her file.

Eden watched from the sofa, heart in her throat, as the printer began to hum. Page after page fed out—her medical records, flagged anomalies, flagged blood types, the lab header:
TheraGen Research Division.

Nyx didn't speak. He gathered the pages, scanned them one final time, then turned back to her.

"I need to be in the boardroom when this meeting starts. I'll bring you in if I need to. But no one touches you. No one."

His voice left no room for doubt.

"Okay," she said quietly.

He lingered at the door for a second longer than necessary. Then he turned and left, walking back into the lion's den with a file in hand and something deadly simmering in his veins.

In the boardroom, the lights were already on. Jace sat at the head, Kain pacing near the far wall. When Nyx entered, both straightened—tension sharpening the air like a wire pulled tight.

"She's in your office?" Jace asked.

Nyx gave a curt nod. "Locked. Watched."

Then the intercom blinked.

"Sevra Wynne has arrived. Alone. As instructed."

Kain moved first, shooting Nyx a look that asked if, he was sure.

He was.

"Bring her up."

As Kain disappeared down the lift shaft, Nyx dropped the Project Thera file onto the boardroom table—the sound like a gunshot.

Then he leaned back in his chair, waiting.

And when Sevra walked in… that's when the real tension began.

Lyn Rose

Sevra Wynne stepped into the room like she owned the damn city.

Glossy black heels clicked across the marble, her coat a tailored sweep of dark green cashmere, hair pinned with surgical precision. She looked like every inch of Biotech's power—clean, clinical, untouchable.

Nyx didn't stand. He sat at the head of the long conference table, one leg crossed, a folder already in front of him.

"Thanks for coming," he said, voice measured.

"Your call said urgent." She took the seat across from him without asking. "What kind of scan are we talking? You said you needed biochemical analysis?"

He slid the folder across the glass.

Sevra opened it—and stilled.

Nyx watched her.

Not just the way her pupils flared, or how her breath caught for a split second—but the silence. Sevra Wynne didn't do silence. Not unless her mind was sprinting miles ahead of her mouth.

She flipped the pages slowly, skimming reports, genetic logs, incident notes… then his bloodwork.

Sevra picked it up, brows furrowing as she flipped through the contents—gene logs, flagged blood records, anomalies traced to a single donor.

"This isn't standard," she muttered.

"No, it's not," Nyx said flatly. "Which is why I need a full breakdown. I want you to take a fresh sample from me tonight. Run everything. Chemical shifts. Hormonal spikes. Neurobiological patterns. Whatever you find—I want it. All of it."

Sevra looked up sharply. "You fed from this source recently?"

He nodded once. "Hours ago."

Sevra didn't move at first.

Her eyes stayed on the page—but something behind them flickered. Calculating. She flipped back through the file like she was trying to memorize it, then laid it down with deliberate care.

"Where did you get this blood?" she asked, voice too neutral.

Nyx didn't answer immediately.

He watched her. Closely.

"I told you," he said, slow. "I fed. Hours ago. Why?"

Sevra's fingers tapped once, twice on the folder's edge. "Because this isn't just unusual. It's… impossible." Her tone was measured, but her posture had gone rigid. Like she was choosing every word too carefully.

"Define 'impossible,'" Nyx said, stepping forward just enough to remind her who was in the room.

She looked up, met his eyes.

Then asked—too casually:

"Where is she?"

Nyx's silence stretched.

She noticed.

Nyx didn't flinch. Didn't blink. "She's nobody. Random. Off the street. Beautiful, sure—but human. Just a fuck and a feed."

She didn't believe him. He saw it in her eyes—the way they narrowed for the briefest moment before her expression smoothed again.

"I can take the blood now," she said. "Run the biometrics overnight. I'll flag the results to your private server."

Nyx nodded once. "Appreciate it, but don't worry about it."

He turned slightly—enough to signal the conversation was done.

Lyn Rose

Then, casually:

"I'm sure it's nothing. Probably just a high from the sex. Pushed the feed too long. Bad mix."

"Thanks for making the time."

Dismissed.

Sevra knew it. Her lips parted slightly, like she might say something more—but then closed again. She stood, smoothed her coat.

"Of course," she said. "Let me know if you need anything else."

He didn't reply. Not with words.

Just watched her leave.

And that told him everything he needed to know.

Kain followed Sevra out, making sure she left without lingering. It was almost 3AM—Monday morning, technically—and the building was dead quiet except for the low hum of the security grid.

Nyx turned to Jace. "I want everything on Biotech. Like yesterday."

Jace didn't ask questions. Just nodded once and disappeared into the adjacent ops room, fingers already flying across the nearest terminal.

The hum of the systems deepened as doors sealed behind him. Through the glass wall, Nyx caught flashes of code racing across Jace's screens—search trees drilling through encrypted Biotech servers. A quiet comfort: the man worked fast.

Nyx turned back to the main console, letting Jace dig. The report queue still blinked at the edge of his vision, waiting.

Kain returned, brushing invisible dust from his coat. "She's gone."

Nyx didn't acknowledge it. Just looked him dead in the eye. "I need you to take Eden home."

Kain raised a brow.

"My place," Nyx clarified. Then, slower: "And Kain—no flirting. No touching. I'll fucking know."

Kain held both hands up, half amused, half insulted. "Alright, alright. Jesus. I'll be a monk."

Nyx didn't smile.

They moved together toward the lounge where Eden was curled on the leather couch, one hand tucked under her cheek, the other resting over her stomach. Her dark lashes fanned out against her skin, and her breathing was slow, deep—the kind of sleep that came after adrenaline crashed.

Nyx walked over and crouched beside her, his knuckles brushing down her cheek.

"Baby," he murmured. "Wake up."

She stirred slowly, eyes fluttering open, hazy and unfocused. "Nyx…?"

He smiled, soft but tired. "Yeah, baby. Come on. Kain's gonna take you home."

She blinked, struggling to sit up. "My place is finished?" she asked, confused.

He shook his head once—firm. "No."

Then, possessive and without room for argument:

"You're with me. You're going back to Duskwatch."

Eden rubbed her eyes. "Okay…" She hesitated, then looked at him. "Are you coming?"

"Not yet," he said, standing. "I've got some work to catch up on."

She nodded slowly, still fogged with sleep, but didn't argue. Kain stepped forward, helping her gently to her feet without saying a word—clearly taking the 'no touching' warning seriously.

Nyx watched her until the lift doors closed.

Lyn Rose

Only then did he exhale, hands curling into fists at his sides.

The console on the far wall chirped. Once. Twice. Then steadied into a steady, pulsing glow.

Nyx crossed the room in three strides and keyed the panel. A new report populated across the glass—flagged urgent, stamped VIREX MED.

The report glared back at him from the screen, clinical lines spelling out something obscene.

Subject: Vampire – Sample 001

• Blood anomalies: unstable markers, rapid cellular decay

• Tissue sample: grafted sequences identified

• Feeding response rejects standard sustenance (vampiric blood)

• Behavioural note: hyper-aggression toward vampire scent

• Conclusion: Engineered to hunt its own kind. Non-viable. Eventual collapse guaranteed.

Nyx's fangs pressed into his lip, copper blooming on his tongue.

It wasn't a mutation.

It wasn't an accident.

It was built to kill.

Starve it of humans and it would tear through vampires, frenzy until there was nothing left. But it would never be sated.

The injection had rewritten its hunger, hardwired a craving for its own kind. Vampire blood couldn't sustain it—not long term. It would rot on the inside even as it ripped through everything around it.

Not a mutation. Not a soldier.

A weapon.

Designed to unleash in every Vampire House, in every seat of power—to slaughter until nothing remained but ash and silence.

Nyx leaned back in his chair, jaw tight, staring at the screen until his reflection stared back: black eyes, cold as steel.

"Someone made this," he said aloud, the words tasting like ash. "Not to live. To slaughter."

"Fuck," he muttered, low and lethal.

From the ops room came a soft chime—then footsteps. Jace had found something.

The door hissed. Jace entered, folder in hand, face grim. "That the sample?"

Nyx didn't look away. "It's not a vampire anymore. It's something else."

Jace moved closer, scanning the data. "Can it survive?"

"Not for long," Nyx said, killing the screen, locking it behind three layers of encryption. "But long enough to prove this wasn't random."

He finally turned, eyes flat as glass.

"They're not experimenting. They're perfecting."

CHAPTER EIGHTEEN

Blood and Origin

Setting: Virex, 3:27 AM.

The silence after Sevra's exit was cold. Still. It pressed down on the room like a heavy fog, thick and suffocating. Jace was working—fingers flying over the keyboard, rerouting firewalls and breaking into Biotech's archives through one of Virex's private mirrors. He didn't speak, save for the occasional low curse muttered under his breath. The clatter of keys was the only sound breaking the oppressive quiet.

Nyx didn't pace or fidget. He stood dead still, eyes locked on the boardroom glass like staring through it could unravel the world's secrets thread by thread. The city lights outside blinked faintly in the pre-dawn haze, but inside, time itself seemed to pause.

His phone buzzed sharply, cutting through the stillness.

[DUSKWATCH ALERT: Entry Confirmed | Subject: Eden Marlowe | 3:29:47 AM]
The alert blinked once across the glass—Eden was inside.

Nyx's jaw eased. He typed a quick message to her phone:

Stay at the house. Don't leave. I'll be there soon. —N

Then another, to Kain:

You stay until I get there. I don't care how secure it is. She's not alone.

Kain's reply came fast, sharp:
Understood. No one's getting through me.

Nyx slipped the phone away and turned to Jace.

"Find it."

"Already on it," Jace muttered, eyes glued to the screen. "I'm deep in Biotech's mirror archive. Going dark now."

Seconds stretched, heavy and slow.

"There's a buried file string… multiple sublayers. Hidden work." He paused, voice tense. "Project Thera."

Nyx stepped beside him, jaw clenched tight.

"Show me."

Together, they scanned the data—gene maps sprawled across the screen like cryptic constellations, hormonal overlays pulsing beneath, blood reactivity logs flickering in coded sequences.

Jace whistled low.

"This isn't healing. This is weaponized evolution."

Then a donor ID appeared, stark and chilling:

NULL SUBJECT: TH-0RA.

Nyx's blood ran cold.

"Print it," he commanded.

Jace hit the command. "What do you think this means?"

Nyx didn't answer. He already knew.

More firewalls shattered under Jace's assault. Streams of code flickered, decrypted, revealing another set of files:

PROJECT THERA: SECTOR 4 ARCHIVE

GENETIC BASELINE: TH-0RA

OUTCOME STATUS: NULL SUBJECT LOST

"Fuck," Jace muttered, voice low.

He turned slowly toward Nyx.

Lyn Rose

"This isn't just enhancement. It's overwrite. Like they were rewriting the next version of us."

Another flick of the wrist, another file opened. Jace's face tightened, the lines of exhaustion and dread deepening.

"These aren't treatments. They're triggers."

Nyx's jaw tightened. "The vamp injected at Club X. The Fae in Vestry Market—not an aggressive species, built on love and life. The injection burned him from the inside out like acid. And the wolf in Vestry Market—aggressive—turned feral and attacked his own kind. Then the human in his own neighbourhood. Heart attack, they called it. No fight, no blood. Just dropped dead in the street."

His hand curled into a fist. "They're testing. Injecting across species. See what holds, what breaks. So far? The more aggressive the bloodline, the more lethal the outcome. A few doses, and an entire species could wipe itself out."

Jace swore under his breath. "That's not warfare. That's eradication."

Nyx's voice dropped, almost a whisper.

"Her blood triggered something in me."

Jace leaned back, disbelief flickering in his eyes.

"You think Eden's the lost subject?"

Nyx nodded.

"They marked the blood TH-0RA. That's not random. She wasn't just born like this."

"She was made," Jace finished quietly.

A heavy silence filled the room.

Jace scanned the last page again.

"Jesus… if this is what unfinished looks like—what the hell happens when it's done?"

Nyx didn't answer at first. He could still feel her blood moving through him. Still taste it. The way it had supercharged every cell. Stripped him raw and rebuilt him in seconds.

"She wasn't meant to survive," he said finally. "She was meant to activate."

Jace's voice was low.

"And if she had?"

Nyx's eyes hardened like steel.

"We wouldn't be having this conversation."

Jace scrolled again, eyes widening suddenly.

"Wait. Look at this."

He spun the screen.

SUBJECT TH-0RA: TRANSITION ABORTED. STATUS: LOST

SUBJECT TH-0RB: FULL TRANSFORMATION COMPLETE. STATUS: UNSTABLE. LETHAL.

Jace stared at it, stunned.

"There's another one."

Nyx's gaze darkened.

"Finished the transition?"

"Yeah," Jace replied. "Subject B was completed. Fully. They didn't lose that one."

"They unleashed it."

He exhaled sharply. "Those injections in the city—the vamp, the Fae, the wolf, the human collapse—that's not random fallout. That's Subject B. Field tests. Controlled strikes."

Nyx's gaze sharpened, cold as steel. "And Sevra's the hand behind it."

The silence sharpened, slicing through the room.

Nyx's voice was flat, almost hollow.

"If Eden was A… and she never finished…"

Jace finished the thought.

"…Then B did."

Nyx exhaled slowly.

"And it's still out there."

They didn't speak as they shut down the systems—firewalls re-locked, data trails scrubbed clean, physical prints destroyed. Jace moved like a shadow, efficient and practiced. Nyx lingered at the window for a final moment, watching the city skyline pulse faintly in the pre-dawn grey.

His body thrummed.

Not just with rage or suspicion—but with an electric charge burning beneath his skin. Eden's blood hadn't quieted. It had coiled deeper, waiting.

Jace pulled his hood up.

"That's it. We're clear."

Nyx nodded once. Then turned.

The building groaned softly as they moved—long corridors echoing under their boots, motion-triggered lights flickering on overhead. They took the stairs down, not the lift. Instinct.

On the ground floor, the lobby was dark. Polished marble gleamed faintly under silent monitors. Wall sconces flickered on night setting, casting shadows that seemed to twitch at the edge of vision.

Nyx stopped just short of the double doors.

His hand hovered above the biometric scanner.

Jace frowned.

"What?"

Nyx didn't answer.

He just listened.

The silence was too clean. Too staged.

A breath too still.

"Something's off," he murmured.

Jace's expression shifted, alert.

"We being watched?"

"No," Nyx said quietly. "We're being waited for."

Then—a scent. Sharp. Faint. Wrong.

Nyx looked at Jace, eyes hardening.

"Get ready."

The doors hissed open.

Outside, the night lay still. Too still. No traffic. No wind. Just flickering streetlamps casting long, skeletal shadows… and the sharp reek of ozone and chemical magic hanging in the air.

Then—movement.

Three shadows detached from an alley across the street. Silent. Masked. Precise.

Not wolves. Not vampires.

Witches.

Biotech's coven-bred blades.

Jace muttered, "Shit—"

But Nyx was already gone.

The first witch—broad-shouldered, male—barely reached the curb before Nyx hit him. Shoulder driving into ribs with a thunderous crack, sending him crashing back into a parked sedan. Metal folded like paper.

The second—lean, female, eyes glowing faintly with spellfire—raised a weapon, compact and pulsing with a core of glowing blue. Coven sigils ran down the casing like veins. Nyx blurred. One hand wrenched the weapon aside, the other crushed her wrist with a sickening crack. A knee came up—brutal, fast—then a fist to the throat. She dropped like a cut marionette.

The third—masked, genderless under dark robes—turned to run.

Mistake.

Jace materialised behind, yanking the collar and slamming the witch into the Virex wall. "Evening," he muttered, twisting the arm until bone popped.

The witch screamed.

But Nyx's attention snapped sideways.

The first one wasn't down.

From the wreck of the sedan, the male witch surged up, coughing blood—and pulled something from his coat. A syringe. Thick glass barrel, needle glinting under the streetlight, liquid inside glowing faintly green.

Nyx's eyes narrowed.

He was there in a blink, hand snapping around the wrist before the needle could plunge into his side. The witch's lips curled, teeth bloody. "Just one dose," he hissed. "Let's see what you *become*—"

Nyx crushed his hand until the syringe shattered. The liquid hissed as it splattered across the pavement, burning a smoking hole into the asphalt.

The witch's scream cut sharp, jaw breaking under Nyx's next blow. He collapsed, twitching, unconscious.

Lyn Rose

Behind him, Jace still had the third witch pinned, blood dripping down the wall. He glanced over, breath sharp. "That—" he jerked his chin at the smoking pavement— "wasn't just poison."

Nyx's voice was low, cold. "It was meant to rewrite me."

Jace shifted his grip, eyes narrowing. "Orders?"

Nyx didn't hesitate. He turned back, blood already drying on his knuckles. No words. No tremble. Just cold, clinical violence.

"They underestimated her," he said at last, voice flat as stone.

Jace raised a brow. "You mean you."

Nyx didn't answer.

Behind him, the pinned witch whimpered. Jace nudged with his boot. "So… we taking this one for questioning, or leaving a note that says 'Sevra, nice try'?"

Nyx's eyes went black. His fangs glinted in the streetlight.

"No survivors."

The screams didn't last long.

Virex sealed behind them like nothing had happened.

Only the blood on Nyx's knuckles and the stink of burned asphalt said otherwise.

The drive back was silent. Jace didn't push, didn't speak—just wiped the witch's blood from his hands and stared out into the neon-smeared streets of Edalva. Nyx gripped the wheel hard enough to crack leather, jaw locked, mind running faster than the city lights streaming past.

This wasn't random.

This was Biotech.

Sevra Wynne had just tried to put a needle in his heart.

Duskwatch.

The gates opened with a low hydraulic hiss.

Nyx remained silent. Jace sat beside him, scrolling through encrypted files one last time.

Kain was waiting at the door when they arrived—gun holstered, jaw tight.

"Nothing since she came in," Kain said. "House is clean."

Nyx nodded.

"You and Jace stay. Every angle, inside and out. If anything so much as breathes near this property, I want it on record before it blinks."

Both nodded. No questions.

Nyx moved down the hall alone. He passed the guest rooms—Jace's, Kain's—already claimed and armed. His steps didn't slow until he reached his own door.

It was cracked open.

He pushed it gently.

The fire inside was low again—embers glowing like half-lidded eyes in the grate. Eden lay curled under the sheets, one arm flung over the pillow he'd left behind.

His chest tightened at the sight.

So fucking breakable.

So fucking his.

And he'd waited long enough.

He shed his jacket as he walked in, silent. Sat at the edge of the bed.

She stirred. Eyes fluttered open. Still hazy, but sharp enough to find him.

"Nyx?"

"Yeah, baby. It's me."

She sat up slightly, brows furrowed.

"You're bleeding—"

He took her hand. Pressed his lips to her knuckles.

"No. Not mine."

She didn't pull away.

But she knew.

"What's wrong?"

He exhaled slowly, thumb stilling against her hand.

"I'll tell you everything," he murmured. "Just not now. Sleep a little more. We've got time."

She hesitated.

Then leaned in, pressed her forehead to his.

"Okay."

She curled into his chest, and he wrapped around her like a shield—arms locking her in, heart racing slower now.

She slept.

He didn't.

Not yet.

Lyn Rose

CHAPTER NINETEEN

Mine To Protect

Eden woke to the scent of him.

Not cologne. Not soap. Just him—that cool cedar scent that had somehow seeped into the pillows, the sheets, her skin, a quiet claim left behind in the night.

The bed beside her was empty but still warm, it felt like he'd just slipped away moments ago. She stretched slowly, muscles aching in that satisfying way exhaustion brings, then rolled onto her back. For a long moment, she just stared at the ceiling, heart beating a steady, low drum that thrummed deep inside her ribs. Even here, in this quiet, she couldn't shake the new tension in her body—a sense that something inside her was off-balance, restless, like she was standing on the edge of a cliff, waiting for the ground to shift beneath her feet.

Water ran in the bathroom.

She moved quietly through the steam-fogged doorway, drawn by the soft sound.

Nyx stood beneath the shower, head bowed, water tracing the sharp planes of his back like liquid silver. He was still— or pretending to be.

Without a word, she stepped in behind him, arms sliding around his waist, her front pressing to his back.

He stiffened.

Then turned.

"Morning," she murmured.

His eyes roamed over her slowly, hungry and raw. He was already hard—his breath hitched when his hand lifted to brace against the tile behind her head, the other trailing down her spine with a possessive grace.

"You drive me insane," he said, voice low and rough like gravel.

"Good," she whispered.

Their lips met, urgent and unrelenting. There was no slow build, no hesitation. Their bodies moved like a promise— need and memory crashing together beneath the steaming water. But when his fingers grazed her neck, when his lips brushed the pulse at her jaw, Nyx flinched just enough for her to notice.

He shook his head, grounding himself against the pull.

"I'm not feeding," he rasped. "Not until we know what it's doing to me."

She didn't press. He didn't need to explain. Still, a familiar chill crept down her spine—worry blooming, sharp and sudden. What was happening to him? And to her? She tried to focus on the feeling of his skin, the taste of him, but a thread of unease wound through every touch.

They moved together anyway—until nothing remained but steam and skin and the sound of her name on his lips.

Ten minutes later, Eden stood at the mirror, lace black underwear and stockings on, brushing damp hair that clung in dark strands to her neck. She studied her reflection, searching for something familiar, something unchanged, but her eyes seemed too bright, her skin too pale. Was she imagining it, or did she look different—altered somehow, in ways only she could sense?

Nyx stepped out of the closet behind her—suit tailored to perfection, cufflinks gleaming under the soft light, jaw set like it had been carved from polished stone.

He froze.

Groaned.

Because Eden was standing there in stockings—those stockings—sheer black with the line running up the back like a whispered dare.

"No," he said, already suffering.

She raised a brow, all wide eyes and wicked smiles. "No what?"

"You're not wearing those to work."

She smiled slow, wicked. "Why not?"

He stepped closer, voice low and dangerous. "Because I have self-control. I don't trust anyone else in that office to."

"You're overreacting."

"You're wearing weapons disguised as tights."

She laughed, pulling on a black pencil skirt—tight, high-waisted—and a singlet that clung like a second skin, breasts framed perfectly enough to make his breath catch.

He stared.

"You're trying to kill me," he muttered.

Eden smiled sweetly. "I have to go in. And I'm not changing."

He stepped into her space, hand curling at her waist.

"You're not going in alone."

"I didn't expect I would be." She rolled her eyes, but inside, a faint relief fluttered—like part of her wanted him close, protective, in case the world tilted again.

He narrowed his gaze.

"You'll take Kain," he added tersely.

"Good," she teased. "He's fun."

Nyx scowled. "He better be mute fun."

She leaned up, pressed a kiss to his jaw. "I'll be fine." But even as she said it, a knot of nerves twisted in her gut.

Worry etched across his face, shadowing the sharp lines of his jaw.

"Nyx," she whispered, searching his eyes. "What's wrong? Talk to me."

His voice dropped lower, heavier.

"Last night wasn't random," he said. "They hit us outside Virex. One of them tried to inject me."

Eden's breath caught. "What—Nyx—"

He shook his head once, cutting her panic. "I'm fine. But this isn't just about me. Someone's experimenting. Injecting across species. Vampires, wolves, Fae, even humans. No discrimination. Testing what holds, what breaks."

Her stomach turned. "The bodies…"

"Yes," he said flatly. "Biotech is behind it. And Sevra Wynne is pulling the strings. That means they could be anywhere. Anyone."

His hand lingered at her waist, grip iron. "You'll take Kain. I'll have him bring you back before dark," he said. "We're not done."

Eden smiled—wicked, radiant.

"Not even close."

Eden stepped out of the sleek black car, heels clicking sharp against the curb. Kain followed, suit crisp, sunglasses still on despite the clouded sky.

She smirked. "You look like the guy they send when negotiations have failed."

Kain didn't miss a beat. "I am the negotiation."

She laughed, tugging her coat tighter as they crossed the pavement toward the firm's glass front doors. But even as she joked, she felt eyes on her, prickling at the back of her neck. Was it just Kain's presence, or something else?

Inside, the Monday rush was in full swing. Phones rang continuously. Secretaries juggled coffee trays and files. The scent of burnt espresso and ambition thickened the air like fog. For the first time, she felt out of sync with it all, like she was moving through someone else's life.

Kain trailed just behind her, a half-step to the right—silent, watchful, professional to a fault.

The receptionist raised a brow. "Bodyguard?"

Eden smiled as she signed in. "Temporary. My apartment was broken into over the weekend."

Instant sympathy. "Oh my God, are you okay?"

"Yeah. Just a precaution."

No one questioned it. Not in Edalva. Not when powerful men showed up unannounced, and quiet ones followed you like shadows.

She made it to her desk before anyone stopped her.

"Eden." Her supervisor—Miriam Lau—appeared beside her desk with a look unreadable and sharp. "Mr. Halden would like to see you."

Her stomach sank. Now what? Anxiety twisted in her chest, sharp and cold.

But when she walked in, Marcus Halden was… smiling?

"Morning," he said, folding his hands on the desk. "I wanted to let you know—we got a call late last week from a major client. Virex."

Eden blinked. "Virex?"

"Yes. Apparently, you worked on a case their team was monitoring. Something about your attention to detail impressed them."

Her heart thudded. Nyx.

"They've formally requested that all future correspondence with Lorne & Carrick go through you. Exclusively."

Eden stared. "I… wow. Thank you."

Halden nodded. "Effective immediately, you'll be reporting directly to me. We'll restructure your caseload by noon."

He gestured to the door. "Congratulations, Counsel Marlowe. Keep it up."

She walked out in a daze. A strange mix of pride and suspicion warred in her chest—she wanted to feel excited, but her mind kept circling back to Nyx, and the uneasy sense that nothing in her life was as simple as it seemed.

Kain was waiting, leaned against the far wall. "Well?"

"I just got promoted."

He grinned. "Damn right you did."

Lyn Rose

She blinked, stunned. "Virex only wants to deal with me now."

Kain chuckled. "You have no idea how dangerous that man is when he sets his mind to something."

Eden arched a brow. "I thought this wasn't a thing."

Kain just grinned wider. "Oh, honey. It's a fucking thing."

Eden pulled out her phone and sent a message to Nyx.

[Eden's message, 9:47 AM]
I didn't even have your number
(Kain gave it to me. Don't act smug.)
I just got promoted.
I'm guessing I have you to thank for that?

[Nyx's reply, 9:49 AM]
That call was after the meeting last week and
before dinner.
So hey—
That's all you, baby.

The congratulatory email was still open on her screen when Anna leaned into her office doorway, brows pinched.

"Hey… there's someone asking for you in reception."

Eden glanced up. "Client?"

Anna shook her head. "Didn't say. Didn't give a name. Just said they had a personal inquiry. Kind of weird vibe, honestly."

"Weird how?"

Before Eden could ask, her office phone buzzed. The front desk.

She picked up.

"Ms. Marlowe?" the receptionist's voice was hushed. "There's… a gentleman here. Says he's here to speak with you about a private genetic matter."

The blood in her veins turned to ice. The word genetic echoed in her mind, and for a split second, she couldn't breathe. Her heart hammered, panic flaring so sharp it left her dizzy.

"Genetic?" she echoed, voice thin.

"Yes. He said he's from… Bio-Systems. Or Biotech? Something like that."

The line went quiet.

Eden stood slowly. "Tell him I'm not available. And call security." She forced her voice steady, but her hands shook as she set the phone down.

The receptionist paused. "Already did. Your bodyguard heard, he's moving."

Lyn Rose

Eden hung up and grabbed her phone, her fingers numb and clumsy.

[Text Message, 11:07 AM]
Eden → Nyx:
We've got a problem. Someone from Biotech just showed up asking for me.
Used the word genetic.

She stepped out of her office just as Kain crossed the tiled corridor, moving like he was going to kill someone and then have a drink with the corpse.

Anna pointed toward reception. "Guy's still there."

Kain didn't break stride. "Stay here," he said over his shoulder, voice low. "Don't speak to him."

Eden followed anyway—close enough to see through the glass.

The man at reception didn't look like a threat. Slim. Expensively dressed. Boring. Except something about him was off. Skin too smooth. Smile too still. Like he'd studied people but never quite figured them out. Eden's skin crawled, dread rising in her throat.

Kain stepped between him and the desk.

"You have an appointment?" he asked flatly.

The man blinked slowly. "I'm here to see Ms. Marlowe."

"About?"

"A private genetic consultation."

Wrong answer.

Kain's hand moved toward the inside of his jacket. "You can submit your inquiry through legal channels. Walk out now."

The man's expression didn't shift, but his eyes flicked past Kain—straight to Eden.

"I only need a sample," he said smoothly. "Just a vial. From *her*."

The blood drained from Eden's face. Cold prickled up her arms, her pulse thundering in her ears. This wasn't theory anymore. This wasn't Nyx's warning whispered over breakfast. It was real. Here.

Her blood.

Kain didn't give him another second.

He slammed him harder into the glass, twisting his arm until the man hissed.

"You're not touching her," Kain growled, voice low and lethal. "Not a drop. Not ever."

Eden's hands trembled where she clutched her phone, the reality of it slicing through her like ice water. They wanted her. Not rumours. Not files. *Her.*

Lyn Rose

The man didn't resist. But as the guard escorted him toward the exit, his eyes never left Eden. His smile widened—slow, deliberate, poisonous.

"We'll be in touch."

Eden exhaled shakily, her knees threatening to buckle. The words felt like a threat pressed directly against her pulse.

Kain turned back, jaw clenched. "You alright?"

"I… yeah. I think so." But her hands trembled. She wasn't sure she'd ever feel steady again.

Kain pulled his phone out.

"Calling Nyx."

The man had barely been gone ten minutes when Kain's phone buzzed.

He looked at the screen once,

Then he said, "He's here."

The air shifted.

Not two minutes later, the atmosphere changed again—violently.

The front doors of the firm opened, and it was like someone sucked the oxygen from the building. Phones stopped ringing. Conversations died mid-sentence. Heads turned.

Nyx Ravelle walked in like he owned the foundations.

Not fast. Not loud. Just certain.

Every step was thunder in a room that didn't dare breathe.

Eden stood frozen by her office doorway, heart skipping. He wasn't wearing rage—not visibly—but it radiated off him. Composure like a blade. Eyes like frost. She felt both relief and terror at the sight of him, it felt like the ground beneath her was about to crack open.

Straight past reception. Straight into her boss's office.

The door shut behind him without a word.

Kain whistled under his breath. Leaned close.

"Like I said," he murmured, "dangerous."

She swallowed. "You knew he'd be like that?"

"Pftttt yeh, but I figured he'd be faster," Kain said with a low chuckle. "Expected he'd leave a few bodies on the way in."

He winked. "Joking."

But Eden wasn't sure he was.

Ten minutes passed. Maybe less. Then the door opened.

Nyx stepped out, eyes locking with Eden's for half a second. Something dark passed through them—not anger. Possession.

Then he was gone.

A heartbeat later, her name rang out from down the hall.

"Ms. Marlowe? Could you step into my office, please?"

Her boss looked… pale.

Eden straightened her spine and entered.

He gestured for her to sit, running a hand through thinning hair, sweating like he'd just escaped a warzone.

"That was Mr. Ravelle. From Virex."

"I gathered," she said carefully, fighting to keep her voice calm.

He looked at her, almost pleading. "They've requested you personally. As a private legal consultant. Effective immediately. Willing to pay double our retainer—in advance."

Eden blinked.

"For how long?"

"He didn't say." His voice softened. "But I strongly suggest you take it. This is… a very good thing."

Lyn Rose

She nodded slowly. "Of course, Mr. Halden. I'll pack up now."

"Thank you. Yes. Yes—I'll have someone reassign your caseload."

She left the room with her head held high—but her pulse pounding in her throat, uncertainty spilling through every vein.

The moment the firm's doors closed behind her, Eden exhaled.

Her nerves buzzed—not fear exactly. More like overload. The way Nyx had entered like a supernova and said nothing, yet said everything in a glance. She felt like she was standing at the edge of some precipice, about to fall.

Her phone buzzed.

Nyx Ravelle.

She stared. "How the hell—?"

Kain grinned. "You didn't think he'd let you leave without checking in, did you?"

She answered.

"Hello?"

"Hi, baby." Nyx's voice was deep, warm, and infuriatingly pleased with himself. "Miss me already?"

She rolled her eyes, biting back a smile. "You're very pleased with yourself."

"I told you I'd take care of it."

"You didn't take care of it. You staged a power play in my boss's office. You can't just step in and bulldoze my workplace whenever you feel like it." Eden's voice was low, resigned, threaded with frustration. This was her career, built on her own merit—not his shadow.

On the other end, Nyx's reply came rough, steady, leaving no space for argument.

"Eden—until we know and have the threat under control, I want and need you with me. Or somewhere I know you're safe."

Her chest tightened. He wasn't trying to own her, not really—he was trying to shield her the only way he knew how. Still, the sting of it pressed hot behind her eyes.

She sighed. "You could've warned me."

"Where's the fun in that?"

Kain snorted beside her.

Eden rubbed her temple. "I've just been strong-armed into being a private legal consultant for Virex, on your request, and you didn't think to mention it beforehand?"

"You got promoted, didn't you?"

Lyn Rose

"That was before dinner."

"Exactly. You earned that one."

She shook her head, climbing into the car as Kain held the door.

"You're impossible."

"But effective."

A beat of silence. Then Nyx's voice slid in smooth, CEO-like.

"See you at Virex."

Her heart gave a traitorous twist—part dread, part anticipation, part something darker she didn't want to name.

"Yeah," she murmured. "See you soon."

She hung up, slipping the phone into her bag as Kain pulled into traffic.

"So," he said, eyes flicking toward her. "Still think he's just a tech CEO?"

Eden stared out the window, lips curving despite herself.

"No. I think he's a storm."

The car pulled into the underground garage at Virex.

It was silent down here—too clean, too clinical, like even the shadows had been sterilized. Her skin prickled with anxiety, a mounting sense of unreality.

Kain stepped out first. He didn't say anything, just rounded the car, opened her door, and offered his hand like she was something precious—or dangerous. She hesitated before taking it, suddenly unsure of her own solidity.

Eden slid out, heels clicking lightly against polished concrete. As they moved toward the elevator, Kain pressed his hand to the biometric pad. The doors hissed open without a sound.

"Straight to the top," he said, gesturing.

The elevator rose, smooth as a heartbeat.

No music. No announcements. Just the slow, pressurized climb. With every floor, her anxiety ratcheted higher, hands twisting around the strap of her bag.

When the doors opened, the floor was quiet. Empty. The city glittered through floor-to-ceiling glass on every side—but up here, it felt like another world entirely.

Kain led her forward.

One more keypad. One more scan.

Then the door slid open.

Nyx was waiting.

Lyn Rose

Standing at the head of the long glass table, suit immaculate, hands braced on the surface like he owned every breath in the room.

His eyes lifted the moment she stepped through.

They locked on hers—and didn't move.

Nyx's gaze didn't shift as Kain stepped back.

Without a word, Nyx gave him a short nod—a silent thanks that only someone like Kain would catch. You did well.

Then Nyx moved.

Not rushed. Not hesitant.

Like gravity had finally remembered where it belonged.

He walked straight to her, unbuttoning his cuffs as he came. The rest of the world didn't exist outside the space between them.

"Hey, baby," he said, voice low.

Before she could answer, his hand slid to the curve of her jaw, and he kissed her.

Not gentle.

Not for show.

All heat and possession, like he needed to brand her lungs with his name.

Eden forgot to breathe. The world spun—or maybe she did—and for a second, she could feel nothing but the press of his mouth, the weight of his body, the way her hands found his chest like they'd been waiting to be let home. She clung to him, desperate for something solid, something real.

When he pulled back, her lips were parted, pulse racing, brain useless. She was dizzy—off-balance, emotions flickering between relief, hunger, and a cold, rising fear.

Nyx smiled—slow, wicked, the kind that meant he knew exactly what he'd done to her.

"Missed you," he murmured, thumb brushing her lower lip.

"Have a seat, gorgeous," Nyx said, voice smooth—too smooth.

Eden sank into the chair, still trying to catch her breath, knees brushing the edge of the glass table like she wasn't fully back in her body. Her hands trembled, gripping the armrests, as she tried to ground herself in the present.

Nyx said nothing.

He slid a manila folder across the table toward her—slow, deliberate.

She blinked at it. Then at him.

"What is it?"

"Just read."

Still off-kilter, she opened it.

The first pages were clinical, dry—biochemical anomaly, subject reactivity, bloodborne strain detection. She skimmed, brows knitting as she tried to process the jargon. Her mind fogged, spinning from the kiss, the day, from him. But something about the words snagged at her, sharp and familiar and wrong. Dread rose, coiling tight in her chest.

Then she turned the page.

And saw her name.

Not spelled out—initials. DOB. Blood type. Medical record numbers she knew too well. A test subject ID she didn't.

TH-0RA.

The world tilted. The room felt too bright, too small. Eden stared, the edges of the page blurring as her vision tunnelled.

Nyx said nothing. Just watched.

Watched the heat drain from her face as her eyes darted, reread, jumped to flagged words—Null subject, transition incomplete, recovery complomised.

All the blood drained from her hands.

Her mouth opened. Closed.

Then her voice broke, barely a whisper.

"Is this… me?"

Nyx's jaw tightened. He nodded once.

"Yes, baby. That's you."

She didn't speak.

Didn't blink.

Just stared at the page like it might bleed. She felt cold, hollow. Like someone had scooped out everything she knew about herself and left her skin as the only evidence she'd ever existed.

Her fingers tightened on the file.

"…What is this, Nyx?" she whispered. "Where did you get it?"

Nyx stood slowly, stepped around the desk, crouched beside her chair—close but not touching. Grounded.

"I found it last night," he said softly. "But I've had pieces… suspicions for days. Your blood. Your adrenaline spikes. The way you affect supernatural's. It didn't make sense. Not naturally."

Eden stared, shaking her head. "This says test subject… this says—"

"I know," he said gently. "TH-0RA. That's what they called you."

Her breath caught. Lips parted, but no words came. She tried to steady herself, but her vision wavered, hot tears threatening. She pressed her palm to her mouth, swallowing a sob.

He reached out, wiped a tear from her cheek.

"You weren't born like this, Eden. You were made. Project Thera was supposed to cure supernatural affliction. But something changed. The files were hidden, encrypted deep in Biotech's archives. You were genetically altered—likely from conception. When your parents died—"

Her head jerked up, pain lancing through her chest.

Nyx nodded.

"—You got lost in the system. They didn't track where you ended up. You became the one that got away."

"No," she whispered. "No, that's—" Her voice cracked, panic clawing at her ribs. "That can't be—" She squeezed her eyes shut, shaking all over, trying to deny it, to erase it, to go back to the morning before any of this was real.

Nyx leaned in.

Lyn Rose

"They didn't stop after you. You were just Subject A."

He slid another page across the desk, voice darkening.

"There was a Subject B—fully completed, not lost. Controlled. Weaponized. When the serum trials began failing across species, they released B to test the end result in the field."

Eden blinked, stunned. "Released?"

He nodded once. "Biotech's been scattering the serums through the city—wolves, fae, humans—seeing which strain holds. Those killings you've heard about. Most are fallout from the injections. But Subject B is different. The witch who ran Biotech made them the blueprint. The proof of concept."

Her breath hitched, memory snapping back. "The file I asked you to degrain… from the firm…"

Nyx's jaw tightened. "That was the start. Your first case linked to a serum trial. Not B. Just another test."

Eden swayed, bile rising. "Oh my god…"

And then it hit her—the way Nyx had stormed her office, the scene in front of her boss, the fury when the man at reception asked for her blood. She'd thought it was arrogance. Control. But now—

She finally understood.

He hadn't been trying to cage her.

He'd been terrified she'd already been marked.

Her chest ached, panic warring with something softer, something that felt dangerously like love.

"Two fronts," Nyx said, voice low and certain. "One—the serum trials. The other—the prototype they perfected. And Sevra Wynne's behind both."

Eden froze. The pieces collided, sharp and jagged. Her hands trembled so badly she could barely hold the file.

"You've been part of it since the beginning," he said. "You just didn't know."

The room held only her ragged breathing and the whisper of paper between them. She stared at the file, at her own reflection in the glass, and at him—realizing that the woman she'd been before this moment no longer existed.

CHAPTER TWENTY

Truth In Blood

Eden didn't speak.

She didn't move.

The file slipped from her hands, landing with a soft thud on the glass table. The sound echoed faintly in the quiet room, a solemn punctuation to the storm inside her.

Her chest seized. Breath locked. Then came too fast. Too shallow. Her vision tunnelled, black creeping at the edges.

She was hyperventilating. Couldn't stop. Couldn't slow.

"Eden." Nyx's voice cut low, steady. Command and comfort fused in one word.

Her breath caught in her throat, then finally broke—letting loose a sound raw and fragile. Not loud or dramatic, just something deep and broken, like a shard of her soul had snapped free.

Her hands clawed uselessly at the arms of the chair, nails biting leather, trying to ground herself while air tore in ragged, broken gasps. Panic surged sharp and uncontrollable, like her own body had turned traitor.

Nyx crouched before her, slow and steady, knees on the cold floor, looking up at her, like he was making a vow.

"Hey," he murmured, voice low and steady. "Hey, baby, look at me."

Her head shook violently. She couldn't. The room was tilting, collapsing.

Her hands shook too violently to hold anything steady. Her vision blurred again—not from the file, but from the weight of what it meant.

His hands closed gently over hers—warm, firm. "With me. Breathe with me. In—" he inhaled, deep, steady, holding her gaze until she mimicked him. "—and out."

It took three tries before her lungs obeyed. Four before the dizziness loosened its grip. Five before her hands stopped shaking enough for him to lift her gently, pulling her against his chest. Her body felt light against him.

She sagged into him, body trembling, face pressed against the hard line of his suit. The world was chaos, but he was an anchor—immovable, unshakable.

He said nothing else. Just held her. Let her quake and splinter and slowly knit herself back together in the silence of his arms.

Minutes bled past. She didn't know how many. Enough for her breathing to steady. Enough for shame to creep in.

She pulled back first.

"I need a second," she whispered, wiping her eyes. "Bathroom?"

He nodded once, releasing her with a gentle brush of damp hair from her forehead.

"Take your time."

She walked away on unsteady legs, shoulders stiff with the effort of holding herself together.

Nyx waited until the door closed, then turned back to the computer. The screen glowed in the dim room.

Jace's secure file waited in his inbox, marked with a red lock and the words: Encrypted: NYX BLOOD – THERA REACTION.

He sat. Clicked.

Lyn Rose

The report opened in a cascade of scrolling windows—
biometric data, DNA strain breakdowns, cellular overlays.

Normal vampire physiology appeared first, his own data
alongside it.

And then it stopped.

He leaned in closer.

Not vampire. Not anymore.

The core markers remained—fang signatures, ultraviolet
resistance, regenerative coding—but the rest... had changed.

Blood oxygen density reached impossible saturation. Neural
conductivity went off the charts. Time-to-react ratings
couldn't register—they read like he moved before the
stimulus even arrived.

Movement wasn't speed now.

It was intention.

A thought.

And then arrival.

He read faster.

Scent profiles altered. Pheromone signatures overwritten.
His presence alone would trigger instinct in lower-blooded
vampires—either deference or fear. Maybe both.

Lyn Rose

Then he hit the flagged marker.

LDS-A01
Origin: External blood sample. Subject match: TH-0RA.

Nyx stared, jaw tightening.

Laç de Sânge.

The tag confirmed more than the bond. It confirmed his dependency.

Another note appeared beneath the signature:

"Without consistent top-up from original bonded source, host will experience blood rejection syndrome within 7-10 days. Early symptoms: aggression, instability, cognitive dissonance. Final stage: feral reversion."

Nyx leaned back, throat tight, hands clenched on the desk.

He was stronger. Faster. More dominant than any vampire before him.

But it came at a price.

Without Eden...

He would become something worse than a monster.

Eden

The bathroom was too bright. Too clean. Too normal.

Her brain felt packed with cotton, thoughts muffled and sluggish. Trying to think straight was like wading through fog—every logical thread slipping away before she could catch it.

She closed the door behind her gently and leaned on it for a long moment, trying to catch her breath.

Her reflection stared back from the long mirror above the sink—wide eyes, pale skin, mascara faintly smudged beneath one lash line.

"I don't know who I am."

The thought hit like a knife through glass. Her reflection stared back—same face, same eyes—but now laced with something artificial. Engineered.

Was anything real?

The memories, the feelings, the choices—

She touched her lips, remembering the first time she'd kissed Nyx.

That was mine.

No lab had given her that.

She looked... human.

Lyn Rose

Which, it seemed, was the biggest lie of all.

She turned on the tap. Cool water ran over her wrists, then cupped into her palms, pressed to her face. Again. Again. But it could wash the truth from her skin.

TH-0RA.

Not a name. A designation. A label.

Test subject. Engineered. Altered.

Not born.

She braced her hands on the marble edge of the counter, staring hard at her reflection. If she looked long enough, would something crack? Would her skin split and reveal what lived beneath?

Her eyes shimmered too bright.

She forced a breath, reached for the small makeup bag in her purse.

It felt like a ritual—each step a lifeline back to herself.

Foundation to cover the flush. Concealer to mask the wreckage under her eyes. Mascara to prove she was still trying. Lipstick—red, because anything softer would shatter her.

She applied it carefully, deliberately. Red always felt like armour.

Lyn Rose

As the colour bloomed on her lips, she exhaled—not calm, not peace, but control: brittle, borrowed, precious.

Her hands stilled.

She looked into her own eyes and whispered,

"You're still here. No matter what they made you."

Behind her, faintly, she heard Nyx's voice on a call, then silence.

Her fingers curled tightly around the lipstick tube.

You were made, he'd said. But her choices were her own.

And if they wanted a weapon?

They'd learn that blades could choose where they cut.

Eden rolled her shoulders back and stepped into her heels again, spine straighter than it had any right to be.

She walked to the door.

When she opened it, she was still shaking.

But this time—she looked like steel.

Nyx

He didn't look up right away when the door clicked open.

His eyes remained on the screen, the scan of his blood shifting with every line of data.

His blood.

But not his blood anymore.

Everything had changed. Markers that once labelled him—vampiric alleles, dormant traits, centuries of coded restraint—were overwritten. Not erased. Enhanced.

Strength, speed, cellular regeneration. But more than that—neurological pathways altered. Thought-impulse compression. Sound displacement. Time flexure.

He could move faster than thought now—not because his body obeyed, but because the world didn't have time to object.

Layered beneath it all, another marker glowed like a brand.

Laç de Sânge.

Blood Tie.

Not theoretical. Not myth. Confirmed.

Eden wasn't just the trigger—she was the match to his flame.

Lyn Rose

And without her?

The data was incomplete, but the implication was clear. Without regular blood exchange... something collapsed.

He didn't know what. But it was coming.

"Nyx?" Eden's voice was quiet. Composed—but fragile, like stained glass after an earthquake.

He looked up.

And forgot how to breathe.

She stood in the doorway like a goddess rebuilt. Red lips. Sharp lines. Heartbreak painted over with war paint. No tears now—just fire, contained and simmering in her eyes.

"You look…" He paused, rose slowly. "Stronger than I deserve."

She gave him a faint, brittle smile.

"Fake it till you feel it."

He crossed the room. Stopped just before touching her.

"You shouldn't have to."

Her hand lifted, brushing the lapel of his jacket, lingering over the tension in his shoulders.

"I know. But I do."

Lyn Rose

Before he could answer, his phone vibrated once in his pocket—sharp and coded. Priority line.

He answered on reflex.

"Ravelle."

Stroud's voice came crisp, clipped.

"Another body. West perimeter."

Nyx tensed.

"Where?"

"Black's territory."

"Fuck," he hissed, already moving to the desk. Eden followed silently, pulse quickening.

"Low-level wolf," Stroud continued. "Not someone vital, but still—Torran won't like the breach. You need to smooth this out."

"I'll go to him personally."

"Nyx…" Stroud's voice dropped. "We've logged deaths across every faction now. Human, wolf, Fae, witch, vampire. No one's untouched."

He exhaled, fingers tightening around the edge of the desk.

"I know."

Lyn Rose

Nyx's jaw tightened. "Cause?"

Stroud's voice dropped.

Stroud didn't hesitate. "No injection. No chemical trace. Drained dry—Subject B."

Nyx closed his eyes.

The factions weren't just being attacked.

They were being sampled.

Harvested.

In his head, the truth was colder still: Subject B was moving. The one Biotech had finished where Eden's transition had failed. Testing across bloodlines—wolves, Fae, humans, witches. Watching what held, what broke. Proving the weapon worked.

But the injections… those were worse in a different way. The serum didn't just kill, it spread chaos. Wolves turned on wolves. Fae bodies burned from within. Humans dropped in the street with no warning. No pattern. No mercy.

One predator harvesting.

The other forcing entire factions to devour themselves.

And through it all, Eden was the fucking blueprint.

Eden stepped closer, voice low.

"What happened?"

Nyx set the phone down, jaw tight.

"Another death. In wolf territory this time."

Her stomach dropped.

"Another supernatural?"

He nodded.

"Young wolf. Not high rank, but it's a message. Fourth death. Different faction every time."

She blinked.

"That's a pattern."

"It's a fucking escalation," he muttered, already dialling again.

The line barely rang before it picked up.

"You heard?" Nyx said, no preamble.

Torran Black's voice came low, grim.

"I'm standing in it."

Nyx's tone darkened.

"Where are you?"

"Sector nine. Industrial edge."

"I'll be there in thirty."

No goodbye.

The line went dead.

Nyx slipped the phone back into his pocket and looked at Eden.

His face was calm, but the weight in his gaze said more than words could.

"Stay here," he said softly.

"Don't open the door for anyone but Kain or Jace."

She crossed her arms.

"Nyx—"

"I'll be back before sundown," he promised, shrugging on his coat.

"But this thing just got too close to someone I trust. That changes everything."

CHAPTER TWENTY-ONE

Withdrawal and Addiction

Eden stepped into his path, arms crossed, fire sparking behind her eyes. "You're locking me in a glass tower now? That it?"

Her voice carried all defiance, but beneath it, her heart pounded so loud she could barely hear her own words. The thought of being contained, protected, of losing choice, scraped at old scars—made her skin crawl. She wanted to scream. Too many things in her life had slipped beyond her control, and now this? She was burning—furious, but also scared, and she hated that he could see it.

Nyx stilled, shoulders tense. "This isn't about control."

His jaw flexed, but a flicker of fear—sharp and real—hid behind the steel in his eyes.

"It feels like it."

Lyn Rose

The words came out harsher than she meant. She clenched her fists tighter, digging her nails into her palms to anchor herself, to stop her hands from trembling.

He stepped close. Too close. The air between them charged instantly, heat threading like a live wire. His gaze dropped to her mouth, then back to her eyes. Her breath caught, even as anger curled in her chest—he always unraveled her at the exact second she needed to stay strong.

"I don't have time to explain everything," he said, voice low and sharp. "Not now."

His hand lifted, knuckles grazing down her cheek. The touch was reverent. Anchoring. Eden's lashes fluttered—a shiver ran down her spine, unwanted and electric. He grounded her, and she both despised and craved it.

"But listen to me, Eden. You are my reason to live.
The only one that matters. If you don't make it out of this—"
His throat worked around the next words.
"I don't."…

The world tilted. She froze, mind blank, everything else falling away. That wasn't strategy. That was truth. Bleeding and brutal. Her anger flickered, replaced by something raw and aching she didn't know how to hold.

"I need to know you're here, safe, helping Jace and Kain. Not walking into something I can't drag you back from."

She opened her mouth, but it failed her. For a split second she hated how much she needed him, how much she wanted to believe she mattered that much.

He leaned in, forehead brushing hers, whispering the plea like a vow.

"Please. Let me do this knowing I'm not going to lose the only thing that makes this worth a fucking damn."

His words burrowed under her skin, splintering her composure. Her breath caught. She wasn't used to being the most important thing in anyone's life. But here, now, she was his centre of gravity. The knowledge was terrifying and intoxicating all at once.

She nodded slowly. "Sundown," she said, voice a little cracked. "Not a minute later."

She gripped his sleeve, just for a heartbeat, needing the contact as much as he did.

Nyx pulled back just enough to meet her eyes again. His smirk curved like temptation, like salvation—dangerous and devoted all at once.

"Baby," he murmured, "I can't stay away from you long. Every second hurts."

The words landed in her bones, hot and sharp. She almost laughed, almost cried.

Then he kissed her—not soft, not gentle—but like he was promising to return with blood on his hands if that's what it took.

She let him. She kissed him back with everything she couldn't say, everything threatening to break her open if she tried.

And then he was gone.

Nyx didn't wait for the elevator.

He took the stairs.

By the time he hit the parking level, his jacket was off and slung over one shoulder, jaw tight, mind already racing ahead of the engine. The reinforced glass doors hissed open as he crossed to his car—matte black, low to the ground, Virex-modified so vampires at customs couldn't trace half its systems.

He climbed in.

Closed the door.

The silence was immediate, airtight.

But inside him, it raged.

He gripped the wheel, knuckles blanching. Eden's face still burned behind his eyes—her tears, her fear, the moment she nodded and said sundown. He hated leaving her. Hated the way every second felt like a dare to fate, and the thought of her out of sight made him ache in a way that was primitive and ugly.

The engine roared to life.

He pulled onto the arterial road cutting through the financial district but didn't floor it—didn't need to. Something in him had shifted. Bent. Evolved.

The vampire inside him had always been fast, but this wasn't speed.

This was movement rewritten.

His thoughts outran the car.

He could feel time press around him like skin—pliable, stretchable, wrong. A voice whispered in the back of his mind: try it. Bend it. Take what you want and be gone before the city catches its breath.

Not yet.

Not here.

He gritted his teeth, forcing focus forward, pushing the hunger—the hum of altered blood—deep down where it wouldn't distract him.

He had to get to Black. Had to see the body. Had to figure out what Subject B was doing in wolf territory. Why now.

Was it random?

Lyn Rose

Or was it Eden's scent pulling it closer?

He took a sharp right, headlights flicking off stone walls as he dropped into the lower quarter—wolf territory. Less polished than the towers. More dangerous. No signs, no rules. Just unspoken lines in the street you didn't cross unless you wanted your throat checked.

But Nyx Ravelle didn't get checked.

He pulled up to the blockade just past an abandoned overpass.

Two wolves stepped forward—no uniforms, just the smell of rain and blood.

They clocked him immediately. One nodded toward the alley behind the block, where flickering hazard lights cast long shadows across the pavement.

"He's waiting for you," the younger said, voice taut.

Nyx stepped out of the car. Adjusted his cuffs. Didn't say a word.

He could already feel Torran Black ahead—not by scent, but by presence. Alpha power, tightly leashed. A quiet storm in leather and shadow.

Nyx walked forward, eyes narrowing.

The body lay slumped. Drained.

Lyn Rose

A low-level wolf—young, maybe eighteen.

Torran stood over him, arms crossed, face unreadable. But when he looked up and saw Nyx, something in his shoulders shifted—not relaxed, not stiffened. Just… readied.

Nyx met his gaze.

"I'm here," he said. "Tell me everything."

His voice was calm, but inside, his nerves screamed. Every detail could matter. Every second wasted felt like one closer to losing Eden.

Torran didn't speak right away.

He just stared down at the body—the kid's skin pale, lips tinged blue, eyes frozen open. His shirt torn down the front, but no gore. No tearing.

Just… hollow. Drained from the inside out.

Nyx's stomach turned. He recognized that method. It was too clean, too deliberate, too much like something engineered.

His gaze swept the body again, searching. No punctures. No bruised veins. No chemical trace on the skin. This wasn't injection. It was something worse. Skin pulled tight over bone, vessels collapsed like emptied rivers. Drained. Hollowed. Subject B's signature.

"His name was Mace," Torran said finally, voice quiet. "Runner. Low-rank. Never made trouble. Patrol schedule put him on shift at midnight."

Nyx knelt, inspecting the body with cold precision. The veins were collapsed. No blood. No scent of fear either. He felt sick, old memories pushing up—failed experiments, consequences of unnatural hunger.

"Any witnesses?"

Torran shook his head. "Just found him like this an hour ago. The smell was already fading."

Nyx knelt beside the body, breathing in.

It wasn't blood he was after—it was something else.

A residue. A presence. The echo of death left behind by monsters.

Then he caught it.

Faint. Wrong. Like burned plastic and rotted sugar. Artificial and ancient all at once.

He glanced at Black.

"You smell that?"

Black's nostrils flared. He stilled.

"Yeah," he said, voice tight. "But it's not ours."

Lyn Rose

Nyx stood, eyes scanning the dark perimeter of the industrial edge.

"It's recent."

Black nodded once. "This way."

They moved, low and fast, slipping through the broken remains of a shipping yard—glass underfoot, rusted crates leaning like tombstones. The scent thread wound between loading bays and collapsing walls, always just out of reach.

Then they saw him.

Far off—just a silhouette under the buzzing orange light of a broken streetlamp. Hooded. Limping.

Black froze. "That him?"

Nyx didn't answer. He was already moving.

The figure turned slowly—almost casually—and stepped behind a wall of old freight.

Gone.

Black growled low, following fast.

They tracked him deeper into the ruins, until the streetlamps vanished and the air thickened with dust and silence. The trail bent around an old supply depot—half-collapsed, steel beams groaning in the wind.

Then he was there.

Not waiting.

Standing.

Calculated. he'd led them to him.

The hood dropped.

And Nyx saw its face.

He turned to face them fully—hood falling back to reveal too-smooth skin stretched over fused bone, black eyes like voids, no whites, no pupils. Mouth stitched at the corners—then the threads split open as it grinned.

Black moved first.

He lunged, claws slashing—

The creature caught him mid-air and threw him through a metal bin like it was made of paper.

Nyx didn't hesitate.

He struck—faster than light, faster than logic—but the creature was faster still. It ducked, turned, and pressed two fingers to Nyx's chest—

Agony.

Lyn Rose

His body locked up. Like something pulling inside, like his life was being drained—not blood, but essence.

His vision went white. Nerves flared like exposed wire.

Then a roar.

Torran was back, slamming the creature sideways.

It let go.

Nyx hit the ground hard, breath shuddering, every nerve screaming.

The creature tilted its head. Blinked once.

Then it vanished into shadow.

Gone.

Not running—phasing.

Torran stumbled to Nyx's side. "You alright?"

Nyx coughed. "No."

He looked toward the wall where the creature had disappeared. His hands trembled.

Nyx's lip was split.

Blood ran down Black's temple.

Lyn Rose

Their breathing came ragged—

bent around fury and shame.

"It's learning," Nyx whispered.

Black didn't speak. He just wiped blood from his jaw and looked back the way they came.

"Come on. We need to go back."

They limped in silence, retracing their steps to the body.

Nyx knelt again beside the boy.

The wolf's eyes were still open.

Still cold.

Nyx pulled out his phone and hit the secure line.

"Stroud."

She picked up instantly.

"Report."

"You were right," he said, voice low. "It was Subject B. We made contact."

Silence.

Then, sharper: "You what?"

"Don't ask how. Just know we're lucky to be standing."

Black's eyes were flat, fixed on the alley beyond.

"I need a team here," Nyx said. "Full-spectrum forensic. Blood sniffers. Arcane readers. Whatever can catch a trace. This thing isn't just feeding."

He glanced at Black, who gave a short nod toward the dark where Subject B disappeared.

"It's sampling," Nyx continued grimly. "Strategic. And it's evolving."

Stroud's voice came like ice. "Send coordinates. I'll dispatch covert sweepers."

Nyx ended the call.

He slid the phone back into his pocket—

And swayed.

His vision tilted.

"Nyx?"

Black's voice—sharp. Closer now.

The crash hit like a freight train.

Twelve hours since Eden's blood. Half a feed. Unstable. Potent. Addictive.

His balance slipped. He dropped to one knee.

"Shit," Black muttered, catching his arm. "Let's go."

Eden's face flashed in Nyx's mind.

His chest tightened.

It wasn't just hunger. It was withdrawal. His senses blurred at the edges, focus fraying. Skin itching. Pulse like a war drum.

One blood bag a day kept him level—500mls. Controlled.

From Eden, he'd taken half that.

And it had changed everything.

Surge. Sight sharpened. Reflexes beyond even the oldest of his kind. Time bent around his command.

But now…

It was burning out.

Fast.

Too fast.

He tried to stand—

And staggered again.

Torran caught him hard.

"Nyx. What the fuck?"

"I'm not—fuck." Nyx gritted his teeth.

He pressed a palm to the nearest wall, breath dragging in.

"We need to talk. Somewhere not here."

Torran didn't hesitate. "Come on."

They left the scene, slipping through side alleys until the world shifted—neon buzz and old stone underfoot. A door unmarked save for a single glyph scrawled in paint, warded, discreet. Fangs and Claws Torran's place.

They stepped inside the narrow bar.

Dim, smoky, private.

The server clocked them both and didn't wait for a word. She placed two glasses of whiskey and one crystal-cut goblet of blood on the back bar, then vanished without a sound.

Nyx collapsed onto the worn leather booth, one hand braced on the table.

He reached for the blood.

Raised it.

Drank.

It hit his throat and—

Violent rejection.

His whole body revolted.

He barely made it to the bin beneath the bar before the blood came back up—red splattered against metal, viscous and unnatural. His stomach clenched hard, body remembering what it hadn't done in centuries.

He vomited.

When it was done, he wiped his mouth on the back of his hand, shoulders shaking with aftershocks. He felt hollowed out, scraped raw from the inside.

Torran stared, stunned.

"The fuck," he muttered, voice low and sharp. "You haven't done that since—"

"Since I was alive," Nyx rasped, still crouched, breathing hard. "I know."

Every word was a razor, his mind spinning with fear—for himself, for Eden, for what he was becoming.

He looked up, eyes rimmed in red.

"There's more to this," Torran said darkly. "A lot more than you've told me."

Nyx met his gaze, fury and fear colliding in his chest.

"There is."

He stood slowly, jaw set.

"And I'm going to tell you everything."

Lyn Rose

CHAPTER TWENTY-TWO

What I Took From Her

The bitter taste of blood still lingered on Nyx's tongue—thick, metallic, and wrong. It clung there like a stain, a copper tang burning down his throat and twisting his stomach in knots. More than the taste, it was the rejection—his body refusing what it once craved, and like some ancient part of him recoiled in disbelief.

He leaned back against the bar, bracing both hands on the rough wood beneath his palms. The grain scratched lightly at his skin, grounding him in the moment. His jaw ached from clenching so hard, and his breath came jagged, uneven, like ragged waves crashing in his chest. His eyes burned raw from the purge—bloodshot and fierce—flickering with a hunger that went beyond simple need.

It wasn't just need.

It was her. Only her.

Lyn Rose

A primal ache clawed inside him—raw, relentless, wildfire beneath his skin. His flesh prickled, hairs rising and his body tried to barricade itself against the void gnawing within. The hunger wasn't just physical; it was a storm of emotion writhing beneath the surface, twisting and pulling at every nerve ending.

Across from him, Torran stood silent, arms folded. The amber liquid in his glass caught the low light like molten fire—untouched, unmoved. His eyes were hard, still—a storm waiting to break, a dangerous calm that hung in the tense air between them.

"I fed from her," Nyx said, voice low, the words burning like acid in the quiet room.

Black smiled—a slow, crooked curve with a wolf-glint sparking in his eyes, dangerous and knowing.

"Mate, that doesn't surprise me. She smells like candy wrapped in a sinfully perfect goddamn body."

His tone was light, teasing, but edged with danger, as though daring Nyx not to fall deeper into his own confession.

"You'd have to be dead not to want a taste."

Black's smirk sharpened. *"Pun intended."*

The sound that left Nyx wasn't a growl.

It was wrong—too deep, layered with something ancient and primal, twisted with something alien. Not beast. Not vampire. Something new. Terrifying. Alive.

The overhead lights flickered, casting jittery shadows that recoiled, jumping, afraid of what was stirring in the room.

Nyx's eyes had gone black—not red, not silver. Just dark, like every star inside him had blinked out. His fangs dropped, longer and sharper than ever, glistening menacingly in the dim light. His stance shifted—bones subtly stretching beneath taut skin, a predator unmade for this world, caught between two forms, neither human nor fully monster.

Black raised both hands, palms up, voice steady and calm. "Easy, Ravelle. Easy. I'm not interested. Christ, I like breathing."

It took Nyx a long, brutal ten seconds to drag himself back from the edge of that abyss.

He forced the shift down. Fangs retracted. Shadows softened like retreating smoke, leaving behind the exhausted man who still fought to hold himself together.

Still breathless, voice rough, he said, "Since I fed from her, things have happened."

Black didn't blink, eyes steady and unflinching, waiting.

Nyx pressed on, voice heavy with raw truth. "She's not human. Not fully. Her parents went to an IVF clinic years ago—TheraGen. Pretty sure it was a front for Biotech. They engineered embryos designed to interact with supernatural DNA, placed in desperate couples looking for a miracle."

Black's brows drew together, disbelief and horror flickering across his face. "Jesus."

"Eden was Subject A. When her parents died in a car crash, she was lost in the system. Ended up in human foster care—out of supernatural jurisdiction. Biotech lost track. But her blood…" He exhaled a long, shuddering breath, the weight of the revelation pressing down on him. "It was made. Engineered. Meant to trigger change in our kind."

Black stared, the gravity sinking in like cold stone.

"I fed from her," Nyx said again, quieter now, almost a whisper. "And it rewrote me. I'm not just vampire anymore. My DNA—every marker, every strand—it's different. I'm faster than speed. I think, then move. Time bends. Sound collapses. My body's stronger. Sharper. I can hear the world breathe."

"And that wasn't enough," Black muttered, voice low, almost to himself, as the weight of Nyx's words echoed in his own mind.

Nyx's voice turned rough as gravel as he continued. "I told her everything. Gave her the option to walk. She didn't. She came back. We had sex. I fed."

Black's face twitched, a shadow flickering across his features, struggling to process the depth of what Nyx just admitted. "And?"

"I can't drink from anyone else now." Nyx's gaze flicked to the silver trash can holding evidence—cold and clinical, a stark contrast to the chaos inside him. "Not even bags. Her blood's the only thing I can take. It's fused to me. But it fades fast. I fed twelve hours ago, and already—" He clenched his fist, knuckles white. "I can feel the decay. It's like I'm unravelling without her."

Black exhaled sharply, the sound sharp in the quiet room, and sank back into his chair, whiskey untouched.

"What the actual fuck, Nyx."

Nyx looked away, jaw tight, eyes burning with exhaustion and fear, the storm inside him barely held at bay.

"So let me get this straight," Black said, voice low and steady, burning with disbelief and awe. "You're saying she's your mate. Your Sang de-whatever. Now you can only survive on her blood. No substitutes. No backups. And if you don't get it often enough, you go feral? Insane? Dead?"

Nyx's smile was hollow, brittle, a cracked mask. "That's the clinical summary, yeah."

Black shook his head slowly, the weight pressing down. "Fuck."

A long beat of silence stretched between them, thick and heavy.

Then Black stood, eyes blazing with awe and wariness.

"Come on," he said. "Let's get you back to her."

CHAPTER TWENTY-THREE

When Salvation Tasted Like Death

Black drove through the night, the city lights a blur of neon and shadow outside the windshield. The engine thrummed beneath him, a steady pulse against the silence inside the cabin. The faint scent of burnt rubber and cold air slipped through the cracked window, threading with the lingering whiskey from earlier.

Nyx sat rigid in the passenger seat, jaw clenched so tight it could've shattered glass. He hadn't spoken since they left the bar. His gaze stayed fixed ahead, as if the act of staring forward was the only thing keeping his mind from splitting apart. The leather beneath him was cool and worn, the stitching rough against his curled fists.

Outside, the world melted away like watercolours bleeding in rain—shapes smearing into nothing. Traffic roared distantly, fading to a hum broken only by the occasional siren or the hiss of tires on wet asphalt. All he could taste was loss and need—the memory of her blood, sharp and raw on his tongue. Burning. Consuming. A wound pulsing in his veins, far crueller than anything physical.

When they reached Virex's underground entrance, Black tapped his code into the console. The gate yawned open with a hiss, metal sliding like a beast breathing, swallowing the car in its cold chest. A metallic tang hung in the air, damp concrete wrapping around them like a shroud.

Black parked, engine still rumbling—a low growl vibrating through the chassis like a predator pacing behind bars. The stale garage air smelled of oil and concrete dust, grit settling on their tongues.

Nyx didn't wait for permission.

He opened the door with a flick of his hand—the locks whispering open without touch—and stepped out into the low-lit garage. The cold bit at his skin immediately, sharp against the warmth still radiating from the car. His boots clunked against the hard floor, footsteps echoing off the steel walls. Black followed, adjusting his collar, posture relaxed but eyes sharp, pupils narrowing as they scanned the shadows for any sign of threat.

They took the lift, rising through layers of cold stone and steel. The air grew thinner, colder, pressing against Nyx's chest like a weighty tide. His pulse thudded raw and loud in his ears, each beat a drum of warning, echoing in the hollow chamber of his ribs. The faint buzz of the elevator's mechanics whispered behind the steel doors until they slid open.

The doors slid open to the executive wing, and Nyx's PA stood waiting—clipboard in hand, stylus tucked behind one ear, faint scent of lavender clinging to her like a soft whisper. She startled slightly when she saw who was with him.

"Mr. Ravelle—oh, and… Mr. Black." Her voice dropped an octave, nerves crackling beneath it. "Hi."

Black gave her a lazy smile and a wink, the corner of his mouth twitching with mischief. "Afternoon, sweetheart."

She flushed, warmth blooming across her cheeks like a sudden sunrise.

Nyx barely spared her a glance. "Clear my schedule. Now."

"Of course, sir." She turned on hurried heels, nearly tripping in her rush, the soft click of her shoes echoing down the long, sterile hallway.

They stepped through the next set of glass doors—and stopped cold.

Eden sat at Nyx's desk, absorbed in the glow of the monitor. Her hair was tied up carelessly, lazy strands falling around her face like silk curtains framing a masterpiece. She wore a slight smile that played at her lips, the faint scent of her perfume—a warm, floral note—floating in the air between them.

The black singlet clung to her body in all the ways that undid him—every curve outlined, every inch claiming him without a word. The pencil skirt did worse. Her legs were crossed, heels kicked back just enough to reveal the seam line trailing up the back of her tights, a whisper of fabric sliding against skin. Her lips were red, cheeks flushed with life.

She looked like every fantasy he'd never dared to name—perfected and standing right in front of him—too beautiful, too utterly his for any logic to hold.

Kain leaned over her shoulder, pointing at something on the screen.

"That one," he said. "See the margin overlay?"

She laughed, the sound light and teasing, a bell cutting through the heavy air. "You're a menace."

He grinned, teeth flashing white. "Guilty. But if this timestamp holds, the same anomaly that showed up on the Grenton body is here too."

She leaned in closer, brow furrowed, breath warm against his face. "The one near the overpass?"

"Yeah. Wolf territory. Jace and I ran the footage through Nyx's spectral filter—it flagged the drain pattern instantly."

Then—they both looked up.

Froze.

The shift in the room was immediate—the air thinning, charged, every hair on their arms rising.

Nyx stood rooted in the doorway.

And whatever he was now… it was ancient. Born of hunger and claim. Something dark, something risen.

His frame bulked, clothes straining tight across shoulders no longer built to hold back. His fangs were fully bared now— too long. Too sharp. His eyes were pitch black, swirling with molten threads beneath the surface—something that did not belong in this world.

The room dimmed. Lights buzzed, a low electrical hum vibrating through the walls. Shadows twisted and danced, curling like smoke around his feet.

He was losing the fight inside himself. The control he'd kept iron-clad was splintering, wild and barely leashed.

The need for her was a hunger, an agony. It burned beneath his skin—a fire clawing through muscle and bone.

He couldn't breathe without it. Didn't want to.

And then came the sound—

A growl. Not of any animal. Not of any man.

A sound like metal warping in fire. Like time cracking open—sharp and jagged—tearing through the silence.

"Nyx," Black said, stepping beside him slowly. "Mate. Not again. She's fine."

He reached out, hand steady and sure, rough calluses a tether to the man unravelling beside him.

"Easy. Breathe."

Nyx didn't blink. His gaze was locked on Kain—one of his most trusted.

Too close.

Too familiar.

He wanted to tear the world apart to keep her safe.

Kain raised his hands, stepping back slowly. "I didn't touch her."

Eden stood. "Nyx?"

His head snapped toward her—and just like that, the air shifted again.

He staggered, the weight of realization crashed over him.

The monster flinched.

Black's hand was firm on his shoulder now. "Come on. Anchor up."

From the hallway, Jace's voice cracked like a whip. "What the fuck—?"

"Jace," Black snapped. "Get Kain the fuck out. Now."

Kain didn't argue. He backed away, head down, brushing Eden's arm gently on the way past. "I'm good," he said softly. "Go to him."

Eden took a hesitant step forward.

"Nyx," she whispered. "You're scaring me."

And that—that was what broke the spell.

Nyx dropped to his knees—breath torn from him like it cost everything.

Hands shaking, eyes still wrong, still other—but the rage bleeding out in choked, soundless shudders.

His body trembled—not with weakness, but with the sheer force of holding himself back from destroying everything.

Eden crossed the room and dropped to the floor with him.

She reached for his face.

And he let her.

Her touch was the only thing in the universe that could call him back.

Black stepped back, watching the way Eden's hands cupped Nyx's face, how her presence alone unraveled the fury within him. The growls had quieted. His breathing slowed.

Still dangerous. But not lost.

Eden looked up and met Black's eyes. She gave a single nod.

That was enough.

He smiled—something rare and sharp—and stepped out the door, closing it quietly behind him.

Her hands were on his face—and he was burning.

Eden drew back slowly, eyes searching his. "Nyx," she whispered. "What's happening to you?"

He didn't answer.

Couldn't.

The hunger was too loud now. His skin vibrated, his mind splintering beneath the weight of it. His body was on fire.

She rose, breath trembling, moving toward the bar sink.

He watched—every motion sharpened in predatory detail. The way her skirt hugged her hips. The glint of the black line running up the back of her stockings. The delicate bend of her spine as she reached for a cloth, wet it, and bent to retrieve a glass from the lower cabinet.

His control snapped.

He didn't move—not consciously—but suddenly, he was behind her.

Her breath caught.

"Nyx—"

He buried his face in her neck, groaning against her skin like the contact physically hurt. His arms wrapped around her waist and dragged her flush against him, chest to her back, breath hot and ragged as his mouth found her pulse. His tongue ran over it slowly, reverently.

She tilted her head, exposing more.

His hands slid lower.

The skirt was no barrier. He shoved it up—hands reverent and desperate all at once—palms skating up the soft line of her stockings until he reached the lace edge of her underwear. One sharp tug—it tore in his hand. Another pair gone.

His fingers slid between her thighs.

She gasped—soaked, waiting for him.

He groaned again, forehead pressed to her shoulder as he moved—slow at first, then deeper, harder. She moaned, bracing herself on the counter as he stroked her from behind, her hips rolling into his hand, seeking more.

Lyn Rose

"Greedy girl," he muttered, voice a deep rumble.

One hand dropped to his belt.

The clink of the buckle. The slide of fabric.

She cried out when he pulled his fingers away—only to arch and shudder as he grabbed her hips and bent her over the counter.

He didn't wait.

He thrust into her in one powerful, claiming stroke.

Both of them gasped—broken, wrecked already—and then he was moving. Hard. Deep. His hands gripping her thighs, her hips, her ribs—anything to keep her close as he lost himself in her.

His lips found her neck again. He kissed, tasted.

And then—

His fangs dropped.

And sank in.

She screamed—not in pain, but in ecstasy. His thrusts never slowed. His mouth latched on, drinking as his body pounded into hers. Her walls fluttered around him, her body breaking apart, pulsing in waves that stole her breath—and his sanity.

"Nyx—ah—fuck—Nyx—"

Lyn Rose

Because the moment her blood hit his tongue, something ignited.

It wasn't just taste. It wasn't just hunger.

It was ascension.

He drank.

And fucked.

And lost time.

Until—

She gasped, voice cracking. "I—I can't—I—"

Her legs buckled.

He caught her.

Fangs retracting, tongue sealing the marks he'd made, he turned her in his arms—her skin pale, breath shivering, lips parted like she was still drowning in the aftershock.

Every cell in him lit up—lightning through bone. Her heartbeat fluttered against his chest, too weak, too slow, yet each fading pulse echoed through him, forcing life into his body.
It shouldn't have been possible. But it was—her rhythm bleeding into him until the hollow space where his heart had been began to ache again.

"Eden," he whispered, lowering her carefully to the black couch, cradling her like she was still made of fire and threadbare breath. "Baby—are you okay?"

Her body went loose, the shuddering pleasure snapping into stillness. Her breathing turned shallow, each inhale weaker than the last.

"Eden—" His voice was a rasp edged in steel. He pressed a hand to her sternum, counting the faltering thuds beneath his palm. Too far apart. Too slow.

Her skin was cold. Her heart stuttered, uneven and sluggish, like it was deciding whether to keep going.

The beast inside him tore free.

Claws ripped from his hands, fangs punching down so fast his jaw ached. The shadows under his skin writhed, veins standing out black against the strain of holding himself together.

"Eden—" His voice broke, low and vicious, but she didn't answer.

Nyx's eyes snapped to the doorway. "Black!" he yelled.

Black filled the doorway, taking in the scene in a split second—the blood, the limp body, the predator crouched over her.

"She's crashing," Nyx snarled. "Her heart's failing."

"I can see that." Black was already reaching for his phone.

"Get someone here!" Nyx roared, the sound shaking the glass.

Black's jaw tightened. "Evara. She's a witch, old bloodline, healer. I trust her."

"A witch?" Nyx's voice cracked with disbelief, his lip curling.

"Yeah," Black said flatly. "And she's the only one who can pull her back. You want her breathing in ten minutes? Then shut up and let me make the call."

Nyx's growl deepened, but he didn't argue.

Black hit the line. "Evara. Virex. Top floor. Emergency. Bring your kit. Now."

Black's eyes flicked to him, but he didn't slow. "She'll come. And she'll keep her mouth shut."

Nyx didn't look away from Eden. Her skin was too pale, lips parted like she was drowning on air. He could hear every faltering beat in her chest, each one threatening to be the last.

"I saw it in Biotech's archives," Nyx rasped, voice like stone grinding. "Buried. Erased from public record. *Laç de Sânges.*"

Black's brow hardened. "And that is—?"

"A protocol," Nyx said. "Not an accident. Not a mutation. A design."

He leaned forward, eyes dark, fangs still down.

"They engineered a bond response. Built to lure us in. Built to make us feed. Built to entangle our systems, rewrite us… then break us."

Black's gaze flicked to Eden, something sharp and dangerous rising behind his eyes.

"They didn't expect any of the subjects to live long enough to trigger a full reaction," Nyx added, voice dropping. "No one ever documented a survivor."

His claws curled until skin split.

"She wasn't bitten," he said. "She was built."

CHAPTER TWENTY-FOUR

Bound in Blood and Breath

The lift dinged.

Its metallic chime was sharp in the charged silence, a note that cut through the heavy air like a blade through silk. The faint vibration underfoot tickled Nyx's boots, a subtle reminder of the machinery humming just beneath the floor.

The doors slid open, revealing Jace, broad-shouldered and braced, holding them for a tall woman who stepped out as though the marble floor owed her tribute. Her boots were scarred leather, the kind that had seen wars, creaking softly with each step. Black trousers tucked neatly into them, a fitted black blazer framing a deep green tunic that brushed her thighs. Over one shoulder fell a single braid streaked with silver, threaded with what looked like tiny bones— tokens, trophies, or talismans that whispered secrets of battles past.

Magic walked with her.

Lyn Rose

The faint scent of rosemary and iron spilled into the room, curling in the air like smoke from an invisible fire—sharp, clean, with that metallic bite that spoke of both blood and ritual. It prickled over Nyx's skin like static, stirring memories he didn't want to face.

"Evara," Black said, and Nyx heard something in his voice he'd never heard before—relief threaded with certainty.

She gave him a curt nod, eyes already scanning the room with a soldier's precision. "Torran."

She was Pack, but she didn't need fur or fangs to prove it. Every movement was economy and purpose, the kind you saw in those who'd pulled warriors back from the brink and buried the ones they couldn't save.

Her gaze landed on Eden.

No gasp. No curse. No widening of the eyes. Just the narrowing—sharp, analytical, the mind behind them running through diagnostics faster than any human could. She knelt before her satchel hit the floor, the sound of glass vials and metal tools clicking faintly as they shifted.

Black's voice carried from behind her, pitched low but firm. "She's the best healer in the Pack. Saved my life more than once. She doesn't fuck around, and she doesn't work for Biotech."

Evara's hands were already moving, laying out vials in a neat line. The faint clink of glass punctuated the tense quiet.

"Tell me what happened."

Nyx's voice was gravel. "I took too much."

She didn't look up. "You've got other healers on call. Why me?"

"None I trust," he said. "But Black trusts you."

That earned a small nod. No pride, no surprise — just acknowledgement. Her focus stayed on the instruments, movements precise, deliberate. Then—just for a heartbeat—her nostrils flared.

Her head tilted, the silver-threaded braid swinging forward.

And there it was — the first crack in her composure.

"What the hell is she?"

Nyx's eyes locked with hers, black as a midnight storm. "Not bitten," he said, the words like ground glass. "Created."

Her fingers tightened on Eden's wrist, feeling the sluggish pulse. The faint thump echoed in the quiet room, uneven and weak.

"She's not just crashing," she said, sharper now. "Her system's in failure. And whatever she is—it's fighting itself."

Lyn Rose

Black stepped forward, voice a steady anchor. "We think Biotech's behind it. Just found files."

Evara's attention flicked up, narrowing further. "What kind of files?"

"Buried," Nyx said. "Locked archives. The protocol name was Laç de Sânges."

That stilled her hands completely.

"That's not possible," she said after a moment, the words low. "That was banned a century ago."

Nyx's voice was dark iron. "It wasn't gone. They used it to build her."

Evara's brow creased. "Build her?"

No one answered.

Silence sat heavy, the kind that made the air feel thicker.

Evara leaned closer, her palm hovering over Eden's chest now, not touching—just feeling. The faint warmth from Eden's skin barely registered beneath the electric tension in the air. "Then she's worse off than I thought. That protocol destabilises the subject after feeding. Until they adapt, their body starts tearing itself apart trying to match the bond."

Nyx crouched beside her, claws still out, fangs still down. "Then tell me how to fix it."

"You don't fix it," she said, matter-of-fact. "You complete it. She needs your blood. Now. And it has to take, or she won't survive the hour."

He didn't hesitate. One swipe of his claw opened his wrist, thick, dark blood welling. The scent hit the air like a strike of flint, sharp and primal.

Evara caught it in a silver cup. "She drinks until the bond catches. Don't stop early, or it'll fail."

Nyx brushed Eden's hair back from her face. She looked impossibly fragile under his hands, her lips pale, her breath ghost-light. His voice was a growl meant only for her.

"You're not leaving me like this."

Her lashes fluttered, a faint tremor in her throat. He pressed the cup to her mouth—

The first drop hit her tongue, and the world changed shape.

Her back arched violently, a cry torn from her chest as magic detonated inside her like a lightning strike. It poured off her in crashing waves, slamming into Nyx with enough force to drive his claws into the velvet beneath her.

She grabbed his shirt with sudden strength, her nails slicing through the fabric to scrape his skin. Her breathing went wild—ragged gasps drawn between pulls from the cup. A guttural sound escaped her, half-moan, half-animal.

Nyx's vision darkened at the edges. His pulse synced to hers, dragged into her rhythm like the bond had shackled him, too.

The air thickened until Black muttered from the doorway, "Holy shit…"

"Out," Nyx growled, not looking away. His voice was a blade in the dark.

The door shut.

Eden's hands found his wrist now instead of the cup. She pulled him closer, mouth locking over the wound, drinking straight from him. The pull was relentless.

Power roared between them in a closed circuit—his blood rewriting her cells, hers pushing back with something older, stranger. The room felt smaller, the magic they stirred could no longer be contained by its walls.

"That's it," Nyx rasped, his voice breaking between words. "Take it all."

Her pulse kicked under his mouth, sudden and strong, like lightning under skin. The scent of her hit him hard—sharper, wilder, laced with something untamed. Every inhale was sharpened steel and wildfire.

And in that instant, Nyx knew Edalva wasn't ready for what she was becoming.

Hell, neither was he.

CHAPTER TWENTY-FIVE

Bound and Changed

The magic storm left the air heavy, trembling against Nyx's skin like the room itself hadn't quite caught up to reality. Every breath felt thick, the atmosphere inside was saturated with unseen energy, prickling the hairs on his arms and crawling beneath his skin.

Eden lay limp in his arms, her pulse steadier now but racing like it had just learned how to run. Her skin held a faint, unnatural glow—not glamour, not life—but something other. Something that hummed deep in the bones, a subtle vibration that resonated with the very air around them.

For a moment, he thought she was still gone. Then—

Her breath hitched.

Her eyes opened.

Gold-flecked, pupils blown wide, she stared at the ceiling for a long, suspended heartbeat before her gaze found his. He watched the recognition flare, saw the way her pupils tightened then widened again, adjusting to a new kind of light. She inhaled sharply, her lungs had been wrung out and refilled with ice and fire.

Her hands turned palm-up, then over again, searching for proof they were still hers. Fingers flexed. She touched her cheek, fingertips skimming over her lips, down the line of her jaw. Her breathing was shallow, quick—every inhale carrying more weight than the last, the faint scent of blood and something metallic lingering on her skin.

"I feel… different," she murmured. Not frightened. Just aware.

"Warmer. Stronger. Like my skin's too tight, but in a way that's—" she broke off, frowning. "—like something under it. Waiting."

Nyx couldn't look away. The bond was raw and loud between them, pulling him under. His fangs ached. The taste of her was still on his tongue, every beat of her heart echoing in his own chest like a tether wound too tight.

Evara crouched beside her, the witch's eyes raking her head to toe with clinical precision.

"You were nearly gone," she said plainly. "Now you're not. But your body isn't the same as it was an hour ago."

Eden's brows drew together. "What happened?"

"You adapted. Fast. Too fast for something natural." Evara's voice was low, measured. "Your pulse, your temperature, your… scent—all changed when you took his blood." Her gaze sharpened. "And you're still changing."

"You're altered," Evara added. "Not vampire. Not anything I've seen. Your body isn't imitating his—it's responding to what was already in you."

The world wasn't just around her anymore. It was inside her.

She could hear the whisper of the curtains shifting from the AC.

The grind of gears deep in the elevator shaft, five floors down.

And beneath all of it—her own heartbeat, but not where it should've been.

It echoed back through him, steady and strong, pulsing in the hollow where his should've lived.

Through that echo she felt him—hunger sharpening into relief, relief folding into something rawer.

Love. Adoration. Need.

It wasn't her imagination.

It was connection, bleeding both ways, impossible to tell whose feeling belonged to whom.

Her head snapped toward the door before it opened.

Boots on marble. The faint smell of metal and rosemary oil.

Black, still in the hall, and she knew it before his shadow touched the floor.

She pressed her palms to her ears, but the sounds were in her now, soaked into bone and blood.

The scent of Nyx's blood—thick, dark, magnetic—lingered on her tongue, and it felt like it was in her marrow.

"Is this going to stop?" she asked, her voice low but edged.

Evara shook her head. "No. You'll learn to control it. But right now? You're running on instinct."

Every inch of her skin felt lit from underneath, lightning crawling just beneath the surface.

And Nyx… Nyx was staring at her like the bond was dragging him under too. Shoulders tight. Fangs still down. Pupils wide and dark.

"You're not just healed," Evara said. "You're altered. And I can't tell you by how much—not yet. Your medical history is… an unknown."

Lyn Rose

"What happened to me?" Eden asked again, this time steadier, logical.

"You were dying," Evara said. "Your body was burning itself out trying to keep pace with him." She tipped her head toward Nyx. "So he gave you blood. Enough to seal the first thread of the bond."

Eden's breath caught, her eyes locking on his. He didn't look away.

Evara's tone softened. "It's why you can hear so far, smell so much, feel like lightning's under your skin. The bond is raw. Everything is sharp right now."

"And this is permanent?"

"Yes. But it will settle. When it does, you'll still be you. Just… not only you."

Nyx's jaw tightened at that, but he didn't speak.

Evara's focus shifted to him. "You understand what this means, Ravelle. She already drew attention before. Now? Her scent will pull predators from miles. If anyone catches her bleeding—"

"I know," he cut in, his voice low enough to frost the air.

"Keep her close. Don't let anyone else near her blood again."

She stood, collecting her satchel, then paused at the door. "Call me if it gets worse. Or if you feel something you can't explain." A faint smirk. "And trust me—you will."

Then she was gone.

The room felt smaller without her.

Nyx was still kneeling in front of Eden, his eyes shadowed, fangs barely retracted. He looked dangerous in a way that had nothing to do with threat—dangerous in the way that made her heartbeat hitch.

"You saved me," she said.

"I took too much," he rasped. "I didn't give you a choice. If I hadn't—" His voice frayed. "You wouldn't be here."

She pressed her palm to his chest, feeling that unsteady beat under her hand. "Nyx… I want this. I want you. Don't you dare regret it."

His shoulders eased, just a fraction.

She glanced at her hands again—the shimmer in her skin, the strange way her eyes caught the light, the vast, sharp thing curled beneath her ribs.

It was still her face in his gaze. But now there was something else behind it.

Something patient.

Lyn Rose

Something that could be dangerous if it ever rose.

She didn't look like a monster.

But she could feel it—the beast under her skin, biding its time.

And she smiled.

The smile felt strange on her lips—lighter than it should, considering the storm in her veins. Nyx stayed kneeling, shadow and heat in front of her, the bond thrumming between them like a live wire. Whatever she'd become, it was tied to him now—not dangerous, but undeniable.

CHAPTER TWENTY-SIX

Blood on Accorded Ground

She smiled—small, private, almost secret—and then pushed herself to her feet. The movement felt foreign, like her body were still adjusting to new shapes and shadows beneath her skin. Every muscle twitched with unfamiliar strength, smooth and taut beneath the surface.

The air seemed thicker now, sliding over her skin like silk, warm and slightly electric. She could feel the weight of her own blood moving under the surface, the beat of her heart pressing insistently against her ribs. Even her balance felt different—like the floor had learned her shape and was moving with her instead of against her.

She moved toward the bathroom without a word, bare feet whispering over the polished floor. The soft echo of each step was a strange comfort in the heavy silence. The faint scent of lavender from the office lingered in the air, mingling with the sharper hint of steel and floor polish.

The lights in the bathroom flared softly as she stepped in. Chrome and glass reflected her from every angle—fractured yet whole. She looked up into the mirror.

For a breath, she froze.

Her eyes—her familiar warm brown—were gone.

In their place: molten gold, threaded with shadow, the pupils thin slits that made her look like something pulled out of a story meant to scare children. The reflection shimmered, alive and shifting like liquid metal under the fluorescent glow.

She leaned closer to the mirror, the gold in her irises catching the light like molten fire. The change wasn't static—it moved, shimmered, alive in a way human eyes shouldn't be. Her breath quickened, and the gold rippled... until, just like that, the brown bled back in, the predator hidden again like a curtain dropping after the final act.

She gripped the counter, fingertips whitening. The counter was cool stone, but she swore she could feel each mineral grain under her skin, a strange new sensitivity that tingled and pulsed.

She turned her palms over—the same hands, the same lines—but somehow sharper, more defined. She brushed her own cheek, down to the curve of her mouth, testing if she still recognised the girl in the reflection.

Lyn Rose

Her cheeks were flushed, lips a deeper red than any lipstick could manage. Her skin looked lit from within, like some low sun had been trapped under it. Her hair—longer, thicker—spilled over her shoulders in waves that caught every glint of light.

And her body…

She peeled her shirt up to mid-ribcage.

The softness she remembered was gone. Every muscle seemed carved sharper, tighter, as though her body had decided survival meant beauty honed into a blade. She rolled her shoulders, and the mirror caught the play of muscle down her arms. She tightened her stomach—the lines deepened, shadows making her look like she'd been training for years instead of nearly dying an hour ago.

She touched the new definition in her stomach, fingertips ghosting over skin that felt electric to her own touch. The faint scent of sweat and something metallic clung to her skin, the tangible reminder of change.

Her breath fogged the mirror. "What did you do to me?"

Nyx's reflection appeared behind her, dark and steady.

"I saved you," he said simply, voice low enough to blur the words.

She turned, fire and fear warring in her eyes.

"Nyx… my eyes, my skin—" her gaze dropped to her hands, fingers flexing as though testing if they were still hers. "I can hear things I shouldn't. Feel things I never did before."

Nyx's expression shadowed, but his voice came low, steady.

"No. It's the bond. The first thread of it. You're still human, Eden. Still you. But now you're tied to me. My blood rewrote just enough to keep you alive—altered you, not turned you."

Her breath hitched, gold flickering faintly in her irises. She pressed a palm to her chest trying to feel the storm racing inside.

"And this feeling?"

"It'll dull," Nyx said, stepping closer, his hand covering hers. "The edges will settle. But the bond… that doesn't fade. You're in it now. With me."

He stepped closer, until the heat of him pressed against her back. His hands slid to her hips—firm, grounding—and his eyes found hers in the mirror.

"You are still the most beautiful and dangerous thing I've ever seen," he said.

Her lips curved—not soft, not sweet. A smile edged in shock and surrender both.

Lyn Rose

Later, when the office had gone dark around them and the world outside had forgotten it was supposed to sleep, they left.

The building was empty, silent. Virex staff had cleared out hours ago.

Downstairs, Black, Kain, and Jace were talking quietly near the car lift. They turned when the doors opened.

Kain's gaze dropped immediately to Eden. His brows lifted. "Damn."

Eden smiled back. "Hey."

Kain smiled, then flicked a glance to Nyx, clearly waiting to see if his throat was about to get ripped out. But Nyx just stood at ease, hand curled around Eden's like she was gravity itself.

Black let out a low whistle. "Well, hello there. So glad you're okay." He looked her up and down, grin sharp. "Ready for another night out?" He winked.

Eden laughed. "As long as there's dinner first."

He laughed right back. "Deal."

Nyx squeezed her hand gently. "Let's get you home."

She glanced up. "Can we stop at my apartment first? I need a few things."

He nodded. "Of course."

Jace handed over her keys without a word. "Building's secure," he said. "No one gets inside unless we say so."

She looked between them all—Nyx, Jace, Kain—and swallowed. "Thank you. For everything. You didn't have to go this far…"

Kain grinned. "Anything for you. You're the other half now."

She arched a brow. "Is that your way of saying I'm bonded property?"

He smirked. "Property? No. But if you ever get tired of the boss, I'm available."

Nyx's growl rumbled low and dark, the kind that didn't need words.

Kain laughed, hands up. "Kidding. Mostly. All love, boss."

Nyx didn't smile. He just pulled her closer.

The car ride was quiet—Eden still adjusting to her body, her blood, her bond—and Nyx driving like he was restraining himself from simply teleporting them there.

When they pulled up to her old apartment building, Eden stared.

No, gawked.

Lyn Rose

"What the fuck?" she whispered, stepping out slowly. "This isn't—this wasn't—my building looked like a shitty postgrad block in a recession, not…" Her voice trailed off as her gaze lifted up the pristine façade. Smooth black glass. Matte steel trims. Private rooftop access.

Nyx walked around the car. "I bought it."

"You what?"

"I bought the building," he said simply. "And remodelled."

Her mouth opened. Then shut. Then opened again. "The whole thing?"

He nodded. "You take up the top floor now."

"The entire top floor?! What about my neighbours?"

"They've been safely rehomed. Generous relocation packages. No one asked questions."

Eden blinked. Hard. "You just… kicked out four families?"

"They were renters. Not families. One guy ran a crypto cult from his lounge room," he said dryly. "Trust me, you're doing this place a favour."

She let out a sharp laugh, somewhere between disbelief and surrender, and walked toward the elevator. The glass door whooshed open automatically when she got close.

Her hand hesitated midair.

Lyn Rose

Nyx leaned in. "It's yours. Handprint access. Alarm is keyed to your biometrics."

Of course it was.

Inside, the lift walls glowed a soft gold, warm light chasing her as she rose.

She trailed her fingers over the glass, watching her distorted reflection slide with her. Her pulse was picking up—not from fear, but from the realisation that this wasn't just security. This was Nyx's claim, set into steel and code.

When the doors opened, she stepped into what could only be described as architectural seduction. All black marble, soft greys, warm amber tones in the lighting. Velvet throws. Sheer curtains. A kitchen that looked like it belonged in a luxury catalogue.

She turned in a slow circle. Everything was new. Not a trace of the life she had before.

A faint trace of her perfume lingered in the air—the one she wore when they first met. A single mug from her old set sat on the counter, placed like it had always been there. A throw blanket that looked suspiciously like the one she'd kept on her old couch, only now woven in cashmere. The details punched through her awe, hitting something raw and deep in her chest.

The couch was curved, the bed massive, the bookshelves lined with titles she actually read. Her wardrobe was full—

new clothes, tailored to her exact size, already hung by style and colour.

Even the linen smelled like home.

"You planned all this?" she said, barely turning to look at him.

He walked in behind her, holding out a sleek black phone.

"Download this app. It's connected to the security grid. You'll get real-time visuals, remote lock and alarm access. Every door responds to you—or to me."

She took the phone, staring at it. "You rebuilt my entire life."

"I upgraded it."

"Nyx…"

"You needed a safe place," he said, eyes steady. "Now you have one."

Her chest tightened. She wanted to argue—to tell him this was too much, too invasive—but all she could think of was the break-in, the attack in the alley, people being injected. The thought of going back to that world without this between her and it… she couldn't.

She opened her mouth. Closed it again. And shook her head, smiling despite herself. "Jesus. You're not just obsessive, you're thorough."

Lyn Rose

He smirked. "You're mine."

And somehow, that explained everything.

Eden wandered deeper into the space, kicking off her heels as she moved through the living room like someone trying not to wake a dream. Nyx followed at a respectful distance, silent unless she asked.

"Is that… a rainfall shower?" she called from the bathroom, eyes wide.

"And heated floors. You like warmth."

She gave him a look through the doorway. "Have you been stalking me?"

"No," he said, tone dry. "I just remember everything."

Bedroom. Walk-in wardrobe. Floor-to-ceiling windows with blackout controls.

The terrace.

He led her through the final set of glass doors to a private outdoor patio—wrapped with climbing vines, softly lit by recessed lighting that danced across the stone floor. A firepit burned low, casting orange light on a bottle of red and two glasses already waiting on the table.

"You really thought of everything," she said, stepping out into the night air.

Lyn Rose

"I try," he murmured. "Sit. I'll pour."

They settled into the cushioned chairs, the city glittering beyond them. Eden tucked her legs under herself, accepting the glass with a grateful murmur.

They lingered there for a while, the fire warming her skin as the city lights painted Nyx's face in gold and shadow. Every time the bond pulsed, she felt it in her bones—not frantic now, but steady, like a second heartbeat she couldn't imagine losing.

Her laughter came easier now. She looked lighter, freer—until Nyx's phone buzzed.

He glanced at the screen. Evelyn Stroud.

He stood as he answered.

"Stroud."

"Another one," she said, voice clipped. "Fae. Left gutted in a riverbed just outside Ironmere. I have everything I need. It's time. I've called the Accord into emergency session."

Nyx's jaw tensed. "How long ago?"

"Less than an hour. The Department's already securing the site."

He nodded once, eyes narrowing. "Where?"

"The Council Chambers. Midnight."

Lyn Rose

"I'll be there." He hung up.

Eden looked up from her wine. "What is it?"

He met her eyes. "Another death. Fae this time. Stroud's called an emergency Accord meeting."

The easy warmth between them dissolved like mist. Eden sat up straighter, concern flaring in her features.

"What do you need?"

Nyx looked at her for a long beat. "To keep you out of it.

But I know that's not going to happen."

She stood. "Damn right it's not."

He smiled—faint, tired, proud. "Finish your wine, Eden. Then we move."

CHAPTER TWENTY-SEVEN

Ashes of the Covenant

The city felt colder after midnight.

Nyx barely spoke on the drive. Eden sat beside him in the back seat, her hand resting lightly on his thigh, steadying them both. The car hummed through Edalva's wet streets, headlights flashing across glass and steel. Sirens rose somewhere distant—urgent, human noise swallowed by the night.

Tension sat between them like a third passenger. Nyx had already called Jace and Kain—short orders, no explanations. The silence said the rest.

By the time they reached the Council Chambers, the moon hung pale above the skyline. The building rose from the square in clean lines of glass and stone, its lights a cold glare against the dark.

Lyn Rose

Black cars lined the steps. Armed guards waited, eyes sharp, faint wards pulsing across their gear. The air smelled of rain and magic, faint copper beneath it.

Jace and Kain stood by the doors.

Kain's gaze swept over Eden before he pushed the heavy doors open. "You sure about bringing her in?"

"She's already part of this," Nyx said. "No sense pretending otherwise."

Inside, the chambers murmured with restrained hostility. Incense clung to the air, masking the iron scent of fear.

Representatives from every faction filled the circular hall—built for negotiation, ready for war. Witches whispered. A Fae envoy watched, expression unreadable. The wolves crowded together, restless. Torran Black leaned back, arms folded, gaze fixed on Nyx.

Eden stayed close. Every stare followed her. The magic in the room shifted around her presence—subtle, uneasy, alive.

Conversation died.

Then Evelyn Stroud turned from the front of the room, her smile sharp, professional—neither warm nor cold, but a blade wrapped in courtesy.

"Eden. It's good to see you again."

Eden dipped her head, voice steady. "You too, Director."

Lyn Rose

The words landed like a quiet detonation.

From the witches' table, Sevra Wynne rose. Her robes whispered across the marble, eyes fixed on the woman beside Nyx.

"Director," she said, tone brittle with restraint. "I don't feel comfortable proceeding with an unvetted outsider present. This is a sanctioned session of the Sixth Accord. Head representatives only."

Her voice faltered on *outsider*. Recognition struck hard, pupils narrowing before she smoothed it away.

Eden felt that stare—clinical, appraising, almost possessive.

Nyx felt it too.

The sound that left his chest made every supernatural present stiffen. Not a growl. Not a snarl. Something ancient and low—like the ground warning before it split.

"She is my Laç de Sânge," he said, voice contained violence. "And we are bonded."

The chamber rippled with murmurs.

"Impossible."

"A vampire?"

"They don't bond."

"It can't be real—"

He took a step forward, the air dimming, shadows drawing close.

"You have a problem with her presence, Sevra?" he asked, voice low enough to vibrate through the floor. "Say it again."

Sevra's mouth opened, then shut. Colour drained from her face. She muttered something sharp in the Old Tongue—half curse, half disbelief—and lowered herself back into her chair, fingers tightening on the table.

No one dared speak.

Only then did Stroud break the silence, her tone crisp as glass.

"If anyone else has a problem with Miss Marlowe's presence," she said, "take it up with me after the meeting. Until then"—her gaze swept the room—"we move forward."

"We've had deaths across multiple factions," she said, her voice clipped, carrying. "Wolves tearing each other apart. Fae collapsing mid-shift. Witches combusting in ritual. Even humans and vampires left broken in ways we can't explain. Different houses, different times, but the pattern is clear. This is not random. It's orchestrated."

Nyx's voice cut clean through.

"There are two killers." His tone was flat, brutal. "The first—we've all seen the bodies. Deaths that make no sense. Sudden. Violent. Like something inside them was rewired to turn on itself."

He let the chamber feel the weight of that before he continued.

"The second is worse. Not blood loss. Not wounds. The bodies left hollow. Stripped of essence itself." His gaze swept the circle, black eyes sharp as glass. "That isn't chaos. It's design. Someone built this."

The silence that followed was absolute.

"Two killers. Two methods. One hand behind them both."

Stroud turned, meeting eyes like a judge delivering verdicts.

"This is not random. We are out of time."

Torran raised a brow across the room—a silent question. You good?

Nyx nodded once, cold and sure.

She faced each seat in turn.

"And tonight, we find out who the fuck is responsible."

Nyx didn't wait for the room to settle.

"Director," he said, sharp as a blade, commanding every ear, "can I have the room?"

Stroud nodded once. "Of course, Ravelle."

She stepped back, yielding the floor like it belonged to him.

Nyx faced the faction heads, unflinching, his voice flat, brutal.

"We've discovered the origin of the deaths."

No pause. No breath.

"Project Thera."

The word dropped like a curse into the charged silence.

He scanned the room, catching every eye, then settled on Sevra Wynne.

"There was a program," he said, voice precise, measured, "run under Biotech's jurisdiction, disguised as a human IVF facility called TheraGen Labs. Hidden from the Sixth Accord, buried beneath layers of forged medical research. The project involved biochemical experimentation, genetic alteration, and DNA manipulation targeting supernatural markers."

He let the weight of those words settle, sharp and undeniable.

"The purpose was to create something that could rewrite what we are. Cure us. Control us."

"He turned slightly toward Eden without shifting his gaze from Sevra.

'She was Subject A.'

'She was genetically engineered—not for power, but for compatibility. Her blood designed to interface with supernatural systems. To stabilize, suppress, or destroy. A test subject placed unknowingly in the human world after her parents died. Biotech lost track of her.'

The uproar hit like a wave. Nyx's control frayed.

'You're saying that's *her*?'

'A living weapon?'

'If Ravelle's bonded to it—'

'She should be in containment, not beside him!'

His body tensed, shadows curling up his legs like smoke. The air thickened, heavy with pressure. His pupils widened, fangs flashing. The marble beneath his boots cracked.

One more word and he'd lose it— centuries of restraint snapping clean.

Then Eden moved.

Lyn Rose

No hesitation, no fear. She stepped in front of him, her hand finding his chest. Her power brushed his like silk over steel, steadying it.

The change halted. The air stilled. The growl died halfway through his throat.

"I only found this out tonight," she said, her voice carrying over the room. "A week ago, I didn't even know any of this existed."

Her hand stayed on him, grounding him. The faint shimmer of energy between them pulsed once, visible even to the watching crowd.

"And when I met him, it wasn't politics or power." She met Nyx's eyes, unflinching. "It was cellular. Every part of me recognized every part of him."

A quiet smile touched her lips.

The silence that followed was razor-sharp, stretching long before anyone dared breathe again.

Nyx's jaw flexed once. The shadows at his feet drew back, controlled, the storm caged behind his ribs. When he finally spoke, his voice was calm again—too calm.

He stepped forward, closing distance.

"But it wasn't just Eden. There was another." His tone dropped to a dark whisper. "A completed prototype.

Stronger. Feral. Out of control. The one killing your people. Draining them. Consuming magic itself."

Then, quiet—lethal:

"Biotech created it."

Sevra didn't move. Didn't speak. But her eyes flared with fierce heat.

Nyx smiled—cold, sharp, unforgiving.

"We traced funding. Approvals. Authorizations signed by Biotech's acting director."

No name needed.

All eyes turned on her.

Gasps tore the chamber apart.

Sevra sneered, voice cutting through the tension.

"That program was shut down years ago. Even if it existed. You have no proof, Ravelle. Just theories and paranoia."

Nyx didn't flinch. He pulled his phone from his coat, tapped the side.

The projector flickered on.

Lines of data spilled across the wall—blood charts, encrypted reports, classified footage—all stamped with

Biotech's insignia. The final image froze: a requisition order, signed in silver ink.

Sevra Wynne.

Date-stamped.

Biotech seal authenticated.

Gasps ripped the room raw.

And then Stroud stepped forward, her voice ringing like judgment itself.

"The Department has been conducting its own investigation—quiet, internal, thorough. Paper trails, lab records, buried authorizations. We found the same thing he did, and more."

Her words fell like a blade.

"You broke the law of the Accord, Sevra. You violated the pact that binds us. And by Accord Statute 8.4—biological warfare against Accord kin—you are under arrest."

She turned her head.

"Bring them in."

The doors slammed open.

Two enforcers entered, moving like shadows in reinforced black armour. Between them, a third held glowing restraints—pulsing with dampening runes designed to snuff high-level spellcasting.

Sevra backed up a step, voice trembling. "You're making a mistake—"

"Take her," Stroud snapped.

The shackles clicked shut around her wrists. The runes flared.

Magic gone. Power gone.

Her voice drowned in a single pulse of light.

CHAPTER TWENTY-EIGHT

Magic, Mayhem, and a Message

The heavy doors sealed behind the enforcers with a dull, final thud.

Silence lingered like smoke—thick, heavy. A few members shifted, leather creaking, shoes scraping marble. Someone exhaled slowly, breath rattling through the charged air.

Whispers flared beneath the hush.

"Subject A…"

"Living proof."

"She shouldn't even be breathing."

Stroud's glare cut through the noise, silencing it for now, though the unease hung like static in the air.

Nyx didn't sit. He stood near the projector, arms folded tight, eyes like cut obsidian. Eden drifted to his side without a word—close but not touching, a quiet tether keeping him grounded. Her heartbeat carried in the hush, steady against the storm gathering beneath the surface.

Stroud was the first to move. She'd shed her jacket, sleeves rolled to the elbow, fatigue carved deep but gaze still knife-bright. She stepped into the centre, waited until the room obeyed the quiet.

"Sevra is secured. Her seconds are being brought in for questioning." Her tone was even, controlled. "We'll confirm Biotech's full reach and freeze every connected operation until the audit's complete."

A pause. The weight of it sank like stone.

"Take a breath. Regroup. Process."

At the door, she glanced back, a flicker of dry humour breaking the strain.

"We reconvene at four. Every faction, no exceptions. After that…" her mouth curved, faint and tired, "we all need a drink."

No one argued.

But as Stroud left the chamber, the whispers started again—low, distrustful, curling around Eden's name like smoke that refused to clear.

Lyn Rose

Outside, the city pulsed beneath a velvet midnight hush—the strange quiet that hangs between disaster and dawn.

They didn't go far.

Just across from the Council Chambers, down a back alley marked by a rusted sigil and a faded, unlit sign. Eden wouldn't have noticed it if Nyx hadn't guided her in without hesitation.

Halfway down the passage, his hand caught hers, fingers unexpectedly warm against her own. She turned, pulse stuttering, and found herself backed up against the wall— cool, rough stone pressing through her shirt, grounding her in place while the world narrowed to the space between them. His palms caged her face gently, his thumbs brushed along her jaw, familiar and new all at once. She heard the others keep walking, their voices and laughter fading, echoing against the stone corridor.

For a moment, it was just the two of them, suspended in hush and shadow. The scent of him—rain-soaked cotton and the sharp tang of metal—filled her head, unexpectedly tender. Her own heartbeat slammed so hard she could almost feel it in her wrists, her temple, everywhere he touched.

"Are you okay, baby?" The words were rough silk, barely more than a vibration against her cheek, worry tight in his voice.

Her throat worked. "I don't know," she whispered, feeling how close he was, how his breath ghosted over her skin.

Their foreheads touched, and for a second, she swore the world stopped moving.

"You did good in there," he told her, thumb painting warmth along her cheek. She breathed him in, saw her own fear and something fiercer reflected in his eyes.

"Did I?" her voice cracked, soft as a secret.

He nodded, unwavering. "You didn't break. That's what matters."

He kissed her. Slow, anchoring—more vow than comfort, the kind that steadied all the places inside her that still shook. He tasted of cedar and whiskey and a tang of blood, sharp at the edge of his mouth. She savoured it, the press and scrape of him against her, the living, iron warmth of something wild and alive. Everything else dropped away— the chill of the hall, the echo of distant footsteps—until there was only this: the heat, the salt, the grounding grip of the moment.

When he finally drew back, his hand lingered at her jaw, tender and unhurried, before he turned to go.

Farther down, Black was already at the door, the flick of his fingers making metal ring against metal. That click echoed sharply, snapping her back to herself.

Inside, the world softened: amber lighting glowed over dark leather, the hush scented with old books and the sleep-sweet shadow of expensive cologne. Everything in her felt raw and new at the threshold, but steadier somehow—like a weight she'd carried finally made sense.

Kain and Jace were already waiting at the back booth.

"You took your time," Kain said, raising a brow—and then lifting his glass in a silent salute.

We just blindsided a powerful witch, had her arrested, and froze her assets," Black muttered. "Yeah, I think we earned this drink."

Jace slid over smoothly to make space as they joined. Eden sank into the curve of the booth, grateful for the darkness, the warmth, the normalcy—or what passed for it now.

Black poured whiskey, the amber liquid catching the light as it swirled in the glass.

Kain pushed a cocktail in front of Eden. "It's not blood, I swear."

She arched a brow.

He winked. "Just gin and something pink."

Nyx sat close, one arm stretched along the back of the booth, thigh brushing hers. Protective. Always.

Black raised his glass.

"To surviving the first round."

Kain grinned. "And to the girl who walked into the lion's den and didn't flinch."

Glasses lifted.

Eden blinked, caught off guard. "You're toasting me?"

"Damn right we are," Jace said, clinking her glass with his. "You just stared down half the Accord. That's not nothing."

Her laugh was small, real. She lifted her drink. "Then to surviving… whatever this is."

"Fair enough," Black said, smirking. He lifted his glass again toward Eden. "To an incredibly beautiful and impossibly strong woman—who somehow makes the rest of us look underdressed and underqualified."

Eden flushed, half laughing as the others whooped.

Then he leaned in just enough for her to hear, voice low and teasing. "You wouldn't happen to have a friend, would you?"

Kain barked out a laugh, Jace nearly spilled his drink, and even Nyx's mouth twitched—barely—but it counted.

The laughter rolled easy through the booth, breaking what tension remained, the sound soft and human against the hum of rain outside.

They drank. The moment stretched—warm, sharp, a flicker of calm before the next storm.

Lyn Rose

Her phone buzzed in her pocket. She pulled it out and glanced at the screen.

Nyx's eyes flicked down without meaning to—instinct.

Alana: *Hey, gurl, guess what?*

Eden smiled faintly. *Speaking of strong women…*

He looked up just in time to catch the smile tugging at Eden's mouth as her fingers flew across the screen.

Eden: *What's going on? I miss you.*

Typing bubbles.

Gone.

Back again.

Alana: *You know, same same. Oh! Met this guy. Best sex ever. Turned out to be a stalker. Do you mind if I come to Edalva and hang with you for a few days?? PLEASE.*

Eden's grin widened. She tapped back quickly.

Eden: *Oh honey, kill me now. Absolutely. I cannot wait. When you coming??*

Alana: *Three days. Packing my shit now. Getting outta this hellhole.*

Eden: *Fuck yes. Got so much to tell you. Oh, and my umm… apartment had a remodel. I guess you could say it looks a bit different. Text me when you arrive—probs working.*

Alana: *Yeh babe, will do. Eeeekkk can't wait. Hey—any cute guys around?*

Eden bit her lip, smirking.

She glanced across the table.

Nyx—midnight eyes and lethal charm.

Kain—smirk like sin, laughter always a second away.

Jace—quiet, watchful, loyal to the bone.

And Black—the one who could freeze hell with a glance.

Eden: *Sitting at a table with four right now.*

Alana: *Are you serious? Fuck yes. You with any?*

A slow blush crawled up Eden's cheeks as she typed.

Eden: *Yes. Oh yes. The best one.*

Alana: *OH MY GOSH. Really?? Can't wait to meet him. Tell him I'll tear his throat out with my teeth if he hurts you.*

Eden: *He's a good one.*

Alana: *See you soon. Luv you.*

Lyn Rose

Nyx was watching her.

She raised a brow. "What?"

He leaned close—breath warm on her skin. "Four hot guys, huh?"

Her blush deepened. "You were reading that?"

He grazed his lips against her ear. "You've got the best one."

Then, wickedly: "I'll show you how good you actually have it later."

Her thighs pressed together involuntarily.

That was all it took.

A ripple passed through the booth—subtle, unmistakable. Heads turned. Pupils flared. Nostrils flared.

Every supernatural at the table had caught her scent.

Black's laughter broke the spell.

"Fuck's sake, you two—get a room."

Tension snapped. Kain snorted into his drink. Jace raised his glass. Eden laughed, hiding her face in Nyx's shoulder.

They stayed two more hours.

Lyn Rose

Drinking. Laughing. Free, for once, in the space between disasters.

By the time they returned to the Accord chambers, it was nearing 4 a.m. The streets were dark and quiet, but inside the great glass-and-marble hall, something was already stirring.

Not movement. Not sound.

The scent of politics.

Like blood in the air before a hunt.

Eden was definitely tipsy.

Not drunk, not messy—just loose enough to feel it in her bones. The kind of warmth that made the chandeliers shimmer a little too brightly.

She walked beside Nyx, fingers grazing his. He didn't mind, though his eyes stayed sharp, scanning the chamber as they entered.

They were one of the first to arrive.

The silence didn't last long.

From the far corridor, Aleria Vale drifted in like a dream in heels—all glittering bone structure and scandalous grace. Her eyes locked on Eden with too much interest.

"Well," Aleria purred, sauntering up. "Told you you'd end up in our world. Now we should go for a drink."

Lyn Rose

Eden blinked, dazed—starstruck and alcohol-warm—before managing, "Umm… yeah. Sure. Would love that."

Aleria smiled like a cat with a bleeding mouse. She touched Eden's hand lightly. "Drinks, then. Soon."

Before Eden could answer, the main doors slammed open.

Director Stroud strode in like she owned the realm—heels clicking, coat undone, whiskey on her breath and purpose in her spine.

"All right," she called. "I've had a whisky or two and I've got a bed—and a man—waiting for me.

Let's sort this shit."

She dropped into a chair, eyes sweeping the room like a knife.

"Wynne's gone. With her out of the picture, the serum trials should stop—no more wolves tearing each other apart, no more witches burning alive in their own circles. Pray to the gods she was the only one running that game. If there are more labs still active…" She let the thought hang, sharp and unfinished.

"For now, our focus is narrowed. One problem. Subject B."

No room for debate.

"Ravelle. Black. I assume you have a plan?"

Black grinned, rising. "Don't we always?"

Nyx followed, his expression smoothing into that unreadable calm that always came just before a storm.

Eden stood straighter beside him. Her pulse quickened. This was no longer a game.

The game was back on.

Stroud folded her arms. "All right, gentlemen. Impress me."

Black stepped forward, posture loose but eyes deadly serious.

Black's voice dropped lower. "This thing doesn't fight like anything I've seen. It doesn't rush. It waits. Watches. Like it's learning."

Nyx nodded, jaw clenched. "When we engaged it… it didn't just hit hard. It drained."

A silence swept through the room.

He continued, voice sharp. "It touched me for less than a second and I felt my essence being pulled. Not blood. Not magic. Me."

Black added, "It moves fast. Too fast for a creature that size. And it's not just strength—it phases. Slips between shadows like a Reaper, but it's not magic. It's wrong."

Stroud's eyes narrowed. "You saying it's learning from us?"

Lyn Rose

"Worse," Nyx said. "It's adapting."

"We have a plan. Not perfect. But solid enough to give us a fighting chance."

Nyx added, "This creature is stronger than any of us alone. So we're not going in alone."

Nyx tapped the table panel and looked at Jace.

"Run it."

The room dimmed as the wall behind them lit up. Clean, sharp lines carved across the screen. A digital briefing—tactical, unmistakably Virex.

OPERATION: SUBJECT B CONTAINMENT

Midnight Strike | Edenvale Rail Yard

Authorized by the Sixth Accord

OBJECTIVE

Capture Subject B alive.

Use Eden Marlowe's bonded blood as a temporary neutralization agent.

Contain for interrogation; no kill unless authorized.

LOCATION

Edenvale Rail Yard

Spell-fortified perimeter

Surveillance coverage: thermal + aerial

Weather: light rain, 14°C, low wind

ASSIGNED ROLES

VAMPIRES—House Ravelle

• Nyx Ravelle: Field command

• Jace: Surveillance + comms

• Kain: Fast intercept

WOLVES—Pack Blackthorn

• Torran Black: Strike team leader

• Leif Rusk: Flank and herd toward trap

WITCHES—Interim Leader: Evara

• Evara: Spell trap / manacles

• 2 loyalists: Reinforcement + healing

FAE—Mixed Delegates

• Siraeth Lys: Veil Eden

- Faelorin Virelith: Sensory disruption

- Aleria Vale: Confusion projection

HUMANS—DSD Command

- Director Evelyn Stroud: Logistics

- 2 Agents: Off-site medics / transport

EDEN MARLOWE

Role: Bait

Positioned in trap circle

Blood activated on signal

Bonded blood toxic to Subject B

CONTINGENCIES

If trap fails: Phosphorus round backup

If Eden is harmed: Kill override authorized

If escape: Leif + Kain pursuit unit activated

COMMANDERS: RAVELLE + BLACK

United front. No factional divide. No fuck-ups.

The room breathed deeply as the briefing ended.

Nyx's eyes caught Eden's, steady and sure.

The night was far from over.

Lyn Rose

CHAPTER TWENTY-NINE

The Hunt Begins

Stroud's gaze lingered on the glowing strategy screen, the complex web of lines and data painting a fractured future none of them dared to fully face. The soft hum of the room vibrated faintly, settling deep in their bones. The weight of decisions yet to come pressed down on every shoulder. The cold, recycled air carried a faint metallic tang, mingling with the scent of old leather and worn wood—a reminder of countless battles fought and alliances forged here.

"Any questions?"

Hands rose hesitantly. Voices came low and careful—questions about containment zones, timing, proximity spells. Practical concerns stretched thin over raw nerves. Nyx and Black answered with clipped precision, their voices sharp and controlled, cutting through doubt like honed blades.

Then a voice from the back, quiet but impossible to ignore:

"So… who's taking the witches' seat?"

All eyes shifted, the question hanging in the charged silence like a gauntlet thrown down. No one spoke. Nyx didn't hesitate.

"I nominate Evara Vorght."

Black leaned back in his chair, exhaling slow and deliberate, then nodded.

"Seconded."

Stroud arched a brow, the faintest smirk tugging at her lips.

"Thirded. I'll make the call."

Stroud pulled out her phone and dialled. The sharp ring cut through the tension as the line connected.

"Evara, it's Director Stroud. I'm formally requesting your presence at the Council chambers. Immediately."

A pause. Then a voice, steady and cool:

"Understood. On my way."

Fifteen minutes later, the chamber doors hissed open like a drawn blade. Evara entered, each step measured, sure—like she'd owned this floor in some shadowed past. Her black coat hugged her frame, silver-buckled boots striking the stone floor with a crisp echo, like the drumbeat of war. A cold draft from the door brushed her coat as her sharp eyes swept the room, landing on Nyx, then Black, then Eden.

She smiled—a curve that didn't quite reach her eyes.

"Well. This feels ominous."

Her smile softened just a touch, uncertain now.

"What's this about?"

Nyx nodded once. Black lifted two fingers in crisp greeting. Eden offered a small, steady smile back.

Stroud gestured her forward.

"Thank you for coming. I'll be brief."

No wasted breath.

"Sevra Wynne has been arrested. Her second and third are in containment. Biotech is under investigation for violating the Accord. The witch faction is, at present, without leadership."

Evara's eyes narrowed, dark and sharp.

"That's a hell of a power vacuum."

The witch faction had been left leaderless. The Accord stood fractured, hanging by a thread.

Stroud's voice sharpened, cutting through the weight like a knife.

"You've been nominated to serve as interim faction head—with full voting rights."

Evara blinked, caught off guard.

"By who?"

Nyx raised a hand, cold and certain.

"Me."

Black's voice followed, low and steady.

"And me."

Stroud shrugged, almost casual.

"You're the only one I trust not to burn this room down for sport."

Evara let out a breath, the weight pressing down like lead. Then she lifted her chin, resolve hardening like forged steel.

"Then I accept."

Stroud stepped closer, hand raised like a judge's gavel.

"Then by the Sixth Accord, I name you acting faction lead until a formal vote can be held. Your authority is immediate."

Lyn Rose

Evara raised her hand, the oath binding her with a shimmer of ancient magic—fragile but unbreakable.

Stroud leaned in, voice low but sharp.

"Now go. Gather your most trusted second and third. You're on containment and magical reinforcement."

Evara's nod was tight, her face hardening further.

"Understood."

And just like that, the circle closed.

Stroud's eyes flicked to the glowing time marker in the corner of the projection—"6:02 AM."

She swept the room, catching the faces of vampires, wolves, witches, reapers, Fae—all bound now by more than politics.

"We strike at midnight. Go home. Rest. You've got twelve hours."

A tired smirk played at her lips—a prayer and a curse both.

"And for the love of the gods, no one get killed before then."

Chairs scraped back, the screen blinked dark, and quiet footsteps echoed as each faction peeled off into the waking city.

Nyx didn't move. Neither did Eden.

Black clapped once, sharp and final, then tapped Nyx on the shoulder.

"Midnight, then."

Nyx's jaw tightened.

"Midnight."

They parted, each carrying the weight of what was to come.

Nyx needed supplies and equipment. They went home.

The drive back to Duskwatch was quiet, the city slipping past in muted shades of dawn. The distant hum of early traffic blended with soft birdcalls, the air cool and still. Neither spoke—not out of discomfort, but because the day had caught up with them. Between the blood, the bond, the Council… and the looming plan… words felt unnecessary.

The underground gate scanned the car, recognizing Nyx instantly. The heavy doors slid open with a hiss, swallowing them into darkness.

He pulled into the far bay and shut off the engine. Silence wrapped around them like a suffocating coat.

Eden didn't move.

Nyx turned toward her.

"Eden."

She blinked, eyes wide and struggling to focus, like she was trying to hold onto something slipping away.

"Baby," he said softer, brushing fingers along her thigh—a whisper of warmth in the cold quiet. "Talk to me."

She exhaled, breath heavy with everything she'd been holding back, then gave a small, tired smile—frayed at the edges.

"I'm scared, Nyx. Exhausted. And I just…" Her voice wobbled, fragile.

"I just wanted to be normal."

A dry laugh escaped her lips, bitter and resigned.

"Not that I ever was, really. I think I knew that somewhere. But I was good at pretending, you know? Now it's just…"

"Too real," he murmured, voice a low anchor.

She nodded, breath catching, tears threatening but never falling.

"Yeah."

He leaned over and kissed her—slow, steady, not hungry this time. Just there. Grounding.

"Come," he said against her mouth.

"Let's sleep."

Lyn Rose

He opened the door and came around, helping her out like she weighed nothing. She didn't let go of his hand as they crossed the garage, nor in the elevator, nor when they stepped into the soft dark of his room.

Nyx turned her gently by the waist and helped her undress— her clothes too tight from the changes in her body. Careful. Reverent. Like every inch of her was sacred ground.

He led her into the bathroom and turned on the water—hot and steady. The scent of soap and steam filled the air. Under the spray, he washed her—slow circles over her back, arms, legs. Then dried her off with a thick towel and pulled one of his shirts over her head. It hung off her like a dress.

She yawned, swaying slightly.

"You're good at this."

"I want to be good to you," he said softly.

He pulled back the duvet and tucked her in, kissing her forehead, then lips, then the tip of her nose.

As he turned to leave, her hand caught his.

"Stay?" she whispered.

His throat tightened.

He nodded, sat to pull off his boots, then climbed in behind her—one arm looping over her waist, the other sliding beneath her pillow.

Lyn Rose

Eden sighed and melted into him.

Sleep took her in seconds.

Nyx didn't dream. Not usually.

He didn't need sleep like mortals did. A few hours a week kept his senses razor-sharp, mind honed. But with Eden's warmth pressed against him, heartbeat syncing with the new rhythm in his veins—something in him surrendered. For once, he wanted the stillness. Needed the solitude her body gave.

For two hours, he slept like the dead.

When he jolted awake, it was with a sharp inhale—instinct clawing up his spine before his mind caught up.

The room was still dark, curtains drawn tight against dawn.

He blinked at the time: 9:03 AM.

He hadn't moved once.

Slowly, Nyx leaned away from Eden, careful not to wake her. She made a small sound—a breath, a murmur—but stayed under. He watched her for five more minutes, letting her presence soak through the lingering haze in his bones.

He'd memorised her before—the exact curve of her lips when she was too tired to guard them, the way her breathing shifted when her dreams turned dark.

Lyn Rose

But now… there was more.

The faint, impossible gold that bled into her eyes when the light caught them just right, gone again in a blink like it had never been. The way her skin seemed lit from somewhere beneath, not with heat, but with something alive and old. Even her scent—richer now, layered, threaded through with a note that woke instincts he'd spent a century controlling.

He could feel the bond humming under her skin, an echo in his own veins. Not just a tether—a pulse.

She hadn't seen all the changes yet. Maybe she never would, not the way he did. But he knew. The night he saved her had made her more than she was. More than human. More than vampire. More than him, maybe.

And he didn't know whether that truth terrified him… or made him want to burn the world to keep it.

Then he stood.

Still in yesterday's clothes, he felt the hum of blood adjusting to the bond.

He stepped into the hall and checked his phone.

Three missed calls. Three messages.

Shit.

First: a message from Evara—direct, clean, promising.

"Thank you for your trust. I'll do right by the witches. And the Accord."

Second: Jace.

"Update: Meeting at Duskwatch or elsewhere? Tech gear—bring from Virex or leave secured?"

Kain added his own flair beneath:

"Morning, Sleeping Beauty. We assume you're alive unless Eden drained you dry. Let us know where."

Nyx huffed. Idiots.

Then the calls.

Two from Black.

First voicemail: "Pick up, fucker."

Second: "Call me ASAP. It's about my wolves."

Nyx's jaw locked.

The third call came from a number he didn't recognize. No message. No ID.

But something in his chest went tight.

He tapped the screen and called Black back.

It rang once before the line picked up.

"Where the fuck have you been?" Black growled.

Nyx's voice dropped to a calm, lethal thread.

"Sleeping. Talk."

A pause.

"We've got a problem. Another one of mine is dead."

Nyx's spine straightened.

"Who?"

Black exhaled hard.

"A scout. Young. Nick. Running patrol past the Breakline ridge."

Nyx closed his eyes. Too close.

"How bad?"

"Found at dawn. Nothing left but skin and bones. Drained, hollowed out—the same. But this wasn't random. It was a message."

Nyx paced, voice sharp.

"You sure it's Subject B?"

"Unless something else out there drains life and leaves corpses? Yeah. I'm sure."

Lyn Rose

Nyx leaned on the counter, jaw tight.

"Where's the body?"

"Cold vault," Black said, voice low and tight. "Secured. Not moved. I wanted your eyes on it first."

Nyx nodded even though Black couldn't see it.

"I'll be there in an hour. No one touches it until I do."

A beat of silence.

Then Nyx's voice hardened.

"Black—"

"What?"

"If this thing is circling your territory after the bodies we've already pulled out of your forests, it's not random. It's hunting wolves."

Black gave a dark, humourless laugh.

"Good. Let it try me."

Nyx didn't share the amusement.

"I'm serious. It's killed too many of your people already. If it pushes further—"

"Let it try," Black cut in, voice dropping to something feral. "I'll tear it open and drink whatever keeps it living."

Nyx's jaw clenched. "Just don't underestimate it."

Black exhaled sharply—resolve, not fear.

"You too."

Click.

Nyx stared at the phone a beat longer, tension humming beneath his skin. Then he looked down the hall.

She still slept. Peaceful. Oblivious.

And he intended to keep it that way.

Nyx strode into his private office at Duskwatch.

The screens hummed. Fingers moved faster than thought as he slipped into encrypted logs.

Caller ID: Unknown.

Return: Blocked.

Trace: Failed.

He narrowed his eyes.

"Nothing's untraceable."

Within seconds, he rerouted raw signal data through Virex's shadow net—a system he designed to track supernatural black calls. He decrypted the audio header, isolated a ping.

Location: Outer Industrial Zone. Unlisted. Abandoned Research Facility.

Last Registry: TheraGen Labs.

The name stared at him like a ghost.

TheraGen. The original shell company for Project Thera. The place Eden was made.

Supposed to be destroyed ten years ago.

His eyes narrowed.

He replayed the voicemail. Male voice, raspy, unused for years.

"She wasn't the only one. You don't know the full scope of Project Thera. If you want the truth… come alone."

Click.

No name. No coordinates. Just static and a threat buried in curiosity.

He gripped the desk edge.

"Fuck."

CHAPTER THIRTY

She Was Never Just Eden

The clock on the bedroom wall blinked 9:31 AM, its cold digits cutting through the quiet like a sharp reminder of time slipping away. Nyx stood at the edge of the bed, arms folded tight across his chest, watching the gentle rise and fall of Eden's chest beneath the oversized shirt he'd given her—the same one she was still wrapped in from the night before. The sleeves bunched at her wrists, and her dark hair fanned across the pillow like spilled ink, soft and unreal.

She looked fragile there, like a candle flame flickering in a draft. He should've let her sleep longer. Should've stayed with her until the world felt less sharp and dangerous. But he didn't. Couldn't.

"Eden," he said, voice low and uneven.

No movement.

He knelt beside the bed and brushed his knuckles lightly down her cheek. Her skin was still damp from sleep, cool and smooth beneath his touch.

"Baby," he murmured, breaking the silence.

Her eyes fluttered open—slow, reluctant—like she was waking from a dream that didn't want to end. She blinked against the morning light filtering through the curtains, gaze hazy and heavy.

"Mmm… what time is it?"

"Almost nine-thirty," he answered, voice steady but soft. "I have to go."

The words pried her awake more fully. Her body shifted, pushing up on one elbow, eyes wide with sudden alertness.

"What? Why? What happened?"

Nyx caught her hand, holding it firmly in his. His thumb traced small, absent circles over her knuckles.

"There's been another death. Wolf territory."

She froze—still as stone.

"Subject B?"

He nodded, voice grim.

"Black called me thirty minutes ago. Said it got a scout. Young one. Nick. Running patrol past Breakline Ridge." His mouth tightened.

"That makes six dead. But this time, the trail's fresh—we can follow it before it goes cold."

Her brows furrowed, worry creasing her delicate features.

"You might not come back."

Nyx stilled.

The room seemed to hold its breath around them, the weight of the morning pressing down where warmth and safety had been moments ago. Finally, Eden's voice came again—quieter now, stripped bare.

"And me?"

"You stay here."

Her body straightened, tension snapping into her spine.

"Nyx—"

Before she could say more, his hand cupped her jaw, tilting her face gently to meet his eyes.

"Kain's already here. He's outside now. He'll stay with you. You don't leave Duskwatch. If you need something, he'll handle it."

Her gaze searched his, vulnerable but fierce.

She said it plainly.

"You're scared."

Nyx swallowed hard, the motion visible at his throat. "Yes." His voice dropped, rough and honest. "I'm scared of losing you. Of something getting through those walls while I'm gone. Of what I'd become if it did."

He cupped her face, thumbs brushing her jaw, the weight of his gaze pinning her still. "You're safe here. No one gets past Duskwatch. Promise me you'll stay until I get back."

Her breath trembled, but she nodded.

His forehead pressed to hers for one quiet second. "Good," he said — and the relief in his voice was obvious.

He leaned down, pressing a kiss to her forehead—a silent promise.

"You'll be safe."

Her voice was softer still.

"You'll come back?"

"Always."

He lingered just a moment longer, the space between them charged with everything neither dared say. Then he stood and moved toward the door.

"Kain!" he called into the hall.

The door cracked open, and Kain appeared, a smirk tugging at his lips, a coffee in one hand and a protein bar in the other.

Lyn Rose

"Heard everything. Go kill a monster. I'll guard the girl."

Eden narrowed her eyes, but Kain only grinned wider.

"I'm not just a girl."

Kain's gaze flicked down and back up, slow and obvious.

 "Oh, you're definitely not a girl."

A low sound tore from Nyx's chest—not a growl, not quite a snarl, but something dark and warning.

Kain's smirk sharpened, unbothered, but he lifted his hands in mock surrender.

Nyx didn't smile, but his eyes softened as he looked back at Eden.

Then he was gone.

Nyx arrived at Breakline Ridge,   and the forest edge reeked of ash and fur, the scent thick and raw in the dawn air. Nyx stepped through the wards, meeting Black beside the body, the dim morning light barely piercing the canopy. The stench hit first—iron sharp and bitter, bile sour beneath it, singed hair lingering like a ghost. Yet beneath that, something new—something colder.

It was unnervingly quiet here.

Wrong.

The wolf's corpse lay sprawled in defiance of nature, ribs caved inward, the body collapsed from the inside out. No wounds. No blood. Just a hollowed shell where life used to be.

Nyx crouched beside it, the air around him sharpening.

"Subject B," he said. Not a guess. A verdict.

Black's jaw tightened. "Same signature. Same damn emptiness."

"No spray," Nyx murmured. "No tearing. No toxin."

"Just drained," Black finished, voice low. "Like the others."

A stillness settled between them — too deep, too final.

The forest didn't stir.

No insects, no wind, nothing alive daring to breathe near the corpse.

Only a distant birdcall, a thin breeze through branches, and the faint static hum of violence that still clung to the air.

Finally, Black broke the silence, voice low and raw.
"My pack's rattled."

Nyx stood slowly, eyes sharp.
"Understandable."

"No," Black snapped, jaw tight, voice edged with something sharper than fear—anger. "You think it's just this? It's not just the bodies. Ten of our women vanished the last couple months. Ten, Nyx. Gone on patrol, never came back. No tracks, no scent. Mothers. Sisters. Mates. And I can't give anyone answers. I can't even promise it won't be them next." His fists clenched at his sides, trembling. "They look at me and see someone who can't protect his own. Some of them are saying it out loud now—whispering that I'm slipping. That maybe I'm too distracted, too weak. That a leader without a mate isn't worth following."

Nyx put a heavy hand on his friend's back.
"Tonight, we contain this. You hold your ground. And we get your pack back—together, in line. We'll find the women, Black. We don't stop until we do."

Black gave a bitter laugh, the sound rough.
"Yeah. That'll make me look strong—getting help from a vampire."

Nyx arched a brow.
"You're not just getting help from a vampire. You're getting help from me."

That earned a smirk.
"Know anyone who might want to be my mate?"

"Not unless you want Kain. But he might break you in."

Black barked a laugh.
"Pass."

Nyx's face darkened.

"Got a call this morning."

"From?"

"No one. Blocked, encrypted. Number rerouted six times. Had to hack Virex's shadow net to trace the signal. Took me thirty seconds."

Black raised a brow.

"Of course it did."

Nyx flipped to the decrypted audio log.

"Guess where it came from?"

"Don't say Biotech."

"No. Worse. TheraGen."

Black went still, voice dropping to a whisper.

"The original site?"

Nyx nodded once.

"Abandoned ten years ago. Supposedly destroyed. But ping came from there—two hours ago."

Black swore under his breath.

"Shit."

Nyx hit play. A raspy male voice crackled through the speaker, raw and frayed like it hadn't been used in years.

"She wasn't the only one. You don't know the full scope of Project Thera. If you want the truth… come alone."

Click.

No name. No coordinates. Just a threat wrapped in a riddle.

Black exhaled hard.

"Well. Fuck."

Nyx's jaw clenched.

"We go. Just us."

"You think it's a trap?"

"Definitely."

Black cracked his knuckles.

"Good. I've been waiting to break something."

The car ride was silent.

Nyx and Black sat like statues, the tension between them thick enough to choke on—not hostile, but electric. Focused.

Outside, Edalva's skyline blurred into the industrial sprawl, the sun casting harsh light through tinted glass. Nearly 11:00 AM.

Black shifted in his seat.

"You sure the call wasn't a trap?"

Nyx's grip tightened on the wheel.

"No. But I'm not walking in blind."

"You never do," Black muttered, cracking his neck.

"Still don't like the timing. Not with tonight."

"Neither do I." Nyx's eyes didn't leave the road.

"But if there's truth buried in that message, I want it before this bastard kills again."

They turned off the main road, diving into the forgotten industrial zone. Rusted fences, faded signs, and buildings abandoned a decade ago loomed around them.

They stopped before a half-collapsed gate.

TheraGen Labs.

The shell company behind Project Thera. Officially shut down ten years ago, supposedly destroyed in fire. But the bones remained—broken, but not dead.

Black stepped out first, boots thumping on concrete.

"You smell that?"

Nyx nodded.

"Old blood. Copper. Mold. And something fresh."

He let the change ripple through him—eyes shifting, mind sharpening. He could hear everything now.

They moved as one.

Down twisted corridors, past bent stairwells and scorched signs.

Until they found it.

A door half-hidden behind a false wall. The biometric panel torn out, replaced by a mechanical lock rigged from the inside.

Nyx knocked once. Twice.

Silence.

Then metal scraped. A hiss. The door cracked—

And a rifle stared back.

Held by an old man with trembling hands.

White hair, grey beard, eyes bloodshot like he hadn't slept in years. His coat hung like a shroud.

The gun didn't drop.

Not until recognition flickered.

"Mr. Ravelle," he whispered. "Mr. Black."

The weapon lowered, fingers trembling.

"I never thought you'd come."

The man ushered them inside quickly, glancing over his shoulder like the shadows themselves might reach out to snatch him. The door slammed shut behind them, the heavy steel locking with a definitive clang. An arcane ward shimmered faintly in the dim light, cutting off the outside world.

Inside, the bunker breathed a different kind of life—dim strips of emergency power cast long shadows over cluttered metal tables piled with yellowed papers, dust-coated monitors flickering with static, and tangled wiring that looked barely held together. It was a place forgotten by time but fiercely guarded by memory.

The old man's hands still trembled as he turned to face Nyx and Black, his eyes sharp despite their bloodshot haze.

Thorn's eyes narrowed, studying Nyx.

"You fed from her, didn't you?"

Nyx didn't flinch.

"Yes."

The man exhaled, like he'd been holding that breath for a decade.

"The differences… they're significant. Aren't they?"

Nyx's mind flickered—unbidden—to the morning light spilling across her in the bathroom mirror. How her irises had flared to molten gold before bleeding back to the warm brown he knew. How her hair caught the light like spun obsidian, thicker, heavier in his hands. How her frame had honed itself, subtle but undeniable, how her body had decided overnight to become something that could survive anything—*even him*. She'd caught him watching, and he'd only smiled, hiding the part of him that wanted to drag her back to bed just to map every change.

"More than you know," he said at last.

The old man's gaze darkened.

"I would love to study the shift. Document it. Test the boundaries."

"We don't have time," Nyx cut him off, voice sharp as a blade.

Black's form loomed, half-shifted and tense, ready for everything and nothing. His eyes darted between them, jaw tightening at whatever Thorn was implying about Eden.

The old man nodded, understanding the gravity of the moment.

"No, we don't. I'm Dr. Toby Thorn. One of the lead geneticists on Project Thera—back when it was disguised as a human-facing IVF program."

His eyes flicked to Nyx, haunted.

"I worked at TheraGen Labs until the day it burned. Or rather… until they burned us."

He moved toward a battered terminal, the screen flickering to life with a ghost of its former self.

"I've been hiding ever since. Watching. Waiting. Hoping none of the others succeeded in waking Subject B."

Nyx's voice dropped lower, grim.

"They didn't just wake him. He's out. Killing."

Dr. Thorn's fingers hovered over the keyboard, hesitant, haunted.

"Then it's already started."

Black growled low, voice thick with anger.

"What is it? What the hell did you people make?"

The old man looked at them both, eyes hollow yet fierce.

"Not just a weapon. Not even a monster. Something that adapts to whatever magic it consumes… then perfects it."

Nyx's eyes narrowed. Black's lip curled, a low, animal sound in his throat.

Thorn turned the monitor toward them, revealing encrypted logs, DNA helixes twisting in cold blue light, and photos of infants with barcodes burned into their skin.

"Eden, as you know, is not the only one," Thorn whispered, voice cracking.

"But she was the first. The only one whose blood could bind—or destroy—the others."

The weight of his words pressed down like a stone in Nyx's chest. Black's fists curled until the knuckles whitened, his wolf raging at the idea of Eden marked as either weapon or executioner.

"And that," Thorn added, voice low and bitter, "is why you're here."

CHAPTER THIRTY-ONE

Lust, Lies, and the Lure of Blood

Eden

Eden tugged at the hem of Nyx's oversized black shirt—still faintly scented like him, a mix of cedarwood and something darker, almost musky with the faint sweat of his skin—and paced the edge of the lounge, barefoot on the cool polished floor. The smoothness grounded her restless energy, while the fabric clung soft and worn against her skin, carrying a weight of him she wasn't ready to shed.

Kain sprawled across the leather couch like a sun-drenched cat, arms spread, boots kicked up, watching her with amused laziness.

The scent of leather lingered, touched with old whiskey and a trace of smoke, like a fire recently died out.

She stopped near the window, folding her arms, skin still humming — not from movement now, but from the absence of him.

Lyn Rose

"You're going to wear a hole in the floor," he said without bothering to sit up.

"I can't wear this tonight," she said, voice smooth as glass. "No one's going to listen to me dressed like this."

Kain opened his mouth, but she cut him off with a smile that wasn't entirely sweet.

"You're a strong protector, right?" she said lightly. "You'll keep me safe while I change?"

He blinked, caught between pride and suspicion.

"Yeah," he said slowly. "Yeah, I will."

"Good." Her smile sharpened. "Then let's go."

Eden smiled, faint but real, lavender drifting in through the open window. "Just… don't hit on anyone this time."

He grinned. "No promises. But I'll try and behave until we're back."

She rolled her eyes and followed him out.

The sun climbed higher, slanting through the Duskwatch trees in gold, painting shifting patterns across the car as Eden slid inside. The damp scent of earth drifted through the cracked window, tangled with faint city noise—sirens, voices, tires on wet asphalt.

Kain leaned against the driver's door, easy grin in place.

Lyn Rose

"Ready to risk your life for fashion?" he asked, opening it with a mock bow.

"I need clothes that don't belong to your boss," she said, slipping in.

"You sure? You wear Ravelle pretty well. Could start a trend—blood-bound streetwear."

She snorted. "You're ridiculous."

"No, I'm easy," Kain said with a wink. "Just not in the way you're thinking."

Eden rolled her eyes and shoved his arm.

"Gross."

Kain laughed, unbothered, shifting gears with that lazy, too-confident ease that lived in his bones.

"You are pretty chill," she said once his grin settled.

"Yeah, well. When your boss is half shadow and your best friend treats brawling like foreplay, you learn to pick your vibe."

Eden laughed, tension easing from her shoulders. For a moment, with the hum of the engine and sunlight on glass, the world almost felt normal.

Halfway through the drive, Kain slid his sunglasses down his nose and checked his phone.

Lyn Rose

Still nothing.

He snorted. "His Darkness is ignoring me. Again."

Eden glanced over. "Nothing from Nyx?"

"He'll show up if there's a problem." Kain tossed the phone onto the console. "He always does."

She breathed out, some part of her unwinding.

"Do you always call him that?" she asked.

Kain smirked. "Only when he deserves it."

The rest of the drive slipped by in easy banter and low music, humming beneath their voices.

Kain pulled up at the curb outside Lyon Crescent in the Westmere District.

They stepped out, doors thudding softly in the quiet street.

"Home sweet—well, newly remodelled—home," he said, killing the engine.

Eden took in the sleek façade, brow furrowed. "It still weirds me out how different it looks."

"Yeah," Kain said, stretching as he stepped out. "Boss doesn't do anything half-assed. When he says secure, he means fortress."

They stepped into the private elevator.

Kain leaned back against the mirrored wall, hands in his pockets, while Eden watched the numbers climb.

Ding.

The doors opened directly into her apartment. Or what used to be her apartment.

She paused at the threshold. The air smelled new—fresh paint, wood polish, lavender and lemon. Sharp. Clean. Too clean.

"Shit," she whispered, eyes sweeping the open layout. "It really does take up the whole floor now."

Kain followed, low whistle cutting the quiet. "Told you. Boss doesn't mess around. You should've seen the security team last week—pretty sure half of them could've killed me with a pen."

Eden dropped her bag on the new leather couch and turned slowly. Everything was replaced. New furniture. New walls. Her fingers drifted along the marble counter, touching, testing whether it was real.

A flicker in the glossy backsplash caught her—just a shimmer, but enough. Her irises flashed molten gold before cooling back to brown. The phantom pulse in her veins thrummed harder, echoing the mark Nyx left. Even the cotton of her shirt felt different against her skin—too vivid, too alive.

She smiled faintly. "Still feels like mine, though."

"Good," Kain said, dropping onto the couch. "Means you can stop living in a vampire's lair and finally pick out socks without supervision."

"I'll wait here," Kain said, stretching out on the couch. "Unless you need help picking out clothes." He lifted one brow, lazy grin in place.

Eden paused in the doorway, hand on her hip. "You wish."

He chuckled, settling deeper into the cushions. "No, actually—hard pass. I like my head where it is."

Eden laughed, soft but real, and vanished down the hall. She pulled off Nyx's shirt, the fabric whispering across her skin, then tugged a plain white tee over her head.

Nyx

The bunker's air was thick with dust and ghosts.
Nyx stood over the old lab terminal, screens flickering faintly as Dr. Thorn's fingers flew across the keys. Layers of ancient code peeled back, exposing raw files beneath security protocols long since abandoned. The low hum of the terminal and the faint clatter of fingertips filled the stale room.

Lyn Rose

Thorn stopped typing. His hands hovered above the keyboard.

"After we lost Eden," he said quietly, "Biotech changed the protocol. Implanted trackers in the spinal tissue of every subject. Off-grid. Undetectable. They didn't want to lose another asset."

Nyx said nothing.

Thorn went on. "When I started hearing about the deaths—the ones with no consistent energy signature—I knew it wasn't random. I accessed the local backup server. It's the only place the tracker data still lives."

He turned back to the keys.

"The tracking data was stored off-grid," he muttered. "This terminal piggybacks the old system. No external alert pings—Accord never knew it existed."

"Show me," Nyx said. His voice was calm, but his eyes burned.

The map blinked to life—a skeletal layout of the city, dotted with red pulses. Two signals were archived as terminated. One was active. Moving.

Thorn pointed. "That's Subject B. We thought it was dormant. But someone reactivated it. Someone let it loose."

"It's hunting," Black growled from behind them, arms folded. The scent of oil and sweat clinging to him. "Look at the path."

The signal pulsed again.

Current location: Westmere District.

A second later, the dot moved.

Direction: North-northwest.

Thorn frowned. "Still on the move…"

Nyx leaned in. "Zoom in."

The screen sharpened. Street grids. Landmarks.

"It's cutting across Fairfax," Thorn muttered. "Wait—just stopped again."

The dot hovered at an intersection. Then turned.

Moved again. Slower now.

Nyx's eyes narrowed. "Where is that?"

The map adjusted.

Lyon Crescent.

Nyx froze.

The signal stopped. Right in front of a mid-rise apartment block.

His stomach flipped.

"No."

He yanked out his phone.

One new message.

Kain: Hey Boss. Taking the little lady to her apartment. Needs clothes or something. She's safe. In and out.

The timestamp hit him like a punch to the chest.

Sent 20 minutes ago.

Nyx looked up, eyes flashing.

"Eden's there."

Black's head jerked up. "I thought she was at Duskwatch."

Nyx said nothing.

The shift tore through him—bones cracking beneath flesh, pupils flaring silver, his jaw sharpening like the bite behind a promise.

He shoved the chair back, snarling,

"Let's fucking go."

Eden

Lyn Rose

The sharp chime of the security system shattered the quiet.

Eden blinked, turning toward the screen by the door—but Kain was already moving. He crossed to the wall panel, eyes narrowing as he scanned the alert. His fingers flew, pulling up the external camera feed.

A woman stood downstairs—hair wild, sunglasses pushed up on her head, a hot pink tote slung over one shoulder. She jabbed at the intercom like it owed her money.

"What the fuck— Which button am I pressing? Jesus—okay, I'm just gonna press them all."

BEEP. BEEP. BEEEEP.

"EDEN! Are you up there? In there somewhere?!"

BEEP. BEEEEP

Kain glanced over his shoulder. "Who's the hot mess express downstairs? Because—damn."

Eden's face lit up. "Eeeek! Alana!" She darted over and hit the intercom. "Yes! I'm here! I'll buzz you in—"

"Buzz me in?" Alana snapped, clearly talking over the speaker. "What is this, Fort Fucking Knox? Just—come down and get me!"

Kain grinned. "She always like this?"

"She's had caffeine and probably an orgasm today. So…
yes."

"I like her already."

Eden giggled, punching in the code to unlock the door. "Top
floor, Alana! Come up!"

A few minutes later, the elevator dinged.

Kain moved to the front panel, tapping the override Nyx had
given him. The lock clicked. A soft chime answered, and the
door swung open with force.

Alana exploded through it like a glitter bomb.

"Bitch!" she shrieked, arms flung wide.

"Bitch!" Eden squealed right back.

They collided in the centre of the foyer—tangled limbs,
shrieking laughter, perfume and chaos. Alana smelled like
coconut, vanilla, and faint lust—like a summer cocktail with
teeth. Her tote hit the floor with a thud.

"You look like sex and secrets!" Alana declared, stroking
Eden's hair.

"You look like a flight risk," Eden shot back, laughing.

Kain leaned against the wall, arms folded, watching the
reunion unfold. His phone blinked on the couch behind him,
forgotten.

Lyn Rose

"Hot friends and chaos," he muttered, amused. "Yeah… I'm definitely watching this."

Inside, the apartment was warm and open—modern elegance softened by Eden's touches. The girls kicked off their shoes and collapsed onto the couch, laughter bubbling like champagne.

Kain perched on the back of the sectional, elbows on his knees, smirk sharp and lazy. His presence didn't press—it hummed, steady and amused.

Alana finally clocked him.

She blinked, then grinned like a predator spotting dessert.

"Oh hell yes. Is this him?"

Eden snorted. "What? No—"

Kain clutched his chest, mock-wounded. "Eden. Please. After everything we shared."

Alana burst out laughing. "He's cheeky. I like him."

Eden groaned. "Alana, Kain. Kain, Alana."

He gave a two-finger salute. "Glorified bodyguard, at your service."

Alana raised a brow. "Bodyguard with a face like that? Baby, I feel *very* protected."

Kain's grin deepened, gaze sweeping her like he already knew the temperature of her blood. "Flirting already? Careful. We haven't even made out yet."

"Don't tempt me," Alana purred.

"Oh my god," Eden muttered, flopping back. "This is going to be a nightmare."

"Correction," Kain said. "This is going to be fun."

"Oops," Eden shifted. "I'm sitting on your phone."

Kain grinned. "If it was vibrating, feel free to keep it there. I'll watch."

Alana choked on her drink. "You are filth."

"The best kind," he said smoothly, reaching for the phone without breaking eye contact.

Eden rolled her eyes and handed it over. "Here. Try not to flirt with it."

As Kain took it, Alana looped an arm through Eden's. "Come on, show me around this gorgeous upgrade. I want to see what 'remodel' really means."

They disappeared down the hall, still laughing.

Kain glanced at the phone.

The smirk vanished.

Lyn Rose

Ten missed calls. Five messages.

From Nyx. From Jace. From Black.

He tapped the latest one.

Jace: *GET THE FUCK OUT, KAIN. NOW.*

Then—

Nyx: *She's not safe. It's coming. GET HER OUT.*

And finally—

Black: *CREATURE'S MOVING. HEADED TO EDEN.*

Kain launched off the couch like a bullet.

"Eden—!"

CHAPTER THIRTY-TWO

When Beauty Turns Deadly

Kain didn't think. Didn't breathe. He just moved, every nerve ablaze with instinct.

"EDEN!"

His voice cracked through the apartment like a gunshot, ricocheting off tile and glass as he tore down the hall. The girls didn't answer.

The silence closed in, sudden and brutal. He cursed, eyes wild, and slammed his palm against the wall panel. No signal on the tracker—of course there wasn't. She was still in the apartment. The familiar green blip pulsed tauntingly, refusing him answers.

Where would she go?

The balcony? No. Not open.

The roof.

Lyn Rose

He launched himself into the stairwell like a freight train, taking the steps two at a time, muscles burning, breath tearing in and out, barely registering the pain. He vaulted the last flight, shoes skidding on concrete.

Then—

A scream.

High. Sharp. Eden.

Kain shoved the door open with enough force to splinter the frame, wood cracking under his grip.

The wind hit first—cold, biting, slicing across his skin and filling his lungs with the taste of sunlight and iron. Then the stench. Copper. Death. Burned magic, thick and electric, lingering on his tongue. It made his eyes water, made his heart pound even harder, if that was possible.

At the far edge of the rooftop, beneath the glint of early sun filtering through bruised, heavy clouds, he saw them.

A figure.

Male. Or once male.

The hoodie clung like skin, soaked in blood, fabric stiff and glistening in patches where it hadn't dried. His face was still hidden beneath the shadow of the hood, but his stance was wrong. Not tense. Not poised. Just… still. Like the cold didn't touch him. Like breath wasn't required. Like he didn't belong to this world—or maybe he'd been carved out of it.

He sniffed the air.

Slow. Intentional.

Head tilted, lips parted just enough to reveal jagged teeth—too long, too uneven. Like they'd been forced into a mouth not meant to hold them.

Alana stood frozen between him and Eden. A glow flickered over her skin, smooth and unnatural, like light refracting through oil. The air shimmered around her like a heat mirage, distorting her silhouette into something ethereal. One hand curled into a claw—not for casting, but for *feeding*. She hadn't moved, but something in her was already waking.

Eden stepped back, her bare feet scraping against the rooftop tile. The city heat pulled at her, sweat slick beneath a white shirt that clung to her spine and ribs. Her hair stuck to her face, tangled and wet.

She barely dared to breathe as the thing raised its head again and sniffed—a wet, hungry sound that made her flinch. Then it smiled. Not at Alana. At her.

Its tongue swept along cracked lips, grotesque and deliberate, the motion making Eden's stomach turn. When the hood fell away, her mind jolted: not just a face, but a warning. Stitched skin pulled tight across bones that made no sense, scars in broken patterns across jaw and cheek. One eye was clouded, filmy: the other burned bright, almost fevered, never blinking.

Lyn Rose

He breathed in with a sound that rattled, too thick and slow, harsh in the stillness.

Eden's skin crawled. This wasn't fear alone. This was something more ancient, shutting out language, waking an old, electric terror in her bones.

He watched her, nostrils flaring like he could sort every note of her scent from the air. His mouth twisted wider, exposing more teeth, almost savouring each breath between them. Her pulse thudded hard, and he mirrored it, his head jerking with perfect, predatory rhythm.

He wanted her blood. Her breath. Her heart. There was no hiding it. The rooftop air seemed to seize up, thick and sharp, until she felt she might choke.

She stood frozen, heartbeat pounding in her ears, as the world seemed to winnow down to the space between them. She saw his eyes—cold and wild, glinting with something manufactured, unnatural. Not a mistake. A promise of what she might have become, if Biotech had finished the job.

Eden ripped her gaze away, fingers curled against the wall to keep herself grounded.

Kain moved— the only thing alive in the freeze of panic.
A shadow behind the creature: silent, graceful, eyes lit with something dark and ancient, fangs bared.
One breath.
Eden saw him for just a second—caught the flash of a hand, a single finger to his lips. *Shhh.*

And then the rooftop spun, and he was gone.

Not gone. Unleashed.

Kain struck like a storm.

One second, the creature was snarling at Eden; the next, it was airborne—ripped sideways by a blur of black denim and fury. Kain drove it into the wall with a thunderous crack, concrete fracturing beneath them, the sound echoing down into the city. They slammed into the steel housing of the rooftop vent, metal shrieking, the shockwave rattling Eden's teeth.

No words. Just violence. Pure, brutal, unfiltered violence.

Kain didn't fight clean.

He fought like an animal.

Fangs to flesh. Elbow to throat. Knee to ribs.

The creature screeched—a wet, awful sound—and raked claws across Kain's chest. Blood sprayed, hot and steaming against the cold air, the scent of iron filling the gap between them. Kain didn't stop. Didn't blink. Didn't care.

He grabbed the thing by the back of the skull and slammed it face-first into the tiles. Bone cracked, blood splashing.

"Come on, you stitched-up nightmare," he snarled, spitting blood. "Let's see if you bleed."

The creature answered with a roar, thrashing like a thing possessed—then twisted, faster than thought, and hurled him.

Kain hit the far wall with a sickening thud. Dropped.

Still.

Breathing—but barely. The rise and fall of his chest was ragged, desperate.

Eden screamed, the sound tearing out of her throat, raw and frightened.

The creature turned. Blood smeared across its face like warpaint, chest dragging in ragged, animalistic pulls. It limped toward her—bleeding, broken, mouth torn and dripping saliva and gore, a guttural rasp tearing in and out of its throat.

But not dead.

Not even close.

Then Alana stepped forward, and everything changed.

The creature faltered.

It swung its head toward her, nostrils flaring—then snapped back to Eden, locking on like a predator scenting the only meal that mattered.

Her scent hit it like a war-drum in the dark, hunger sharpening every trembling line of its body.

Eden's heart slammed hard. She stumbled back one step, then another, heel hitting the rooftop's edge—nothing behind her now but open city and cold air.

"Kain—" she choked, voice splintered. "Kain, please…"

He groaned where he'd fallen near the ledge, curled around the pain. Broken. Not rising. His blood pooled beneath him, dark and spreading across the frosted stone.

The creature moved toward her.

One step.

Another.

Then it paused.

Sniffed the air again, nostrils flaring wide tasting her fear.

And turned its head.

Toward Alana.

Alana was still. Watching. Her glamour cracked like a mirror under strain—tiny fractures of violet light threading across her skin. Her eyes glowed unnaturally, pupils blown wide. She didn't blink.

Eden barely noticed. "Alana, run—" Her voice was thin, desperate.

But Alana didn't run.

She smiled.

Slow. Dangerous. Her lips curled in a way that made even the air tense.

"Oh no, darling. I don't run. Not from things like this."

The creature hissed—low, guttural, animal, the sound vibrating in Eden's bones.

Alana stepped forward.

She didn't change.

She unveiled.

Her skin shimmered into something unreal—smooth, flawless, almost too perfect. Her body arched with unnatural grace, lips darkened, eyes flaring with ancient hunger. Not for blood.

For essence.

Magic. Power. Lust. Life.

Eden stared, frozen. "Alana...?" Her voice was barely a whisper, her mind struggling to process what she was seeing.

The creature reeled back—confused. It had never seen one of her kind.

Alana's smile widened, predatory and beautiful.

She opened her arms, soft and slow, every movement a lure.

"I've never tasted something like you," she purred, voice velvety and smooth "Let's fix that."

Power shimmered off her in waves. The air shifted—heavy, sweet, intoxicating, thick as honey. Eden could taste it, cloying on her tongue, making her head spin.

The creature's limbs shook. It took one half-step forward... then stumbled.

Alana's power was already working—siphoning, weakening, draining the edges of its form.

The creature roared and lunged, claws flashing.

The rooftop door exploded inward—metal groaning, hinges torn, the sound echoing like a cannon.

Nyx stormed through like a god of vengeance, a blur of black and crimson shadow, fangs bared, eyes molten silver, his body humming with power still thick from Eden's blood. Behind him—another force hit the rooftop.

Black.

But not the man.

Lyn Rose

The wolf.

Pure white. Massive. Fangs the size of a grown man's forearm, claws tearing stone underfoot as he landed in a crouch and let loose a howl that rattled the city's bones, echoing off glass and steel for blocks.

Eden dropped to her knees, clutching her ears as the sound split the air. Even the creature faltered—turning with a broken, jerking motion just in time to be slammed by a freight train made of fury.

Nyx struck first.

Not elegant.

Brutal.

He collided with the creature mid-turn, shoulder down, driving it across the rooftop into a stack of metal HVAC units hard enough to crumple steel. The creature screamed— blood spraying from its jaw as Nyx tore into it, claws out, slicing tendon from bone, the sound of tearing flesh mingling with screeching metal.

It fought.

Wild.

Desperate.

Claws lashed. Fists swung, the air thick with the scent of blood and sweat and fear.

But then Black was there.

All white and wrath—fangs sinking into the creature's side, dragging it off Nyx like a lion tearing into a boar. The rooftop shook beneath them, chunks of stone breaking loose.

The creature kicked—wild, shrieking—but its strikes slowed, growing weaker and less coordinated.

Alana's power had drained it, but not enough.

Nyx didn't give it a second breath.

He rose, blood on his cheek, and let his voice drop to something lethal, the sound vibrating in the marrow of Eden's bones.

"On your knees."

The creature snarled, tried to lunge—

Nyx's fist hammered its chest.

Not just a punch. An impact. Like a sonic boom packed into muscle and rage. The creature slammed backward—down and not rising, the breath forced from its lungs in a wet, rattling gasp.

"Eden!" Nyx shouted, tossing her his phone.

Eden caught it with shaking hands, nearly dropping it, her fingers slick with sweat.

"Call Stroud. Get the cuffs. Now!"

Her fingers fumbled over the glass, breath coming fast and shallow, catching hard in her throat. The phone rang once—too loud, too sharp in the chaos.

"Stroud, it's Eden—" she gasped. "We're at my apartment—the rooftop—the creature—he's down—Nyx—"

Her voice cracked, panic cinching her ribs until air barely moved.

A violent crash in front of her.

The impact shook the tiles at her feet.

Eden jerked her head up—

and screamed.

Nyx's body hit the ground hard, thrown like a ragdoll, blood arcing through the air before splattering across the rooftop in a brutal crimson spray.

"HURRY!" she shrieked into the phone. "BRING THE CUFFS!"

The creature roared, voice guttural, echoing off the city skyline.

Its claw drove toward Nyx's throat, the movement almost too fast to see.

He blocked, barely, and Black bit down hard on its shoulder. Blood sprayed, salty and metallic in the hot air, spattering onto Eden's face.

They were grappling again—a vicious blur of claws and fangs and brute force colliding, the sounds of battle filling the air, primal and relentless.

And then Eden saw Alana drop her arm.

"No!" Eden screamed. "Alana, don't!"

Alana was already walking toward the melee. She turned, eyes glowing violet, lips parted in a wicked smile, her steps unhurried.

"I can help," she said—smooth, hypnotic. Her voice slid through the chaos like silk cut from shadow.

Eden slapped a hand over her mouth—not just to muffle the scream, but to hold herself together. If she let go, she might not stop. Worse, Nyx might hear her. Worst of all, the creature might.

Alana didn't walk.

She moved.

Like sex in motion. Like a song only the dark remembers.

Every sway of her hips rewrote gravity.

Every glance dared the world to worship.

Lyn Rose

The air shifted—not just around Eden, but across the entire rooftop. Night itself seemed to inhale and *hold*.

The fight paused.

Black's massive wolf form went rigid, fur bristling.

Nyx's claws froze inches from the creature's throat, his gaze caught mid-snarl, spell-stunned.

Even the creature—panting, bloodied, rabid—stilled.

Entranced. Hypnotized.

Alana's glamour pulsed like a second heartbeat. Eden felt it thrum under her skin.

She lifted a single finger—long, clawed, glowing faintly rose-gold—and curled it with slow precision, her body swaying like she moved through water.

Come hither.

And they did.

Nyx's grip faltered, mouth parted, nostrils flaring like he'd been caught in a scent he couldn't resist. Black growled— low, guttural—but even he stood frozen, stunned.

All three—Black, Nyx, the creature—held like statues, torn between instinct and desire.

Alana stepped into the space between them. No raised hand. No spell. No threat.

Just her.

She reached the creature, tilted her head, smiled—and kissed it.

It gasped.

Not from pain. Not at first.

From *pleasure*—the kind that strips resistance, that makes surrender feel like worship.

Eden's heart slammed against her ribs.

She could feel it—the pull. Alana wasn't taking blood. She was taking *essence*. Magic. Vitality. Power. Bit by bit, pulse by pulse, that kiss drained the creature down to its bones.

Its claws sagged.

Its legs folded.

Its eyes rolled white.

And when Alana pulled back—lips-tinged gold, eyes half-lidded, hunger barely masked—the creature collapsed like a puppet cut loose.

The trance shattered.

Nyx blinked. Roared. Shook himself free like water off fur—then slammed the creature's skull into the rooftop. Stone cracked. Blood arced wide and wet.

It shrieked—raw and strangled.

Then—

Wind.

Boots.

Voices.

The Sixth Accord had arrived.

They came in a blur—witches casting veils, Fae dripping from shadow, reapers stepping through air like cracks in reality. The whole rooftop snapped electric with adrenaline.

Spells wove across the skyline, sealing the zone. Blue shimmer. Magic thick in the air.

Stroud's voice rang out—sharp as a blade.

"Containment cuffs—NOW!"

She moved fast. Tossed Nyx the cuffs—glowing silver, runes etched deep.

"Secure it before it regenerates."

Nyx snapped them onto its wrists. The magic flared blue—then red. Runed. Sealed.

Locked.

Contained.

The glow dimmed. Black's massive frame shuddered once, bones cracking, fur receding in a slow ripple of white to skin. The wolf collapsed inward, reforming.

When he stood again, the man was there—bare, breathing hard, blood streaked down one arm, eyes still rimmed with gold. Steam rose faintly off him in the sun, every line of muscle taut with adrenaline. He didn't reach for clothes. Didn't care.

He just stared at Alana.

She turned slightly, basking in the magic she'd siphoned.

"That one was strong," she murmured, dreamy. "Enough to keep me burning for days."

Power still clung to her skin—heat shimmering off her in waves. Eyes glowing. Lips flushed. The scent of raw, stolen magic poured off her like perfume from another realm.

Black didn't move.

Didn't blink.

"What the fuck *are* you?" he breathed.

Lyn Rose

Alana smiled slow. Licked her bottom lip. Lazily.

"You're welcome."

On the edge of it all, Eden sat frozen.

Blood coated her arms. Her legs. Her face.

Not hers.

She was still staring at her best friend. Still processing what she'd just seen. What Alana was.

"Eden."

Nyx's voice broke through the haze.

He was in front of her now—slow, cautious. Like she might vanish. Like she was a deer about to bolt.

"Are you hurt?"

She looked at him. Then at Alana.

Then down.

The blood.

Her lips parted. No words came out. Just a faint, broken sound.

She shook her head.

Nyx's hands stayed lifted—open, unthreatening. "It's okay," he said softly. "You're safe. I've got you."

He took a slow step closer.

Then another.

Until he was right in front of her—and dropped to his knees, eyes never leaving hers.

She didn't move. Couldn't.

Nyx reached out. Folded his arms around her. Pulled her into his chest and held her like a lifeline—afraid, if he didn't, she'd unravel into the wind.

He pressed his face into her hair and breathed her in, holding her close as the chaos faded.

She finally exhaled, the breath shuddering out of her like she'd been holding it for years.

CHAPTER THIRTY-THREE

The Seduction Of Violence

Kain had already been taken—rushed to a supernatural trauma unit with cracked ribs and half his blood volume gone. He'd be fine. Eventually. Just broken, pissed off, and in desperate need of a heavy feed. The faint scent of iron still clung to the air, a bitter reminder of the violence he'd endured. The rooftop carried the memory of screams, the echo of raw power still humming beneath every footstep.

Stroud approached from the front, still barking quiet orders into her comms as she crossed the rooftop. Her voice was sharp but contained, a steady anchor in the fading chaos. She stopped beside Nyx, tapping him once on the shoulder—a brief, commanding gesture.

"Regroup. Debrief tomorrow."

She didn't wait for a response, just turned and strode into the lift as the Accord cleared the rooftop, her heels clicking

Lyn Rose

against the cold concrete. The hollow echo lingered, marking the end of battle and the beginning of aftermath.

Nyx nodded once, still holding Eden. Still breathing her in like she was the only thing keeping him tethered to this world. His chest rose and fell with a rhythm that spoke of desperate need and silent promises.

The rooftop was quiet now. Bloody. Broken. But still.

Black hadn't moved. He was staring at Alana, eyes narrowed, jaw tight—trying to figure her out, maybe. Or maybe just caught in the gravity of what she'd done.

And Alana?

She was staring at Eden.

Then, finally—she broke the silence.

"Well. Alright." She clapped her hands together once, the sharp sound slicing through the heavy stillness. "Let's have it out. I hate quiet introspective moments."

She turned to Black first and held out her hand, unapologetically glowing—a soft violet light rippling beneath her skin, casting delicate shadows on the rough concrete.

"Hi, I'm Alana. Eden's best friend. And you are?"

Black looked at her hand. Didn't move. Mouth slightly open. Still staring.

After a beat, he took it—his massive hand engulfing hers—and gave a short, deliberate shake, the rough calluses contrasting with her smooth skin.

"Torren Black," he said, voice low and gravelly, like a growl held just beneath the surface. "Nice to meet you."

Alana's smile widened like it meant something deeper. Her gaze dipped, slow and shameless, tracing the line of him before meeting his eyes again. "Well, handsome," she said, voice soft with mischief and warmth both, "wanna buy me a drink?"

Black blinked. Then, a slow smile spread across his face, rough and genuine. "Fuck yeah I do."

Alana turned to Eden then—who was still curled in Nyx's arms, eyes blank, breathing shallow.

"Eden, baby," she said, voice softening just slightly, a tender undercurrent beneath the usual sharpness. "Come on. Let's get you changed."

A pause. Then a grin, mischievous and warm. "We're having shots."

They crossed the threshold of Eden's apartment—the four of them.

The air still reeked of blood and magic, thick and metallic, clinging to their clothes. The silence screamed louder than any noise, vibrating in their bones.

Nyx still had her in his arms.

She wasn't resisting—barely even aware—cheek pressed to his chest, fingers curled in the fabric of his shirt like a lifeline. Blood—not hers—clung to her skin in dried streaks, dark and stubborn. Her breath was shallow, uneven. Shock still held her in its grip.

Alana entered last, closing the door with a soft click that felt like punctuation, the final mark on the storm outside.

Her eyes scanned the room once, then landed on Eden.

"You can let go now," Alana said, voice calm, not unkind, coaxing a fragile bird from a cage.

Nyx didn't move.

Alana stepped closer. "Nyx." Firmer this time. A quiet insistence.

He glanced down at the woman cradled against him. Then back to Alana—this glowing, violet-eyed goddess who had just revealed herself as something ancient, dangerous, and unknown.

"You're a succubus," he said evenly. "Or a siren?" The words heavy, weighed with old histories.

Alana smiled, slow and languid, letting a flicker of power slip through her skin. It pulsed outward—a hypnotic echo of hunger and heat.

"Mmm. I could be both," she murmured. Not a confession. Not a denial. Then, with more fire than seduction: "But you're not the only one who would die for her."

A beat passed. Tension wound tight as wire.

Then—reluctantly—Nyx eased his grip. Eden swayed, but Alana was already there, catching her with practiced ease. Eden's arms went around her without thinking, seeking safety.

"I've got her," Alana said softly, a whisper of reassurance. "You've had your turn."

Nyx's jaw ticked—but he didn't argue.

Alana guided Eden toward the hallway. Nyx followed on instinct, steps silent, shadow-like.

At the bedroom door, Alana turned. Her eyes flared—violet fire in the dim light, fierce and unreadable.

"I need to talk to her," she said. "Alone."

Nyx didn't respond. Didn't need to. The low growl in his throat said enough.

Alana raised her chin, not backing down. "She's still my best friend."

Then she shut the door between them. Click.

Behind him, Black chuckled softly—a low sound thick with disbelief and wonder. He reached for the throw draped over the back of the couch, wrapping it loosely around his waist, the motion unhurried, almost amused.

"Siren," he muttered, shaking his head as a grin tugged at his mouth. "Oh yeah. I'm in love."

Eden & Alana

Warm hands. Steam curling through the air like whispered secrets.

Eden didn't know when the clothes came off, only that water was pouring down her body—hot, cleansing—and Alana's hands were there, steady, practiced, protective, tracing lines of healing.

"Come on, baby girl," Alana whispered, guiding her gently under the stream. "Let's get this blood off you."

Eden blinked. The fog in her mind cracked open slightly, light leaking in. The rooftop. The creature. Kain. Nyx. Alana.

"You're naked," Eden murmured weakly, voice fragile as glass.

Alana snorted, a warm, amused sound. "Shower protocol 101. Also, not the weirdest thing I've done."

The heat soaked into Eden's skin, loosening the chill in her bones. The water washed away more than just blood. Alana shampooed her hair like she'd done a hundred times before—back when exams broke Eden's brain and she'd show up at Alana's door half-dead with stress and microwaved noodles.

Only now there was blood. And power. And secrets.

When Eden finally leaned against the tiles, eyes clearer, breath slower, Alana stepped out.

"I'll get clothes," she said. "Warm ones."

Eden stood still for a moment, then turned off the water.

When she stepped into her bedroom wrapped in a towel, Alana was already back—arms full.

"Here," she said, tossing a pair of worn jeans, a tight cropped tee, and soft underwear onto the bed. "Put these on. Trust me, comfort over trauma couture."

Alana spun and disappeared again—back into Eden's closet.

Eden dressed slowly, fingers shaking, but functional. When she looked up, Alana emerged—wet hair tied into a messy bun, wearing her ripped jeans, her favourite jeans, and a mesh top that made no attempt to hide anything.

Alana did a slow turn.

"Hey, you got new clothes. I love this. Can I… have it?"

Eden stared at her.

Lyn Rose

And then cracked.

Laughter—high, hysterical, uncontrollable—broke from her chest like shattering glass. It hit the silence like a scream and didn't stop.

Alana laughed too. Crossed the room. Pulled her in, tight.

They held each other for a long minute—arms locked, foreheads pressed, laughing until it turned to tears. The kind that burn and cleanse at once.

Until Eden's shoulders shook and she choked out,

"What the fuck, Alana. Why didn't you tell me?"

Alana sighed—regret and love braided into one breath.

"I was going to. So many times."

She pulled back just enough to look at her.

"I could smell you, Eden. You're not fully human. I didn't know what you were, not exactly—but I felt it. I was drawn to you. I always have been."

Eden blinked. "Yeah. That's why I always had crazies following me."

Alana grinned, warm and unapologetic.

"Oh, I know. You were like a supernatural magnet. I used to love hanging out with you—fed so well off those idiots."

Eden's jaw dropped.

"Oh my God."

"But then," Alana said, quieter now, her voice dipping into something that trembled at the edges,

"We became friends. And I fell in love with you."

Eden froze.

Alana didn't flinch.

"You're not just my friend, Eden. You're my family. My person. The reason I never told you wasn't because I didn't trust you—it was because I was scared it would change things. That I'd lose you."

Eden exhaled, slow and shaky. Her fingers found Alana's and squeezed.

Grounding. Forgiving. Fierce.

"You would never lose me. No matter what."

She swallowed. "I'll always be here."

Alana smiled, brushing wet hair off her cheek.

"Yeah," she whispered. "I know."

Eden sank onto the bed—still trembling, but more *present* than she'd been since the rooftop.

Lyn Rose

"Okay," Eden said quietly.

"So tell me. Everything. No more secrets."

Alana didn't speak right away. She sat beside her, curling her legs beneath her, fingers brushing Eden's wrist.

"My parents weren't kind," she said at last. "They were King and Queen of a city you'll never find on a map. Myrelinth. Beneath the sea. It's beautiful—cold, cruel, and obsessed with bloodlines."

She looked away.

Jaw tight.

"I was bred to seduce, to command, to marry for power. Nothing else. They arranged my mating like a treaty. Told me I'd be a Queen. I told them to go to hell."

Silence. Not awkward. Just heavy.

"I ran. Came to the surface. Glamoured a new name, a new ID. Thought I'd lie low, feed when I had to, maybe carve out a few months of freedom."

Her voice wavered, but didn't break.

"And then... I saw you. In the admissions hall. Denim jacket. Law folder. Ridiculous hair."

She smiled, small and real.

"I tested you, you know. Let the glamour slip. Everyone else melted."

She touched Eden's hand again, reverent.

"But not you. You didn't flinch. You didn't want me. You just… asked if I wanted to get a drink."

Eden blinked. Lips parted.

"That was the first time in my life," Alana whispered,

"someone *chose me*. Not the succubus. Not the siren. Me."

She let the silence stretch.

"And everything got better after that. Not easier. Not safer. But better. Because you saw me. And I wasn't alone anymore."

Alana sat beside her.

And for the next hour—she told her everything.

Black hadn't moved. Still standing in the hallway like a statue carved from muscle and disbelief, staring at the closed-door Alana had vanished behind. His mouth opened once—then shut again. One hand flexed at his side like he didn't know what to do with it.

Nyx ignored him. He had his phone pressed to his ear, voice low and clipped.

Lyn Rose

"Yeah. Stay at the hospital." A pause. "What?" His eyes narrowed. "Jace, tell him no. Stay. That's an order." Another beat. "Yes, I'm sure. Black will fight him for her." A glance sideways. "Yeah, fuck no. Stay in the hospital."

He ended the call with a flick of his thumb.

Black finally spoke. "You think he'll actually stay put?"

Nyx exhaled. "He'll stay if he knows what's good for him."

Black snorted. "I don't wanna fight him, Nyx. But I will."

Nyx didn't answer. Didn't need to. He heard the Alpha claim in his voice.

And Black—for just a second—remembered the first time he'd heard it, too.

He hadn't backed down then. He wouldn't back down now.

She'd been Fae—or maybe something else entirely. Magic in her veins, venom on her tongue. The kind of woman who walked into a room like a blade already drawn.

And both of them—one young wolf, one newly turned vampire—had been stupid enough to want her.

Torren could still feel the sting of that night: blood in his mouth, stone at his back, Nyx's hand on his throat and fangs bared in a snarl.

Lyn Rose

He'd laughed through a cracked rib and said, "If you're going to kill me, at least buy me a drink first."

Nyx hadn't killed him.

And the girl? She vanished by dawn, leaving only the bruises and a silent agreement between two predators.

They never spoke of her again. But from that night forward, they didn't fight each other. They fought beside each other.

Now, decades later, Torren felt it again—but this time, it wasn't a fight. It was her.

The one his blood answered to before his mind could name it. Violet-eyed. Heat-slick. Untouchable. And his.

And he knew: if it came to it, he would fight.

This time, he might not stop.

Black didn't think about that right now. There were bigger problems than ego and obsession.

Nyx had ended the call with a flick of his thumb.

Black blinked—the memory fading like smoke. Old blood. Old heat. Swallowed by the present.

The vampire wasn't looking at him. He was staring at the bedroom door. At the woman on the other side of it. And the succubus. Or siren. Or whatever the fuck she was—who'd taken Eden like she belonged to her.

Lyn Rose

Nyx's voice came low and quiet, edged with threat.

"God help me if she hurts her."

The bedroom door opened.

Alana stepped out first—and Black forgot how to breathe.

She'd changed into one of Eden's sheer mesh tops. No bra. Just bare skin and the slow flicker of violet magic curling off her like heat. Her jeans clung like they knew what was coming. Hair damp. Lips glossy. Eyes glowing like a secret whispered against skin.

She spotted him immediately.

Blew him a kiss.

Her gaze dropped to the throw knotted low on his hips. A faint frown curved her mouth. "That's a shame," she said, eyes flicking up again. "You looked better before."

He huffed a laugh, and that was all the invitation she needed.

"You were buying me a drink," she purred, walking toward him like heat with hips—the kind of fuck you remember, the kind that brands you so deep no other woman ever measures up.

Black opened his mouth. Closed it again.

She hooked her arm through his, and he almost keeled over.

Then Eden followed.

Fresh-faced. Clean. Hair twisted up with damp strands curling around her cheeks. Simple jeans, tight black crop top—her usual understated charm.

But her eyes…

They found Nyx instantly.

And when she smiled—soft, real—something in him unraveled.

His shoulders dropped. His whole stance softened. He crossed the space without a word and met her in the middle.

"Hey, baby," he said low. "You, okay?"

Alana answered behind her, grinning wickedly. "Oh, she's good."

Eden glanced down at his shirt—now dry and stiff with blood. She wrinkled her nose. "Eww. You're covered in blood."

Nyx looked at the stains. "Most of it's not mine."

"Still ewwww."

Torren Black chuckled. "Come on. Club X. I've got clothes there."

"Oh, hell yes," Alana said, already tugging him toward the door.

"Shots first," she added, eyes glinting. Then, lower—just for him: "Then we'll see what a wolf can handle."

Torren didn't answer. Couldn't. His pulse slammed. Everything in him tightened—too hot, too sharp, like his skin was suddenly the wrong size. He followed without thinking, without speaking, gaze locked on the sway of her hips like gravity had shifted.

He told himself it was lust. Just lust.

Nyx looked at Eden.

She nodded once—steady.

Ready.

They followed.

CHAPTER THIRTY-FOUR

The Wolf Meets His Match

The door to Club X thudded shut behind them, sealing out the city and swallowing them whole in pulse and heat. The muffled roar of traffic and distant sirens died away, replaced by a low, animal thrum that vibrated through polished stone floors and molten red light bleeding down the walls. Shadows curled in the corners—fangs, claws, eyes— flickering just beyond sight. No one looked twice. Not at them. Not tonight.

Nyx's hand was still on Eden's lower back, thumb brushing skin just above her jeans. He had let go of her only once since the rooftop. Not in the car. Not when the Accord cleared the scene. Not even now, when the scent of blood and aftermath still clung to the air like a second skin, raw and pungent.

She leaned into him, willingly, his presence was the only thing anchoring her to the moment, to reality.

Until Alana cleared her throat, sharp and deliberate—a reminder they weren't alone.

"Okay, tall, dark, and territorial," she said, placing a perfectly manicured hand on Nyx's chest, the nails gleaming under the club's strobe lights. "She's alive, not made of glass, and I've got tequila, clean clothes, and trauma bonding to do. So hands off."

Nyx didn't move. Didn't blink.

Alana narrowed her eyes, voice low and sweet as venom, her words slicing through the thick haze. "I've kept her alive for years, blood boy. You got her now, fine—but you don't own her."

Nyx's jaw ticked, muscles tightening like a coil ready to snap. His gaze flicked to Eden, searching, weighing.

She nodded gently, a quiet reassurance that steadied the tension in the air. "It's okay. I'm good."

Reluctantly—slowly—he let his hand fall, like a king conceding a crown.

Alana looped her arm through Eden's and spun her toward the private suite hallway with a fierce grace. "We'll be upstairs. If I hear one man even breathe too loud, I'm hexing your balls."

Black clapped a heavy hand on Nyx's shoulder as the girls disappeared into the shadows. "She's fucking terrifying."

Lyn Rose

A pause.

"And fuck, I'm turned on."

Nyx snorted and then exhaled, tension releasing just a fraction. "She's not the one I'm worried about."

Black glanced down at the throw still knotted at his hips and huffed a laugh. "Come on," he said, already heading for the back hall, his bare feet thudding against the floor with purpose. "I've got clean clothes in the vault and a bottle that might just burn the shit we survived right out of our bloodstream."

The club hadn't changed. Same throb of bass rolling through the floor like a heartbeat, primal and steady. Same bodies, drenched in red light, swaying like heat ghosts in the dark, their movements a dance of hunger and craving. Same pulse of sweat and lust and something older, more primal, seething beneath it all.

But Eden had.

She moved beside Alana now, heels clicking sharply across the mezzanine floor, past velvet ropes and bouncers who parted without a word, their eyes heavy with unspoken respect and wariness. Her head was high. Shoulders squared. But as the shadows flickered and the first notes of a familiar track curled through the air—

She remembered.

Lyn Rose

The last time she was here, she'd stumbled in beside Nyx, wide-eyed and raw. She'd kissed him for the first time under strobe lights and the weight of a thousand hungry stares. A vampire had come too close—

Nyx had slammed him on the floor and nearly torn his throat out.

The memory wasn't clear—it shimmered around the edges like a dream half-woken. But her body remembered. The ache of it. The heat. The sharp intake of breath. The surge of adrenaline that had set her skin on fire.

She smiled faintly to herself, a ghost of that fierce girl who had survived that night.

Alana glanced sideways and grinned, a spark of mischief lighting her eyes. "You're thinking about him, aren't you?"

Eden snorted, a small sound caught between denial and amusement. "No."

"Liar," Alana shot back, voice teasing and warm.

They reached the roped-off private lounge. The same one as before, Eden realized, as she stepped inside. Alana dragged her to the low couch, waving off the server like she owned the place, her confidence filling the room.

Two glasses of something dark and dangerous were placed in front of them anyway, the liquid catching the light like liquid obsidian.

Lyn Rose

Alana raised hers. "To not dying today."

Eden clinked hers without hesitation, the sound a soft chime in the thick air. "To terrifyingly hot best friends being secret demons."

Alana winked, sly and playful. "Succubus, darling. Classy secret demon."

They laughed again—lighter this time, easier, the kind that loosened knots in their chests instead of tightening them. Eden leaned into Alana's shoulder, breath warm and shaky. Safe. Just for now.

Footsteps echoed behind them.

Alana glanced up—and her grin turned wicked, sharp as a blade.

"Showtime."

Nyx and Black re-entered the club booth—showered, changed, and radiating that freshly fucked kind of danger. Clean, yes. But not safe.

Nyx slid in beside Eden like he'd never left her side. He leaned in, kissed her temple, voice low and rough.

"Hey, baby. You, okay?"

Eden smiled and kissed him properly—mouth to mouth. His quiet groan vibrated against her lips, and heat pooled low in her stomach like a lit fuse, sharp and electric.

Across the table, Black dropped into the booth opposite them, right beside Alana. He didn't look at her—just said under his breath, "Still here. Still smell ya."

Alana leaned in close, lips grazing the shell of his ear, her voice a velvet purr. "Mmm. Smells like a good time."

Then she flicked her tongue against his skin, a teasing, dangerous gesture.

Black froze.

Just for a second.

Then smiled.

Like the wolf had finally found a hunt he didn't want to end.

EPILOGUE

Somewhere beneath Edalva

The containment cell hissed shut.

Reinforced steel. Spell-forged locks. Warded by witches, hex-bound by reapers, and lined with silver-threaded obsidian. The creature couldn't move without burning. Couldn't breathe without tasting ash.

It didn't scream anymore.

Didn't roar.

It sat in the centre of the cell, chained at throat, wrists, and ankles—head bowed like a beast that had outlived even its rage. Blood matted its skin, blackened where it had congealed against runes etched into the floor.

But its eyes still glowed.

Still watched.

Lyn Rose

Still waited.

A comm feed crackled to life somewhere in the dark. Voices, muffled but distinct:

"Initiate extraction protocol."

"She's bound. Contained."

"We knew this would happen. We planned for it. You know what to do."

The line went dead.

The creature lifted its head.

For the first time in days, its lips curled. Not wide. Not manic. Just enough to make the guards flinch.

Because if Sevra Wynne walked free—

so would it.

Club X

Upstairs, far above the earth and chains and silence…the bass dropped like a heartbeat synced to sin.

Alana and Eden moved together on the dance floor—heat and hips, glitter and bite, dancing like they owned the night. Eden's laugh slipped through the strobe lights, Alana's hands gliding over her hips as they twirled into the kind of rhythm that didn't just invite attention—it commanded it.

Every male in the room noticed.

Heads turned.

Breath caught.

Predators paused mid-step—shifters, Fae, vamps—all caught in the dragnet of whatever magic the two women had become.

On the mezzanine above, Nyx gripped the railing hard enough it groaned under his palm. His eyes burned silver, locked on Eden, hunger rippling off him like heat from a forge.

Beside him, Black hadn't moved in twenty seconds.

"Fuck me," he muttered, half to himself. "I think I'm dying."

Nyx didn't look away. "You're not dying."

Black exhaled. "Feels like it."

Another beat dropped. Another sway of Eden's waist.

Alana's laugh curled through the music—sweet as sugar, sharp as a snare drum—the kind of sound men followed into shipwrecks.

A crowd of men had started to converge—drawn like moths to flame, some supernatural, some not. But all of them hungry.

Black and Nyx clocked it at the same time.

Their eyes met.

Not a word passed between them.

Then—in unison—they leapt.

Down from the mezzanine. Straight into the pulsing crowd.

Black shouted mid-air:

"Déjà fucking vu!"

COMING SOON

Venom and Vow

Torran Black has walked through fire—and now he's ready to burn it all down.

Chasing a succubus through a shattered world of blood, betrayal, and broken alliances wasn't part of the plan.

But Alana? She's no plan. She's the wildfire that consumes everything in her path.

Kingdoms will crumble. Loyalties will shatter.

And lust? Lust becomes the deadliest weapon of all.

This is only the beginning.

The Sixth Accord is about to ignite.

Are you ready to watch it burn?

Lyn Rose

ABOUT THE AUTHOR

Lyn Rose writes to heal—to bleed safely on the page, to turn pain into power, and to remind others that survival is its own kind of magic.

She writes fierce, addictive fantasy with bite. Stories that blend power, obsession, and rebellion—with heroines who fight back and monsters you might just fall for.

She refuses to write anything that doesn't set fire to her soul.

Drawn to the brutal, the beautiful, and the dangerously in-between, Lyn builds worlds where lust is a weapon, loyalty is earned in blood, and nothing stays buried forever.

Obsidian Kiss is the first book in The Sixth Accord, a supernatural saga of blood bonds, fractured alliances, and desire that cuts deeper than claws.

Find out more at https://www.lynrosebooks.com/

(Signed copies, extras, and what's coming next.)

Lyn Rose